THE
WORLD
WE
BURN

KYLA STONE

The World We Burn

This book is a work of fiction. Any references to historical events, real people, or real places are used fictitiously. Other names, characters, places, and events are products of the author's imagination, and any resemblances to actual events or places or persons, living or dead, is entirely coincidental.

Printed in the United States of America

Cover design by Christian Bentulan

Book formatting by Vellum

First Printed in 2023

ISBN: 978-1-962251-02-0

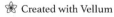 Created with Vellum

Strength does not come from physical capacity. It comes from an indomitable will.
    —MAHATMA GANDHI

FOREWORD

I ask for forgiveness from the residents of Munising in advance as I had perhaps too much fun destroying their town. Many locations are real places, though a few have been invented like the Devil's Corner ghost town. Still, the UP boasts several incredible ghost towns. I recommend you visit them and stop somewhere for a delectable pasty and some thimbleberry jam!

1

SHILOH EASTON POPE
DAY ONE HUNDRED AND TWENTY-TWO

S hiloh Easton Pope felt it in the air—a tight, tingling sensation. Something was going to happen today.

She stood behind the sandbag wall, her crossbow slung across her back as she listened to the shush of the wind in the pines. A pinecone hit the forest floor with a thud. A chipmunk or squirrel scurried in the fallen leaves. A raven took flight from a nearby birch tree.

Someone coughed behind their closed fist. To her left, across the road, one of the other sentries shifted, stomping their feet in the mud to keep warm in the chilly air. It was late afternoon with temperatures in the low fifties, but the wind chill made it feel colder.

"Motion ahead," came a voice through the walkie-talkie clipped to her overalls pocket. The trained fighters got headsets; everyone else had to use stupid walkie-talkies. She wasn't allowed to fight. According to Eli, she was too young and too inexperienced. It was a giant, steaming pile of horse turds.

The sentry to her left, Jason Anders, raised his binoculars. "I don't see anything yet."

"I spot five people headed up the road toward us on foot," the scout said.

"Are they armed?"

"Two shotguns, maybe a couple of handguns, it's hard to tell. They don't look like soldiers, just regular people."

"Maybe that's what they want you to think," Shiloh said. "We should stay alert."

Jason scowled. "Didn't ask for your opinion, did I?"

Jason Anders was barely nineteen, though he acted like he was some hardcore soldier, all swagger and big talk, always flexing his puffy muscles, with an arrogant smirk perpetually plastered across his handsome face.

He seemed to resent Shiloh for some reason and didn't attempt to hide it. She had no idea why he disliked her—maybe because she was Eli's favorite, or that she'd caught him sleeping on his shift last week.

Shiloh offered him her middle finger.

As she expected, Jason ignored her input and kept the field glasses to his eyes. "Alert the main gate. We'll know more after we talk with them."

"Unless they aren't in the mood to talk." Shiloh rested her elbows on the sandbag wall of the sentry post and scanned the forest for shadows that didn't belong. Her raven-black hair was pulled into a ponytail, bound with a rawhide ribbon tied to an authentic arrowhead. Mud crusted her combat boots and streaked her overalls from her early morning hunt with Eli in the woods near Wagner Falls.

She strained her ears, vigilant to any strange sound. Eli had trained them in situational awareness. The four sentries constantly watched the woods, scanned the trees, and studied the road.

"Step back, Shiloh," Phil Nash said. The rookie deputy on the Alger County Sheriff's Department, Nash was in his mid-twenties, blond-haired and rail-thin, with a narrow nose and a wispy mustache.

Most of the time, Nash didn't man the most boring security post in the world. He was typically busy with perimeter sweeps, checking the patrols and checkpoints, and overseeing the security teams.

Today, he'd brought the afternoon shift lunch—fresh thimbleberry juice in glass jars, with goat's cheese and tomato sandwiches on sourdough bread. He'd stayed afterward to grill them on protocol, or so he claimed.

Shiloh scowled. Eli had most definitely sent him to check on her. She hated it, despised feeling like a little kid as if she needed babysitting. She was a better shot with her trusty crossbow than anyone here.

Shiloh had been shooting things since she was five years old. With her crossbow, she could nail the skull of a groundhog or a wild turkey from fifty feet, easy-peasy. Her hands were rock steady. She could handle herself just fine, and frankly, she was itching to show these cocky jerkwads what she was made of.

However, she was certain Eli would make damn sure she'd never get the chance.

"Stay behind me and keep your hands off your weapons," Nash instructed her. He said that every time strangers approached the gate. It was getting on her last nerve.

"Yeah, yeah, I got it."

Out of the corner of her eye, she caught Jason's self-satisfied smirk.

Her right hand slipped into her pocket and brushed her pocketknife. She resisted the temptation to hurl it at Jason's stupidly square jaw, knock out a few of those even white teeth, and see how conceited he was then.

Next to Nash stood two more sentries: Amanda Martz, a serious, quiet woman in her thirties with close-cropped brown hair, and Fiona Smith, a red-headed young woman wearing cargo pants and a white fleece jacket beneath the rifle strapped across her chest.

Amanda stared straight ahead, scanning the road past the oncoming refugees. Fiona sensed Shiloh watching her and offered a crooked-toothed smile. Fiona had come to the Northwoods Inn last week, and unlike her meth-head brother and crabby father, she'd made herself useful, volunteering for everything.

None of the other sentries spared Shiloh one iota of attention whatsoever except for Fiona. She was whip-smart and had already improved the Northwoods Inn's water containment system with a gravity-fed something or other.

Shiloh was reserving judgment, but she didn't hate her. Yet.

Sentry would be way more fun with Ruby present. Unfortunately, her friend loved horrid things like gardening and cooking. Mrs. Brooks had taken her under her wing, so Ruby was always busy in the kitchen or gardens.

Ruby would advise Shiloh to swallow her anger, control it, and wait for her moment.

Shiloh glowered. Fine, she could be patient. She could.

"You know the rules," Nash said. "You're here to observe and learn. Nothing else. No altercations. No interactions with the refugees. And keep your eyes open."

Eli Pope's rules. Her bad-ass father was the literal worst. If he had his way, she'd be stuck at home with a dozen guards while she knitted tiny sweaters for babies and baked cookies for the homeless.

Not a chance.

Today was September sixteenth. Her birthday. She was fourteen years old, practically an adult. In her short life, she'd been kidnapped, attacked, and nearly run over by a truck. Every time, she'd come out on top. Hadn't she proven herself?

Apparently not to these knuckleheads.

"Shiloh," Nash said in warning.

She smiled at him obediently, shifting her weight so the crossbow strapped to her back was mostly hidden, as if he'd forget she was armed and dangerous.

She reached for the binoculars draped around her neck and raised them with one hand, a peace offering of sorts. "Just here to observe. Got it."

While Jason kept his eyes on the road, Nash wrinkled his brow and stared at her, assessing her sincerity. She widened her smile and blinked her dark eyes at him in pure innocence.

With a resigned sigh, Nash shook his head and returned his attention to the approaching interlopers.

"They should appear any second," the scout said.

A mile further down the road, out of sight, twenty-year-old Drew Stewart served as their forward scout, concealed in a sniper hide within the cover of the trees.

Drew was a pretty boy and a shameless flirt, but Shiloh wasn't fooled. Eli assigned him to scout because he didn't know a magazine from a clip and couldn't shoot the broad side of a barn if his life depended on it.

"There they are," Amanda said.

Shiloh peered through the binoculars at the road winding between towering pine

trees. A hundred yards distant, five bedraggled people trudged. They were slump-shouldered, dirty, and exhausted. Worn backpacks clung to their bent backs.

A black-haired woman in her late thirties pulled a red wagon stuffed with duffle bags over the uneven dirt. An older man in his sixties plodded beside her. He sported black hair streaked with silver; his right arm was cradled close to his chest as if it were injured.

Next to them, a younger woman with similar jet-black hair pushed a shopping cart of boxed and canned goods mostly covered by a ratty blanket, and a dusty suitcase.

Behind them, a little boy of four or five held the hand of a long-haired man in his early forties. The kid's sandy-blond head was bent, intently studying the ground as he kicked rocks.

Ever since Eli and the others had rescued Lena and stolen the shipment of medications from Darius Sykes, refugees had straggled into Munising, a few more every day.

The word had gotten out, no matter how they'd tried to keep things on the down-low. The Northwoods Inn had solar and wind power. Not only that, but Munising boasted a medical clinic with supplies of critical, life-saving medications.

People wanted to be saved.

She couldn't blame them. Since the super solar flares four months ago, the world had gone to hell in a handbasket. With few functioning hospitals and a global dearth of resources, things were grim. Without power, society had shattered like Humpty Dumpty falling off his wall. There was no putting things back together again.

"Take care, everyone," Nash said. "Stay sharp. Don't do anything stupid out of fear, either. Wait for my command."

The sentries nodded. They stood tall behind the sandbag walls, hands on their weapons, attentive and scanning their surroundings in case of a possible attack from the side. The refugees could be a decoy for something much worse.

Shiloh stilled, breathing in the woodsy scents of pine needles and rich soil, her pulse thudding against her throat. The cool fall sun dappled her face, the breeze chilled the back of her neck. The crossbow pressed against her back was a comforting weight.

The refugees drew closer. Their eyes widened as they took in the Northwoods' security measures. Most refugees who came to Northwoods in search of sanctuary approached the main entrance to the south. The secondary entrance to the east was smaller, though no less fortified.

The east entrance boasted sandbagged fighting positions on either side of the road. A six-foot fence topped with concertina wire ran along both sides of the road.

On the right side of the road, they'd built a guard shack, a hut constructed with two-by-fours and sandbags mounded chest high. Sentries kept constant watch, rotating in six-hour shifts.

Eli had instructed them to clear the area around each gate to create open killing fields. This way, the sentries could see anyone coming from several hundred yards away. They'd raked the ground with soft dirt so the roving patrols could easily spot the footprints of trespassers.

If an organized force approached, the enemy would have to breach the gate without cover or the ability to sneak up on the guards.

When the refugees were forty feet away, Nash raised his AR-15. "Stop right there!" Jason and Amanda followed his lead.

Startled, the group froze. The little boy kept walking, oblivious to the danger.

The long-haired man seized his collar and yanked him backward. The little boy fell on his butt in the dirt. The man left the kid on the ground and reached for the shotgun slung across his shoulder.

"Hands up where we can see them!" Jason shouted as he flicked his AR's safety switch off. "Drop your weapons!"

Fiona raised the walkie-talkie to her lips and sent a message to her commanding officer, who would inform Eli and Jackson. She carried a rifle without ammo until she passed sufficient training. Like Shiloh, she was here to watch and learn.

"We mean no harm!" the long-haired man said. He had a lean, pock-marked face and heavy-lidded eyes. His right hand stilled over his ribs a few inches from his weapon. "Point those guns somewhere else."

"You're about to lose that hand." Nash gestured with his rifle. "On your knees! Weapons tossed aside. Now!"

Shocked into obedience, the refugees obeyed. The long-haired guy responded slowly, his jaw clenched in anger or possibly fear. With three AR-15 rifles trained on their chests, they removed their guns and tossed them aside.

"Hands up and stay kneeling," Nash instructed. "No funny business, or we shoot now and ask questions later."

The little boy remained seated in the dirt, staring in wide-eyed alarm at the guns pointed in his direction. His mouth gaped, his eyes wide and glassy.

"Get your kid on his knees!" Jason demanded. "On your knees, boy!"

The kid didn't move a muscle.

Jason swiveled his weapon toward the boy. His hands were shaking as if his nerves were getting to him. Like he might do something stupid. "I said—"

"He's deaf!" the middle-aged woman cried. "He can't hear you."

Jason shrugged his shoulder like he didn't give a damn what was wrong with the kid, though he shifted his aim from the little boy to the old man.

A red dot appeared on the old man's forehead. The old man raised one trembling hand, his left hand fisted and held tight against his cadaverous chest as if he was hiding something.

"Please," he said in a tremulous voice. "Have mercy."

Jason said, "Raise both hands, or we fire! Now!"

2

SHILOH EASTON POPE
DAY ONE HUNDRED AND TWENTY-TWO

The older woman's features went rigid. Her pin-straight black hair and sharp cheekbones revealed her Native American heritage. She was slender but for the swollen belly protruding beneath her sweatshirt. She was heavily pregnant.

With her hands in the air, she angled her chin at the two people next to her, obviously family members from the physical resemblance. "My name is Theresa Fleetfoot. This is my father, Ira Fleetfoot, and my daughter, Miriam. Last week, my father sliced open his arm with a chainsaw while cutting firewood and it's badly infected. We mean no harm. Please, help us."

Shiloh shifted her gaze to the old man. Dark bags shadowed his eyes, his sagging skin sallow and sickly. Dark red stains marred the ace bandage wrapped around his forearm. His mouth was pursed in a pained grimace.

He seemed genuinely injured, but appearances could be deceiving.

"Take their weapons," Nash instructed.

With Amanda covering her, Fiona exited the guard shack and retrieved the group's weapons from the ground.

"We need those," Long-haired guy said. "You can't steal our stuff!"

"You'll get them back if you don't pose a threat." Fiona's voice wavered. Her shoulders were stiff, her movements jittery. She was nervous.

"The only threat is you!" the guy snarled.

Nash asked, "What do you want?"

Theresa wrapped her thin arms around her belly. "We heard—we heard there is medicine here. Good people who are willing to take in strangers. This is a place that might be safe. We passed other towns..." She swallowed hard and blinked rapidly, as if to erase a terrible memory. "They weren't safe."

Amanda and Jason exchanged a strained glance. Shiloh's heart stuttered in her chest. They hadn't heard this before. Most of the refugees had traveled from the west and south, from Marquette, Copper Harbor, and Iron Mountain.

"What towns? Why aren't they safe?" Jason asked.

The daughter—Miriam—raised her chin. Her eyes were bloodshot, her dark ponytail limp and snarled. "We were scraping out an existence in Bay Mills. Things are tough without power, grocery stores, or medicine, but we were making do. There's fishing, fruit and nut trees, and enough forest for plenty of firewood."

Nash nodded at her to continue.

The young woman bit her chapped lower lip. "Five days ago, raiders attacked our town. We were driven out. We fled with what we could carry. We heard there was electricity at the Soo Locks, so we headed there, but Sault St. Marie is not what it was. It's controlled by them now. They take whatever they want. It wasn't safe, so we left again."

A shiver of dread crept up Shiloh's spine. "Who is 'they'?"

"The cartel," Theresa said.

No one needed to ask which cartel she meant. There was only one that mattered.

"We're hardy folks, eh?" Theresa said with a faint Yooper twang. "We've never needed a hand-out in our lives. But now..." Her voice trailed off. Her chin dipped, drawing everyone's attention to her round stomach. "We can be of service. I'm an elementary school teacher. Miriam has finished her third year of nursing school. My father is a farmer. He knows everything about growing things in the tough soil up here. He's hurt now, but he can help your community. I may be pregnant, but I'm not an invalid. We can all help. We're willing to work to earn our keep."

"I'm a mechanic," Long-haired guy said. "My name is Bill Scruggs. This is my son, Adam."

"Where's Adam's mother?" Shiloh asked.

Bill's face crumpled. "She was with us until five days ago. Raiders attacked us, too. They killed her. They stole everything we had, including my wedding ring and my watch. I tried to defend us, but there were too many of them. They burned us out of our home in Whitefish. They burned down the whole town."

"The cartel," Amanda said.

"The cartel." He nodded gravely, tears in his eyes. "We've been on the run ever since. I was able to hotwire a truck with a bit of diesel fuel left in the tank, then we met up with these fine folks, but the truck was stolen by raiders in Seney. We've been walking for days. My disabled son is hungry and tired."

Beside her, Nash relaxed his stance slightly. The muzzle of Jason's weapon lowered a few inches. They wanted to believe these people. They did believe them. Shiloh's gaze was drawn to Theresa Fleetfoot and her pregnant belly.

Lena would've flung open the gates already. Shiloh's aunt wanted to save everyone. Lena's desire to rescue the lost and hurting was almost pathological. She wasn't a trained paramedic and search-and-rescue handler for nothing.

Eli, on the other hand, wanted to lock the gates, protect the people he loved, and damn the rest of the world to fire and brimstone.

Shiloh didn't know what she believed, or which way was correct. Conflicted emotions tore at her—pity and compassion and the ferocious urge to protect those she loved: Lena and Eli, Jackson and the Brooks, Ruby and Bear. Even that damned obstinate goat, Faith.

What was the whole world if she didn't have them?

Nothing but ashes.

"We can't just let you in," Amanda said, her voice firm. "We have a process, protocols, and a committee. However, we do have a clinic, and we can escort you there and get your father's injuries tended to. Then we'll see about finding you folks a place to stay if you're accepted."

"Please help us, for my kid if not for me," Bill begged. He patted his son's head with obvious affection. The kid didn't move; his gaze was glued to the guns. He was probably in shock. "You can see this woman is pregnant. You wouldn't turn away a child and a pregnant woman, would you?"

The weighted question hung in the air like an unexploded grenade.

Nash relented first. With a sigh, he lowered his weapon further and gestured for the group to enter through the gate. "Just for tonight. Come on in."

"What about our weapons?" Ira asked.

"Your weapons will be returned to you when we know if we can trust you. We'll keep them safe until then."

Theresa sagged in relief. One hand lowered to cup her round belly. Miriam hugged her grandfather. "It's okay, it'll be okay now," she said to him.

The little boy had started to cry. Tears streamed silently down his cheeks, his tiny hand limp in his father's strong grip. Scruggs' knuckles were hairy. A band of white circled his wrist, the tan line from his stolen watch.

"We'll have to pat you down before we let you inside the perimeter," Amanda said. "No offense."

"None taken," Miriam said.

Nash angled his head at Jason. "Your turn."

Jason exited the guard shack and headed toward the refugees, his AR-15 held low, aimed toward the ground. Fiona had gathered the confiscated weapons in her arms and stood waiting in front of the guard hut a few feet from the refugees.

"Thank you so much. Thank you for your kindness," Theresa said.

As they shuffled forward, Theresa glanced at Bill. A flicker of some emotion flared across her face, and then it was gone—a flash of something Shiloh couldn't read clearly.

What was it? Solace at their deliverance? Concern that they wouldn't be accepted after all? Or something else? Something like trepidation. Or was it suspicion?

An uneasy feeling slithered through her guts, an apprehensive buzz beneath her skin. Her instincts whispered into her ear: *pay attention.*

To what? What was it? What the hell was off? The middle-aged pregnant schoolteacher with her nurse daughter and injured father? Bill Scruggs, the mechanic and grieving widower, and his deaf son?

They appeared scared, needy, and utterly harmless. Just regular people, the victims of terrible circumstances, no different than everyone else within the Northwoods Inn's boundaries.

And yet.

Her pulse quickened. Despite Nash's explicit instructions, she reached behind her for the crossbow and drew it silently to her shoulder, moving to the right of Nash to give her a clear line of sight. Before he could stop her, she crooked the butt of the crossbow against her shoulder and nocked a bolt.

Just in case.

Her hands steadied on the crossbow, her grip firm. Sweat trickled down the back of her neck and beaded along her hairline. She suddenly felt hot and dizzy.

Something was wrong. She wasn't sure what it was. She had to think like Eli, recalling his hours of lectures and training. *Keep your eyes open. Notice everything. Look for what doesn't belong.*

She wasn't only an Easton—she was a damned Pope. The blood of her native ancestors ran through her veins, born and bred warriors who fought bravely to defend their homes and their people. Eli's blood ran through her veins. No way in hell would she let him down.

"Wait," she said.

No one listened to her. Nash was focused on the refugees, but his stance was relaxed. Amanda had lowered her weapon, too.

Jason opened the gate with a creak of unoiled hinges. The refugees had almost reached the gate. Fiona stood between the gate and the refugees. Theresa was first. Bill strode alongside her with teary-eyed Adam. Miriam shuffled behind them. She aided her grandfather, her arm around his waist in a loving embrace.

"Wait," Shiloh said, louder.

She despised the dread curdling in her gut, hated this sense of impotent helplessness. Something was wrong, but she couldn't do a damn thing about it. Like when the psychopath Walter Boone had her in his grasp, or when Sykes kidnapped Lena deep within the copper mine.

She wouldn't feel that way again. She refused.

Shiloh raised her crossbow. "STOP."

3

SHILOH EASTON POPE
DAY ONE HUNDRED AND TWENTY-TWO

"Shiloh, what is it?" Nash asked in a tense voice.

Shiloh ignored him. Her palms had gone clammy. The buttstock of the crossbow snug against her shoulder, her cheek pressed to the stock, her dominant eye in line with the sight. Her right hand held the grip with her index finger balanced on the trigger, ready to fire.

She aimed the crossbow at Bill Scruggs' chest.

"Move and I shoot a bolt through your warm beating heart," she said calmly. "I suggest you don't move."

Fiona and Jason halted in their tracks. Fiona stood a few feet behind Jason, who carried his AR-15 low in one hand, intent on opening the gate wide.

Fiona half-turned and glanced back at Shiloh, frowning in confusion. "What's going on?"

Fiona was too close to Scruggs. So were Theresa and the boy, Adam.

"Back away," Shiloh ordered. "Everybody, get back."

Jason shot her a withering look. "What the hell do you think you're doing?"

"This man is an imposter. He's not who he says he is."

Scruggs locked eyes with Shiloh. He seemed bewildered and frightened, not a hint of guile or subterfuge in his pained expression. "I'm a father trying to protect my son, the only thing I have left. Please." His voice broke. "Please."

She might have given in, might have allowed pity to cloud her judgment. Except she'd recognized what was wrong; she'd figured it out.

"No tan line," she said. "Your ring finger. You said your wedding ring was stolen five days ago along with your watch. You've got the tan line for the watch, but not for your wedding ring. No wedding ring, no wife."

For a split second, no one moved. The air crackled with tension.

"You're lying," Shiloh said. "You're a liar."

"I've been wearing gloves!" Scruggs said defensively, his eyes narrowing.

"I call bull—"

"I told you, I'm a mechanic trying to survive with my deaf son. That's it. All I've done is protect my family and these people here with me. How dare you question my integrity?"

Eli had taught the sentries some basics in interrogation and testing strangers for a lie. People who spoke the truth answered quickly and openly; those with something to hide were typically evasive and acted offended or insulted to put the questioner on the defensive.

"Where did you work before the blackout?" Shiloh asked.

Scruggs shrugged aggressively, his expression annoyed. He was offended and didn't bother to hide it. "Here and there. I was a journeyman of sorts, but mostly I did contract work at a motorcycle shop in Whitefish Point."

His answers did nothing to ease Shiloh's suspicions. He'd picked a vague, distant location where the sentries were unlikely to know anyone. Clever, if he was being deceptive.

Jason stiffened. Though he was arrogant, he seemed to pick up on the same unsettling thread tugging at Shiloh's subconscious. Maybe he wasn't as thickheaded as she'd thought.

Jason shot a wary glance at Fiona. "Your dad owned a gas station, right? You know cars."

Fiona nodded and shifted the handful of guns in her arms. "Yeah, I do. Okay, if you're who you say you are, answer this. How do you change the spark plugs on a diesel engine?"

"What's your problem?" Scruggs' tone turned irritated. "We're just asking for a little help here. What's with the third degree from a twelve-year-old?"

"I'm fourteen, you asshat."

"Answer the question," Nash said sharply.

Scruggs shuffled his feet. His gaze darted to the left, then the right, like he was agitated—or perhaps, plotting his next move. "The same as any engine. If you'll collar your attack dog and let us in—"

"Diesel engines don't have spark plugs," Fiona said. "They have glow plugs. Any mechanic would know—"

In a blur of motion, Scruggs shoved Theresa in front of him. Thereas stumbled forward, her hands flying to her stomach to protect her unborn child.

Theresa's body blocked Shiloh's view of Scruggs as she fell into Fiona. Fiona fell to her knees. The guns in her arms were knocked from her grip and thudded to the dirt at her feet.

Swiftly, Scruggs crouched. He plunged his right hand into his boot and pulled out a six-inch knife, then sprang to his feet and tackled Fiona. Seizing a hank of her hair from behind, he hauled her to her feet.

Scruggs pressed her body against his and yanked her head back, exposing her neck, then jammed the blade against the white column of her throat.

Fear stuttered through Shiloh's chest. She shifted the crossbow's aim, scrambling for a target, but everything happened too fast. She couldn't risk firing and injuring the innocent.

Time seemed to slow. Her vision narrowed. Everything turned crisp and clear, sharp as glass. Every sound amplified: the whoosh of her pulse, Theresa's gasps of terror, Nash's frantic murmurs into the radio.

With a cry of alarm, Miriam ran toward her mother, who knelt on the ground in front of Fiona and Scruggs. Ira grasped Miriam's arm with his good hand and held on tight, keeping her out of the fray.

Two feet to Scruggs' right, little Adam sat trembling, arms raised, his tiny hands grasping at empty air, desperate to cling to something, anything, to save him. He opened his mouth and let out a ragged howl of terror.

"No one move!" Inside the guard shack, Nash aimed his AR-15 at Scruggs, as did Amanda and Jason. It was too little, too late.

Scruggs had effectively shielded his body with his captive. To shoot him, they risked injuring or killing one of their own.

"Let her go!" Amanda said.

"I'm afraid I can't do that." Scruggs transformed in front of their eyes. His tone was deadly calm, a flatness in his eyes that hadn't been there before. His affect transformed like a snake shedding its skin. He was No longer a distraught widower protecting his deaf son, but a predator on the hunt.

"Don't move, Fiona. Stay still, and do what he says," Nash said in a panicked rush. "It'll be okay."

Scruggs' mouth curled in a nasty smile. "I'll slice her throat, and you'll watch her bleed out right here. Lower your weapons!"

"Let her go or we'll blow your head off!" Jason seemed suddenly small and scared. His whole body was shaking, sweat slicking his reddened face.

"Jason," Nash said. "Stay calm. Do as he says."

Nash, Jason, and Amanda obeyed. Slowly, they lowered their guns. Shiloh remained half-hidden behind Nash, angled to shield the crossbow behind the sandbag wall. For once, her small stature played to her advantage.

Scruggs laughed. It was an ugly, unpleasant sound, like nails grating on a chalkboard. He pushed the blade deeper into Fiona's throat. The glint of steel flashed in the late afternoon sunlight. A red line appeared across her neck. Bright droplets of blood pearled on her skin, sliding like tears and pooling into the depression of her collarbone.

Fiona gasped. The cords on her neck stood taut, her head yanked back, the whites of her eyes showing. She didn't cry out or scream; she wasn't losing it. If she could keep her cool, she had a chance.

Shiloh gritted her teeth and took a small step sideways, slipping silently behind Nash. If she could move left without drawing attention, she could adjust the angle and maybe get a shot at the side of Scruggs' head, as long as he kept his attention on the sentries with guns and not on her crossbow.

At fourteen, Shiloh had fought for her life more than once, but she'd never killed anyone before, not face-to-face. She didn't count the guy who'd attacked her in the woods, whom she'd stabbed in the groin with the point of a fiberglass bolt. He'd slunk off to die somewhere else.

No time to think about that now.

On her hands and knees, Theresa wept. Beside her, Miriam and Ira clutched each other. The little boy made terrible grunting cries.

Jason was frozen with indecision, useless under fire. Nash's finger twitched on the trigger of his lowered weapon. He wanted to do something, but Scruggs stared at him as if daring him to act, so he could split Fiona's throat right in front of them.

His eyes shone with a crazed recklessness that made him dangerous. He might kill Fiona at any second.

There was too much noise, too much chaos. Only a few seconds had passed. It felt like hours. Back-up was coming. They wouldn't get here in time.

"Who are you?" Fiona choked out.

"I'm your worst enemy," Scruggs said.

"Cartel," Amanda said, stricken. "You're with the Côté Cartel."

Scruggs smiled. He didn't bother to deny it. He didn't need to. "We know who you are. We know what you've done, what you've taken from us, and we're coming for you. There's nothing you can do to stop it."

His laughter echoed ominously. Startled, several blackbirds took flight, their dark bodies silhouetted against the blue of the late afternoon sky. The sound masked Shiloh's movement as she took another quiet, careful step.

"We didn't know, I swear!" Theresa huddled on the ground with her body curved protectively over her pregnant belly. "I'm so sorry. We didn't know what he was. He offered us some of his food and asked us to join him and his son. He's the one who told us about this place. We thought—we thought he was saving us. I'm sorry."

Shiloh exhaled steadily as she made her final calculations. A hair's breadth in the wrong direction, and Fiona died instead of Scruggs. She couldn't make an error of even a tenth of an inch.

No mistakes. She had to be perfect.

Time to be brave, to be fearless. To be Shiloh freaking Pope.

"It's too late." Scruggs' features twisted, a maniacal, crazed glee distorting his face. "You're too late."

Shiloh caught Fiona's wild-eyed gaze. Shiloh gave the slightest nod. She wasn't certain if Fiona understood what she needed from her. *Come on, come on...*

"You're already dead!" Scruggs crowed. "You're all dead! You just don't know it yet. This place, this whole town, we will destroy you all." He adjusted his grip on the knife handle, his eyes insolent, hateful. "And I'm starting with this one—"

Fiona blinked twice.

Now.

This ended now.

Fiona went limp, a dead weight. As she dropped, she jerked her elbow backward and slammed Scruggs in the crotch.

A stunned grimace crossed his face, followed swiftly by rage. He grasped at Fiona's hair, wrenching her upward, his head half-turned from the effort, forearm muscles flexing as he began to draw the blade across her throat—

Shiloh squeezed the trigger.

4

ELI POPE

DAY ONE HUNDRED AND TWENTY-TWO

"I t's time to kill him," Antoine said.

Eli Pope wiped his hands on his pants and squatted in front of the prisoner, scowling as pain shot up his injured leg. "Not quite yet."

Their prisoner's bruised eyelids were closed. He was unconscious—or pretending to be.

After Antoine and Nyx had captured the spy five days ago, they had stashed him at the Pictured Rocks Golf Course located approximately four miles northeast of Munising. It was far enough outside of town that looky-loos wouldn't bother them—or hear their prisoner's screams.

"He's useless," Antoine said. "We're wasting time here."

Eli said, "I have an idea."

Jackson stood next to Antoine, his arms folded over his broad chest, his Alger County Sheriff's uniform wrinkled and smudged. Still, he gave off a stern and formidable air. Though the uniform hung loosely on his narrow frame, he looked like he'd been born to wear it.

Polished golf clubs hung from hooks on the cedar plank walls of the Pictured Rocks Pro Shop—from woods, irons, and hybrids to drivers, putters, and wedges. Boxes of toothpaste-white golf balls organized in pyramids were stacked along several tables. Behind the cash register hung a wall of collared shirts in bright salmon-pink, sherbet-orange, and candy-apple red.

Jackson nodded grimly. "We're running out of options."

Eli slapped the prisoner hard in the face.

The prisoner groaned and blinked groggily before his swollen eyelids slid shut again. He slumped against a wall of designer golf bags in various colors. He was a barrel-chested guy in his thirties, heavily bearded, with nut-brown hair and tattoo sleeves snaking up his muscled arms.

His arms and legs were bound with wire, his hands tied behind his back, with his legs stretched out in front of him and restrained at the ankles. Globs of dried vomit stained his faded Metallica T-shirt. His hiking pants were stiff and mottled with blood.

An intravenous line dripped saline into his veins, keeping him alive until they got what they needed from him. The fluid bag hung from the IV pole, which stood beside the prisoner like a hangman's noose.

Over the last several days, he'd drifted in and out of consciousness, barely coherent, certainly not aware enough to offer legitimate intel. Perhaps Antoine had tortured him with a bit too much enthusiasm.

"Hey, Don." Eli slapped him again. "Don, my boy. Time to wake up."

The spy's eyes fluttered open. He glared at them blearily. His name was Don Carriker. They'd gotten that much out of him before he'd passed out, as well as the confirmation that he was a Côté Cartel member.

The man reeked of feces and the sharp ammonia smell of urine. He'd pissed himself several times. He was a hostile, a spy, an infiltrator. Eli felt no emotion for him other than cold, calculated anger mingled with a strong desire to smash his skull into pieces with the nearest golf club.

Eli rose gingerly to his feet and stepped back. His crutches leaned against a glass display case of designer sunglasses and golf hats emblazoned with Timberland and Titleist logos.

Panels of sunlight slanted through the windows, swirling with dust motes. The clubhouse was eerily pristine; it remained untouched by raiders or scavengers.

Outside the windows, the wind snarled the overgrown greens. In the barren parking lot, every electric golf cart had been stolen. Fred Combs had modified several with solar panels; Jackson and Eli had driven one here.

"I know how to get him talking," he said. "It won't be pretty."

Jackson didn't hesitate. "Go ahead."

He'd expected Jackson to balk at torture, but Jackson hadn't said a word. He'd remained mostly silent, a haunted, hunted look in his eyes.

They needed to talk, the two of them, but they'd been consumed with the business of survival. That conversation hadn't happened yet.

Despite the conflict between them, Jackson had bravely entered the tunnels of the copper mine to rescue Eli after he'd hunted down Darius Sykes. That meant something. Eli just wasn't sure what, yet.

He picked out the heaviest driver he could find among the shiny rows of new clubs. Adjusting his grip, he practiced a swing in the narrow space between the shelves and display cases.

Pain flared through his chest and right shoulder, but his muscles worked on command—albeit like rusted, sluggish gears. The stitches in his ear itched and stung, his sprained left ankle tender. Though with each passing day, he grew stronger.

Instinctively, he scratched at the bandage wrapping his chest beneath his black T-shirt, then readjusted his grip on the club and swung again.

He needed to beat the truth out of the hostage. He didn't believe the cartel spy had traveled to Munising alone. These types moved in pairs.

There was another spy. But where was he?

Eli and Jackson had bolstered the perimeter patrols and doubled the sentries and guards manning the checkpoints. Even on crutches, he'd continued to train civilians for hours a day in weapons, tactics, surveillance, and hand-to-hand combat.

Apprehension soured his gut. It wasn't enough.

Antoine cocked a bushy eyebrow. "What's the plan, brother? We gonna go out and play a quick nine, or are we finally getting down to business?" His French accent was faint but unmistakable.

Powerfully built, the former French Legionnaire boasted short brown hair, a thick beard, and squinty eyes that vacillated between playful and savage, depending on his mood. He wore his favorite FAMAS 5.56x45mm NATO rifle slung across his back, which he'd affectionately nicknamed "the bugle."

He was bold and often reckless in battle, with a bloodthirsty grin perpetually plastered to his face. Antoine was a special brand of crazy, but he had earned Eli's trust, and so had Nyx.

Antoine and Nyx had abandoned Sawyer and switched sides. They'd turned the tide in the battle to defeat Sykes and rescue Lena. Eli would fight side by side with them any day of the week, and twice on Sundays.

Eli lifted the driver, making sure the prisoner followed the arc with his eyes. Beads of sweat broke out on the man's skin, his pallor fish-belly white. "You don't have to do this—"

Eli didn't listen. He aligned his body, knees slightly bent, his left leg throbbing in protest as he swung with a perfect backswing, coming down hard with a vicious thwack. The wooden head connected with Don's left ankle.

The man howled in agony. He tried desperately to move, to draw his leg back, but he couldn't. The ankle flopped strangely, the foot disconnected from the tibia and fibula, the tiny bones shattered and loose within the bag of his skin.

"Guess you won't be running out of here anytime soon. Tell us what we want to know, and we can still make this easy on you. No one will know you cooperated with us."

Jackson held out a syringe, which sat gleaming on his palm.

"This will take your pain away. All you have to do is give us the answers we want."

Don panted, his breaths ragged and uneven. "You—you bast—!"

Antoine gave a devilish grin. "Now, now. Language. Insults will get you nowhere."

"I will break your other foot in ten seconds," Eli said. "Your choice."

"You're a monster," Don groaned.

"Now you're getting it."

Eli felt zero remorse. He would happily torture this man for days if it got them the intel they needed. This asshat and others like him had put his daughter at risk. He remained a clear and present danger.

For that, this one would pay, and dearly.

He ran his fingers over the smooth buttery leather of the club's grip. "Let's try this again."

Don shrieked in protest. His bloodshot eyes widened in sheer terror.

Eli raised the golf club, his muscles flexing, feeling the hot ache of his injuries. The club lifted high behind him as he focused on the prisoner's right foot: the hairy toes, the dirt-crusted toenails, the odd-shaped little toe.

Humans were so fragile. So easily broken and corrupted.

Jackson stiffened, his features rigid with disgust, but he made no move to stop Eli. Antoine, on the other hand, grinned with enthusiasm, practically rubbing his hands together in glee. "I can't believe Nyx is missing out on all the fun."

"Last chance," Eli said.

Don's entire body quavered.

The driver hovered, ready to fall like a sledgehammer.

"Wait!" the spy cried. His piggish squeals splintered the dense silence of the Pro Shop. "Stop, please! I'll tell you! I'll tell you everything!"

Eli paused. The golf club wavered in the air. "We're listening."

"There is...one more."

Don spat blood. A loose tooth dribbled out with it. He'd lost several.

Eli's breath caught in his throat. "Where is he?"

"I don't know exactly—"

"What's his mission?"

Don spoke in rapid, frantic gasps. "To infiltrate...the North-woods Inn, to discover exactly where you're keeping the meds and the weapons...to find the weak points...for an assault."

Eli's heart seized in his chest. Everything he loved was at the Northwoods Inn. Everything and everyone. It was the thing he feared most come to terrifying life.

"Radio the Inn," he said. "Every security post. Do it now."

Jackson's radio was already in his hand. "On it."

Eli turned back to the prisoner. "What does he look like? Describe him."

Don mumbled something. Blood trickled from the corner of his mouth. Eli used the driver to maintain his balance as he leaned in close to hear his words.

"We'll keep coming...doesn't matter if you kill a hundred of us...or a thousand. Gault won't stop...Not ever."

He meant Luis Gault, the head of the Côté Cartel and self-proclaimed king of the Upper Peninsula's criminal underworld. Rumors swirled of the brutal cartel that had terrorized Canada for years. The cartel had cleverly utilized the chaos of the solar flares to infiltrate the Upper Peninsula, taking over Sault Ste. Marie and the Soo Locks before spreading their destruction far and wide.

"We'll be ready for you," Jackson said, a hardness in his voice that Eli hadn't heard before, an edge of steel. "We'll slaughter your friends. Anyone who tries to come for us will pay with fire."

Antoine's grin widened. "Too bad you won't be there to see it."

Don's breathing was ragged and shallow, and his skin was a sickly color. He was fading, losing consciousness.

Eli longed to swing the club once more, with all his strength.

The crunch of bone and squelch of brain tissue would be incredibly satisfying. But he still needed this waste of human garbage.

Instead, he dropped the driver. The club clattered to the floor in a pool of sticky blood. Using the butt of his rifle, he smacked the man's skull and knocked him out. Don's head lolled to the side. His small pink tongue poked out between uneven teeth.

Eli took no time to relish the small victory. Everything in him crackled with urgency. Shiloh and Lena's safety consumed his every thought: getting to them, seeing them alive and well with his own eyes.

Antoine headed for the door, his weapon in hand as he scanned their surroundings for threats, a habit as ingrained in them as breathing. "It's go time!"

Jackson handed Eli his crutches as he spoke hurriedly into the radio, then clipped the radio to his belt and paused. He met Eli's gaze with a brutal determination that mirrored Eli's. "You ready for this?"

Eli hobbled toward the door to the Pro Shop. "Damn straight."

5

SHILOH EASTON POPE
DAY ONE HUNDRED AND TWENTY-TWO

S hiloh squeezed the crossbow's trigger.

The bolt flew straight and true. Passing within an inch of Fiona's head, it plunged through Scruggs' left eyeball, piercing the sclera, shredding the optic nerve, and punching into spongy brain tissue. The bolt lodged deep within the bony eye socket.

Bill Scruggs made an inhuman sound, like a cougar's high frantic scream. His hands reflexively released Fiona's hair and the knife. The blade clattered harmlessly onto the road. Fiona staggered free and dove for the ground, crawling away from him.

Scruggs sank to his knees, clawing at his bloodied face, howling and shrieking. Blood poured down his face and soaked his shirt. Red splattered the dirt at his knees.

Shiloh swiftly reloaded a fresh bolt, aimed, and fired again. The bolt struck the man in the upper left side of his chest. He twitched and fell back.

Before Shiloh could reload again, Nash aimed his AR-15 and fired. The AR-15 spat rounds into Scruggs' torso. *Boom! Boom! Boom!*

His body jittered as he collapsed sideways. His flailing fingers grasped uselessly at the fiberglass bolt wedged five inches deep into his brain.

Several agonizing seconds later, he went still.

Shiloh sank to her knees. The crossbow sagged in her hands. Sounds went tinny and distant. Her gaze unfocused as she registered Nash leaning over the body, checking for a pulse.

Voices buzzed in the distance, everything far away like she was deep underwater, kicking hard and swimming for the surface. It was difficult to breathe, a tremendous weight on her chest.

Someone was weeping. Someone else was screaming, maybe more than one person. Maybe the scream was her own.

The enemy was dead. She'd killed him. Her first human being, up close and personal. There was no turning away from the grisly results of her handiwork.

Someone was calling her name.

Hands gripped her shoulders and shook her hard. "Shiloh! Are you okay?" Nash's concerned voice brought her back to the present. He leaned over her, worry in his eyes, his brow furrowed, so close she could have counted the hairs in his mustache.

"Fiona—" she mumbled.

"Fiona is fine." Nash's bony fingers squeezed her arm. "You saved Fiona. You saved all of us. Are you okay?"

She gazed up at him, dazed. Dizziness washed over her. A sick feeling churned in her belly. Nash seemed like a stranger, no one she recognized.

She was fine. The bad guy was dead. Fiona was alive. The refugees were okay—the pregnant lady and the boy were safe. Of course, Shiloh was fine. She attempted to tell Nash exactly that, but her thoughts were blurry, wobbly, and indistinct.

Instead, she said, "It's my birthday."

"Yes." Nash rose to his feet, his walkie-talkie in hand. "Yes, it is."

The radio crackled with static. Dimly, she heard Eli's concerned voice burst through the static: "There's another one. There's another spy!"

"There is," Nash said evenly, gazing down at the bloodied corpse. "Your daughter just shot him."

6

LENA EASTON
DAY ONE HUNDRED AND TWENTY-TWO

Lena Easton leaned against the wood door of the Northwoods Inn hotel room and tried not to weep. The lacquered wood was smooth and cool against her palms, the carpet nubby beneath her socks. The hallway air stale without the A/C unit running.

"How is she?" Eli asked.

Lena's head jerked up, startled. She hadn't heard him coming. Even on crutches, he'd managed to round the corner in near silence. Granted, she'd been distracted.

Ever the soldier, Eli wore a rifle slung across his back, his pistol and knife clipped to his battle belt—every inch the former Army Ranger: tough, strong, and indestructible.

Of course, he wasn't indestructible. He'd nearly died in the copper mine, risking life and limb to save her.

"Shiloh is sleeping, finally." Lena took a steadying breath, swiping at the tears stinging her eyes. She raised her trembling chin to hide the fear that radiated from every cell in her body.

Eli glanced past Lena like he wanted to bust the door in, stomp inside, and ensure Shiloh was safe with his own eyes. His hands balled into fists at his sides, his muscles tensed as if he were preparing for battle, as if he could solve every problem with brute force.

Lena knew better. A teenage girl was not a problem to be solved, especially not one like Shiloh. The girl was brave and fragile, fierce and vulnerable, all at the same time.

As soon as Nash had brought Shiloh back to the Inn, Lena had done a full-body medical work-up on her. She was shaken, though physically she was fine, nothing broken or even bruised.

Utterly exhausted, Shiloh had skipped dinner and passed out on her bed, sleeping the deep and dreamless sleep her body needed to heal from the day's trauma.

Lena moved in front of Eli, blocking the door. "She's okay for now, I promise."

Eli frowned as if he didn't believe her. His jaw tensed, every muscle taut with worry.

"The experience was traumatic, but physically she's untouched. Her body is exhausted from the ordeal, though. Her brain needs to shut down for a while to heal itself."

Eli's hard stance relaxed slightly. "She'll probably sleep for a week."

"Then we'll let her."

"Is she alone in there?"

"Bear refuses to leave her side."

Bear, their giant cinnamon-brown Newfoundland dog, was sleeping soundly on the bed next to her, all one hundred fifty pounds of him. Lena had left him with his thick paws stretched out, his furry snout resting on his forelegs, snoring like a freight train.

A tentative smile cracked Eli's tough façade. "Bear is worth a half-dozen armed guards."

"At least." Lena smiled back, but it was a fragile smile, cracking at the corners.

Her pump beeped, reminding her to monitor her blood sugar levels. The stockpile they'd stolen from the cartel had fortunately contained not only life-saving insulin but also plenty of diabetic supplies: pumps, infusion sets, insertion devices, reservoirs, medical tape, transmitters, needles, swabs, glucose monitors, and test strips. Everything she needed.

The pump was a godsend. No longer did she have to bruise her fingers with constant pricks and needle jabs simply to stay alive.

The insulin would expire after two years—it could still be used but would slowly lose its efficacy over time. Two years felt like a lifeline, a miracle. So much could happen in two years.

Eli took a step closer. He narrowed his eyes, his attention fully on Lena. "You're not okay."

"I'm fine."

It was a lie, of course. For once, her Type I Diabetes wasn't the problem. She wasn't worried about herself; she was worried sick about Shiloh. Her legs were shaky, her chest tight with fear. Lena was supposed to be the strong one; she felt anything but strong. She'd been holding it together, but her heart was about to shatter.

"Lena—"

"We could have lost her."

Shiloh was her niece, not her biological child, but Lena loved the girl like her own. She'd read that having a child was like allowing your heart to walk around outside your body, soft and vulnerable and so readily crushed, so easy to destroy. Never had those words felt truer than now.

They could lose anyone at any time. It was a harsh reality that existed in the old world as much as this one. Lulled into complacency with the comforts of modern society, people had ignored the ugly truths, the hard things they didn't want to see, to feel, or to believe. No longer.

Her voice sounded raspy in her ears. "Things are getting worse out there, with the cartel. And winter is coming...how are we going to protect her?"

"I will. We will."

Eli leaned the crutches against the wall. He went to her and placed a hand against the door on either side of her head, forcing her to meet his intent gaze.

She took him in, his intense coal-black eyes, slanting cheek-bones, the firm line of his mouth. The way he looked at her—fervent, hungry, consuming. An electric charge passed between them. Little flames surged in her veins. Heat flared in her belly, flushing her face.

"I want to lock her in a closet until she's twenty-one," Eli growled. "Is that something we're allowed to do?"

"I think that's generally frowned upon."

Eli shrugged. "The upside of a society in freefall is that we can do what we want, or so Shiloh insists. I bet we could get away with it."

"And have her hate us for the rest of her life."

"If it keeps her alive, I could live with that."

"That doesn't sound so terrible," Lena admitted. "Much as I hate to say it, I think we have to give her some freedom. It's called growing up."

Eli gave a defeated sigh. "She's a natural-born warrior. If we try to keep her from the fight, she'll sneak her way in, just like she did today."

Shiloh was the toughest kid Lena knew. Part of her wanted to lock her away to keep her safe from herself, from her reckless courage. The other part wanted to watch her fly.

"That's our girl," Lena said.

A heavy look crossed his face, shadowed and hard to read, but she knew him better than anyone. She saw it in his eyes: a flash of wonder that this startling creature was his, a fierce pride that she was so much like him, the best parts of him and Lily.

He cleared his throat. "Jackson has called an emergency meeting of the committee. He wants you there."

Lena wasn't ready to leave Shiloh yet; she certainly wasn't ready to leave Eli, to share him with the committee when they had so few moments to themselves, just the two of them. "In a minute."

Eli nodded, his shrewd gaze lowering to her mouth. "Yes, in a minute."

He wrapped his arms around her, enfolding her in his strength. Her skin felt electric, on fire. The strength of the desire burning through her took her breath away. Heat built in her belly and spread through her arms and legs, sparking from the tips of her fingers.

He tilted her chin up with one finger, leaned down, and kissed her hungrily. Her stomach constricted, wild and fluttering. She melted into him, this man she'd loved since she was twelve years old. Hell, since she was five.

The stress, fear, and worry faded away, evaporating within his arms, soothing her in a way nothing else on Earth could. A sense of calm settled over her like a soft blanket.

The solar flares had taken so much from so many people. It had devastated the world. And yet, because of the apocalypse, she had found a daughter. Not only that, she'd rediscovered the man she loved with every atom of her being.

They were imperfect, broken, messy people. Together, they fit perfectly. Together, they could face any threat.

"I will protect her," Eli said gruffly. "I will protect both of you. If I must hunt down every member of the cartel and behead them one by one to keep you safe, then I'll do it."

"You do what you have to do," she murmured into his chest, her cheek pressed against the bandage wrapped beneath his T-shirt. "Just come back to us. Come back to me."

Eli released her long enough to step back and meet her pensive green eyes with his dark penetrating gaze. "Always."

"We're a family," she said. "We're your family."

He kissed her again, hard and wanting and eager, their bodies pressed together, each seeking the warmth, comfort, and security of the other, a moment of calm in the eye of the storm.

A perturbed teenage voice filtered through the hotel room door: "I can hear you, you know!"

Lena stiffened. Her lips quirked into a smile against Eli's. She felt him smiling back, suppressing a chuckle. They stood, listening to each other's heartbeats, their lips touching.

"Yuck!" Shiloh cried. "Cease whatever disgusting things you're doing, right now!"

Lena grinned. Her pump beeped again, reminding her to monitor her blood sugar levels. She ignored it for a minute, just one minute.

Joy and relief bubbled in her chest. Whatever happened, as long as they were together, they would be okay. If she had her insulin, her people, and her dog, she could take on the world.

She believed that. She had to believe that.

Eli kissed her again.

"Gross!" Shiloh yelled.

Eli hugged Lena tight. "That's our girl."

7

LENA EASTON
DAY ONE HUNDRED AND TWENTY-TWO

"I say we vote them all off the island," Ramon Moreno said. "No more refugees. Let them find somewhere else to take them in."

Lena perched on the arm of the leather armchair, her hands clasped over her knees, her gaze fixed on the grim faces surrounding her. "There is nowhere else. There's no one else but us."

Tim and Lori had set up a circle of twenty or so chairs next to the massive two-story stone fireplace in the foyer of the Northwoods Inn. Built during the logging glory days of the early nineteenth century, the Inn was a converted mansion constructed of massive logs, intricate stonework, and impressive floor-to-ceiling stained-glass windows.

The fire crackled cheerily, the scent of woodsmoke and sandalwood wafting through the grand foyer. It was nearly ten p.m. Everyone was exhausted but no one could sleep, not after the near attack on the east gate.

With the number of people living at the Northwoods Inn growing larger every day, a leadership committee had formed, consisting of Tim and Lori Brooks, Jackson and Eli, Lena and Nash, Moreno and Devon, Jim Hart, and a few others.

Last week, the citizens had come together and voted unanimously: the committee would make the decisions for the good of Munising until the threat of the cartel was dealt with and a more democratic process of voting could be established.

"Where will the refugees go if we send them away?" Lena asked. "These are women, children, the elderly. Theresa Fleetfoot is pregnant, her father is injured, and the deaf boy with them is five years old. They have no one else to turn to."

"That's not our problem," Moreno insisted. "Other people aren't our responsibility. We can only be responsible for ourselves, for our people."

"I disagree," Lori Brooks said gently. "If we have the resources, then we should take in as many people as we can. That's what we're here for, isn't it? It's our purpose in this difficult time."

Flour smudged her plump cheeks. She spent most of her time in the commercial kitchen or tending the gardens. The woman knew nutrition inside and out and could whip up a delicious meal for two hundred fifty people with nothing but potatoes, grilled bear meat, and fresh-cut herbs. And fish—so much fish.

Tim Brooks leaned over and squeezed his wife's hand. In his late sixties, he was tall and slender, with kind eyes that crinkled when he smiled. "We've gladly taken all of you in, and you've made us stronger and better for it."

"This is different," Eli said. "This is a smart, coordinated, cunning enemy we're facing. The Côté Cartel sent two spies to Munising. We were lucky to capture the first one. The other one almost made it through our gates. He would have done untold damage, brought the entire cartel to our front porch and opened the door wide."

Lena's stomach went queasy. How close they'd come to utter destruction. Shiloh had saved the day, but only at great cost, forced to kill a man and risk the life of an innocent in the process. Things could have gone so much worse.

They'd gotten lucky. But their luck wouldn't hold. It couldn't, not with what was coming for them. Anxiety sparked through her veins, seizing her throat. She felt it out there: an unseen, number-less force, faceless and evil, lurking just beyond their doorstep, waiting for the perfect moment to strike.

They faced an enemy the likes of which they'd never encountered. She saw it on their faces, the same distraught fear. At any moment, the tension could bubble over into panic, despair, and hysteria. They couldn't let that happen.

"We have to assume they will send more men." From his armchair beside the fire, Jackson leaned forward, his spine bent, and raked a weary hand through his mussed, sand-colored hair. Several weeks of beard growth stubbled his clenched jaw. Shadows pooled beneath his eyes. "The cartel won't stop. They've made that clear."

After the death of Police Chief Sarah McCallister during the copper mine assault, Jackson had become their de facto leader, whether or not he wanted to wear the mantle of leadership.

Lena and Jackson had grown up together; she loved him like a brother. The burden of protecting his people weighed heavily upon his shoulders. There was something else, too, something that seemed to be consuming him from the inside out.

"We know the spies had radio contact with their leadership," Eli said. "Everything the spies knew, the cartel now knows, too. The next time the cartel comes, they'll bring an army."

"What about the refugees who were with the spy?" Tim asked. "Were they in on it, too?"

"I don't think so," Jackson said.

"But you don't know for sure," Moreno said.

"Not one hundred percent, no, but they insist they were duped. He appeared to be a grieving widower with a child, harmless as a dove. They saw what he wanted them to see."

Moreno sank back into his seat, glaring around the room as he scratched at his grizzled beard, his bronze skin pale. One of the few remaining Munising police officers, Moreno acted like he didn't care about much, but he'd proven himself brave and loyal.

"They were scared of him," Nash said. "Theresa Fleetfoot and her father said they felt something was off, but they didn't know what, couldn't put their finger on it. They wanted food and a vehicle, and he offered it to them. They were desperate and couldn't afford to be suspicious. He used them and the little boy as camouflage."

"It almost worked," Moreno muttered.

Jackson nodded. "I tried to interview the boy, but I don't understand sign language. I'm looking for someone who does. Scruggs likely killed the child's parents or had a hand in it."

"We treated the grandfather's chainsaw injury at the clinic," Lena said. "He needs antibiotics, IV fluids, and rest. They're not going anywhere until he recovers enough to travel. Since he's injured and Theresa is pregnant, we managed to find a spot for them here at Northwoods temporarily. The daughter, Miriam, can help take care of them."

"Okay, that's settled," Jackson said.

The grand foyer fell into a strained silence as the group contemplated the unknown future, the threats facing them from multiple angles, and the existential dread of an enemy they couldn't yet see.

"What about the Côté Cartel?" Lori asked. "What do we do?"

"First thing, we circle the wagons," Eli said. "Everything and everyone who can be brought into the perimeter of the Northwoods Inn stays here, especially the elderly, young children, the sick, and the infirm. Those who can't be brought in here should remain within the Munising city limits at all times."

Lena's vision blurred. She couldn't meet Eli's gaze. Instead, she blinked, taking in the rustic wood paneling, the arcing cedar beams, the elegant slate floors. Darkness pressed against the stained-glass windows.

Inside the Inn, it felt warm, cozy, and safe. But it wasn't. They weren't safe, not even close. Eli didn't have to lecture her; she knew it in her bones. Returning to the lighthouse wasn't even an option, not until they'd survived the cartel.

Until, not if.

"I can't shut down the clinic," Lena said.

"You can," Eli said sternly. "For this, you can."

Her spine straightened. "I won't."

She thought of the clinic she and Dr. Virtanen had opened at the hospital, the long line of civilians they treated daily for sicknesses like diphtheria and bacterial infections, diarrhea, and viruses, as well as cuts, burns, accidents, and injuries of all kinds.

That morning, she had treated a young single mother who'd accidentally burned her hand on a camp stove while cooking the last of her oatmeal for her three kids. The burn had become so infected that she would have died without the antibiotics the clinic dispensed.

Most of the doctors and nurses in the area had left for Sault Ste. Marie or Marquette, the two remaining hospitals in the Upper Peninsula, but the medical examiner had returned to her hometown to help. Together, they were saving lives.

Lena fumbled for the insulin pump attached to her hip and checked her number—140, still good. Immense gratitude filled her each time she checked her blood sugar or bolused herself for a meal. She had nearly died from lack of insulin for her Type 1 diabetes.

Thanks to the successful attack on the copper mine, she had enough medication for herself and to share with others. The meds had been separated into secret caches, one at the hospital, one at the Inn, and one at the high school.

Keeping the meds for herself was unthinkable. She *had* to give back, to help others; it was knit into her DNA. It gave her life meaning and purpose.

She leaned forward, meeting the eyes of each member of the committee one by one. "If we stop helping people, if people die that we could have saved because we were scared...then how are we any better than the cartel? They've already won."

"Staying alive is what matters!" Eli shook his head. The firelight flickered along the sharp planes of his face, making him appear hard, cruel, even brutal. He glanced at Lena and his expression softened. "It's only temporary."

Like leaving the lighthouse was supposed to be temporary. Lena set her jaw. "We can double or triple the guards at the hospital, but shutting it down isn't an option. We didn't sacrifice so much stealing those meds to keep it all to ourselves."

Eli grunted in frustration. He opened his mouth to argue, but Jackson raised a weary palm. "Let's table this discussion for the moment. Eli, Antoine, Nyx, and I will meet with the security committee tomorrow morning and come up with a workable response to the cartel threat. Right now, everyone needs some sleep. We'll come at this fresh in the morning."

"Not yet." Lori shifted uneasily in her seat. The paper clutched in her hands crinkled as she smoothed the creases. "We have one more task to complete tonight."

8

LENA EASTON
DAY ONE HUNDRED AND TWENTY-THREE

"We have people on the waiting list." Lori looked down at the unfolded piece of paper in her lap, a dozen names sketched in pencil, and frowned. "Traci Tilton and her son and Bradley Underwood. We haven't decided about them yet and they've been waiting for an answer. They need somewhere to sleep tonight."

"Underwood is an incompetent hack," Moreno spat.

Lena watched Jackson's reaction. His jaw twitched, his gaze hardening, but he said nothing. The former sheriff had failed to recognize the serial killer within their midst, repeatedly confounding the investigation and hamstringing Jackson as he'd hunted for the killer.

"Incompetence is its own kind of evil," Eli warned. "Be careful who you allow into the henhouse."

Tim frowned. "He's our former sheriff. I don't want to turn him away. We don't have to give him a leadership role, but we can offer him shelter."

"Sheriff Cross, what do you think?" Lori asked.

Jackson's stony expression gave little away. "This is your place. If you want to invite him in, that's your prerogative. I won't try to stop it."

43

"Maybe you should," Moreno said sullenly.

"Everyone deserves a second chance," Lena said. "Not at leadership, but to be part of a community."

Moreno made a face. "He better stay in his lane."

"I'm sure he will." Lori appeared flustered, smoothing the handwritten list in her lap again and again. "He will."

"Moving on." Tim glanced at Lena with obvious reticence and perhaps guilt. "Traci is waiting in the library. She asked to speak with us before we decide."

Lena stiffened. Her pulse quickened against her throat, her muscles going taut as she gripped the chair armrests. She forced her voice to remain even. "That seems fair."

Nash rose from his seat and went to retrieve Traci Tilton. The rest of the committee studied Lena with curious, empathetic gazes. Everyone knew about the gift shop, how Sykes used Traci's diabetic son to lure Lena into a trap.

Conflicted emotions tangled in Lena's gut as Traci Tilton entered the foyer and approached the committee, her gait uncertain, her gaze pleading. Her hands clasped in front of her in a conciliatory gesture. She took a seat in the single empty chair.

A flash of memory seared Lena's mind—Traci begging for help; Curtis Tilton's blood soaking the floor of the Enchanted Cascades gift shop; Angel Flud's maniacal grin; how Sykes had looked at her as if she were a meal.

Lena pushed the dark thoughts out of her head. She never wanted to think about Sykes or Angel Flud again.

Traci's anxious gaze darted around the room, looking everywhere but at Lena. "I am so sorry for what I did," she said in a choked whisper. "I will do everything I can to make up for it. I will work sanitation, do the dishes every single meal, whatever is needed, whatever it takes, I'll do it. I humbly petition the committee to allow me to stay at the Inn with my son."

"No!" came a voice behind them. "No way in hell."

Shiloh appeared out of nowhere. Lena hadn't heard her enter the foyer from the hallway lined with hotel rooms.

44

With Bear a big furry shadow pressed close to her side, Shiloh strode into the center of the circle of chairs, her snarled ink-black hair sticking up all over her head. She wore a pair of Eli's black boxers and an oversized shirt of Cody's that featured a drawing of a *Star Wars* storm trooper sitting on the toilet with the words "Storm Pooper" in large type. She looked so small suddenly, small and fierce.

Shiloh stabbed a furious finger at Traci. "That woman does not belong here. She does not get a place at the table."

Traci sat back in her chair with an exhaled breath as if she'd been punched in the solar plexus. Her features contorted in a mixture of shame and regret. "I'm so sorry—"

"I said shut up!"

"Shiloh—" Lena started, attempting to placate her.

Shiloh spun and faced Lena. Her face red, her dark eyes flinty. "You of all people should know. You almost died because of her! She betrayed you!"

"Traci lost her husband and almost lost her son. Darius Sykes put a gun to her son's head and forced her to set a trap for me."

"I don't care!"

"I do." Lena kept her gaze on Shiloh. Everyone was watching them, listening intently. "I know what it feels like to almost lose your child, to love as a mother loves. I know what that means now. I can't say what I would do in that situation, but—"

"You wouldn't have sacrificed someone else's life in exchange. You wouldn't have done it. You would have figured out a way!"

Shiloh's pain pierced Lena's heart. The girl was suffering, hurting, and incredibly angry. Lena didn't have the energy for hatred and grudge-keeping. Her near-death experience had clarified things, pruning the unessential until only what mattered remained.

Their true enemies were out there, not in here. That's what she wanted Shiloh to understand. "I forgave her. I forgive her."

Tears streamed down Traci's cheeks. Her curly blonde hair was messy. Deep circles shadowed her blue eyes. She sniffled and wrung her hands in her lap. "If I could take it back or do something differently, I would—"

Shiloh glared daggers at her. "No one asked you to speak."

"I would never ask to stay for myself. I'm only asking for my son—"

"Stop! Just stop!"

Traci nodded miserably. Her shoulders hunched, head bowed, a woman utterly defeated by the world, devastated and grieving. She still had her son. Keagan, a Type 1 diabetic like Lena, was still alive.

Bear chuffed softly, ears flattened, tail low, swinging his big head from Shiloh to Lena to Traci, and back to Shiloh, as if alarmed at the charged emotion in the room. He pressed his furry torso against Shiloh's thigh to give her moral support. His fur had grown over the stitched wound in his front leg, his limp barely perceptible.

He was a smart, sensitive dog, alert to his humans' feelings, always eager to offer comfort, though this wasn't a problem Bear's soft fur and sweet, puppy-dog eyes could fix. It wasn't something anyone could fix.

Eli rose from his chair next to Jackson and hobbled across the floor to Shiloh, leaving his crutches leaning against the chair. He wrapped his arms around Shiloh's quaking shoulders.

Shiloh attempted to shove him away, but he held her close and hugged her to his chest. He said her name, softly, into her hair.

Only then did some of the fight leak out of her. She blinked rapidly like she was holding back tears. Normally so tough and mature, it was easy to forget that Shiloh was still a child, barely a teenager.

Bear sat forlornly at their feet, his tail sweeping the floor, whimpering in concern. Like Lena, he seemed to want everyone to get along.

"I understand how painful it was to almost lose your aunt, honey," Lori said gently. Her eyes glittered like she was fighting back tears herself, her voice scratchy. "It was a terrible thing to happen to anyone, but I think we can find room in our hearts for understanding and compassion, and possibly someday, forgiveness."

"Never!" Shiloh spat. "That woman—she betrayed Lena. She deserves to die—!"

"That's enough," Eli said quietly, firmly. He met Lena's gaze over Shiloh's head, distress in his eyes. He didn't need to speak it aloud; she felt his concern for Shiloh as strongly as her own.

"We've left the final decision up to Lena," Tim said. "What Traci did affected Lena the most. She's the one who suffered. Her decision is our decision."

Shiloh glared at Lena. "Say it. Tell them all to suck it."

"I vote yes," Lena said. "Traci and her son may stay."

Traci sagged in relief. "Thank you! Thank you so, so much—!"

Shiloh wrestled out of Eli's grip, spun on her heels, and nearly spat at Traci. "I will always hate you. I will never, ever forgive you for what you did."

Traci blanched. "Shiloh, I—"

"Stay the hell out of my way or I swear, you'll regret it." Hands fisted at her sides, Shiloh stalked from the foyer, marching past Traci's seat without deigning to look at her, as if she were suddenly invisible. Bear trotted at her side, his tail low. Her parting words echoed behind her, her sharp footsteps and Bear's clicking nails receding into stillness.

Eli took a step like he was about to go after her, shooting Lena an inquiring look, his eyebrows raised as if to say: *should we go after her?*

Lena gave a slight shake of her head. Like Eli, she longed to wrap her niece in her arms and hold her until the anger, bitterness, and fear had purged themselves.

But Shiloh was prickly. She was hurting. She was both an Easton and a Pope, which meant a double helping of stubbornness flowed through her veins like lava. She'd refuse to listen to anyone, especially Lena, until she was good and ready.

Traci rose unsteadily, smoothing her clothes, her hands rigid like claws at her sides. Trembling, she wiped the tears from her face with the back of her arm. The sound of her voice when she spoke was barely audible. "You won't regret this, I promise."

"You and Keagan can take room Thirty-Six, in the eastern wing," Lori told her. "There are fresh sheets on the bed. You can get the key at the front desk."

"Thank you." Traci turned and fled.

"Poor Shiloh," Lori said once Traci was gone. "She's been through so much."

"She'll get through this," Lena said with more confidence than she felt. "I know she will. We all will."

There's no other choice. No one said that part aloud.

9

ELI POPE

DAY ONE HUNDRED AND TWENTY-FOUR

E li looked at his daughter, steeling himself as if challenging a charging bull.

For seven years, he had served as a hardened tier-one operator with the 75th Ranger Regiment, surviving combat in Afghanistan, Iraq, Syria, and elsewhere on top-secret spec ops missions. Then he'd endured eight brutal years in the Alger Correctional Facility prison, surviving among savage killers and maniacal monsters.

Yet nothing frightened him quite as much as this tiny girl in front of him, five foot nothing and one hundred pounds soaking wet. Navigating relationships was treacherous, he'd learned, and fraught with hazards at every step.

He considered his words carefully. "You can talk to me, you know."

Shiloh scowled. "Talking is overrated."

They sat cross-legged, facing each other across the expansive pelt of the black bear Shiloh had killed a few weeks ago. The shed was lined with shovels, rakes, post-hole diggers, and hoes, along with several wheelbarrows and other gardening paraphernalia.

The smell of fertilizer, cut grass, and oil was strong in his nostrils. Dust motes swirled in the stale air. The light from the battery-operated lanterns cast everything in a warm yellow glow, deep shadows pooling in the spiderwebbed corners.

For weeks, Shiloh had begged him to work on the bear hide, but between bolstering their defenses and training the civilians, plus the rest required for his injuries, he hadn't had time.

He needed to make time, especially for her belated birthday. These moments with his daughter were precious and fleeting. He'd missed so many years—he refused to miss a second more.

Earlier, they had poured several pounds of non-iodized salt onto the skin side of the hide. Wearing rubber gloves, they'd rubbed the salt into the bear skin, then draped the hide over a pair of sawhorses to dry for several days.

After that, they'd painstakingly scraped the flesh from the hide, then washed, rinsed, and soaked it in trash bags several times to remove the grease. After tanning the hide in a plastic trash can with a potassium-aluminum and soda mixture for six days, Shiloh scrubbed the hide and dried it.

For the last several hours, they'd worked on stretching the hide while oil heated in a pot on the camping stove set beneath the open shed window. Together, they constructed a frame with spare 2x4s, then laid the hide out flat, with the skin side up.

With a large needle, they each took a side and began poking holes every four inches along the perimeter of the hide, sewing each hole with a thin nylon cord.

Eli focused on the steady work of his hands and watched his daughter out of the corner of his eye. She didn't look at him, her head down, brows furrowed in concentration. Her black hair shone in the electric lamplight, falling across her face in rippling curtains.

"You had to take a life to save a life," he said. "Whatever you feel, it's normal. Angry, sad, victorious, guilty. Whatever it is, it's okay."

"Feelings are overrated."

"No," he said. "They're not."

He felt awkward and embarrassed, never sure of the right

words, always stumbling over his thoughts, constantly worried he'd say the wrong thing and mess up everything. One thing he was certain of: the love that pulsed through the fiber of his being. A love as fierce as it was surprising.

He'd never known the meaning of true joy until he'd laid his eyes on his daughter for the first time. He hadn't believed a second chance at love was possible for someone like him. It was not only possible, it was real. A fresh chance, a life he'd never imagined unfurling before him. It was as fragile as a bubble, as rare and astonishing as a deep-sea pearl.

"I used to think that way, too. Do you know who taught me something different? Your Aunt Lena."

"Gross." Shiloh made a face. She acted disgusted at the thought of Lena and Eli together, but Eli had caught her furtive smiles and pleased glances.

Shiloh finished sewing the black bear's left hind leg and moved to the wide torso. Her oversized T-shirt depicted Darth Vader holding a platter of desserts: *Join the dark side. We have cookies.*

"Are you going to kill the other spy you have locked up?" she asked.

Eli grunted. "Yes, but that's not what we're discussing right now. We're discussing Scruggs and how you feel about killing him. Don't try to wriggle out of it. You're attempting to distract me. Tell me about what happened."

"Fine, whatever." Shiloh offered a careless shrug, her gaze glued to the knitting needle in her hands. "I saw what I had to do, and I did it. He would've noticed Nash, Amanda, or Jason making a move. He didn't pay much attention to me. I made him pay for it."

"How did you feel?"

She hesitated. "I was scared I would miss, terrified I would hurt Fiona instead. I figured if I went for a shoulder shot or something, he might kill Fiona. He was going to do it. I saw the look in his eyes. It's like death reflected back at you. I've seen it before."

A pained twinge thrummed in his chest. He longed to protect her from this, but he couldn't. Another emotion flared through him: a rush of tremendous pride.

"You did exactly what you should've done. You took a life to save lives. There is no shame in that. None."

Her mouth twisted. In the dim light, her black eyes glittered as if twin flames lit her from within. "I'm fine. Better than fine. You want to know exactly how I felt? It felt good. It felt like justice."

She ran one hand absently across the coarse black fur. "I mean, I felt bad when I shot the black bear, but I had to do it. It was gonna kill Bear, and it was threatening Lena. I didn't feel bad when I shot that asshat through his eyeball. I still don't feel bad. I felt a lot of other things, but not bad. Not guilty. I still don't."

"Good."

A soft smirk slipped across her lips. "I'm not like Lena. I'm like you."

As usual, she was correct. She was his miniature in so many ways, which both pained him and pleased him immensely.

"Remember, it's much easier to kill than to heal. Easier to destroy than to do the work of rebuilding. Easier to hate than to forgive. In her way, Lena is braver than I am. She puts her heart out there, again and again. She refuses to let the world tear her down."

Shiloh considered that. "She's too naive."

"She's not naive. She makes decisions with her eyes wide open. It's not what I would choose, but I respect her for it. It's a radical thing, to choose to trust when your heart has been broken. I think it might be the bravest thing anyone can do."

"Hmm," Shiloh said noncommittally.

"She's smarter than both of us put together."

"That Tilton woman betrayed her. Lena could have died. We can't trust her. She should be banished at the very least, but all Lena did was forgive her. It's a mistake. She's making a mistake."

"Maybe," Eli allowed.

Lena carried a deeper strength than merely physical. He

respected her ingrained sense of compassion; it was part of why he loved her. He did not share her merciful nature, but he did admire it.

Shiloh didn't say anything for a while as she worked on stretching the hide over the frame, her lower lip caught between her small white teeth. They lapsed into a comfortable silence for several minutes.

"I'm angry," she said abruptly. "I'm angry all the time, and I don't know how not to be angry. Sometimes, I want to break things. Sometimes, I want to break people. I hated Scruggs. I wanted to destroy him."

"Anger is good when it's righteous. It fuels you. It drives you to right a wrong, to protect the innocent, to defend your home and your loved ones, like you did in saving Fiona. Control it, don't let it control you. I lived with that all-consuming anger for a long time, for years, the cancerous kind that eats away at you. I almost lost myself to it, but Lena showed me something different. She showed me that love isn't weakness—love is the thing that gives us the strength to overcome anything. You showed me that, too."

Shiloh blinked several times, her eyes glassy in the lamplight. "I'll try to remember that."

They finished weaving the cord through the perimeter holes before stretching the hide length and widthwise, tightening the cord along the frame, which they would repeat over the next several days until the hide was sufficiently stretched, softened, and supple.

Shiloh stood and took a step back as she examined their hand-iwork, beaming with pride. He studied her: her pointed chin, the rigid set of her mouth, the flint arrowhead glinting in her raven-black hair. She beamed with pride.

For an instant, standing there in that dilapidated shed, in the warm dusty glow of the lamplight, he glimpsed his daughter as a grown woman, as she would be. Strength and assured confidence radiated from her being. She was tough, stubborn, whip-smart, and so achingly beautiful.

"Before...before I knew about this—" she made a vague gesture encompassing herself and Eli. "I defined myself by what I'd lost. Fatherless and motherless. No grandfather, no—" her voice caught in her throat. "No brother. Whatever I did, no matter how much I tried, I lost him, again and again. I lost my mom, over and over, in every nightmare, every time I dreamed. I kept losing them, no matter how hard I tried to save them."

Eli ached for her. "You couldn't save your brother, but you saved Ruby. You saved Lena. You saved Fiona. You helped Jackson find your mother's killer. You have a warrior's heart."

She raised her chin. "I know."

He'd been to prison. He'd been to war. He'd seen human beings break beneath combat, PTSD, the terrors of the mind. He'd seen the worst humanity had to offer and the best.

This child—she was the best of them. She was what he fought for, would keep fighting for, until his last gasping breath.

His heart felt both full and shattered with equal parts love and pain. This, then, was how it felt to be a parent: your chest torn open every second of every day.

She regarded him with a somber expression. "Promise you won't leave. Promise you won't die."

"I won't," he vowed. "I'm not going anywhere, not ever."

She understood this was a vow he couldn't keep, and yet it seemed to satisfy something inside her. She gave a curt nod. "I'm gonna hold you to that if I have to drag you out of the grave myself."

"I'm well aware." If anyone could defy death, it would be his daughter. "As long as I'm not allowed to die, the same rule applies to you, too, young lady," he said in his best stern, fatherly voice.

A steely flash shone in her eyes. Then she smiled, a smile that brightened her entire face, like the dazzling sun breaking through the clouds. "Touché."

10

ELI POPE

DAY ONE HUNDRED AND TWENTY-SIX

"I swear, I'm telling the truth!" the spy cried. "Please, have mercy. I'm begging you!"

Unfortunately for Don Carriker, Eli was not merciful. Not at all.

He leaned forward and pulled the soaked towel from the prisoner's head. Tears and snot mingled with the water pouring down his face. His shirt and torso were drenched. He gasped and sputtered for oxygen, half-choking, his chest seizing.

Don slumped against a wooden beam in the center of the schoolhouse. The single-room boasted wooden benches, an ancient chalkboard, and an iron woodstove. It was almost as if the teacher and pupils had simply stepped out for recess a mere hundred years ago.

Daylight streamed through the filmy windows. Cardboard boxes and crates were stacked in the cobwebbed corners. Fresh footprints tracked through the layers of dust.

The boxes and crates were empty, but the hostage didn't know that.

Eli glanced pointedly at the half-full bucket of water beside him. "I can do this all day long and happily start fresh again in the morning. Twenty-four hours a day, seven days a week."

"No! No, please! I'll tell you anything!"

In the four days since Bill Scruggs had attempted to infiltrate the Northwoods Inn, Eli and Antoine had tortured further information from their prisoner. They splinted his ankle and taped his broken toes, giving him ibuprofen for the pain so he'd remain somewhat coherent.

It had taken a few days of torture to break him, but they'd succeeded.

Two nights ago, in the middle of the night, while the prisoner was still unconscious, they'd dragged him from the Pro Shop to a secure location Eli had previously scouted.

Located well outside of Munising, Devil's Corner was an abandoned iron-mining community that had become one of the Upper Peninsula's infamous ghost towns.

The collection of dilapidated eighteenth-century buildings included a few dozen stick-built houses, an old church, a general store, a ramshackle two-story hotel, a cemetery, and a one-room schoolhouse. A single dirt road snaked through the abandoned town.

The place was utterly devoid of people, of any signs of life but for cockroaches, snakes, and the occasional ghost wandering through the eerie quiet.

"How many fighters does the cartel have?" Antoine stood behind Eli, leaning against the sagging wall of the one-room schoolhouse and tapping the blade of a combat knife against his palm with studied boredom.

"A thousand, at least," Don mumbled. "More every day. People fight for him, they get to eat, to live. They fight against him, they die. Their family dies. We have a force of five hundred troops just across the border. We have more, but they're busy holding the towns we've taken, including the Soo Locks."

"How many soldiers does the cartel use in their raids?" Eli clarified.

"Fifty or sixty per raiding party, give or take. Sometimes they collect people with battle experience who are willing to fight for them for free food, security, and shelter."

"Where is the closest raiding party now?" Antoine asked.

"I...don't know. We were camped out at a swanky five-star hotel near Whitefish Point last week before I was sent on this mission. Without electricity, things were getting pretty rank by the time I left."

"How often do you move?"

"The raiders move every few days. They never stay in one place for long. Gault's orders."

"What kind of supplies does the cartel have for these raids? They're traveling far from their base at the Soo Locks."

"They have a huge storehouse of supplies. Two of the raiders' trucks are designated for food and water. A third one stores ammunition and weapons. They steal whatever they find as they move from town to town."

"How many working vehicles do they have? And are they armored?"

The man grimaced, breathing heavily for a minute before he answered. "Eight, I think. Mostly black armored SUVs. A couple of trucks for supplies."

Eli saw it, a tiny tic of the right eye. "What else?"

"Ah—I—"

Antoine scowled and pushed himself off the wall. "Time for another shower."

"No! I don't need—"

Antoine sheathed his knife, grabbed the sodden towel from the bucket, and pressed the wet fabric over the man's mouth and nose. The spy sputtered and choked. Antoine lifted the bucket and poured gushing water over Don's face, blocking his airways, slowly drowning him.

After thirty seconds, an eternity to the man being tortured, Eli signaled to Antoine to cease. Antoine set the sloshing bucket down on the floor and whipped the sopping towel from Don's face. "How's that feel, asshat?"

The spy wheezed, his chest shuddering, slimy snot glistening on his chin and cheeks. "Please don't—"

Antoine loomed over him. "You clean enough yet or are you ready for another round? Or maybe I should just gut you with my knife. It needs sharpening."

"Helicopters!" Don panted. "We have three Hueys."

Eli and Antoine exchanged a grim look. They'd met those helos in battle before. The odds were as bad as he'd feared.

"What other equipment and weapons do they have?" Antoine asked.

"We've raided a few National Guard armories. They hardly put up a fight. We ambushed 'em with overwhelming force. They were expecting back-up and never got it. We've got hundreds of assault rifles, grenades, RPGs, land mines. Drones. Mortars and artillery. We're an army. No one can stop us."

"How many fighters can the cartel supply in the field and in garrison?"

Don looked at him blankly.

Eli clarified. "Is there a quick reaction force nearby to aid the raiders if they need back-up?"

"Yes, but I don't know where they're located. They keep the important intel from the grunts. I'm just a grunt—"

"How many of your fighting force are former military?"

"I—I don't have any idea—"

"Try harder."

"I—I swear. There are some, but I don't know how many. A few Russians, Mexican Marines, and some mercenaries, a couple have French accents."

"French Legionnaires," Antoine said darkly.

"Yeah, them. And a few dozen American soldiers, but I don't know from where, Navy or Marines or what. They don't exactly advertise their previous affiliations. They picked the winning team because they want to live, same as I do."

"Do they train their soldiers themselves? If not, who does the training, and how long do they train them? What do they do in training?"

The spy gaped at him. "I don't know. I got some basic training, enough so they knew I could shoot and fight. And then I got sent out on missions."

Eli believed him—almost. A rough picture was taking shape in his mind, and it didn't look good. He figured the cartel had a semi-professional army equal to a light infantry American National Guard, four to five companies in strength, with a few special forces sprinkled in to make things interesting.

Eli asked several follow-up questions, interrogating him on tactics, movements, locations, and weapons. He examined him closely for signs of deception, a twitch of his lips or a tightening around the eyes, but there was nothing.

Don was a broken man.

Eli stood slowly, using his new favorite golf club for balance. He'd brought the driver with him from the Pictured Rocks Clubhouse. He'd grown quite fond of it—and the damage it could do. Finally, he was off crutches, though still limping, and the driver aided his balance.

As a bonus, it struck pure terror into Don Carriker's ugly heart.

The spy's eyes widened in fear. "You still need me! I can get you more intel—"

"The next time I come in here, I'm going to kill you." The club gripped in one hand, Eli strode from the dilapidated room, Antoine at his side. The spy's gurgled cries faded behind them.

Once they were outside, Antoine whistled. "Well, that's a giant floating turd in my soup."

"We knew we were outmanned and outgunned. We have no aid from the National Guard, the state police, or any other law enforcement agency. We're on our own."

"What are you thinking, brother?" Antoine asked. "I can see that tactical mind grinding gears in your eyes. You have a plan."

"Perhaps."

"While you're otherwise occupied, can we kill this jerkwad already?"

The cartel spies had gotten too close for comfort. Shiloh could've been killed. He wanted nothing more than to make this squirming rat pay for it. Everything in him longed to smash his skull inside out with the fat glossy golf club. He wanted to make this interloper suffer, and suffer immensely.

Instead, he said, "Not yet."

11

ELI POPE

DAY ONE HUNDRED AND TWENTY-SEVEN

The next morning, the sun rose high in the cobalt blue sky, not a cloud in sight. Birds twittered, the September air was fresh and cool and smelled of pine sap and distant woodsmoke.

Eli leaned against the crumbling outer wall of the schoolhouse and cocked his head, listening to the whinnies of a couple of horses. Alexis Chilton had arrived with a young girl in tow. Alexis waved at them as the horses trotted nearer.

In her late twenties, Alexis was a deputy with the Sheriff's Office. Her strawberry-blonde hair was plopped on top of her head in a messy bun. She wore oversized, black-frame glasses. A tech nerd, she'd still fought bravely in several battles to defend her town.

The girl with Alexis slid down from the saddle and wrapped the horse's reins around a fence post before approaching Eli. Her mass of red curls was pulled back into messy pigtails. The pigtails and the sunflower yellow sundress she wore made her seem younger than her sixteen years.

Eli's gut clenched in apprehension. "You sure you're up for this? There's no pressure. You don't have to do this."

His daughter's best friend clenched her jaw and raised her

chin with a tremulous smile. "Shiloh doesn't get to save the world all by herself."

"Fair enough." Eli found himself smiling back at her. Ruby Carpenter had come so far from the filthy, trembling victim Shiloh had yanked from Walter Boone's basement dungeon over four months ago.

Gentle and sweet, she wasn't a natural warrior like Shiloh. Certainly, she was no killer, but beneath that soft exterior, Eli sensed an inner strength, a powerful resilience that would serve her well in this world.

"I want to do this," Ruby said. "I can fool him."

Eli stepped back and gestured for her to enter the building. "By all means, have at it."

Antoine appeared around the corner with a tray of food they'd brought over that morning from the Inn—a bowl of Lori Brooks' chili soup, a cup of blackberries, and a glass of water with a spoon set on a cloth napkin.

Antoine grinned at her. "Here we go. Breakfast of champions."

Ruby took the tray, plastered a wan smile on her face, and winked at them. "How am I doing so far?"

"Good," they both said.

"I took community drama in high school. I've got this."

Eli hoped like hell that she did. A lot was riding on this moment, more than he wished to contemplate.

He and Antoine watched in silence as Ruby shuffled into the lion's den. A few moments later, her soft voice filtered through the walls. "They told me not to feed you anything, but they're gone, and I couldn't help it. Everyone deserves to eat."

"Thank you, thank you," Don gushed weakly. "I haven't eaten more than moldy bread in days."

Ruby gave a sympathetic cluck of her tongue.

They waited, listening to the muffled sounds as Ruby squatted beside the prisoner, followed by slurping noises as she spoon-fed him the soup.

"You're so pretty," Don said.

Antoine rolled his eyes heavenward. Eli suppressed a wry smile. It worked every time. Certain types of men were so incredibly predictable. Put a pretty girl in the room and they lost all sense.

Ruby murmured a demure thanks.

"This is delicious. Did you make it at the Northwoods Inn?"

He was fishing for intel. So far, so good.

"I made it myself."

"It's amazing. You're so talented. I hope they appreciate you here."

Ruby made a noncommittal noise. "I'm not supposed to talk to you."

There was silence for a few minutes as the man ate hungrily. "We have fresh food at the Soo, where I live. We eat whatever we want. And electricity for hot showers from the locks, which generate electricity. You would like it. Bet you haven't had a hot shower for a long time. Or have you? I mean, you're clean, and you smell good."

"Oh, I'm not supposed to talk about it."

"Of course not. I wouldn't want you to get into trouble. I just...I really enjoy talking to you. That's okay, right?"

"Um, sure. I suppose that's okay. Thank you."

Eli imagined Ruby blushing, biting her lower lip as she allowed him to lead, lulling him into believing he was the one in control of this conversation.

The prisoner asked her a series of softball questions: about her hobbies, and things she liked from the old world, before gradually coming back around to her living quarters, her family, and her daily chores. They were seemingly innocuous questions that were anything but.

Ruby handled them deftly, providing only what Eli had approved and not an iota more. He had to admit, she was good. This half-baked plan just might work.

"What are all these boxes everywhere?" Don asked, sounding nonchalant.

Ruby didn't miss a beat. "Um, just like, medical supplies and stuff. And like, weapons, I think?"

"It's great you still have that stuff. Lots of places don't."

"We've been lucky. We've got several buildings stacked full of these supplies. And a bunch of caches buried in the woods. I think we're doing okay."

"I'd say so. I'm happy for you. How do people get the medicines they need if they're stored out here?"

"Um, so I should probably go now," Ruby said in a breathy rush, suddenly sounding nervous as if she'd realized she'd said too much. "I'm not supposed to talk about that stuff. I'll get in trouble."

"You won't get in trouble, I promise. I won't tell if you won't." His voice was conspiratorial as if they were both in on a secret.

Of course, he was biding his time. But so was Ruby.

"Okay," Ruby said, acting demure and uncertain. "Okay, sure."

"You know, I could help you. I could make sure you and your family are protected. In case something happens. If it ever came to that."

"I'll—I'll think about it."

"You could stay a little longer. I like it when you talk to me." His tone was confident now. He thought he was working her, squeezing the pretty little girl for information, expertly turning her to his side. "You're so smart and pretty. I hope your people treat you like a princess."

"Oh, I don't know about that."

"I'd treat you like a princess. I'd give you the best of everything if I ever had the chance."

Eli imagined Ruby blushing, flustered but also flattered at the shower of compliments.

"Sorry, I didn't mean to embarrass you. It's just—you're so special. I could tell the second I saw you. I like talking with you."

"I...I like it, too. No one has been this nice to me." A shuffling sound as she rose to her feet, the clatter of the bowl and spoon on the tray. Ruby gave a nervous, girlish laugh. "It's late. I can't get caught in here with you."

"Please don't rush away. I hope I get a chance to talk to you again. I've enjoyed your visit. Will you come back to see me?"

A beat of silence as Eli imagined Ruby turning on her full-wattage smile, maybe batting her eyelashes a little, playing the part of the timid, naive girl ripe for manipulation. "I'd like that."

"Me too." Another moment of silence. "This place seems kind of quiet. I know you can't tell me where we are, but it doesn't seem like anybody lives here."

"Oh, this is temporary. They bring the boxes and crates here from various secret spots. We keep the supplies buried in different locations in the woods. Every other Tuesday, what's needed is brought here to distribute to local towns via horse-drawn cart."

A fraction of a pause.

Eli tensed, afraid that the spy had recognized the tactics employed against him.

After a moment, Don said cautiously, "So this place is a depot."

"Yeah, something like that." A frown in her voice, a flare of just the right amount of concern, as if realizing her mistake. "I've gotta go."

"Wait—will you come back tomorrow?"

"I'll try." Ruby scuttled from the room, clutching the tray to her chest like a life vest that could save her if she held on hard enough. Exiting the schoolhouse, she let the battered door close behind her.

Instantly, her hunched shoulder blades straightened and her timid, wide-eyed expression vanished. She flashed Eli a triumphant smile.

"I'm officially impressed," Antoine said once they were out of hearing distance. He gave her a gentle clap on the back. "That was top-level spy craft right there. You're a natural."

Ruby beamed. "I acted the way he expected me to act—weak, scared, naïve, and guileless. When you act like the person they think you are, they can't imagine that you might be more. They let their guard down. That's how—" She paused, biting her lower lip as a shadow passed across her face, storm clouds blocking the sun. She took a steadying breath. "That's how I survived."

Eli's mind flashed to Walter Boone's cabin in the woods, the dead girls Boone's partner Cyrus Lee had buried in the backyard. "You did good, Ruby."

This time, her smile was forced. They both remembered things they'd rather forget. That was the nature of trauma, your scars a constant reminder, the past forever casting a shadow over the present.

She handed Antoine the tray. "Now what?"

Eli glanced at his watch. "Let him stew until tomorrow. Then you do your thing again."

"So, we wait."

Eli nodded. "We wait."

After she'd left, hitching a ride into town with Alexis on the horses, Eli and Antoine waited until the oppressive silence settled over the ghost town once again.

Eli swung the driver in a practice swing, lopping the tops off a cluster of wildflowers with a satisfying thwack. "One more thing to do before you can get back to Nyx."

The former legionnaire's rugged face blushed a deep crimson. "I don't—it's not like that—"

Eli raised both hands in acquiescence, still holding the club. "It's none of my business. Deny it all you want, but I'm happy for you. I really am."

"You're getting sappy in your old age, brother."

"Maybe," Eli allowed. "For the first time in my life, I know what I'm fighting for. And why."

"I get it, bro." Antoine grew uncharacteristically pensive. "I do. When we got those beta blockers and saved Nyx's grandma, it was surreal, man. Her grandma may be old, but she's feisty. She keeps bees as a hobby. She walks right in and opens the hive boxes and a million bees are buzzing all around her, landing on her cheeks, and crawling up her arms. I'm about to pass out from anxiety. I hate bees, brother, but this tough old broad, she doesn't even blink."

"She should join the co-op. We could use more honey."

"Nyx tried to convince her to move from her house out on Snow Road, but she's set in her ways, and she doesn't want to disrupt the bees. So, you know, I go with Nyx when she visits her when we're not on patrol." Antoine attempted a nonchalant shrug that was anything but. "Her grandma gives me honeycomb, right from the hive. How can I resist?"

"It's Nyx you can't resist."

"I can neither confirm nor deny the rumors," Antoine grunted. "Are we good to go or what?"

"We're good," Eli said.

Phase one of the plan had begun.

Tomorrow, they'd do it all again.

12

SHILOH EASTON POPE
DAY ONE HUNDRED AND THIRTY-TWO

Shiloh shielded her eyes against the harsh sunshine. She and Ruby walked along the docks of the Munising Marina. The sky was a pale hazy blue. The breeze rippled the smooth surface of the harbor like aluminum foil.

The marina was bustling. Small boats bobbed in the harbor, fishermen coming and going as seagulls soared and swooped overhead. With most folks out of gas, rowboats and kayaks had become the watercraft of choice. Voices hummed as hundreds of dirty, hungry, scared people gathered to share rumors and bits of gossip and to trade for needed goods and services.

Shiloh and Ruby strolled through the makeshift marketplace, passing pavilions, tents, and canvas shades strung over tables stacked with crates and cardboard boxes. Wheelbarrows, trailers, and wagons brimmed with dried grains, beans and rice, canned fruits and vegetables, and various types of meat jerky, from deer to black bear to wild turkey.

Cardboard signs tacked to each stall announced items to barter: "Will trade Band-Aids for bullets" and "Need prednisone, have eggs and cow's milk."

The fresh air smelled distinctly of fish—largemouth bass, whitefish, northern pike, lake trout, and perch. Nearly every booth had some type of fish to sell. Ruby paused at a booth to exchange several bars of Lori Brooks' handmade soap for packages of Rachel Billing's grilled walleye wrapped in aluminum foil.

Shiloh stuffed the supplies into her backpack. It didn't matter that she'd had fish for each of the last ten meals—protein was protein, and besides, these were for Bear. He loved fish.

At the next booth, an old geezer handed out handwritten fliers detailing the gossip and news reports he'd gathered from around the country with his Ham radio: gangs ruled Chicago and Detroit; New York City was on fire; a catastrophic hurricane had struck Tampa, killing tens of thousands.

There were rumblings of wars, coups, and insurrections. Though only the northern hemisphere had lost power, the entire planet had been affected. The world's superpowers battled over dwindling resources. Certain bad actors took advantage of the mayhem to make strategic military and geopolitical chess moves.

Rumors were flying that Russia had invaded the Baltic States and Lithuania and was eyeing Estonia and Latvia next, along with Finland. The Middle East may or may not have been nuked.

Everyone was greedy for news of the outside world, though it was never good news. And who knew what was true or fearmongering; they had no way to verify anything. Frankly, the UP had enough problems without worrying about Russia, China, or Iranian terrorists.

Everything had become insular and isolated. Essentially, each town was now a tiny sovereign state.

In some ways, maybe it was better not to know.

They moved on, passing booths selling car batteries and another spread with baskets of apples. "How did it go with the spy thing?" Shiloh asked.

Ruby's green eyes shone bright. "It was...fun. It felt good to turn the tables, to be the one tricking someone for a change."

"Eli says you were a natural."

"I took drama in high school. I've always enjoyed slipping into someone else's skin. Back then, it felt better than being inside my own."

Shiloh side-eyed her. "But not anymore."

Ruby smiled. "Right. Not anymore."

Dressed in gray hiking pants and a long-sleeved black shirt, with a combat knife hooked to her belt, Ruby appeared confident, strong, and happy. She was no longer the trembling, terrified waif that Shiloh had rescued from a dank hole in the ground.

Here was the girl who'd gnawed through the ropes binding her hands and feet with nothing but her teeth, the girl who'd made a knot with that same rope and beat the trap door for hours, for days, refusing to surrender, never relinquishing her will to live.

The timorous girl with death in her eyes—that girl was long gone.

Ruby watched her with a slight frown. "What's wrong?"

"I was just thinking."

"You were staring at me like I'm a bug under a magnifying glass. Like maybe you wanna squish me."

Shiloh laughed. The sound rang clean and clear through the crisp fall air. "I just..." The words clotted in her throat. She was her father's daughter, better at punching things and blowing stuff up than negotiating the land mines of human emotions. "You look good, is all."

Ruby rolled her eyes. "Are you hitting on me? Is there something you want to tell me? A crush, perhaps?"

Shiloh scowled. "No, never. Not that there's anything wrong with that, but...no, you weirdo."

"Fine. Whatever." Ruby picked up a jar of homemade applesauce and perused it before setting it down and moving on to a table arrayed with solar-charged power stations. "You look good, too."

Shiloh stiffened. Nightmares still plagued her, but they weren't as dark or as terrifying. Gradually, the terrifying visage of Walter Boone's hands squeezing her throat was fading, like a desiccated leaf crumbling away to nothing.

"What was it like, shooting that guy in the face with your cross-bow?" Ruby asked.

Shiloh hesitated, considering her answer. "People say it's a terrible thing, to kill another human being, but after you do it once, it becomes easier and easier. A part of me doesn't want it to become easier. Another part of me says, bring it on. I'll stack bad guy corpses like firewood if that's what it takes."

"Like when I tricked the spy. It felt good to be useful, to have a purpose."

Shiloh nodded. She got it completely.

"Look who it is." Jason Anders sauntered across the marina promenade toward them, his rifle slung across his back. Fiona Smith strode beside him, a pistol snug at her hip. They were one of three security patrols Jackson kept at the marina to maintain order.

A twinge of jealousy nipped at her heart. Eli had grounded her for two weeks—no security checkpoint or patrol shifts. She was allowed to participate in weapons and tactics training. Big whoop. Her place was out here, fighting the bad guys, not stuck at the Inn churning butter by hand, making goat cheese from scratch, or pulling weeds for the millionth time.

"Hey Shiloh," Fiona said as they came up to Ruby and Shiloh and halted. "I've been looking for you."

Jason smirked. "If it isn't the kid-soldier wannabe."

Shiloh wanted to slap the smirk right off his face, but she smiled sweetly instead. Jackson had begged her to play nice with others. She'd sworn she was capable of self-control; now she had to prove it.

"I'm surprised you're not crying and sucking your thumb in a corner somewhere," Jason said.

Shiloh glared at him. "As soon as you win a fight, then we'll talk, smartass."

Jason's face purpled in embarrassment. "Look, you little—"

Fiona whirled on him. "Do you ever shut up?"

Jason blanched. "I was just playing around, having some fun."

"Well, you're being stupid. So, stop it." Fiona returned her attention to Shiloh, tilting her head, a tiny smile playing across her lips. "Kid or no, she saved my life. I didn't see you firing an arrow through a dude's eyeball."

Shiloh didn't correct her crossbow terminology. The flattery warmed her cheeks and set her heart beating faster. She hadn't done it to win Fiona's respect, but she'd take it.

Jason shrugged, chagrined but attempting to appear nonchalant. He wasted no love on Shiloh, but he cared what Fiona thought of him. "Whatever."

Fiona stuck out her hand. "Anytime you need us, we'll have your back. You've earned it."

Shiloh shook her hand. "It was nothing."

"It was definitely something. I owe you one." Fiona signaled to Jason, and they continued their patrol, weaving among the crowd until they disappeared from view.

Shiloh stared after them for a minute, unable to wipe the beaming grin from her face. Fiona had looked at her with admiration. Many of the other teens did as well, and so did some of the adults. It was a pleasant feeling.

Every day, she felt a transformation happening inside her: the assuredness, the alertness, the wily shrewdness of a warrior knitting itself within her bones, rushing in her blood, beating with every pulse of her heart.

She was finally earning her place in the world, becoming who she was meant to be.

Ruby elbowed her in the ribs. "Look who else decided to show their face."

A big white yacht floated at the end of one of the docks. James Sawyer strode down the dock with long confident strides, flanked by four enormous bodyguards with baleful expressions.

The hustle and bustle of the market stilled as clusters of people quieted, their tense gazes pinned on Sawyer. The security patrols drew closer, alert and wary, though they didn't interfere. As long as Sawyer didn't cause a disruption, they had orders to leave him and his goons alone.

Ruby seized Shiloh's arm and pulled her into the shadows of one of the tents, her hip bumping a table spread with single-serving straws filled with various herbs and spices—turmeric and nutmeg, cinnamon and parsley.

They watched in silence as the criminal kingpin of Alger County stalked toward them. The crowds moved aside with deference. No one dared to criticize Sawyer to his face, not if they wanted to keep their limbs intact.

Shiloh clenched her teeth so hard she bit her tongue. Sawyer may have been Cody's biological father, but he'd never publicly claimed him as his son. He'd kidnapped and tortured Eli. For that, she would loathe him forever and ever.

"Just let him go," Ruby murmured. "No sudden moves."

"I'm not stupid," Shiloh said through gritted teeth.

Sawyer stopped in front of them. He reminded her of a shark with his sea-gray eyes, weathered features, and rugged build, his powerful muscles coiled as if prepared to strike at any moment.

His bodyguards spread out behind him, hands on their weapons, their hard faces impassive. Sawyer perused the booth's offerings, chose a jar of lavender honey, and handed it to his nearest thug.

The woman manning the booth didn't say a word. Her eyes widened in trepidation as her lips pressed into a thin line. Her shoulders hunched as if to make herself smaller.

Sawyer's flat gaze passed over her and settled on Shiloh. Recognition flashed in his eyes, a spark of something dark and dangerous. "You're the little Pope girl."

Unease sank in Shiloh's gut like a stone. Her mouth went dry, her palms clammy, but she refused to flinch or make herself small, no matter how Sawyer intimidated her.

She raised her chin in defiance. "I'm no little girl."

A smile split his tanned face, revealing straight white teeth. It was a flat, emotionless smile. It didn't reach his eyes. "I can see that."

He tilted his head as if examining her, eyes shrewd, studying her from head to toe for some perceived weakness. Ruby squeezed her arm, attempting to silence her, but Shiloh would not cower for anyone, certainly not the man who hadn't bothered to claim Cody as his son.

"What are you doing out here alone?"

"None of your damn beeswax."

"And she's not alone," Ruby snapped.

Whatever he was looking for, he must have found it, because he dipped his chin at her with something almost like appreciation, which didn't make a lick of sense. "Until we meet again, Little Pope. I look forward to next time."

"There won't be a next time, not if I can help it."

Sawyer gave a mirthless laugh. "We'll see, won't we?"

He gestured to his men and departed the booth, heading toward the southern end of the marina. Shiloh stared daggers at his back as he and his entourage strolled past. The security patrols watched him go with relieved expressions.

"He's going to pay," she said. "Eli will make him pay."

"Someday," Ruby said, maintaining her grip on Shiloh's elbow, "but not today."

Shiloh spat on the ground where Sawyer had stepped only moments before. "It'll come sooner than he thinks."

13

JACKSON CROSS
DAY ONE HUNDRED AND THIRTY-THREE

"You ready?" Jackson asked Devon.

"Do we have a choice?" she asked over the hum of the electric golf cart. It had rained the night before. Mud splattered the wheels of the electric golf cart, which was outfitted with solar panels.

"Nope," he said.

Devon grunted and stared straight ahead at the road, her gaze distant as if she wasn't seeing the potholes, the downed branches, and the detritus scattered between the husks of abandoned vehicles. Vines crept forth from the woods, reaching with knotted fingers, steadily overtaking the roads, the cars, and buildings—civilization itself.

Now that Jackson had been promoted to sheriff, he spent most mornings making the rounds of the perimeter checkpoints with Devon Harris at his side.

Devon rubbed her arms and shivered as they approached the M-94 checkpoint, located past the Econo Lodge Inn and Suites and the Pictured Rocks KOA, where dozens of families lived in campers or crammed into cramped, unheated hotel rooms.

At the checkpoint, about fifty people milled before the gates. They were dirty and dusty, their faces drawn, their eyes haunted.

They rode bikes and carried backpacks, duffle bags, and suitcases stuffed into wheelbarrows and bike carts. They looked like they had fled with nothing but the clothes on their backs and what goods they could carry.

Six months ago, Jackson couldn't have imagined a scene like this: desperate refugees in America, starving children, and people killing each other over a handful of bullets or a can of corn.

Now, there was nothing to imagine. The atrocities were far too real. It felt like only the tiny town of Munising maintained some semblance of order.

It was difficult to describe the heaviness in his chest, the inescapable sense of impending doom looming over their heads as if everything they'd been working for, everything they'd fought for and sacrificed—it could all be incinerated in a heartbeat.

"I'm sorry, you'll have to turn back," Jim Hart said firmly, his rifle held low, aimed at the ground but ready to engage if needed.

A retired Marine and longtime cop from the Munising Police Department, Hart was balding, overweight, and perpetually grumpy; he was also brave and loyal as hell. Even after a bullet had nailed his shoulder in the yacht battle against Sawyer, he hadn't quit.

Jim Hart and Alexis Chilton manned the checkpoint along with five members of the civilian security team. Several garbage trucks had been pushed across the road to block access as well as to provide concealment and cover in case of an altercation.

Like the Northwoods Inn perimeter, Eli had ordered the construction of guard shacks, reinforced sandbag walls, and sniper hides hidden within the tree line, where two sentries lurked out of sight.

"We're tired and hungry!" one of the refugees cried. "Please, let us stay for a night. One night, that's all we ask."

It wasn't just for a night. It never was. People who came here stayed. There were few places to go, fewer still that offered a modicum of safety.

Jackson pocketed the golf cart key fob as he strode between a garbage truck and a school bus to stand next to Hart and Alexis. Devon trailed behind him.

Several dozen pairs of eyes locked on him, warily scanning his uniform, taking in his aura of authority and leadership. As one, the crowd turned toward him.

"Where are you from?" Devon asked the crowd.

"Newberry," answered a middle-aged man with two young children clinging to his

waist.

Newberry was a small town approximately sixty miles southeast of Munising, located within the Newberry State Forest Area. The town was most known for Oswald's Bear Ranch.

Weeks ago, the bears had escaped or someone had released them; one black bear had wandered to the lighthouse, unable to hunt for itself and reckless with hunger. Shiloh now proudly wore its skin.

"We had to leave," said a woman wearing a blue handkerchief. "People streamed into town, hundreds of them, all saying the same thing. They were from Hulbert. In the middle of the night, a gang of raiders invaded their streets in trucks and black SUVs. They opened fire and started shooting into people's houses. They burned the township office to the ground. They set fire to the bar, the grocery store, and the Tahquamenon Hotel. The townspeople from Hulbert were forced to flee with whatever they could carry. They warned us that their town wasn't the first and wouldn't be the last."

Jackson's guts turned to water. "When did this happen?"

"Three nights ago," the old man said.

"Some of our neighbors stayed in Newberry," said an older woman, her white hair cropped close to her scalp. She wore a baggy pink sweater that fell to her knees. "They either didn't believe the warning, or they decided things would be different for them if they gave these thugs what they wanted. I believed the warning. I saw the burns on two of the refugees. They chopped off a man's hand because he didn't give them what they wanted fast enough."

Several people in line nodded, their frightened eyes wide and glazed, as if imagining the terrible things that could happen to their wives, brothers, uncles, and children.

"What did the raiders want?" Devon asked.

A bearded black man shook his head. "No one ever said. The fleeing townspeople warned us to leave as they came through. They didn't stop. They said our town would be next."

"A bunch of families headed for the bridge," said a woman in her sixties, a backpack slung on her back and a smaller rucksack carried against her chest. She leaned on a walking stick, favoring her right ankle. "We thought about going with them, fleeing downstate, maybe heading south to Georgia or Florida where winter won't be a problem, but that's everyone's first thought. We've heard the rumors, the horror stories of the cities. The over-crowded conditions. The tent cities of starving people. Poor sanitation. Diseases running rampant."

"I couldn't put my kids at risk like that." The father hugged his children closer. "We figured our odds were better up north, even with winter. Until this. These...these monsters killing people for no reason. Burning whole towns..." His voice drifted into angry, helpless silence.

The hairs on the back of Jackson's neck prickled. "Was it the cartel?"

The refugees stared at him dully.

"I don't know," the old woman said. "We don't know."

The last group of refugees had come from Bay Mills, much further east than this group. If these raiders were with the cartel... they were creeping westward, stealing nearer, ever nearer, a dragon breathing down the backs of their necks. The hour was closer than it appeared.

"We heard..." The bearded man shifted his gaze to Jackson. "We heard Munising defeated a bunch of escaped convicts, that the new sheriff has caught not one but two killers, even with the world ending."

Word was spreading slowly without phones, texting, or social media, but it still spread.

They weren't wrong. Munising was safer than most towns, more prepared, and with better security. The combined sheriff's department and local police force remained intact for the most part. The civilian security team was training daily, their numbers swelling.

The waterfront marina and proximity to Lake Superior gave them easy access to fishing and fresh water for bathing, cooking, watering the gardens, and drinking once disinfected.

The Northwoods Inn offered a refuge of self-sufficiency. Tim and Lori Brooks were teaching the lost skills of foraging, medicinal plants, water containment systems, cheese and soap making, and water purification. The list went on.

It didn't matter how much he wanted to help these people; the committee had voted—no refugees in or out until they'd dealt with the cartel threat. He loathed turning good people away, but he had no choice. His first obligation was to his county, his town, and his people.

Jackson raised his voice. "If it is within our power, we'll stop these raiders so you can return to your homes."

Newberry was a significant distance considering their limited transportation options. Sixty miles used to be an hour or so drive, but now it was an ordeal. The electric golf carts didn't have the range, even with the solar batteries, and the ATVs were nearly out of fuel. They'd sacrificed their last few gallons in their ploy with the cartel spy.

Unlike the popular zombie apocalypse TV shows, in the real world, gasoline only had a shelf life of three to six months. Diesel could last longer, but they had already run out. They were in desperate want of vehicles that could run on biofuel.

"When?" the bearded man demanded. "What are we supposed

to do until then? We need shelter. We have women and children with us. We're begging you."

"I'm sorry." Every word was like barbed wire on his tongue. Guilt like red-hot coals scorched his internal organs. "We can't take in more people at this time. We're full to bursting, and we must prepare for winter."

He forced himself to watch the crestfallen expressions. He refused to look away; it was his penance.

"Where are we supposed to go?" the father asked, chin trembling.

"How could you?" one of the women cried angrily. "We're just like you! We *are* you! How can you turn us away?" Her anger masked her fear. The anger wasn't aimed at him, not really. Still, it struck him like an arrow to his chest.

The residents of the Upper Peninsula were tough and self-sufficient. They had to be strong to survive the isolation, the wilderness, and the harsh winters sometimes cut off from the rest of civilization.

This was different. What they faced now was catastrophic, unspeakable.

"You're no better than the rest." Bearded Guy spat on the ground and made a motion as if to wash his hands of them. "May karma bite you on the ass."

Beside him, Devon went rigid. Hart and Alexis looked crestfallen. Jackson's stomach twisted. His face went hot with shame. He felt discouraged and disheartened.

Lowering his voice, he spoke so only Hart, Alexis, and Devon could hear him. "There's an abandoned hotel over on Adam's Trail outside the county line. No one else has claimed it yet. It's not ideal, but it will put a roof over their heads and keep those kids out of the elements until the adults can figure out a plan."

Hart gave him a sober nod. "Will do."

He patted Hart on the shoulder. "You've got it from here."

Devon fell into stride beside him. Panicked voices rose behind them, a few people hurling insults they ignored. With stiff legs, they walked back to the golf cart parked along the road.

In the Econo Lodge parking lot, rusty campers and ragged tents crammed the weedy asphalt. A ring of campfires and home-made rocket stoves had sprung up around the hotel.

Children's voices rent the chilly air. A couple of dozen kids played soccer in the overgrown field while the adults focused on cooking lunch, cleaning clothes by hand, or gathering loads of firewood. They were dressed in sweaters and jackets; some wore hats and scarves.

Though it was a sunny day, there was a sharp chill in the air, a warning. Winter was coming whether they were ready or not.

As the days stretched into late September, the nights were colder, temps reaching the low forties. Camping was a short-term solution; these people would freeze to death in winter. They needed housing. He made a mental note to figure something out.

"That was awful," Devon said.

"Tell me about it. We gave the last available housing to the refugees from Bay Mills. If we start overcrowding, we'll have the same sanitation issues as the bigger towns and cities. Cholera, dysentery, and typhoid. People sick and dying in their own filth. Not enough food or disinfected water. Winter is coming. We must have enough food and seasoned firewood to keep people warm and fed for five months, at least." He rubbed a weary hand along his stubbled jaw. "We don't have enough as it is."

"It still feels horrible. Like we're the bad guys here. Those two little girls, their devastated faces..."

He stopped and put a hand on her shoulder. "I know. Logically, it's the right choice, but my heart is telling me this is wrong."

"How do you put a value on a life?" Devon asked.

"You don't. You can't."

"Aren't we doing exactly that? We're valuing our lives above theirs. We're turning them away to die."

"We've helped as many as we could. We've done as much as we could."

Devon's dark eyes glittered. She blinked rapidly, fiercely, and took a step back. "Have we? Because it doesn't feel like enough. It never feels like enough."

His arm fell limp at his side. He felt profoundly tired. "We can't save the whole world." His words felt hollow in his ears. He hated himself for saying it, but that didn't change the bitter truth.

Abruptly, his sister flared through his mind: her writhing body as she gasped for oxygen, wheezing, her lips swollen and gaping like a dying fish. He blinked and pushed out the memory. Astrid invaded his nightmares; he couldn't let the darkness hamper his job.

They lapsed into an uncomfortable silence as Jackson drove. They backtracked through town before heading north along the coast, turning right on Adam's Trail.

Devon kept her gaze on the trees and passing buildings, scanning for potential danger, though the checkpoints and security patrols kept crimes within the county line to a minimum.

"Where are we going, boss?" Her voice was subdued. She was upset. He couldn't blame her; he felt the same way. Yet, he was the boss. He had to make the hard choices.

"These carts have a range of fifty to sixty miles. We need vehicles if we're going to travel outside of Alger County. We can use the horses, but..."

"You hate horses."

Jackson grunted. "Hate is a strong word. I prefer strong loathing. Or perhaps revulsion."

It was more the lack of control, fear of heights, and painful seating arrangement he disliked, rather than the animals themselves. Some folks had turned to horses and carts for transportation, but Jackson far preferred vehicles with engines.

He'd heard that the mechanic, Fred Combs, could make biofuel for diesel engines. That was Jackson's next stop. He had a to-do list as long as his arm, and though he worked from sunup to sundown and after, the list only grew longer and longer.

The towns within Alger County were connected through a pony express circuit that delivered news and mail twice a week. Jackson regularly checked in with nearby counties' law enforcement through Ham radio, but certain areas had recently gone dark.

None of the other towns knew much about the raider attacks, though rumors were running rampant, stirring up panic and hysteria.

It was the outside world Jackson feared most.

"I'm going to Newberry. We need to see for ourselves what's happening out there. If this is the work of the cartel, we need more intel. We can't just wait for them to come for us. You in?"

Devon's shoulders straightened, her chin lifting. "Did you need to ask?"

"Just making sure we're on the same page."

She managed a tight grin. "Always."

They drove past the marina. A dozen fishing boats floated in the water. People bartered goods and services at the makeshift farmer's market while armed sentries patrolled strategic points along the lakefront. A few hidden snipers provided overwatch. In the distance, Grand Island rose, dense with green spruce and fir trees.

Devon reached into the bag tucked between her feet and pulled out two peanut butter and honey sandwiches on sourdough bread and a glass jar of raspberries—their daily meal on the go. "I brought lunch. It's no pasty, but it'll have to do."

As they exited Munising and headed northeast toward Adam's Trail, he glanced at the passing trees—the sugar maples, yellow beech, and ironwoods, their leaves bursting with fiery reds, burnt oranges, and wine purples.

"That's the worst part of the apocalypse," Devon said mournfully. "No pasties."

Falling Rock Café had finally run out of ingredients to make the classic UP delicacies: savory beef and root veggies folded into a pastry shell and baked until juicy and tender. Invented as portable meals for Cornish miners in the mid-nineteenth century, the pasty was pronounced with a soft "a" like "pass."

Jackson flashed her a grim smile. Devon had a soothing way about her, a preternatural ability to brighten the worst day. "You have your priorities straight."

Devon patted her belly, which growled loudly on command. "You betcha."

14

JACKSON CROSS
DAY ONE HUNDRED AND THIRTY-THREE

Combs' Automotive Body Shop was located on Adam's Trail, past the Bear Trap Inn and the Pictured Rocks Golf Club, on a long dirt road surrounded by dense hardwoods.

Jackson and Devon entered through the battered front office and made their way to the back, edging past several bays with various vehicles on hydraulic lifts.

The shop smelled of oil and grease. Stacks of tires lay everywhere. The walls were lined with cluttered work benches. A couple of rolling creepers were shoved against the wall, with engine parts scattered across every surface of the shop.

Combs was working in the left bay, bent over the engine of a diesel truck. The white hair ringing his bald head stood on end. He wore a grease-stained apron and protective eyeglasses along with rubber gloves. His gnarled feet were shoved incongruously into a pair of pink fuzzy slippers, giving him the look of a half-mad scientist.

"What'd ya want?" Fred Combs jerked upright at their approach, scratching at his fuzzy scalp with grease-crusted fingers. He scowled at them. "I didn't do nothin' wrong."

"Never said you did," Jackson replied evenly.

"I'm not showing you nothin', even if you got a warrant this time, which you sure as hell don't."

The last time they'd had an altercation with Fred Combs was over the identity of the owner of the truck that had run Shiloh off the road. Calvin Fitch's truck had led them to the serial predator Walter Boone.

"We noticed that nice Dodge Ram D-250 in the parking lot," Devon said. "I've seen it around town. We heard a rumor that you've transitioned to biofuel."

Fred's chest puffed with obvious pride. "What's it to you?"

"We need biofuel to drive our diesel vehicles," Jackson said. "Gasoline is gone, and we've used up our emergency diesel supply, too. The only option left is biofuel. Will you help us?"

Combs wiped a smudge of oil from his hands on a filthy rag, tossed it on top of a rack of tools, and turned to face them. A lifelong resident of Munising, he spoke with a heavy Yooper twang. "You've asked me before and the answer is the same, eh? No way in hades. I'm too busy takin' care of myself and the missus. I ain't got time to hold nobody's hand."

Jackson glanced at the array of tools hung next to him. Along the far wall stood containers of vegetable oil, methanol, and lye stored in non-oxidizing glass jars, along with several portable propane stoves. Fred was making biofuel.

"No one is asking for a handout," Devon said sweetly. She was always good at keeping her calm when Jackson wanted to strangle the obstinance right out of a suspect or witness. "Maybe we can help you in return."

"Don't see how you people can offer anything worth having," Fred grumbled. "I stay up all night with my shotgun poked out the window, making sure no fools try to steal what ain't theirs. Ain't no one gonna take what's mine, and that goes for you hooligans, too. I don't care what fancy titles you carry." His rheumy eyes narrowed in contempt. "You Crosses are all the same."

"Not all of us," Jackson said. "I can help you."

"What the hell are you gonna do to fix all this, huh?" Fred

waved a hand vaguely. "The damn government, corrupt and greedy though they are, they promised us nothing like this would ever happen, but they knew the supply chain was precarious, the power grid was vulnerable. They knew it, and they did nothin', eh?"

He shook his head in impotent fury. "They could've built more transformer plants here in the States. Could've stored more back-ups, and had a whole stash of that magnetized steel or whatever they needed to make them. Eighteen months for one transformer, that's what I heard. And now China won't make them for us, 'cause they're desperate and starving themselves."

He blinked his rheumy eyes as if he couldn't comprehend the colossal disaster in which he'd found himself trapped, the perpetual nightmare that never ended. "On the ham radio, people are talking about all the dead in the cities downstate. And not just Michigan, but every city across the Midwest, the whole country. Folks are sick from sewage running into the streets, garbage every-where, and no clean water with the treatment plants down. Gangs shooting civilians in the streets, corpses left out to rot. My daughter and granddaughters live in Detroit. I dunno if they're even alive. My brother in Fort Wayne was on the liver transplant list. Guess I won't ever know what happened to him, whether he died alone, in the end."

"I'm sorry," Jackson said.

There was much he didn't miss about society: governments were corrupt, corporations destroyed people's lives, individual freedoms were vanishing, people turned on each other with toxic vitriol on social media.

In many ways, the world had already gone to pot.

This, though, was a new level of hell, one he hadn't imagined in his worst nightmares. The senseless deaths, the horrific suffering, the lack of healthcare, basic hygiene, food, and water...

Even those who had prepared could not possibly be ready for everything, for a catastrophe that would devastate the entire planet. Australia and New Zealand were probably okay but the rest of the planet, not so much.

"You heard the rumors, eh?" Fred continued. "Russia going nuclear against our NATO allies. China attacking Taiwan, Israel and Iran battling to eradicate each other. The whole world is burning, or about to be."

"We heard," Devon said quietly.

It was enough to drive a person insane.

"Everything out there ain't the worst thing. The worst thing is right inside my own damn house." Fred stared bitterly at the grease creasing his veined, liver-spotted hands. "The missus, she won't eat, won't sleep, won't leave the house. Barely leaves her bed. She's got lupus, lives in constant pain, and without her meds...I'm watching her wither away before my eyes, and I can't do a damn thing about it."

He glared up at Jackson as if he loathed him for his own weakness, for forcing him to speak it aloud, although Jackson hadn't forced him to say or do a thing.

"You gonna do something about that, *sheriff*? Or are you a worthless sack of hot air like your good-for-nothing father?"

Jackson resisted the urge to flinch. "Lena Easton has some herbal remedies for pain and aid with sleep. I'm sure Dr. Virtanen can prescribe something. We have access to a supply of medications. We can help your wife, I promise."

"We were high school sweethearts, been together forty years. If she goes..." Fred left the rest of the sentence unspoken. Deep wrinkles radiated like cracks across his hard leathery face. He swiped at his eyes with his gnarled fists and briefly turned away as if hiding his grief.

Jackson had no comfort to offer, no useless platitudes. His duty was to bear witness to the pain and suffering of others, their collective grief.

It wasn't about missing Starbucks and Netflix, Amazon Prime deliveries and take-out: billions of people grieved for lost dreams, lost lives, lost loved ones. Their future ripped from them in an instant.

So much of survival was mental, the incessant anxiety, the unrelenting stress, the looming despair. Fortitude and resilience were as necessary as food, sanitized water, and security. The mind was its own battlefield.

Jackson offered Fred the only thing he could. "If you can help us transition our diesel engines to accept biofuel and teach us how to make the fuel, we can take you and your wife to the Northwoods Inn. Lori and Tim are good people. They can at least make your wife as comfortable as possible."

Jackson thought of the hungry, exhausted families they'd rejected earlier in the day. Hours later, he was offering an obstinate old man a place at the table. Every life had value; however, some had more value, at least when it came to collective survival.

It was an ugly, bitter truth. Much as he hated it, they had to make the difficult choices or no one would survive. Perhaps he was simply lying to himself to ease his conflicted conscience.

Fred scowled. "I don't want no handouts."

"Trust me, it's not a handout, it's a trade. We need your skills and expertise and the use of the tools in your shop. I can send more volunteers you can train to do the physical work so you don't have to."

Fred grunted. He picked up a ratchet and put it down, then a screwdriver. He seemed at a loss, unsure how to respond to the sudden change in his luck.

"It's a good deal," Devon said. "The Inn has wind and solar power that's shared between the community members. You don't have to worry about gathering your firewood or scavenging for every meal. The tasks are shared."

Fred gazed at his rows of tools, grabbed a dirty wrench, and polished it furiously with a soiled rag. "I don't got enough vegetable oil. I've only got enough for the truck out front. I need more methanol. You want me to cook in bulk, I need more of everything. And potassium hydroxide or sodium hydroxide. Most of all, more lye."

"Lori makes lye out of wood ash," Devon said.

"We can get all of that," Jackson said. "We already have a stockpile of barrels at the Inn. Oil has topped our scavenger list from the beginning, we just haven't managed to scale production like we need to. We're having problems with the purification part."

"That'll only work until you've plundered every restaurant and fast-food joint in the surrounding counties."

"It'll work for now. We're researching growing and harvesting oilseeds, like sunflowers perhaps, to make oil next summer. We have a list of equipment to scavenge."

"Good luck with that." Fred rolled his eyes. Then he said, "You wear a man down, Cross. For the missus, you understand. I could survive on my own for years, always have, eh? I don't need nothin' from nobody."

"Noted," Jackson said, trying and failing to hide his abject relief. "Thank you. Lori asked me to tell you to save the glycerin for her so she can make soap. She says it's good for composting as well."

"You got any more demands, Sheriff?"

Devon hooked her thumb at the rusted red '93 Dodge Ram visible from one of the windows. It was nothing special, except that it ran on biodiesel, which made it priceless. "To start with, may we borrow your truck for the day?"

"You want favors? Then I want somethin' in return to make it worth my while. Extra rations for my missus. She gets a room in that hotel, with a real mattress and pillows, not one of those flimsy cabins."

Jackson balked at that. "We can't just make exceptions for—"

"Then no dice." Fred turned his back on them. His knobby spine poked through his grimy shirt, his shoulder blades sharp and angular.

Devon and Jackson exchanged a hesitant glance, Devon's brow cocked as if asking, *well?*

Jackson nodded in reluctance. They were up a creek, and Fred had the only paddle—which he damn well knew, too.

Devon stuck out her hand. "You have yourself a deal, sir."

Fred didn't bother to take it. He wasn't looking at them anymore as if he wished they were long gone. "You better bring it back in pristine condition. Not a scratch on it, mind you. Take it before I change my damn mind, eh?"

They didn't need to be told twice.

15

JACKSON CROSS
DAY ONE HUNDRED AND THIRTY-THREE

Ten minutes later, Jackson and Devon were on the road, headed east toward Newberry. The fuel tank had a range of one hundred fifty miles. With a bit of luck, they'd make it there and back home before nightfall.

Devon put up a lackluster fight over who would drive but threw up her hands in defeat when Jackson insisted, offering her the return trip at the wheel. She'd radioed Moreno and Alexis and instructed them to send a few citizen volunteers to the autobody shop to move Fred Combs and his wife to the Inn.

Devon blew out a frustrated breath. She was quiet for a few minutes as they drove. "Can I ask you a question?"

"Shoot." Jackson shifted in his seat. It felt good to sit behind the wheel again, to feel the strong rumble of an engine beneath him, the sound strange in his ears.

Devon rested her hand on his forearm, her touch light as a feather, her palm cool and dry. "Everything that happened...what you had to do...have you talked about it with anyone, boss?"

Jackson's stomach knotted. He couldn't pretend he didn't know what she meant—the unspoken thing between them, the elephant in the room he'd ignored the last two weeks. He gave a sharp shake of his head. "I'm fine."

He could feel her stare singeing his skin. He glanced at her out of the corner of his eye. Her expression was kind, her dark eyes inquisitive, her long black braids tied back in a ponytail. In her mid-twenties, Devon was one of the newer deputies, but she made up for her youth with intelligence, loyalty, and grit.

"Have I told you recently how much I appreciate you?" he asked to deflect her question.

Her brown skin crinkled around her eyes when she smiled. He'd forgotten how much he liked her smile. "Now I know something's wrong. Don't tell me, you've discovered an inoperable brain tumor and you have three weeks to live."

He choked out a laugh. "That would almost be easier."

Her smile faded. "Tell me about Astrid."

His throat closed as if he couldn't inhale enough oxygen.

They rode with the windows down; the sun shining, cottony clouds dappling the sky, the trees transforming into vibrant shades of burnt-orange, crimson, and deep purple. It was as if the fall hadn't happened. Beneath the denim blue sky, mankind wasn't imploding, killing each other over a can of beans, murdering and plundering for the hell of it.

As if he hadn't murdered his own sister.

"Boss," Devon said in a soft but persistent voice. "You're stuck in a truck with me. You can't escape, so you might as well talk to me."

"I don't want to talk about it."

"I don't care."

Jackson snorted.

"It was a big deal, what you had to do. You're going around like it doesn't matter. I know it matters, I know it's affecting you, whether you want to admit it or not."

"I don't."

Devon huffed in frustration.

"Everyone's dealing with trauma. There's nothing special about mine. We've all lost people."

"Not like that."

The desolate road ahead of them went blurry. He sensed a hardness deep inside him, something flinty and ugly curled like a fist within his chest.

He'd stood by and watched as his sister went into anaphylactic shock. He was the one who'd proffered the poison. He'd held the EpiPen like a dagger and watched her die.

After years of chasing monsters, he'd hunted the ultimate predator to its lair, only to discover the wolf inside his own home. He'd caught the wolf by the tail. He'd killed his sister.

"You did what you had to do."

"I'm the sheriff. I've lived my whole life by the rules, right and wrong, law and order. What I did feels both wrong and like I had no choice, at the same time."

"We live in shades of gray. We have to be okay with that."

"I don't know if I can."

"If the justice system was still intact, would you have put cuffs on her, read her rights, and dragged her to jail?"

There was no hesitation. "Of course."

"Justice is still just, no matter the rules or laws or who enforces them. You eliminated a killer who would've killed again without a second thought. You kept Lily's daughter safe. If she could speak to you from the grave, Lily would tell you 'Job well done.'"

"I hope she would," he said.

"I know she would," Devon said with certainty.

His lips twitched at the bittersweet memory of Lily Easton: her wild black hair and fierce dark eyes, her golden bell of a laugh. The girl he'd loved his whole life, yet failed to save.

Her ghost had haunted him for eight years, but finally, at long last, she'd been laid to rest. He'd hoped his soul would find solace, too, but alas, he'd miscalculated. Perhaps this was his burden to carry, his penance to bear the scars forever.

They turned onto a side road clogged with felled branches from the latest storm. He swerved to avoid the larger branches. The truck jolted over yet another pothole as they passed rows of boarded-up houses set back off the road.

"I'm sorry about your mom," Devon said.

Devon probably thought she'd switched the subject to safer territory, but nothing about Jackson's family was safe. His father had drugged his mother to keep her docile, to keep his terrible secrets hidden from his son. Jackson hadn't been smart or fast enough to save Dolores, either.

The only family members he had left were a corrupt father and an absent brother he hadn't seen in fifteen years. His family legacy was one of treachery, manipulation, and murder.

"Thank you," he said because that was the answer expected of him. He did miss his mother. What he missed most was the mother she should've been, the fantasy version he'd needed, not the weak, pliant woman she had become.

"Boss." Devon's voice took on an apprehensive edge. She leaned forward in her seat. "There's something ahead."

Jackson slowed the truck. With his right hand, he unholstered his service pistol and held it against the steering wheel. His heart rate quickened as they rounded a bend in the road.

He'd expected to reach a checkpoint at Seney, a tiny town of several hundred residents located in the middle of the Upper Peninsula. They were still a good thirty miles from Newberry.

Up ahead, the vehicles crowded the road's shoulder were burned husks and blackened skeletons. His pulse thudded in his ears. He scanned the road, the trees, and the vehicles, searching for a hint of movement, the telltale glint of a muzzle hidden in the shadows.

The place was deserted, ominous as a graveyard. Two crows perched on the hood of what was once a Toyota Camry. The birds cawed angrily as if offended by their presence.

Jackson had the disconcerting feeling that they'd infiltrated dangerous territory. "Keep your head on a swivel."

"Got it, boss." Devon pulled the AR-15 from the floorboard at her feet, shifting sideways in her seat as she flicked the safety to off and eased the muzzle out the open window.

Cicadas buzzed in the grass. The canopy of branches overhead rustled, whispering dark secrets that Jackson couldn't translate. The hairs on the back of his neck stood on end, his instincts screaming at him to get out while he still could.

The air smelled wrong. The faint stink of charred plastic stung his nostrils.

"Something happened here," Devon said. "Something bad."

"I feel it, too."

"When's the last time we heard from Seney?"

"A few days. I tried to contact the police chief on the Ham radio yesterday, but there was nothing but static."

"That's not a good sign."

Jackson felt it in his gut, that familiar flutter-flap of trepidation. All was not well in Seney.

Devon gave Jackson a questioning glance. "We still doing this, boss?"

A part of him wanted to turn and flee, but the urgent need to run was overpowered by the desire to protect his town and his people. There would be answers here. "We're going in."

16

JACKSON CROSS
DAY ONE HUNDRED AND THIRTY-THREE

Jackson scanned the area ahead through his binoculars while Devon searched with the drone, manning the controller and peering at the tiny screen. Streets, houses, and cars appeared like miniature toys from above.

"I don't see anything," Devon said.

"Me neither."

After stashing the truck in the woods and hurriedly camouflaging it with some underbrush, they'd circled the outskirts of Seney before closing in on Main Street, scouting the area for threats. The last thing they wanted to do was stroll into a trap.

The houses stood empty and shuttered. The front doors of several homes hung open, screen doors creaking in the breeze. Some were boarded up while others were sprayed with graffiti, their windows shattered.

A glance inside a few houses revealed the same story: everything ransacked, sofa cushions slashed, pictures hurled from walls, bookcases toppled, and drawers yanked from cabinets and dressers, their contents spilled across the floor.

There were no people anywhere—no animals, either. Gusts of wind scattered dead leaves. Stray bits of trash scudded across the barren streets. An unnatural silence hung heavy and thick in the air. Even the birds had fallen quiet, as if in mourning.

Most of the townships in the UP were small villages, where you bought gas and groceries and fishing tackle from the same corner store, maybe from the same mom-and-pop you'd known for thirty years, the type of towns where you borrowed eggs and sugar from your neighbors.

Not here. Not anymore.

Jackson craned his neck, finger twitching on the trigger guard. His vigilant gaze searched broken windows and hunted for shadows lurking in doorways or crouched on rooftops. "It feels like a ghost town."

Devon studied the images from the drone before bringing it back to base. "I didn't see anything alive down there. If there are ghosts, they're well hidden."

On high alert, with weapons drawn, Jackson and Devon entered Main Street, keeping to the left side of the road in case they needed to dart inside a building for cover. The only noise was their steady breathing and the footfall of their boots. Jackson's blood whooshed in his ears.

They passed a barber shop with busted windows, a ransacked automotive shop, a bed and breakfast with the front door ripped off its hinges, and an office with signs advertising local cabins to rent torn into pieces.

Jackson made a mental note to check the diner on their return for vegetable oil and other items on Fred Combs' wanted list. If they could—

A clanging sound echoed nearby.

With his heart in his throat, Jackson whipped around. As they'd trained, he took the left as Devon spun right, aiming at windows and doorways, alleyways and rooftops.

Where was the danger? A sniper could lurk anywhere, their skulls within his sights. They could be seconds from death and not know it.

His gaze settled on a set of wind chimes hanging from a striped pole set in front of a coffee shop. The chimes twirled lazily in the breeze, clanging merrily—the sound discordant against the uncanny quiet, the empty streets, the buildings devoid of people.

They continued in tandem. As they moved deeper into the town, the air grew hazy. The smell of smoke and something burned stung their nostrils.

Devon wrinkled her nose, then pointed ahead. Further down the street, several buildings had been set on fire. Some were burned to the ground, others half-collapsed. The charred remains still smoked. Among the ruins, tiny flames flickered and danced.

They halted on the corner next to a bank. Across the street stood the local grocery store. A half-dozen vehicles gathered dust in the parking lot. Empty shopping carts stood in clusters. Dozens of spent shell casings glinted among the shopping bags, plastic wrappers, and detritus littering the asphalt.

The smell struck them like a physical blow: the stench of dead carcasses, rancid meat baking in the sun, and decomposing flesh engorged with fetid gases.

Human bodies were scattered among the wreckage. Ten, twelve—no, twenty, at least. Men and women. All dead. Flies buzzed in dense clouds above them.

With his free hand, Jackson covered his mouth with a handkerchief, struggling to keep from retching, the noxious stink making him dizzy. His eyes watered and stung. Devon made a choking sound in the back of her throat.

As they approached, several carrion birds squawked at them, rising from the corpses and alighting on the trunks and hoods of the cars. They flapped their black wings in protest at the interruption of their feast.

The corpse closest to them was a woman. She lay twisted on her side, her body bent into a grotesque, unnatural shape. Three bloodied holes near her spine told the story: she'd been shot in the back while fleeing. A plastic grocery bag was trapped beneath her right arm. It fluttered in the breeze.

Horrified, Jackson stared at the corpse, mesmerized by the fluttering plastic bag, unable to tear his gaze away.

Devon blanched. "These people were murdered."

Jackson forced himself to keep it together. Uneasiness crawled beneath his skin. He resisted the urge to run. Instead, he studied the scene as an investigator. "Whoever did this rounded up citizens and executed them here. See the bodies near the front? They were lined up and shot in the back of the head. The corpses have started bloating. Rigor mortis has passed. These bodies have been out here for a couple of days."

"They were systematically slaughtered and left to rot like roadkill," Devon said, appalled. "Who would do something like this?"

"The cartel would."

"We still don't know that for sure."

"That's what we're here to find out."

Devon glanced over her shoulder and studied the vacant street behind them. "Law enforcement should've at least taken away the bodies, buried them, or stored them somewhere..."

Jackson swallowed his outrage. He pointed to five corpses slumped near the entrance. "Several of the victims are police officers. That corpse is dressed in a Schoolcraft County deputy uniform. Likely, the raiders targeted anyone who put up a fight. There may not be anyone left to tend to the deceased. The townspeople fled or were caught in the crossfire."

"Someone has to know what happened here."

He scanned the sky. The late afternoon sun cast long golden fingers across the asphalt, dense shadows hovering at the corners of his vision. The atmosphere hummed with menace. "We can go house to house and check for survivors, but don't get your hopes up. We need to leave now if we're going to make it to Newberry and get back before sundown."

Devon nodded gravely. "We have to come back to bury the bodies or burn them, at least. We can't leave these people like this, as if they're nothing but roadkill."

"Agreed, but—"

A soft scraping came from their left.

Jackson spun, took two quick steps, and hunkered down behind the engine mount of a burgundy minivan. Devon crouched beside him, her weapon up and ready. Cautiously, he peered over the hood.

Someone coughed, the sound wet and ragged. The sound originated from the corner of the grocery store, somewhere in the alley.

Jackson signaled for Devon to cover him. Hardly breathing, he jogged in a half-crouch across ten yards of open asphalt until he reached the corner. Blading his body to make himself a smaller target, he led with his muzzle and edged around the side of the building.

Ten feet away, a man dressed in a police uniform leaned against the brick wall, his legs splayed in front of him, his pants legs splattered with blood. Beneath him, a sticky red puddle oozed across the pavement. He didn't appear to be armed.

Jackson crossed the alley, squatted next to him, and patted him down for weapons. Devon faced the parking lot and kept guard, the rifle buttstock pressed to her shoulder, scouring their surroundings for movement.

The officer appeared to be in his thirties, with a lean, angular face, hooded eyes, and a thick mustache. His lips were chapped and peeling, his cheeks sunken from dehydration, his bronze skin sallow from lack of blood. His uniform nametag read "Gomez."

"Water," he begged, his voice raspy.

Jackson pulled a water bottle from his pack and handed it to the officer. He gulped several swallows before swiping his mouth with the back of his arm. His movements were slow and jerky.

"What's your name?" Jackson asked.

"Gomez. Officer Carlos Gomez."

"Where are you hurt?"

"My...my legs. I can't feel anything below my waist."

Jackson kept him talking while he assessed his injuries. Gomez had been shot once in each knee to ensure he couldn't escape. The bullets had effectively shattered his kneecaps. He'd been left here to suffer and die in immense agony.

Jackson tugged a first-aid kit from his rucksack. He wasn't as skilled as Lena or Eli in medicine, but the officer's ruined knees needed to be stabilized before they could move him. Even if he survived, he'd never walk again.

Gomez saw it in Jackson's face. "It's bad, isn't it?"

"If we get you to our clinic right away, you'll live," Jackson said with as much assurance as he could muster. "Tell me what happened."

Gomez winced, his jaw clenched against what must have been incredible pain. "It happened two days ago, I think. I've faded in and out of consciousness, so I'm not certain of the exact time. They came in so fast, in the middle of the night. Eight or nine trucks, several men to a truck, each with AK-47s. They dragged people out of their houses and shot anyone who attempted to defend their homes. As they drove by, they hurled Molotov cocktails at houses, businesses, and whatever struck their fancy. They wore black from head to toe, with combat gear and ceramic plates, their faces grease-painted to make them look like monsters, like ghouls out of a nightmare. They seemed...inhuman."

"They *are* monsters," Devon spat.

Jackson wanted confirmation. "Who were they?"

"The cartel," Gomez rasped. "They weren't trying to hide. They crowed it from the rooftops. They wanted everyone to know who'd done this to them."

Jackson wasn't surprised. Though he'd been expecting the news, his heart still kicked with adrenaline. The cartel was a cloud of destructive locusts ravaging everything within sight, consuming everything and everyone in their path.

"How many men?" Devon asked.

"It was hard to count in the chaos. It felt like a hundred, but at least fifty. With their vehicles and weapons, they had a huge advantage. We didn't have time to respond with a quick reaction force. We didn't have enough men to mount a defense. We're just a tiny town. We didn't think we were big enough to be a target. We have nothing worth stealing here anymore, but they didn't come to steal. They came to destroy."

Jackson held his breath. This intel jived with the information Eli and Antoine had extracted from the cartel spy. "Then what happened?"

"They rounded up anyone who resisted—several cops, a few former soldiers, a handful of civilians with shooting experience. They lined us up and shot everyone in the head. Everyone but me."

Officer Gomez leaned his head back against the wall, his jaw clenched against the pain. Sweat trickled down his temples. "They left me alive on purpose. They said they had a message to send."

A chill touched the back of Jackson's neck. "Who was the message for?"

The man's bruised eyelids fluttered. He looked straight at Jackson. His bleary gaze focused on the nametag affixed to Jackson's uniform. "For you, Sheriff Cross. The message was for you."

17

JACKSON CROSS
DAY ONE HUNDRED AND THIRTY-THREE

Reeling, Jackson leaned back on his heels, his head spinning. "Who gave you the message?"

Carlos Gomez coughed up blood and spat a glob of red onto his chest. "Their leader had an older guy with him. He was the one who did this to me."

"What did he look like?"

"I thought I recognized him from somewhere. He wasn't dressed in black or combat gear like the others. He wore nice clothes, expensive and clean as if he was headed to a business meeting or something. Tall, elegant, silver-haired. I got the impression he was there to give the cartel local intel, like some twisted tour guide. He asked about our police chief—he knew him by name. I heard one of the raiders call him Cross." His bloodshot eyes narrowed in suspicion. "I see that's your name, too."

Shame slashed through Jackson's entire body. His throat seized. He'd suspected his father had turned traitor, but this... He'd never imagined Horatio could be capable of a massacre of innocent people.

But then, he hadn't suspected his sister, either.

What did he know of the darkness of the human heart, the

atrocities committed in the name of self-preservation? He was drowning in a perilous black sea and couldn't see past his own flailing hands.

"What did he say?" Jackson asked in a choked voice. "Tell me every word. Leave nothing out."

"The cartel knows you have the stolen weapons and the meds. They know Munising is where you're hiding everything. He said they would keep coming, keep destroying, until and unless you give up what they want."

Jackson breathed in the stench of charred things, of death and destruction. A wave of dizziness washed through him. "How did he know I'd be the one who found you?"

"He didn't. He said the Alger County Sheriff sticks his nose where it doesn't belong, so he guessed you or your people would hear of it, and somehow the message would get to you."

"What else?"

"He gave me something to give to you." Gomez stuck a shaky hand into a pouch on his battle belt and tugged out a small black phone-like object. It was a portable Ham radio.

Unlike an EMP, an electromagnetic pulse, the solar storms had significantly impacted long conductors, such as power lines, internet cables, and magnetic gas lines, while small-scale electronics like computers and microchips had been left unaffected.

It had also fried half the world's satellites, so satellite phones weren't an option. Short-wave radios still worked, and while Ham radios had sustained some damage during the geomagnetic storms, many had been fixed.

Reluctantly, Jackson took the portable Ham radio.

Officer Gomez groaned. His words were hoarse and raspy; Jackson had to lean in close to hear him: "He said to call him when you're ready to make peace."

"Peace," Jackson echoed dully.

"The cartel won't stop. They won't be satisfied with simply retrieving what was stolen. They're hellbent on making their point to the entire region. Dare to cross them, and they won't just defeat you, they will wipe you off the map. That's what they're going to do to Munising. Make an example of you, then no one will dare to stand up to them. They'll control the entire Upper Peninsula, including the Soo Locks and the bridge. No one but the actual army will be able to stop them. Fat chance of that happening up here."

"I'll keep that in mind." There was no time to move on to Newberry, but they no longer needed to go. They'd gotten the confirmation Jackson needed. And Carlos Gomez was in urgent need of medical care. "Let's get you back to our clinic. We can debrief more later."

With Devon's aid, he managed to splint and stabilize Officer Gomez's legs with several long, straight sticks and strips of cloth. It took a while. Jackson hated how exposed they were, how vulnerable he felt as if a giant target was painted on their backs.

"Don't move," Devon said to Gomez. "We'll bring the truck to you."

As Jackson stood, Gomez reached out and grabbed the sleeve of his uniform with weak, rubbery fingers. His breathing had grown ragged. His face was far too pale, his lips turning purple. He wouldn't last long. "Don't make a deal with them. Don't do it."

Jackson nodded gravely. "I won't if I can help it."

They left Gomez and made their way back to the truck. Aghast, Devon shook her head in disbelief. "Horatio is with the cartel. He's part of this. I didn't want to believe it."

Jackson couldn't ignore the ugly truth staring him full in the face. "He fled when he realized I was getting close to uncovering him. Even though he'd drugged my mother to keep her from telling me the truth, he knew I'd find out eventually. He knew I'd come for Astrid and then him. He cut his losses and ran like a coward."

"He's the former sheriff. How could he do something like this? How could anyone do something like this?"

Jackson clenched his jaw so hard his molars hurt. He looked down at the radio in his hand with revulsion. It felt strangely alien, like some monstrous thing that might suddenly transform into a poisonous spider or a hand grenade about to explode.

He said, "I don't know, but I'm going to find out."

18

ELI POPE

DAY ONE HUNDRED AND THIRTY-FOUR

E li lowered the binoculars and handed them to Jackson. "This is it."

Beside him, Jackson lifted the field glasses and perused their surroundings. They stood on a ridge overlooking the ghost town, a long-abandoned iron mine located about twenty-five miles southwest of Munising, just south of Au Train and Chatham, near Trenary.

The location was far enough from town to prevent collateral damage but close enough to make transportation and supply transfers feasible, but only as long as they maintained access to Fred Combs' growing supply of biofuel.

Known as Devil's Corner, the town was a smaller version of the more famous ghost town at Fayette Historical State Park. In the eighteenth century, the once-bustling town had sprung up seemingly overnight, spurred by the booming production of iron mines spread throughout the Upper Peninsula. When the mines closed in the early 1920s, the town died.

Now, Devil's Corner consisted of a collection of one- and two-story log buildings. The remains of stone foundations and crumbling log-built houses were scattered among the standing stick-built homes. On the edge of town, a cluster of gravestones marked an ancient graveyard built next to a white clapboard church complete with a bell and steeple.

Legend had it that the town was haunted. The ghosts of two dozen miners killed in an underground collapse in the 1850s lurked along the narrow dirt roads, drifted among the houses, and moaned within the decaying walls.

The place was desolate, eerie, and fascinating in equal measure.

Eli pivoted east and pointed to the winding dirt road that led to the ghost town from M-28. "That's where we set up the ambush."

"Are you sure we're up for this?" Jackson asked tightly.

Eli knew what he was asking: whether Eli's body could handle another battle. Eli didn't have a choice. His body might be battered and bruised, but his mind was sharp as ever, still his best weapon.

With every passing day, they risked the cartel gathering enough strength to mount an attack on Munising. To have any chance against a larger, stronger, better-armed adversary, they needed to be the most cunning, the most vicious.

"I'm good," Eli said. "Let's go."

He and Jackson descended the ridge, fighting thorny under-brush and tripping roots, then strode along the dirt road in search of the perfect ambush location. They needed an open area, with a nearby bridge, a hill, or a sharp turn.

Pain throbbed through Eli's leg, his ribs, his upper shoulder. He ignored it. They walked in silence, every so often pausing to strain their ears and listen.

Birds sang in the trees. Insects shushed as they waded through shin-high weeds. The sun had hidden itself behind a bank of thick cottony clouds.

Even in the wilderness, Eli remained vigilant, his neck on a swivel, his gaze constantly sweeping the trees, the bushes, and the cloaked shadows crouched within the unruly borders of the forest. He wore his dog tags and lucky St. Michael's medal beneath his shirt, the metal cool against his skin.

He carried his Glock at his hip, a small secondary pistol in his boot, and his favorite H&K rifle slung across his chest on a two-point sling. He preferred his VP9 handgun, but he'd lost it during the train battle against Sykes. Beggars couldn't be choosers.

A quarter-mile from the ghost town, they found it—the perfect chokepoint. The road curved at a sharp 90-degree angle, with dense woods on the left and a steep hill rising on the right, creating a choke point that would be difficult if not impossible for a vehicle to circumvent.

Eli grunted in approval.

"How are we going to do this?" Jackson asked.

"Very, very carefully."

He'd been preparing for this moment for weeks. In the aftermath of the assault on the copper mine, they'd recovered several crates of 81 mm mortar rounds, once the property of a National Guard unit. Sykes and his merry band of convicts had killed them and stolen the weapons.

While the mortars weren't salvageable, the ammunition was ripe for the taking. Eli knew how to create improvised explosive devices from the materials.

He'd gathered enough components to build switches, which he could activate with a UHF radio, along with supplies for an initiator, or fuse, in addition to the mortar rounds for the explosive.

The homemade IEDs would be buried on either side of the road, then set with markers, specifically rocks stacked into cairns, placed level with the buried IED but hidden from the road sightlines, so only the good guys knew when and where to detonate them.

While he had learned advanced battle tactics in Ranger school, it was the brutal lessons taught by the Taliban—the guerilla ambush tactics that had killed many of his friends—that he now utilized.

The capacity for human brutality was the same whether here in the States or across the ocean. The cartel was no better than the Taliban. No man, woman, or child was safe until they were utterly destroyed.

Eli pointed along the road. "We'll string ten or so improvised mines along a hundred-yard stretch. The cartel caravan will have to pass through this funnel to reach the ghost town. We blow the explosives and take out the front and rear of the convoy first, so the middle vehicles between them are trapped and can't easily circumvent the trap and escape."

He scanned the flat meadow to the left and right, zeroing in on the shallow ditch spanning the right side of the road. Three half-collapsed stone huts stood fifty yards back from the road. "Once we blow the first IEDs on the road, the cartel soldiers will most likely flee the vehicles and run to the ditch or those huts for cover. We'll bury a few IEDs in those locations, and once the hostiles take up their firing positions, we'll blow them."

Jackson nodded, warming to the idea. "And our people?"

Eli pivoted and pointed up the opposite hillside. "We dig seven to ten fighting holes about one hundred fifty yards out for our guys to lay down fire on the caravan. We have a couple of SAWs to utilize here. Ideally, every fighting position would have a .50 caliber gun, but we're using what we have. Where we don't have a more powerful gun, we'll arm our people with AR-15s and M4s."

"Good idea."

"We'll put a second fighting force of about forty men ahead of the convoy, hidden at the edge of the ghost town near the cemetery. It'll serve as our quick reaction force if needed, or potentially flank any survivors of the ambush if the firefight continues for too long."

Eli contemplated the potential scenarios, the pros and cons. The highway battle between Sawyer's men and the cartel flashed through his mind: the blood and carnage, the road a mass grave of bodies picked clean by vultures.

"We know from interrogating the spy that they still have three vintage Hueys armed with RPGs and fuel for the choppers. They have drones, too. While they have a fighting force of over five hundred troops across the border, many of them will be tied up holding the Soo Locks and other towns. From what intel you gathered from the police officer in Seney, their raiding force is approximately sixty to seventy mercenaries, many with some military training.

"If they came at us with everything they've got, we wouldn't stand a chance, but tactically, they won't. They can't hit us with full force and simultaneously maintain control of Sault Ste. Marie, which is a critical stronghold for them. We're going to use that constraint to our advantage."

"And thanks to the false intel we leaked to their spy, we've created a small window for the cartel to hit our ambush, rather than having to guard this site 24/7 for months."

"Exactly."

Jackson made the mental calculation. "You let the spy escape last week. It's Friday now. Can we prepare ourselves by Tuesday? Will they come that quickly?"

"I don't know, but we have to assume they will. We'll be ready for them. We need every man and woman we can spare, including the teenagers. Starting yesterday. That's it. That's the plan."

Jackson set his jaw. "Let's do it."

Eli hesitated, studying his old friend out of the corner of his eye. The burden of leadership weighed heavily on him. He held so many lives in his hands, life or death balanced on a razor's edge. It was an incredible amount of pressure for one man.

Eli fumbled for a moment, unsure what to say. He could discuss tactics 24/7, but when it came to human emotions, he felt discombobulated, uncertain, completely out of his element. "You sure you're good?"

"Of course."

Jackson squinted against the sun as it set over the trees in the west. Ribbons of sherbet-orange and grapefruit-pink streaked the sky. He shoved his hands into his pockets and said nothing. His expression was carefully blank, too blank. Even after all these years, Eli knew him too well.

"You're hiding something," Eli said.

19

ELI POPE

DAY ONE HUNDRED AND THIRTY-FOUR

Eli waited for Jackson to speak.

After a minute, Jackson cleared his throat, shifting uneasily. "I feel darkness inside me. It's like nothing I've ever experienced before. Honestly, it scares me."

"Let it scare you. Use it."

"It makes me feel like a monster."

"That darkness is what lets you face bigger monsters," Eli said quietly. "Sometimes, we must do terrible things to protect the ones we love. I will choose the darkness every single time if it keeps Lena and Shiloh safe."

"You're right. I know you're right." Jackson rubbed his jaw, hesitating, as if conflicted. He seemed embarrassed and ashamed, but determined to push through anyway. "What if this darkness inside my family is genetic? It's inside me, too. My sister was a sociopath, and I didn't see it until it was too late. My father...maybe he is, too. I believe he is." He spread out his hands helplessly. "What if—"

"You aren't your family. You aren't your sister or your father. You are who you decide to be."

Jackson stared solemnly at his outstretched hands as if he was seeing blood dripping from his fingers. Like he was watching himself kill his sister again and again. He was a man tortured by his conscience, haunted by the ghosts of those he'd slain. "The things I've had to do, I would do again, but that knowledge doesn't make the nightmares go away. It doesn't erase this feeling that I've done the unthinkable and can never be forgiven."

"Forgiven by whom?" Eli asked.

"I don't know."

"Your sister?"

Jackson frowned and shook his head. "She was a monster, without remorse or mercy. I know that. I know it logically, but the heart doesn't always follow the script."

"You don't need forgiveness from any of them."

"I have to learn to live with the scars. I don't have a choice."

Eli thought of his own scars, the terrible things he'd done in prison to survive. "You don't have a choice."

"I'm not sure I have a choice with this, either." With a beleaguered sigh, Jackson pulled a small object out of his pocket and held it in his hand. "I left this part out of the incident report to the committee."

Yesterday, Jackson had informed the committee about his conversation with Carlos Gomez in the razed town of Seney. Unfortunately, Officer Gomez had bled out during the return trip to Munising.

Eli glanced at the object, his brows furrowed. "Tell me everything."

Jackson explained how Horatio had left a bloody message for him. "He wants a meeting. A professed peace treaty, though I doubt that's what he truly wants."

"Your father is the enemy."

"I know." Jackson swallowed hard. "I know."

"He's luring you into a trap."

"Probably."

"Has your father ever done anything that wasn't in his self-interest in your entire life?"

Jackson didn't answer that question aloud. They both knew the answer. His frown deepened. "If meeting with him could put a stop to this, to avoid needless bloodshed and the loss of people we care about, it might be worth it."

"He's going to torture you for intel."

"I don't think so. They have plenty of intel. Horatio is feeding it to the cartel himself. He doesn't know the real locations of the stolen meds, but he'll believe he does after the spy reports back to his camp."

"If you call him, he'll twist you up again, make you doubt yourself, and manipulate you."

"I'm not twisted up," Jackson said. "I see more clearly than I ever have."

"Don't make the call yet," Eli said. "If we do it, we do it the smart way. Let me think about it."

Jackson nodded. The tension in his shoulders seemed to ease as if telling Eli had made the tremendous burden that he carried a bit lighter. His jaw was set; he was resolved, though he remained pensive.

Together, they hiked down the ridge to the spot where they'd stashed the truck. Every few minutes, they paused to look and listen, maintaining situational awareness.

Birds flitted among the canopies of the oak, birch, and spruce trees. Eli spotted a blue jay and several chickadees. A red-winged blackbird hopped from branch to branch, seeming to follow them.

When they reached flat ground, Eli studied the desolate ghost town, the sad huddle of barren buildings. Vines snaked over walls, windows, and doors. Moss filmed crumbling stones. Weeds sprouted from every crevice and corner. A sapling grew from the center of a log cabin, rising through the caved-in roof.

If given the opportunity, nature would reclaim everything humanity had created. In ten years, how many towns across the U.S. would be like this? In twenty? in fifty? Silent, abandoned, visited only by ghosts.

They reached the truck. Eli removed several of the pine boughs they'd used to camouflage the vehicle while Jackson climbed into the passenger side. Eli started the engine and backed out of the woods and onto the dirt road, the tires bouncing over roots and fallen tree limbs.

"We might survive this," Jackson said, a flicker of hope in his voice. "It's a good plan."

Eli couldn't share Jackson's optimism, not yet. He stared through the scummy windshield, hands gripping the wheel, his knuckles white. "All plans are good until first contact with the enemy."

They would lay the trap. Then they would wait for the cartel to walk right into it.

20

SHILOH EASTON POPE
DAY ONE HUNDRED AND THIRTY-FIVE

S hiloh put one hand on her hips and scowled, raising the can of spray paint in her other hand and shaking it at the goat. "Faith, for the last time, get out of the squash before I spray-paint a target on your big white butt and turn you into a pincushion!"

Ruby snorted. "You know she won't listen. She's as stubborn as you are."

"Gah! If Bear wasn't such a scaredy cat, I'd sic him after her. Speaking of the devil..."

Shiloh scanned the grounds of the Northwoods Inn in search of the giant dog, but the Newfie was nowhere to be found. He was probably taking one of his languorous afternoon naps somewhere in the shade.

The goat ignored her. She was too busy scarfing up the precious plants in the garden, her head down, big white butt swaying in the air like a fuzzy middle finger to the world.

Ruby leaped to her feet and chased the goat, shouting insults and clapping her hands. "Get out of here, you big dumb oaf!"

Faith raised her head and glared at the girls with her weird, rectangular pupils. The goat boasted a stout body and small sharp horns curling back from her skull. The scruffy beard on her chin made her look perpetually ornery—which she most definitely was.

Ruby raised a hand as if to slap her on her furry rump. Faith gave an obstinate bleat, turned on her sharp hooves, and trotted off to torment the kids hanging damp sheets and towels to dry on the clotheslines. She'd likely gobble up the washcloths before they could stop her.

"Good riddance." Ruby wiped her dirt-crusted hands on her khaki pants. "Why do goats have such a problem making friends?"

Before Shiloh could venture a guess, Ruby answered, "They always butt heads!"

"Good one," Shiloh deadpanned.

"What do you call a young goat that knows martial arts?"

"I have no—"

"The karate kid!"

Shiloh shook her head in dismay.

"What do you call a goat's beard?" Ruby asked. "Wait for it—a goatee!"

"Enough!" Shiloh threatened to spray Ruby with the can of paint in her hand. "You're the literal worst."

Ruby grinned. "Sorry, not sorry. I have the morning egg-gathering shift with Keagan, Traci Tilton's son. He has a book of dad jokes. We tell each other terrible jokes to pass the time."

At the mention of Traci's name, Shiloh stiffened. Hatred sizzled through her veins. She narrowed her eyes. "Yeah well, let's hope he's nothing like his traitorous mother."

"He's just a kid," Ruby said.

In the distance, two sentries marched past, their rifles on slings and pistols at their hips, with extra magazines and ammo slipped into pouches on their battle belts. It was Jason Anders and Fiona Smith.

Fiona waved; Shiloh managed a tentative wave back. She couldn't wait until Eli ungrounded her and allowed her back on sentry duty.

"Fine. Whatever." Shiloh shook the can of black spray paint and returned to the task at hand. Several dozen bright yellow rubber duckies stood in cheerful rows on a tarp spread on the grass.

Last week, Eli had given Shiloh the job of gathering every duckie she could find in Alger County. Turned out, it was an easier task than she'd thought: a bunch of abandoned Jeeps in town sported the rubber duckies on their dashboards. It was some sort of weird Jeep thing from the old world.

A shriek split the air. Adrenaline spiking, Shiloh whirled and reached for the crossbow in the grass beside her. Her head whipped back and forth as she searched for the danger, her nerves on edge.

"It's okay, Shiloh." Ruby pointed across the lawn. Past the rabbit warren huts and the chicken coops, several kids shouted gleefully as they chased Faith, who zigzagged between the clothes-lines spread among several trees.

The goat galloped merrily amid flapping towels and fluttering pillowcases, nipping at a sheet here, biting a hand towel there, yanking a pair of pants from the line, and flinging them in the air as the kids shrieked in delight. Shiloh recognized one of the kids: little Adam, the deaf boy.

Shiloh exhaled, lowering the crossbow. Her pulse roared in her ears. She touched the arrowhead in her hair with a shaky hand. Her legs felt weak and watery.

It was a false alarm. Everything was fine, she was fine. Her mind understood yet her body had responded like she'd been shoved over a cliff.

"Just the stupid goat," she muttered. "Just a goat."

As her pulse gradually returned to normal, she stood still and took in her familiar surroundings. To the south, a half-dozen teens carted loads of trash in wheelbarrows to the designated trash dump outside the housing zone and away from water sources. Older folks weeded, collected and spread compost, or gathered ripe fruits and veggies in baskets. Others lugged firewood and kindling to the fifty rustic cabins they'd built in the last few months.

In the afternoons, between lunch and dinner demands, the kitchen staff sat around the picnic tables, chatting and laughing while pressure-canning fruits and veggies like peaches, apples, and tomatoes to make jams, salsas, and sauces, as well as canning green beans, mushrooms, okra, and pumpkins for various hearty soups.

Volunteers had built concrete spring houses along the creek and dug out root cellars behind the rows of hastily constructed cabins, which were useful for storing potatoes, onions, garlic, and squash through the winter.

As late September approached, everyone was focused on food preservation and storage for winter. The mornings were downright cold, a reminder that winter was bearing down upon them, which meant freezing temperatures, mountains of snow, and months of the deepest, darkest cold a person could imagine.

In winter, the Upper Peninsula might as well be Siberia. Nothing would grow. The cold would invade your bones and freeze the liquid in your cells. In the worst weather, a few minutes outside could kill a grown man. Simple tasks like hauling water from the lake or traipsing to the woodshed for firewood would become monumental tasks.

With a rueful shake of her head, Ruby returned to her spot in the garden. She knelt, busily transferring leftovers from dinner—citrus rinds, broccoli stalks, and potato peels—from the wheelbarrow beside her to the patch of growing root vegetables.

Shiloh set the crossbow in the grass next to the tarp. She wrinkled her nose at the stink of rotting fruit. "That's super gross."

"The leftovers provide vitamins A and C to the plants. Helps them grow bigger." Ruby hefted a giant green zucchini. "See?"

"I don't even like zucchini."

"You're missing out."

"It's a texture thing."

"I think you're just scared to try something new."

"Mind your own beeswax, why don't you?" Shiloh flipped her off. Then she shook the paint can and sprayed an even second coat over the rubber ducks. She had no clue why Eli wanted them, but she doubted they'd be utilized as bathtub toys.

Ruby wrinkled her nose. "Eli has you do some weird stuff, you know."

"I'm well aware."

"What are those things for, anyway?"

"No clue. Eli is always up to something."

Raised voices echoed in the still air. Two guys were arguing by the latrines, their arms flailing, fingers pointing, hands curling into fists. No doubt another argument over whose turn it was to do what, who refused to pull their weight, or who was lazy and entitled, mooching off the hard work of others.

Tim Brooks strode across the lawn, chickens squawking and feathers flying in his wake as he moved between the two men. He shoved them apart and spoke in a low, strained voice Shiloh couldn't make out.

She recognized Bradley Underwood, the old sheriff. Eli didn't like him, so obviously, Shiloh didn't either. A couple of the sentries on patrol stood by, watchful and alert but staying out of it.

There were arguments nearly every day, with hurt feelings, flaring tempers, and fragile egos to soothe. Shiloh didn't envy the Brooks; it must be exhausting and incredibly disheartening to deal with constant bickering at the end of the damn world.

Why couldn't everyone put aside their differences and come together to face their greatest enemies? The problem wasn't the rules, the problem was the people. People always screwed things up.

Finally, the men broke apart without coming to blows, thanks to Tim. Underwood stalked off toward the wind turbines perched on the bluff, a wrench in hand. The other guy was heatedly arguing with Tim, though Tim seemed to have things under control.

Humanity was as dumb as a box of rocks.

Shiloh shrugged and turned away from the altercation. A flash of movement inside the nearest goat pen caught her eye. A familiar figure sat on a stool milking one of the better-behaved goats, a black nanny with white spots named Merigold. It was Traci Tilton.

Shiloh glared at her back. Traci didn't seem to notice her laser-eyed stare, because she didn't lift her head or bother to turn around. She was engrossed in teaching one of the new women how to milk the goats—Theresa Fleetfoot, so heavily pregnant she waddled when she walked. She looked like she was about to go into labor at any second.

Shiloh glowered at them both. "Everybody's worried about the cartel spies sneaking in here, and Traci Tilton is already inside. We have a crack in our defenses the size of Kansas and everyone's like 'second chances,' 'forgiveness,' and 'keeping our humanity,' blah blah blah. Who cares about ethics and morals if we're all dead?"

"They're keeping a close eye on her. How would she sneak messages to the cartel even if she wanted to? And why would she? Her son is here, too."

"Why would anyone? Because alliances shift like oil on water to whoever appears the most powerful at the moment. Mark my words, she *will* turn on us the second she gets the chance. And we'll pay a high price for it."

"I hope not," Ruby said.

Shiloh gritted her teeth and hefted one of the black rubber duckies, checking to make sure the paint was dry before chucking it into the canvas sack next to the wheelbarrow. She squeezed the duckie in her fist. "The second she makes a mistake, I'll be there to kick her bony butt into next Tuesday, and I'll do it with a big fat smile on my face."

21

SHILOH EASTON POPE
DAY ONE HUNDRED AND THIRTY-SIX

The pleasant smell of woodsmoke wafted through the air, mingling with the rich scent of gun oil.

Shiloh sat with Lena and Eli outside one of the cabins near the creek. Eli was busy cleaning and oiling his guns, with stacks of magazines and piles of ammo scattered across the table, while Lena mashed various herbs to create one of her tinctures for Theresa Fleetfoot, who had started the early signs of labor.

Shiloh expertly skinned several squirrels she'd caught in her snares and tossed the tiny corpses to Bear, who pounced on them eagerly. He wolfed down the squirrel meat in a couple of bites, blood flecking his jowls. Shiloh tossed him her last piece of black bear jerky, which also disappeared within seconds.

It was becoming more difficult to hunt enough wildlife to feed the giant Newfoundland. It was a good thing she had stashed stores of dried fish and bear jerky for him.

The dog caught the occasional mouse or rabbit himself, but he wasn't very good at it. Unless he was working, he preferred to laze around near his humans all day.

"Good boy." She petted his head as she glanced across the Northwoods grounds. The atmosphere around the Inn was tense as the fighters prepared to depart for Devil's Corner in a few short hours. Shiloh watched them out of the corner of her eye with more than a bit of jealousy.

Lena caught Shiloh's gaze and narrowed her eyes, as if she could read her mind and knew exactly what she was thinking. "Shiloh, you are not to leave the Northwoods grounds on your own for any reason. Do you understand?"

"Like you did when you went to get the wild cranberries at the lighthouse?" Shiloh snapped.

She was sick of being treated like a little kid when she'd killed a grown man by herself. She hadn't panicked or choked. They should take her seriously.

To her credit, Lena didn't flinch. "I was thinking of my sick client, and I did something foolhardy. I will not make that mistake again, and neither will you."

"I feel claustrophobic here. Like I can't breathe properly."

"Wander through the woods on the property," Eli said. "Go fish in the stream. Sit by the waterfall while you clean your weapons. Keep Bear with you and stay close."

"Boring."

Eli set down his Glock. "I need to know that I can trust you, so I'm not expending needed time and energy worrying about you when I'm supposed to be winning an ambush."

Shiloh glared at them with fire in her eyes. "Is that why you two ganged up on me? To ground me like I'm a little kid?"

"It's not like that," Lena said.

Shiloh spun on Eli. "You're going to fight at Devil's Corner in the morning. I want to fight, too."

"Absolutely not," Eli growled.

Shiloh folded her arms across her chest. "Then put me back on guard duty. Let me help defend our people."

"It's only been a few weeks since you killed someone—"

"—who deserved to die."

"Of course," Lena said, "Be that as it may, you're still recovering from the trauma—"

"Do I look traumatized? Or scared? Am I curled up in a fetal position on the freaking floor? I'm fine. I am. I want to do something. I need to help." She shifted her gaze to Eli. "Either put me back into rotation or I'm sneaking into one of the cargo trucks at midnight. You won't find me until it's too late and the battle has already started."

Eli eyed her warily. "If I grab her legs and you get her arms, do you think we could take

her?" he asked Lena.

"Hmmm," Lena mused. "A few hours tied up in a closet might change her mind."

Shiloh leaped to her feet and darted back, out of his reach. "I dare you to try. Don't forget, I've gone running every day, even when you can't. You've still got a bum leg. I can outrun you any day of the week."

Lena snorted.

Eli rolled his eyes. "It's like trying to argue with a brick wall."

Shiloh stood her ground. "I have a right to fight for us, too. I've earned it."

She refused to break eye contact with Eli until he softened. And he would soften first, she knew he would. He understood her warrior's heart in a way no one else did, not even Lena.

Finally, Eli sat back with a defeated sigh.

Shiloh narrowed her eyes. "Is that a yes?"

"If you agree to stay at Northwoods no matter what, I'll tell Baker and Flores to put you back on the rotation on the east gate."

Shiloh smiled in triumph. "Done."

22

ELI POPE

DAY ONE HUNDRED AND THIRTY-SIX

"We're losing her!" Lena cried.

"She's breech," Dr. Virtanen said. "This baby is only coming out one way."

Eli stood in the operating theater and watched helplessly as Lena and Dr. Virtanen tended to their patient. A pair of battery-operated work lights glared into his eyes. Eli inhaled the strong smell of bleach and disinfectant mingling with the darker scents of blood, sweat, and vomit.

Theresa Fleetfoot had gone into labor early that morning. The woman lay on the operating table, moaning in pain, barely conscious and naked below the waist, her round stomach slathered in iodine to disinfect her skin.

Sweat soaked her temples. Her eyelids fluttered as her eyes rolled back in her head. Blood drenched the table beneath her and dripped into a growing puddle on the floor at their feet. Too much blood. A soul-piercing scream of agony ripped from her lips. The horrific sound sent chills racing up Eli's spine.

Dr. Virtanen's features went rigid. "She's running out of time. We get this baby out now, or she hemorrhages to death, and we lose the baby, too."

"You mean surgery?" Lena stilled. "A cesarean."

The World We Burn

The medical examiner looked up from between Theresa's legs, her eyes bleak but resolved over her face mask. "We've prepped for this. We can do it. We don't have a choice."

The sun had set hours ago. Outside, heavy clouds shrouded the moon and stars in a dense black blanket. Everything was dark and still. No breeze stirred the desiccated leaves clinging to the branches of the beech and maple trees.

Trash littered the deserted corridors—deflated IV bags, dropped blankets, a forgotten pressure cuff. Obsolete monitoring equipment and barren gurneys cluttered the rooms and hallways like something out of a horror movie.

Eli stepped forward. He had scrubbed in to help. He was no doctor, but with his extensive emergency field training, he knew enough to follow instructions. He snapped on a pair of gloves. "Tell me what to do."

After a long day spent bolstering their defenses and training their fighters in defensive tactics, Eli longed to don his forty-pound pack to run his usual ten miles a day, though he could only jog a mile or two before his leg threatened to give out on him.

He could, however, still ride a bike. That evening, he'd ridden one of the electric bikes from the Northwoods Inn to the hospital to see Lena. She and Dr. Virtanen had reopened a wing of the Munising hospital to provide whatever aid they could to anyone who came through the hospital doors.

Every day, the lines were longer and longer. The people were hurting and desperate. It was difficult, disheartening, agonizing work. Several times, Lena had returned to the Northwoods Inn in tears after losing a patient to an infection or a stroke or burst appendix, people who should have been saved.

"We must work quickly," the ME said. Venla Virtanen was a stout Finnish woman in her fifties with short white-blonde hair. Her bedside manner was no-nonsense and brisk, perhaps due to her chosen vocation as an examiner of the dead, not the living.

A portable pulse oximeter monitored the patient's heart rate and oxygen level. An IV dripped into her arm from a stand behind the operating table, administering saline fluids.

To put Theresa under without proper anesthesia or a trained anesthesiologist, they used ether. One of the volunteer scavenging teams had obtained ketamine from a local veterinarian clinic, which Dr. Virtanen used to make the patient sleepy and to help her forget the trauma of the surgery. By the time the ketamine wore off, the ether would take effect.

Placing a clean towel over the patient's eyes, Lena dripped the ether onto several layers of gauze attached to a medical face mask, which she lowered to cover the patient's nose and mouth as she fell into a deep sleep.

Dr. Virtanen grasped a shiny scalpel from the tray next to her and sliced the woman's belly open above the pubic bone, cutting a low curved line to avoid harming the baby. The doctor cut through the layer of fat and muscle, mumbling curses under her breath, sweat beading her forehead, blood slicking her gloved hands.

Beside her, Eli wicked up the blood with gauze and a suction tool they'd hooked up to the single portable generator. Urgency knotted his guts.

"She's waking up!" Lena cried. "I can't keep her under!"

Tension crackled through the air. If Theresa woke in the middle of surgery, she could go into shock and perish on the table. They were working against the clock.

"I'm almost there! Give her more ether." Dr. Virtanen set down the scalpel and pushed her hand into the open wound. She tugged and pulled, moving aside internal organs to reach the uterus. She snapped instructions at Eli as she worked.

Eli had administered first aid to his fellow soldiers on many a battlefield—staunching gushing injuries from severed limbs, sealing sucking chest wounds, and splinting shattered bones—but he had never delivered a baby.

It was both terrifying and awe-inspiring.

Something moved and rolled beneath his hands—the baby. Amniotic fluid gushed over his fingers. Swiftly, he mopped up as much fluid as he could so Dr. Virtanen could see clearly. She took hold of the fetus and tugged, gently and then harder, sliding her hand beneath the wriggling form, grasping the tiny shoulders with her fingers splayed across the child's fragile back.

The ME snatched the infant from its mother's womb. She handed the infant to Eli and immediately returned her attention to the mother.

"Get the child to breathe!" she ordered over her shoulder.

The infant lay curled in Eli's arm, little legs kicking, tiny fists flailing. Its skin was wrinkled and purplish and filmed in a white cheesy substance called vernix. Dark wet hair matted the oblong skull. The delicate eyes squinted shut. A fine fuzz coated the pink shell-shaped ears.

Holding the infant felt like holding a live grenade. Cradling the child cautiously, Eli rubbed its chest with two fingers. The babe opened its rose-bud mouth and gave a wretched, gargling cry.

"It's a girl," Eli said in relief. "A healthy baby girl."

Eli rocked the baby while Dr. Virtanen tended to the afterbirth. Lena expertly tied off the umbilical cord with a few pieces of string, cut the cord with sterile scissors, then took the baby from Eli's arms and wiped the infant down, swaddling her in a blanket like a tiny burrito. Her little round face peeked out, red and startled.

Lena laid her carefully in a warming incubator attached to the portable solar generator. Once she'd ensured the baby was okay, Lena staggered to the wall and ripped off her mask. She scrubbed her forehead with the back of her arm, leaving a streak of bright red blood along her left temple.

Eli grabbed a towel from the medical tray, went to her, and wiped away the blood. "You okay?"

Lena's eyes were glassy. "The mother lost a lot of blood. I don't know if she's going to wake up. I'm so sick of losing people."

He sensed the stress and tension radiating from her body in waves. Even with the medications they'd stolen from the cartel, they were woefully undersupplied and radically understaffed, forced to make do with what little they had.

It was like keeping a sinking ship afloat with little more than spit and duct tape.

"You saved the baby," he said.

"Yes, we did." She sucked in a steadying breath. "It's not enough. It's never—"

A beeping sound interrupted them. His gaze dropped to the bulge of the insulin pump attached to her belly beneath her hospital scrubs. Her pump beeped again, and she paused long enough to check her number.

His brow furrowed in concern. "I have some raisins in my pack."

"One hundred and steady."

"You sure?"

"It's good, Eli. I'm good."

Undaunted, Eli fished in his pack for the raisins and handed them to her. "To keep your energy up, then."

She accepted the food and chewed slowly, methodically, her tense gaze on Dr. Virtanen and their patient lying still on the operating table. Though she'd regained some of the weight she'd lost, she still seemed frail. Too skinny. Eli worried about her constantly.

Lena finished the raisins and retied her ponytail, pulling the hair back from her pale face. She rubbed the back of her neck. "I need to help Dr. Virtanen stitch Theresa's C-section and tend to the baby. Her daughter Miriam is outside in the hallway, waiting. I need to tell her what happened...I don't know when I'll be able to return to the Inn."

He took a step closer. "You sure you're okay?"

"You already asked me that."

"I wasn't satisfied with your answer."

"You don't have to worry about me."

"I'm not worried," he lied, "but you are on my mind. Every second of every day, Lena."

Lena blushed. "Right back at you."

"I wish you would stay within the protection of the Inn."

"I know full well what you wish, but the real world doesn't work that way. We have the equipment and supplies here. You can't be the only one who risks your life all the time. You don't get to be the only hero in the room."

Eli snorted. He pushed a stray hair back from her face, gazing intently into her eyes. He longed to kiss her for all eternity, to hold her forever, to lose himself in a beautiful world they created for themselves, a world without war and pain and death.

Much as he'd like to, he couldn't keep her locked in a safe little box. She'd never allow it. She was too brave, too kind, and too good to stand by while others suffered. Lena was always the first to jump into the fray. In her way, Lena was as much a fighter as any of them.

To refuse that part of her would be to fundamentally alter the woman he'd fallen in love with, the woman he'd loved his entire life.

His chest pulsed with the fierceness of his affection for this woman. He had never known a love like this—powerful, all-consuming—nor the utter terror of loss, either. If he lost her or Shiloh...the shot of liquid fear stopped his heart in his chest.

Eli narrowed his eyes. "The sentries will stay on guard until you leave. They have strict instructions to escort you back. Don't you dare send them away."

Lena attempted a weary smile. "I won't."

"I'm right here. Just say the word, and I'll be right by your side."

She sank against him, then. Her heart thudded against his ribcage. He held her close. "I know."

Their reprieve was brief. Seconds later, Eli's radio hissed to life. Eli removed his gloves before answering.

"It's Waldo," Nash said, referring to his new call sign. Everyone had been assigned one in case their transmissions were overheard by enemy ears. "I'm on watch. I think I've spotted something."

"Spit it out," Eli said.

"Last night, I thought I saw movement just inside the town perimeter. Not necessarily suspicious. It was just once and then nothing. I thought maybe it was one of the residents or a stray dog or something, but tonight I saw it again. Two figures moving between houses and skirting backyards, but not like a resident walking a dog or taking out the trash. They're furtive, leapfrogging each other, moving like trained soldiers, but we don't have a patrol on Snow Road tonight."

Concern sparked under Eli's skin. "Did you say Snow Road?"

"Roger that. No outsiders could've gotten through our security net. We've doubled our patrols and tripled our checkpoints and overwatch. I'm sure of it."

"It's not an outsider."

"Then who is it?"

"Stay at your post and radio Jackson for backup."

"Copy that, but—"

Eli had already changed the channel. He attempted to reach Antoine repeatedly. Only static, no answer. Then he tried Nyx. Still nothing. Though the sheriff's office had constructed several repeaters, radio range remained an issue.

As he'd feared, they were likely together and out of range at Nyx's grandmother's house.

"Did you pull them up on the radio?" he asked Nash, who was much closer to their probable location.

"I tried. No answer."

There was no time. Eli would have to go to them.

Apprehension curled in his gut like a snake eating its tail, threatening to consume him. Antoine and Nyx were skilled warriors. They could hold their own—but an ambush, at night, when they were least expecting it—that was something else entirely.

A clear and present threat existed within their borders. They'd allowed themselves to grow complacent. Eli should have known: James Sawyer didn't get complacent. He was patient, cunning, and vengeful—a potent combination.

Like a crocodile, he waited, and watched, and when the moment was right, he struck.

"Eli," Lena said behind him. "What's wrong?"

"Nyx's grandmother lives on Snow Road. Sawyer had his goons staking out her house, waiting for them to approach. It's the only location he knows they'll eventually visit. Sawyer believes Antoine and Nyx betrayed him. I can't let them pay for their loyalty with their lives."

"How do you know it's Sawyer?"

"Because it's what I would do."

Lena nodded. "Take backup."

He paused for a second to look at her—to really look at her. Tendrils of hair stuck to her sweaty cheeks. Droplets of blood spattered her scrubs. In the wavering lamplight, her eyes were deep, bottomless wells. He could spend his entire life staring into those eyes.

"I will," he lied. Backup would be too late. He had to go now. Holstering his radio, he seized his rucksack from its spot by the door—he took his battle gear with him everywhere. "They risked their lives for me, for us. I won't abandon them. Tactically, we need their skills for the battle to come. I don't know if we can pull this off without them."

"You don't have to convince me." Lena stepped forward and gave him a fierce hug. "Go save them. Then come back to me."

Eli kissed her hard on the lips. "Always."

23

ELI POPE
DAY ONE HUNDRED AND THIRTY-SIX

Eli stalked the night. The cloud cover was dense and oppressive. The stars were blotted out, the moon invisible as if it had been erased from the galaxy, like it had never existed except within the world of dreams.

This night, however, was a nightmare.

A nightmare for the miserable cockroaches who dared to attack Eli's people. Things would not end well for them. Eli would make sure of it.

His compact Glock 19 sat snug against his kidney in an inside-the-waistband holster. His tactical knife was tucked into its sheath at his hip, with another blade slipped into his boot. He wore a helmet with night vision goggles, the world glowing in shades of green.

Eli crept from vehicle to vehicle, house to house, slinking closer and closer to his target. The ceramic plates dug into his tender ribs, pain streaking up his left shin with each step.

The pain he tucked into a box and then put it on a high shelf in the back of his mind. No time for that now. He slowed his breathing and focused his entire body on the task at hand, the danger that awaited him around the next corner.

Nash was positioned at a second-story window at the end of

the street. He'd provide overwatch and detect any hostiles lurking in the neighborhood or holed up in a house. He'd alerted backup, but Jackson was at least ten minutes out.

Eli kept his neck on a swivel, examining darkened windows, checking the interior of each vehicle as he moved in a half-crouch from cover to cover. He raised his gaze and studied the rooftops for the glint of a rifle, the shifty movements of a sniper lying in wait.

He was extremely aware that he might be walking into a trap.

Normally, he'd know the layout of the building, as well as the number of hostiles and their weapons. There were too many tactical unknowns.

He had no choice. He had to go in hot.

Taking a knee behind a cherry-red Subaru WRX carpeted in dead leaves, he exhaled and peered around the engine block, listening hard, studying the quiet houses, the cars, the trees. The maples lining the sidewalk were fast losing their leaves, their gnarled branches reaching for him like bleached bone fingers.

A tidy two-story Cape Cod caught his eye. It was of indeterminate color—gray or light blue or green—it was impossible to tell in the dark with the NVGs. Among the flowers and bushes surrounding the front porch, small ceramic creatures peered back at him.

Eli had never been to this house, but he'd heard Antoine describe the dozens of merrily grinning garden gnomes dotting the scruffy landscaping. How many houses on Snow Road boasted resident gnomes? Couldn't be more than one.

Moving silently toward his target, Eli snuck down a weedy driveway to approach the house from behind, intending to enter through a bedroom window or back door.

He placed each step with care. Dry crackling leaves were strewn across the street and blanketed the yards. Twigs, leaves, and trash collected along the curb and clotted in the storm drains.

As he approached the corner of the house in front of the garage, he angled his body, slipped down the right side of the driveway past a minivan, and knelt beside the engine block.

Peering around the fender, he studied the overgrown backyard. A shed and a pile of firewood hunched in the shadows beside a rickety, sagging wood fence. Several bee hives were stacked next to the fence—

Movement at his three o'clock.

He froze. Adrenaline spiked his veins. As his eyes adjusted, he made out a familiar shape about ten yards to the northeast of his position, behind the house.

Antoine bent over the shape of a second figure lying on the ground. Soft grunts and thuds sounded: bodies grappling in the dark. Before Eli could render aid, Antoine grasped the other man's head by the hair with his left hand and shoved his knife into the side of the man's neck with the other.

Antoine pushed his knee into the man's back. The man flopped like a dying fish. A faint gurgle dribbled from his lips as he attempted to call for help.

Eli crouched, fighting tunnel vision. He looked left and right and up toward the roofline, every cell in his body alert and wary. Maintaining situational awareness at all times was critical, especially in a hostile environment.

His weapon up, he rose and approached from the cover of the parked minivan. "At your six," he said as he swiveled to cover Antoine from any threats from the woods behind the house.

Hunched over the body, Antoine withdrew the blade from the man's throat. Near translucent fluid poured into the grass. Through night vision goggles, the blood was bizarrely luminescent.

Gripping the man's limp head with both hands, Antoine smashed the back of his skull into the ground again and again. Antoine's usual jovial smile was gone; rage blackened his eyes.

"He's good and dead, friend," Eli whispered.

The body ceased flopping. Antoine stood after he wiped the blood from his knife onto his victim's shirt. Eli recognized it as a Douk-Douk, the traditional knife of many Legionnaires.

Eli glanced down at Antoine's handiwork. He recognized the

wolf's tattoo on the dead man's forearm, the twin snakes caught in the predator's jaws. "Sawyer's mercs."

Antoine gazed at Eli with a hard expression. He was in soldier mode, wearing his helmet and night vision goggles, though not his chest rig or body armor. "How did you know they were here?"

"Nash alerted me. I made an educated guess."

"There are too many inside the house for me to take alone without risking Nyx or her grandma. There are four of them. Three now. They took Nyx's radio before she could call for backup. I've been otherwise engaged hunting this joker. He was outside doing sentry duty, so I took him out."

"Is Nyx alive?"

"As far as I know. I think they're waiting for me. I would've walked straight into their trap except I did some counter-surveillance around the house first and discovered their entry point. The rear window to the laundry room was open with the bottom latch broken. It wasn't broken before tonight."

He pointed to the window closest to the garage. The screen had been jimmied from the track and lay in the tall grass next to the air conditioning unit.

"These guys are good. They snuck in beneath Nash's watch and covered their tracks."

"Did you get a look inside?" Eli asked.

"Three hostiles armed with automatic weapons. They've got Nyx and her grandma in the kitchen, which is through the laundry room to the left of the living room. Nyx is gagged and handcuffed to a kitchen chair, her hands behind her back."

His face darkened. "They stripped her to her bra and under-wear. Her clothes, plate carrier, and weapons are in a pile next to the fridge. I saw a huge bruise on her chest above her bra. They must have snuck in through the back and shot her in the vest. They used the seconds she was down from the blow to grab and disarm her. Her grandma is on the floor in front of the stove on the right. I saw a pool of blood around her head. It looks bad. I don't know if she's alive. They were burning her with cigarette butts. Part of a sick show for Nyx."

Anger ran through Eli like an electric current. "You said three guys. Do we know who they are?"

"Andy Kade, David Reynard, and the third one is Martin Aguilera."

Eli knew them. Kade was long and lean, with mousy brown hair and a drooping mustache, his utterly bland exterior concealing his penchant for brutality.

David Reynard sported Celtic tattoos snaking up both arms and a bushy beard to his chest. He was a former Marine, discharged dishonorably for photographing the torture of Iraqi detainees in the Middle East.

Aguilera was a quiet, brooding man in his late twenties, thick and muscled, with a 101st Air Assault tattoo on his right forearm, the kind of man who wouldn't hesitate to kill a monastery of monks if it suited his goals.

None of these guys would go down easily.

"Falcon is ten minutes out," Nash whispered into his comms, meaning Jackson.

Eli gritted his teeth in growing frustration. Ten minutes was too long. Anything could happen in a fraction of a second, let alone the eternity of a single minute.

Nyx and her grandmother didn't have the luxury of time.

Antoine knew the layout, where the hostages were located, in what condition, and where the bad guys stood with their weapons. With his intel, they had a chance.

Taking a breath, Eli thought of Lena's smile, of Shiloh's shining dark eyes, and vowed he'd make it out of this alive, someway, somehow.

"I'm going in with Antoine now," Eli said to Nash. "Remain on overwatch."

"Roger that."

"When backup arrives, put your men in a perimeter position around the house. Stay tight with your cover and pay attention so you make it home tonight. Make sure your guys don't shoot us, either."

"Good copy."

Eli looked at Antoine. "We're going to keep this simple. I'm gonna yell grenade, and throw it to give us time to get in."

Antoine's eyes widened in alarm. "You're going to use a grenade? You'll hit Nyx—"

"I'm well aware."

"Then what—"

Eli pulled a painted black rubber duck from his pack. It was slightly bigger than a baseball. Shiloh had done a good job. He hefted it in his palm. "I'm throwing this."

Antoine stared at Eli like he'd lost his marbles.

"I cut the bottom open and put a stone inside so it weighs close to the same as a grenade and sounds similar as it lands. The eye will see what it thinks it sees. The bad guys will instinctively dive for cover, which will give us an extra second or two to nail these mouth-breathers."

Antoine shook his head in wonder. "You just might be crazy enough to pull this off."

Eli offered him a grim smile. "Welcome to hostage rescue in the apocalypse."

24

ELI POPE
DAY ONE HUNDRED AND THIRTY-SIX

E li and Antoine slithered through the window, dropping quietly to the tile floor below. Cold sweat beaded beneath his chest plates and trickled down the back of his neck. He focused on the fight at hand and locked everything else out. His vision narrowed, his nerves sharp.

It was dark inside. Watery moonlight streamed through the window. Both men wore twin NVGs mounted on their helmets. As Antoine adjusted his depth perception, his hip accidentally knocked a laundry basket full of folded clothes.

It swayed, about to fall.

Throwing out a hand, Eli steadied it, his heart in his throat. They stared at each other in strained silence. Had anyone heard? There was no reaction from deeper inside the house.

Carefully, they made their way through the laundry room, entering a hallway with a half-bath, the door ajar, then crept through the small storage room that opened into the kitchen.

Warm candlelight flickered from beneath the door into the kitchen. Harsh, raised voices filtered through the flimsy hollow-core door. It was followed by a low moan of pain.

Crouching, Antoine reached for the door and cautiously cracked it open. With more than enough light to see, Eli and

Antoine raised their NVGs. Eli knelt and peered through the six-inch crack in the door.

Bile churned in his gut as he took in the scene. Nyx was no longer tied to the chair but lay on her back on the tile floor, her hands handcuffed behind her. She was weaponless and vulnerable. The bandolier of ammo she wore like a Miss America sash had been kicked into a corner next to the trash can.

Bruises bloomed along her jaw and swelled her right eye. Blood smeared her bare chest. The bruise from the bullet striking her chest plate was a nasty reddish purple and worsening by the minute.

Reynard stood over her. He held a combat blade in one hand and a bottle of vodka in the other. The other men wore black, charcoal smeared across their hard faces.

Kade was closest. He stood to the side of Eli's hidden position, his attention on Nyx on the floor. Aguilera leaned against a faded calendar tacked to the wall next to the sink.

Grandma lay motionless a few feet from Nyx. Red circles seared her scrawny arms. Blood splattered her floral housedress. Her filmy white hair was spread in a halo around her head. Her wrinkled lips were split, like she'd been punched hard in the face.

Eli couldn't tell her condition from his position peering through the crack in the doorway. She might be unconscious or already dead.

Reynard set the vodka on the kitchen counter along with his knife, one hand resting on his belt buckle while the other men watched with dark greedy eyes. Their attention had shifted completely to Reynard and Nyx.

"You and I are gonna have a real good time even if your boyfriend doesn't show up," Reynard drawled.

"Go to hell!" Nyx slurred through split lips. Hatred flared in her eyes. She was down but certainly not out.

"Don't worry, I'll meet you there," Reynard said. "When we're done with you, we'll start on your boy toy as soon as Frenchie shows his ugly mug. Sawyer gives his regards. He's only sad he couldn't be here to rip your entrails from your belly himself."

White-hot anger burned beneath Eli's breastbone. Only animals tortured defenseless old ladies and did the things this thug was preparing to do to Nyx. Not even Sawyer would condone this behavior.

Eli had known Sawyer his entire life, from their high school days as an awkward, sullen outsider desperate to be included, to the criminal mastermind lording over his fortress on Grand Island.

Sawyer was ruthless and cunning, but he had his own twisted code, which did not include brutalizing women. For all his ruthlessness, Sawyer was a gentlemen's gangster, or so he liked to think of himself.

Sawyer wanted to dole out punishments with his own hand. He wouldn't hesitate to kill Nyx or Antoine, but he wouldn't do this.

Reynard's eyes glittered like a fish's scales beneath the heavy shelf of his brow. "We're going to have so much fun with you."

Nyx spat blood. "Go ahead and try. You'll be peeing sitting down the rest of your life."

Reynard cursed in fury. He kicked her repeatedly in the stomach, driving Nyx against the perimeter wall of cabinets. She curled into a fetal position to protect her internal organs.

They couldn't wait a second longer. Action beat reaction, every time. It was go time.

Eli nodded at Antoine. He mouthed, *one, two, three.*

Antoine yanked the door open wide.

25

ELI POPE

DAY ONE HUNDRED AND THIRTY-SIX

On cue, Eli yelled, "Get down! Grenade!"

Antoine and Eli burst through the kitchen door. Simultaneously, they crisscrossed each other as they rushed into the kitchen.

Eli lobbed the black rubber ducky. The approximate size and shape of a grenade, the little black duck arced through the air. It thudded and bounced and rolled beneath the kitchen table.

The mercenaries reacted on instinct. The three men jerked toward the small dark shape flying toward them. Panicked, they dove for the floor. Nyx rolled away, making herself small against the perimeter cabinets.

Kade and Aguilera scrambled on their hands and knees toward their weapons on the counter. They were reacting to the threat of the grenade, not the soldiers who'd just burst into the kitchen.

Antoine and Eli fired as they moved. Shots slammed into Kade's torso. Eli fired a quick double tap into the side of the man's temple. A pink mist erupted from Kade's head. The round exited the back of his skull and drilled a cabinet door. Meanwhile, Antoine eliminated Aguilera with two shots to the face.

In a single swift motion, Eli sank low and spun. Out of the

corner of his eye, he glimpsed movement—a dark blur as Reynard charged him.

Reynard fired at the spot where Eli's skull had been a millisecond previously. A loud bang split the air. Then another and another. Rounds whizzed past Eli's head and shattered the laundry room window behind him. Shards of glass rained into the laundry sink basin.

Reynard tucked into a roll and leaped to his feet, crouched and armed, weapon rising. He lunged at Eli. Eli tackled the mercenary, headbutting him in the stomach as he got in under the weapon. Startled at the ferocity of the counterattack, Reynard lost his grip on the gun. It skittered across the floor and slid beneath the sink cabinet.

The man regained his balance impossibly fast. He came at Eli with a flurry of punches. Pain exploded through his ribs. Reynard's left hand reached for something at his belt—a fixed blade. He threw a right jab that connected with Eli's cheekbone. Stars burst in front of his eyes.

Eli dove to the tile floor, fumbling for his Glock, and rolled onto his back, bringing the weapon up and around. His finger found the trigger. Reynard fell upon him with the knife.

The blade bounced off his chest plate. Reynard was relentless, stabbing at him in a frenzy. Eli managed to maneuver the pistol from underneath Reynard's crushing weight. He punched the suppressor against the man's chin and fired.

The single 9mm round drove up through the bottom of Reynard's chin, into the roof of his mouth, through his sinuses, and into his frontal lobe.

Reynard collapsed on top of him. Two hundred fifty pounds of dead weight slammed against his tender ribs. The tip of the knife glanced off Eli's collarbone. It fell to the floor beside the table.

Hot coppery blood leaked into his mouth. It spattered his cheeks and forehead. It took him a second to realize it wasn't his own.

"Hey, brother." Antoine's voice sounded distant, so incredibly far away. "You alive under there?"

With a groan, Eli managed to push the corpse off him. Reynard's body thumped to the floor and rolled heavily against the table legs. Eli sat up, winced, and rubbed his jaw. His ribs flared. The whole right side of his body throbbed. "Barely."

"Barely is good enough for me." Antoine strode across the kitchen, reached out his hand, and pulled Eli to his feet. "I got Aguilera. I couldn't get in a good shot at Reynard without risking hitting you. Sorry, brother."

"They're dead. That's what matters."

Eli and Antoine scanned the kitchen, hearts pounding. A heavy silence descended over the house. Eli's ears rang from the gunshots at close quarters. His legs were weak and watery from the adrenaline rush.

The kitchen looked like something out of a horror film. Candlelight glinted off the blood spatters painting the cabinets, the floor, the furniture. Chairs were knocked over. Several bullet holes scarred the upper cabinets to the left of the sink. The corpses lay where they'd fallen.

Nyx groaned.

Eli went to the old woman while Antoine sprinted for Nyx.

Eli squatted beside the grandmother and checked her pulse. Her chest was still. Her skin was gray, her lips blue. His stomach roiled. "There's no pulse. She's not breathing. She's gone."

Antoine hovered nervously near Nyx. She was locked in the fetal position, curled in on herself. He retrieved her clothes. She gasped in pain as he helped her sit up, sliced her wrists free of the zip-ties, and helped her stand. They didn't speak but shared an unspeakable look.

Shaking him off, Nyx hobbled across the kitchen to her grandmother. As she passed, she kicked Reynard's bloody torso before slumping to her knees opposite Eli. Taking her grandmother's liver-spotted hand, she pressed it against her cheek, smearing the blood, snot, and tears streaking her face.

"Let's get you fixed up," Antoine said. "You've got some nasty cuts. You could have a concussion or broken ribs. Reynard hit you pretty hard."

Nyx ignored him. She rocked back and forth. An animalistic cry of grief escaped her lips. She moaned deep in her throat.

Eli watched her suffering in impotent fury. He loathed Sawyer and his men for what they'd done to her, for the sorrow and guilt Nyx would carry for the rest of her life.

"Nyx," Antoine said with startling gentleness. He bent over her, hands hovering above her shoulders helplessly, as if afraid to touch her. "Are you okay? Are you—"

She shoved him away. "Leave me alone."

"I'm so sorry, Nyx—"

"Shut up! Just shut the hell up." On her knees, she collapsed across her grandmother's body. Nyx hugged her and wept. Her whole body trembled uncontrollably. "I'm sorry. I'm so sorry I brought this on you."

Eli had never seen Nyx cry and doubted he ever would again. Both men stood awkwardly in the small, cramped kitchen, watching in obvious discomfort, unsure what to say or do.

Eli's headset hissed with static. Jackson's voice broke through. "We're en route on Snow Road. One minute from your location. SITREP?"

"Hostiles down," Eli said. "One casualty. We need another med kit and a body bag."

Jackson hesitated. "Who?"

"Nyx and Antoine are alive and kicking," Eli said in answer.

"Copy that," Jackson said, relieved.

Rage flared in Antoine's eyes. He looked ready to murder someone—again. "Sawyer will pay for this. I will make him pay for this."

"Vengeance will come," Eli said. "But not today."

Antoine scowled. "Screw that."

"Not today."

The Legionnaire's hands balled into fists at his sides. "Yeah, okay."

"We'll deal with Sawyer, but we have a more dangerous enemy lurking outside the gates. Tomorrow is Tuesday. We've set the trap. It's time to spring it. I need your heads in the game, both of you."

Nyx knelt over her dead grandmother. She wiped the blood from the side of her face, her expression fierce. "Tell me Sawyer is mine."

Eli said, "He didn't order his men to kill your grandmother. They did it on their own."

"I don't care. "I want his severed head on a platter."

Antoine's jaw bulged. He didn't take his gaze off Nyx. "We're going to kill every single cartel asshole. Then we'll come for Sawyer. That I promise you."

She nodded to herself, as if coming to terms with her insatiable desire for vengeance, that black rage that Eli knew intimately. She was shaken, hurt, and grieving, but that familiar fire blazed in her eyes. She was a warrior, through and through.

Nyx looked up at Antoine, her gaze hardening. "Good."

26

JACKSON CROSS
DAY ONE HUNDRED AND THIRTY-SIX

Jackson sat at his desk long into the night. The oil lantern perched on the corner of the desk sent wavering shadows flaring across the walls behind him, shifting like wraiths from nightmares.

The portable Ham radio sat on the desk in front of him. He'd been staring at it for what felt like hours. Anxiety crackled through him, a knot of dread in his guts. He had the disconcerting sensation of sand rushing through an hourglass at a far faster rate than he could handle or stop.

The hour was later than they believed.

He picked up the radio and turned it over in his hands. Such an innocuous object. Yet it was infused with the bitterness, shame, and longing of his entire childhood.

His father waited on the other end of this radio. His father waited for *him*.

He suspected it was a trap of sorts, a psychological mind trip, a shrewd and manipulative ploy to twist Jackson's actions to Horatio's devious aims.

He doubted his father would allow physical harm to befall his son—but then, he'd drugged his wife. And when things had gotten tough, he'd walked out on his crippled daughter to save his own skin.

Horatio Cross was cunning, calculating, and egotistical. Jackson was no longer blind to his father's flaws. And yet, if he could do something to avoid an attack by the cartel, if a discussion with his father could potentially save lives, the lives of the people Jackson felt responsible for, then wasn't it worth the risk?

Eli didn't think so. But then, Eli's preferred response to everything was violence: to fight tooth and nail until you won or you died.

There were other ways to win.

Or at least, to not lose.

There had to be a way out of this.

Lena had been beside herself with worry when he'd explained what he wanted to do. Only Devon was supportive, but she too watched him with grave concern.

They had good reason to be worried. He'd learned the hard way not to underestimate his father.

Jackson ran his hands along the sides of the radio, touched the buttons lightly, set it on the desk, and picked it up again. The air was heavy and still. It felt dense in his lungs. Every breath was a chore, a test of his will.

He inhaled the stale smell of paper and ink, sour body odor, and old leather as he mulled over his options, the weight of his decision like a thousand tons pressed upon his chest.

Earlier tonight, two of their best soldiers had narrowly survived a surprise attack. Antoine and Nyx were shaken but alive. Sawyer was a problem they'd have to deal with, and soon. But not yet.

Tomorrow before dawn, their fighting force would assemble amid the ruins of the ghost town to ambush the enemy before the enemy could destroy them first.

The residents of Alger County would face their greatest test yet.

Eli was certain they could win. Even if they did, at what cost?

How many good people would they lose? People Jackson loved and cared for.

He thought of Moreno and Nash, Jim Hart and Alexis Chilton. He thought of Lena and Shiloh. Devon's mischievous smile appeared like a shimmering mirage behind his eyelids. He blinked that image away. For now.

So many things could go wrong. So many ways to die.

If he could put a stop to any of it, broker some kind of treaty, if there was any chance to prevent massive bloodshed and save his friends, didn't he have to try?

Jackson picked up the radio, stilled his trembling hands, and made the call.

27

JACKSON CROSS
DAY ONE HUNDRED AND THIRTY-SIX

J ackson entered the enemy camp alone.

On their radio call, Horatio had promised safe passage to and from the meeting, regardless of the outcome.

His words had been convincing enough, but then, they always were.

Jackson didn't believe Horatio would kidnap or kill him, though that disquieting possibility lurked in the back of his mind, wriggling like a live maggot.

At any rate, Jackson had no choice.

Back in Munising, Eli and his ambush teams were heading to Devil's Corner to lay their trap. If Jackson could manage a miracle ceasefire before then, he could save them all.

He'd been instructed to meet at Wagner Falls outside of Alger County limits at midnight. He waited tensely at the side of the road for twenty minutes, muscles taut, his hand resting on the butt of his service pistol.

Two electric SUVs appeared in near silence. Jackson barely heard them over the loud splash of the waterfall spilling down rocky terraces. Located just off the road, the waterfall flowed into Wagner Creek.

The SUVs pulled up next to him. Their windows were heavily

tinted so Jackson couldn't see who—or what—waited for him inside. He didn't have to wait long.

Several burly men wearing ski masks hopped out, frisked him, removed his weapons, and bound his hands behind him with zipties. They shoved a burlap sack over his head and pushed him into the backseat.

They drove in silence for less than an hour. Jackson tried to keep the time in his head, straining his ears to listen to the whirr of gravel beneath the tires, the hum of asphalt, the night sounds of the forest, the shuffling movements of his hosts, their heavy breathing.

He could discern few clues beneath the heavy burlap. His world was darkness and stale air. He fought the claustrophobia clawing at his throat. His nerves were raw, frantic thoughts running a million miles a minute. Suddenly, this felt like a terrible idea.

The vehicles came to a smooth stop. Two men jerked him from the SUV and shoved him stumbling ahead of them. Meaty hands grasped his arms to keep him from tripping blindly and falling flat on his face.

"Stop here," a gruff voice demanded.

He halted, his boots scraping on the pavement. He listened to the hushed voices around him, the occasional crack of laughter, and the hum of an engine, or perhaps a generator.

He inhaled the scent of woodsmoke from campfires, a mix of sweat and gun oil. The wafting smell of seared meat reached him. His mouth watered.

Footsteps approached, sharp and confident. He sensed the shift in his guards' demeanors: tensed muscles, a tighter squeeze on his arms. Whoever stood before him demanded respect.

"Take off the bag," a gruff voice said.

Someone ripped the burlap sack from his head. The rough fabric scraped his cheeks. Jackson sucked in fresh air and adjusted his eyes as he took in his surroundings.

Two formidable bodyguards flanked him, holding AK-47s in

their burly arms, their expressions stony. Jackson stood, not on pavement as he'd guessed, but on a cobblestone circular driveway.

An impressive structure loomed above him: a great castle fashioned after a French Chateau, constructed of whitewashed stone and complete with towers, turrets, and stained-glass windows.

Jackson had visited this place a few times before. Built in the 1880s by a wealthy timber baron, the castle had been converted into a luxury hotel and event hall, with an adjacent historical museum.

The cartel had modified it for their own uses. Muzzles glinted from the slotted windows of the towers and turrets. He spotted several armed men patrolling the grounds in pairs. A handful of drones zoomed overhead.

Though it was after midnight, the castle grounds were bustling. Granite-faced men and women moved about, stacking gear and supplies, arming themselves with weapons and body armor.

Many looked and moved like soldiers. Others acted like gangsters and thugs. They sneered at Jackson with the soulless eyes of violent criminals.

At least three dozen armored SUVs and diesel trucks were parked to the right of the main entrance. Several semi-trucks and a giant gas tanker stood next to an actual tank. Crates, duffle bags, and piles of weapons were stacked next to several of the vehicles.

They were preparing to go to war.

A cold frisson of fear shot through him. Jackson tried to count their numbers, but there were too many of them. From his narrow vantage point, he saw at least a hundred, possibly many more.

"Jackson." Horatio Cross stood in the shadows within the arched entrance. He held open one of the massive wooden double doors. "My son."

Jackson steeled himself. "Father."

Jackson regarded Horatio with a mixture of awe and loathing, taking in his tall, lean frame, still straight-backed in his sixties. His full head of silvery hair was swept back off his forehead, giving him an elegant, almost regal appearance.

He wore clean khaki slacks and an unwrinkled white linen shirt. His jaw was clean-shaven. He looked well-fed and healthy. An H&K pistol sat snugly in a holster at his hip.

Jackson's lip curled in disgust. "I see the cartel is treating you well. You must have given them truly valuable intel when you sold out your people."

Horatio smiled thinly, taking the insult in stride. "Luis Gault is generous to those who prove their loyalty. You'll see."

"I don't think so."

"You'll change your mind, I'm certain of it."

"The bag over the head was a bit much, don't you think?" Jackson said dryly. "It's rather obvious where we are."

Horatio waved a hand in a vague, careless manner. "I apologize for the theatrics. My boss errs on the side of extreme caution. I can't blame him, as his methods, while primitive and rather brutal, have ultimately proven quite effective."

Jackson made a noncommittal sound in the back of his throat.

"Are you hungry? I know it's late, but I took the liberty of assuming you would appreciate a bite to eat. I've had the kitchen prepare a meal for us."

Horatio gestured for Jackson to follow him into the castle. They passed through the immense wooden doors into a grand hall replete with arched beams crisscrossing the cathedral ceiling.

The bodyguards kept close to his side, hands on their weapons. He accidentally brushed a full-sized replica of a knight complete with shining armor. The armor clanged dully, echoing in the massive chamber.

On the opposite end of the foyer, three wide hallways festooned with decorative arches split to the north, east, and west, presumably leading to the residential areas. Battery-operated lanterns shed pools of yellow light across the slate floor. Elaborate tapestries of knights engaged in battle hung from the stone walls.

In the center of the grand hall stood a dozen men in combat

gear. They leaned over a massive, wood-carved table spread with various maps.

Jackson studied the men as Horatio explained how most of Gault's top men had been trained by Russian Spetsnaz commandos hired by the cartel. Some were former Mexican Marines and Seals, others mere street thugs whom the Russian mercenaries had taught close-quarters combat and infantry tactics —for a price, of course.

"That man in the center is Luis Gault himself," Horatio said with evident pride.

Luis Gault stood at the center of the group, speaking quietly, giving orders as his men listened attentively, occasionally nodding.

While the myths surrounding the head of the cartel were larger than life, rife with hysterical rumors and fear-mongering gossip, the man himself was less impressive, at least physically.

Luis Gault stood five foot seven, at most. Small-boned and wiry, his stringy muscles were like sinew, his features bland and nondescript, with round glasses perched on a snub nose. His eyes, though, were the flat, cunning eyes of a predator.

Horatio frowned as Jackson watched Gault with narrowed eyes. "Make no mistake, that man is incredibly dangerous."

"I don't doubt it."

"He's brilliant and ruthless. He slaughtered half of his own family to take over the cartel. He's since expanded the organization into a vicious fighting force to rival those in Mexico. Once he defeats Munising, Marquette will fall easily. They're overcrowded with too many mouths to feed and not enough men to defend their borders. Then the entire Upper Peninsula will be his."

"And then what?"

"Then Michigan. After that, the entire Midwest. He already has much of Canada under his thumb. With every battle, his legend grows. Criminals are flocking to him. Mercenaries, soldiers, thieves, and killers, he takes them all, swelling his ranks with each passing day while the little towns piss their pants in terror."

Revulsion roiled through Jackson's belly. "How can you be a part of this?"

Horatio gave a dismissive shrug of his shoulders. "I'd rather reign in hell than be dead. Wouldn't you?"

"No."

"Let me explain, son. Come with me."

Jackson made a mental note of tactical details to report to Eli, but the bodyguards pushed him quickly past Gault and his top men. They led him to the right through a smaller corridor, the filigreed archway opening into a luxurious restaurant.

He glimpsed lush carpets, fancy tables, and medieval lanterns glittering like tiny stars as they moved through the interior and exited through French doors into an exterior courtyard. Towering sycamores wrapped in solar fairy lights surrounded the patio perimeter.

In the center of the cobblestone patio, among the collection of tables, a single round table was set with a white tablecloth. The silverware was rolled in cloth napkins, and each plate was topped with a cover to keep the food warm. In the glow from the fairy lights, stemmed glasses half-filled with red wine glistened like blood.

"Come, dine with me. See what you've been missing. Needlessly, I might add."

Jackson's empty stomach grumbled. "I'm not missing anything."

Horatio laughed. The sound sent chills up Jackson's spine. His father turned to one of the bodyguards. "Cut this man's restraints. He is no threat to us."

"Don't speak too soon," Jackson muttered.

One of the men sawed the zip-ties with a knife. The bits of plastic dropped to the ground. His hands now free, Jackson rubbed his sore wrists.

Horatio gestured at the nearest chair. "Have a seat."

Jackson hesitated. The bodyguards decided for him. Hands on his shoulders, one of the men pressed him into the ornate upholstered chair as the second bodyguard whisked off the plate cover and dropped it onto a nearby tabletop.

Steaming mashed potatoes slathered in butter, tender green beans, and a big juicy steak were piled upon his plate. The enticing scent struck him first. His ravenous stomach felt like it was eating itself.

His body craved the calories, the precious protein. He could eat ten plates and never be satisfied. He imagined plunging his hands into the mounds of mashed potatoes and shoving giant handfuls into his mouth.

Horatio watched him intently, a smirk playing across his lips. His sharp eyes glinted, missing nothing. "You've lost weight you didn't need to lose. You're lean and you look hungry. They don't have enough food at that Northwoods Inn of yours? I thought they were self-sufficient."

Jackson pressed his lips together and said nothing. He refused to be goaded or tricked into revealing information his father would use against them. Saliva filled his mouth. He swallowed it, steeling himself to resist the volley of temptations paraded before him.

Horatio picked up his sterling silver knife and cut his steak precisely into bite-sized chunks. He swiped the chunk of meat through the fluffy mashed potatoes before bringing the bite to his mouth. He chewed slowly, his gaze on Jackson, gray eyebrows raised as if taunting him.

Jackson couldn't take his eyes off the tantalizing morsels. He hadn't realized how little he'd eaten in the last few weeks. With everyone concerned with surviving the winter, rations were diminishing almost every day.

"Aren't you going to eat the meal I prepared for you? It's rude to reject our graciousness."

With tremendous effort, Jackson pushed back the plate. The food could be poisoned. At any rate, he refused anything from his father, even a gift as meager as a dinner. Accepting food from a traitor while his people went without felt like a grievous sin.

The words physically hurt him to speak aloud. "I seem to have lost my appetite."

Horatio frowned in displeasure. "Your loss."

"You seem well fed. And your men."

"I am. We are."

Jackson eyed the steak, coveting every bite.

"Jackson, if we wanted to kill you, we'd just shoot you. You might as well eat."

He licked his dry lips and forced himself to ignore the hunger hollowing his insides, the craving making him dizzy. He tilted his chin at the steak on his father's plate. "I didn't know there were any cows left alive in the UP."

"We have livestock and people to care for them. We're not scavenging for scraps like everyone else. We have an infrastructure in place, access to liquid propane and diesel fuel, and we've started to restore the local supply chain of goods and services."

"Access? Interesting word choice. You mean you stole everything you have from other people."

Horatio *tssked*. "You're thinking about things the wrong way. Your brain is stuck in a box, your thoughts trapped in the old ways. It can be difficult for some people to adjust. We control assets so the hordes don't chew through everything like rats, and we all starve. We aren't barbarians, despite the rumors your people enjoy spreading. We offer shelter, protection, and equitable resource distribution."

"Who decides what is equitable?"

Horatio chewed another bite and gave a little groan of pleasure. "Remember how your mother used to cook roast duck every Christmas Eve? She would decorate the whole house for you kids. You hated roast duck and refused to eat it though she'd slaved all day in the kitchen. All you wanted to eat was Trenary Toast with cinnamon and cherries, remember? Drove your mother crazy."

It was the live-in maid, not his mother, who'd slaved in the kitchen during every holiday. Jackson gritted his teeth against the flash of pain at the mention of his mother.

"Mother is dead," he blurted before he could stop himself.

Horatio blinked, though not in surprise.

"You knew."

"I know a lot of things."

"You knew what she did, didn't you? That it was Astrid. Astrid killed Lily."

Horatio gave him a pointed look. "I know you should be arrested for murder, *Sheriff*."

Jackson stiffened. "You knew. All along, you knew what she was."

Horatio's mouth curled in disdain. Grease glistened on his lips. "You're the killer, Jackson. You're the one who destroyed this family. What kind of person murders his own sister?"

Familiar shame wormed into his chest, squirming deep into that dark, fetid place in his soul where his worst fears resided, the hole inside him where slimy things slithered, a place of rot and decay.

He forced his tone to remain even. "I stopped the monster you unleashed."

"You dare to judge me?" Horatio demanded. He was a master at flipping the tables, turning your anger against you. "You're no different than me, than Gault, than anyone here. The difference is, we know who and what we are. We own it. You're deceiving yourself, and for what? Your self-deluding conscience? Some meaningless moral high ground? No one cares. Society went through the motions and made a pretense of morality before everything went to hell. Now, there's no need to pretend. It's all a façade. It's always been a façade."

"I am *nothing* like you."

"You're a bigger fool than I thought."

The insults stung. He could not pretend the cruel words didn't do damage, that his father didn't know the bruised, tender spots in his soul to dig and poke. Your family knew how to hurt you the most.

Jackson pushed back the tsunami of abhorrent emotions

threatening to overwhelm him and forced himself to focus. "I agreed to this meeting to discuss a ceasefire. Your thugs must stop razing towns and slaughtering innocent people. Your days of inflicting terror are finished."

"You're in a precarious position to be making demands, son."

"Be that as it may, these are the baseline terms. They are non-negotiable."

Horatio speared a chunk of steak and gave a derisive sniff. "You don't understand anything."

"I don't understand you."

"You don't have to." Horatio leaned across the table, his fork suspended over his plate, the bite of seared beef quivering on the tines. "Listen to me, son. I convinced Gault to approve the message I sent you because you are my son, and somewhere deep inside you is the part of you that's like me. You share my DNA. I know you're not stupid, so do not be stupid now when it matters most. Use logic and reason to make the smart decision. Gault does not offer second chances. Toe the line, and keep your head down like a good boy, because once we take over Munising, we will need to leave someone in charge. I've already negotiated terms on your behalf so you can stay on as sheriff. You can continue doing everything you're doing now."

"What's the catch?"

"Who says there's a catch?"

"There's always a catch."

Horatio shook his head as if flummoxed at his son's absurd folly. "I'm trying to save your life."

28

JACKSON CROSS
DAY ONE HUNDRED AND THIRTY-SIX

"You want to save my life?" Jackson asked, incredulous. "That's rich, coming from you."

He tamped down his anger. Beneath the anger squirmed the dark thing he despised most in himself—that tenacious longing, the lost little boy inside him who craved his father's approval, who'd once been willing to do anything to get it, even betray his best friend.

Even now, he felt the agonizing pull, stronger than he'd thought possible, the old feelings of unworthiness rushing back in a heartbeat.

He kept his voice even and steady; he wouldn't allow Horatio to see how he'd unnerved him. "What about my people? My town? What about their lives?"

"There are consequences for every action," Horatio said. "You stole from us. In return, we will destroy the Northwoods Inn for what your people did. We will obliterate James Sawyer and his little island utopia. However, in exchange for your help in procuring the return of our stolen goods, we'll spare you and the majority of your men. Rather than suffering incredibly painful deaths, your friends will receive immunity for past crimes against the cartel."

"We'll never relinquish control of Munising to a murderous sociopath."

Horatio's expression darkened. "Then what do you have to offer in this peace-making deal you want so much? I've offered you a good deal, better than what you deserve. No one else has been afforded an olive branch. This mercy is because you are my son. Understand that, if you understand nothing else."

"We could get the weapons back that Sawyer stole and return them. That should appease Gault."

"You don't know him. Gault wants the meds."

"Why does he need them so badly? He's expending a lot of resources on this fight."

Horatio leaned forward and lowered his voice. "I shouldn't tell you this, but I will, to enlighten you. Gault's wife is diabetic. She needs that insulin as much as your precious Lena does. Gault will burn the entire world to the ground to get the insulin back."

Jackson sat back in his seat, a sour-sick churning in his stomach like he'd been sucker-punched. The terrible understanding sank into the marrow of his bones.

How far had they been willing to go to save Lena? They'd descended into hell to rescue her and retrieve the insulin.

A pitiless man like Gault would commit far more horrific atrocities to get what he wanted. There would be no peace treaty. No way to come back from this—only flat-out war.

"You'll have to pry that insulin from my cold dead hands," Jackson said.

"That's up to you." Horatio took another bite of steak and chewed slowly, methodically. He swirled his wine glass, sniffed it, then took a sip and swallowed, his Adam's apple bobbing as he sighed in pleasure.

Jackson watched him in tense silence.

"Don't you miss the comforts and conveniences of your old life? It's not all gone. It doesn't have to be." He swept his arms wide as if to encompass the courtyard, the castle, the delicious meal, the trappings of wealth. "This is what I can offer you. Enough food for everyone. Shelter through the winter. Your very *survival.* No one you love has to die."

"All we have to do is sell our souls and surrender our freedom."

"What is freedom? It's just a word. Meaningless talk to make people feel good about themselves. None of that matters now."

"It matters to me."

"You don't get the moral high ground, Jackson. You lost that right long ago. Are you not the one who planted evidence against your best friend? Or is that some other Jackson Cross who sold his soul to close a case?" Horatio's eyes glittered. He bared his teeth like a predator crouched over his kill. "You're the one who murdered your sister. The stink of corruption is on you. It's *inside* you. You are your father's son."

"No." Jackson licked his lips. His chest was so tight with anxiety, it was difficult to breathe, to think clearly. "I am nothing like you."

"Why are you resisting? You know you're made for this!"

Jackson shook his head. "I may be guilty of some terrible things, but I know who I am. Astrid was a clear and present threat to others. I did what I had to—"

"—to do, yes. I know. I've always done the same. People are peasants! Even Yoopers, and they're hardier than most, but they're still stupid. Stupid little ants going about their meaningless, purposeless lives, surprised when a giant foot stomps them out of existence. They never even realize how utterly insignificant they are. I see the big picture. I see what we can become. We can make this suffering mean something. We can make things better for everyone—"

"By burning down their towns? By lining up the local leadership and shooting them in the head so no one will dare to defy the cartel? Don't use your pretty words to twist reality. I saw the carnage with my own eyes."

"Violence has been necessary to subdue nations since the beginning of time. We're living in a new world that's unlike anything history has ever seen. One must destroy the old to build something new from the ashes. It's a story as old as time. The strong win the victory and the spoils that go with it. This is our time to upend everything to create our own rules, our own government, our own kingdom."

"You sound like James Sawyer."

A muscle twitched in Horatio's jaw. "We are Crosses. We are the ones who survive. Come, join us. Join us and live. You belong with me, at my side, as my son. Together, we can rule."

Jackson folded his napkin over his untouched meal, his stomach growling painfully, and pushed his chair back. His father averted his eyes. He wasn't going to apologize. He would never say, *forgive me, son, for I have sinned. Your entire family has sinned against you and I am chief among them.*

Where did he go from here? There was nowhere. There was nothing. It was as if he were speaking a foreign language. The words coming out of his mouth were incomprehensible. The words Jackson had yearned to one day hear from his father did not exist, not in any language.

His mouth filled up as if with river stones. He couldn't speak, his throat thick. He couldn't swallow. This was a complete waste of time.

Jackson stood.

Horatio looked at him in surprise. "What are you doing?"

"I held out a glimmer of hope that we could compromise, meet in the middle, and somehow find a way to spare the destruction of the town where you served as sheriff for twenty years. I'm the ultimate fool for believing you ever cared about anything but yourself."

"Don't move," Horatio commanded.

"We have nothing more to say to each other."

Jackson turned to leave.

The bodyguards approached him with aggressive postures. One pulled a pistol.

Horatio thrust out his hand. "Wait!"

The guards halted midstride. They waited for the next

command, whether to kill Jackson or spare him. Their expressions were bored; they didn't care one way or the other.

"You promised me safe passage," Jackson said. "Are you going to renege on your word?"

Horatio stood swiftly, glaring at him. "I made a promise, and I will keep that promise, but we're not done here. Before you go, I have a little surprise."

As if on cue, a man stepped through the archway into the courtyard, striding between the rows of dining tables. He was tall and lean with a leonine build. His blond hair was cropped close to his skull. His sharp blue eyes were set in a long, angular face.

Jackson stared, slack-jawed with shock. Dizziness washed through him. His legs went weak and rubbery. He wasn't sure if the man standing before him was real. He blinked several times and rubbed his eyes. He was real.

Horatio greeted the man with a bear hug. He slapped him on the back, then turned and smirked at Jackson. "Jackson, say hello to your brother."

29

JACKSON CROSS
DAY ONE HUNDRED AND THIRTY-SIX

"Garrett," Jackson said, stunned.

"In the flesh." Garrett rounded the table in long confident strides and embraced him.

Jackson's arms remained stiff at his sides. He was discombobulated, bewildered, unsteady in a way that frightened him. His world had just been upended—again.

Jackson had not laid eyes on his brother in fifteen years. It felt like a thousand years, an eternity. Garrett Cross, once the golden boy of the Cross family.

Fifteen years ago, Garrett had won a full ride to MSU, only to be expelled after spiraling into drugs and dealing to feed his addiction. He'd left home one day and never returned. The family had received a few postcards from Mackinac Island and Traverse City, then nothing.

Not a birthday phone call. Not a visit. Not a Christmas card. Here one day and then vanished the next.

Horatio flashed a self-satisfied smirk. "This little visit is turning into quite the family reunion."

Understanding shot through him like an electric shock. "This is why. This is why you joined with the cartel. You had a personal invitation. Garrett is one of them."

"Your brother has worked his way up the ranks to become one of Gault's most trusted advisors. In the last eight years, he has amassed considerable wealth and power. It's quite impressive. You're lucky he's willing to take you back."

Jackson sputtered. "He's the one who left!"

"We're your family. The only family you have left. You need us."

Garrett gripped Jackson's arms. "I've missed you, Jackson. You have no idea how often I've thought about you, how many times I've wanted to reach out. Father said it wasn't the right time. Finally, now it is. Join us, brother. You'll never have to be alone again."

"I'm not alone now."

"But Father said Mother and Astrid are dead—"

"I have another kind of family."

Garrett frowned as if he couldn't comprehend his brother's words. He released Jackson and took a step back, bumping the table. The candle guttered. "What does that mean?"

"Jackson has refused our generosity," Horatio said. "He'd rather die with his pathetic friends."

Garrett pulled up a chair from a nearby table and sat, his muscled forearms crossed over his chest, his thick thighs spread wide. He was large, imposing, and muscular, a study in physical fitness, if nothing else.

"Let me get this straight. After this grand reunion with your actual family, you're turning your back on us? We've generously offered you shelter, safekeeping, and peace for yourself and your people, with so little demanded in return, and you're refusing us?"

Jackson pressed his lips into a thin line and said nothing.

Garrett's eyes narrowed. "Where is your loyalty? I'm your brother, damn it! The one who saved you from bullies in the third grade. The one who brought you licorice every day after school that time you had bronchitis."

Jackson remembered none of this. An unsettled feeling wriggled in his stomach. His memories of childhood were worn, incomplete, pocked with holes if not outright fabricated. An illusion, a magic trick.

If he remembered anything, it was the perpetual competition for their parents' stingy affection. Garrett and Astrid always won through sheer ruthlessness. Garrett had always been a skilled liar. Like Astrid, he'd used his good looks to obscure the rot beneath the pleasant façade.

But Astrid had never been pleasant; she'd played on her marks' empathy and pity to manipulate them. Garrett used shame and guilt as his tactic of choice, much like Horatio.

The golden boy, the high school quarterback and star of his local community was also the vicious, calculating drug dealer, the same cruel boy who turned his back on his mother and siblings, walking out the moment he had a better offer.

Garrett didn't care one whit about family ties unless it suited his own ends. Both he and Horatio were cut from the same cloth. Like father, like son.

Jackson was tired of being used and manipulated, tired of the toxic shame his family had weaponized to control him. He'd had enough.

He spoke calmly and clearly. "I won't betray my people."

"Then we'll kill them," Garrett spoke in a nonchalant tone, as casually as he might discuss whether to grill salmon or trout for dinner. "All of them. Including your friend Lena and her niece. What's her name again?" Garrett snapped his fingers. "Ah, yes. Shiloh."

Jackson struggled to rein in his outrage. "If you touch them, I will kill you myself."

Horatio's expression remained stony, unreadable. Garrett let out a harsh bark of laughter. "I'd like to see you try."

Several of the guards had inched closer, hands on their weapons, expressions impassive. Never had he been more aware of his vulnerability. He felt naked, exposed. His hand instinctively hovered above his empty holster. "I'm leaving now."

This had been a mistake. He never should have come here.

At the same time, he now knew the true face of his enemy.

"Go, then," Horatio spat. "Run off to your pathetic friends. If they're still alive, that is."

Jackson froze. "What?"

It was Garrett who smiled, a cruel smile that injected Jackon with pure terror. His brother uncoiled his crossed arms and stood. A rapacious excitement shone in his eyes. "We figured out your little ploy."

"What ploy?"

Garrett took a menacing step toward him. "You think you're about to trap the tiger, but you're wrong. We cannot be trapped. We cannot be contained. However smart you think you are, we're smarter. However strong you believe you are, we're stronger. We outnumber you, we are legion. We will wipe you off the face of the Earth."

Jackson's mouth went bone dry. "You're bluffing."

"Luis Gault does not bluff. Neither do I. How do you think I earned my place by his side? Surely, you know better."

Horatio said, "A contingent of our fighters are moving in on Devil's Corner as we speak. There's nothing you can do to stop us."

Jackson kept his features taciturn. He could not reveal an iota of the fear coursing through his veins. "I have no idea what you're talking about."

Garrett's smile widened. "The location you chose is more than apt. In a few short hours, your people will be little more than ghosts, left to haunt the lonely streets of that pathetic place for the rest of eternity."

"You underestimate us," Jackson said. "We won't go down without a fight."

"That's exactly what we're expecting," Garrett said.

Jackson had to reach Eli and had to warn him somehow, but the cartel had stripped him of his radio as well as his weapons. He was well out of range, anyway. He had nothing. He was utterly useless.

He had to get to Eli and the others as fast as possible.

"Return me to Wagner Falls," he said. "Now."

Horatio gestured to the nearest guard with studied indifference. Gone was the tattered remnant of fatherly affection. Gone too was the disappointment, the anger, the conniving and pleading. His eyes were utterly empty.

Jackson had made his decision. So had his father and his brother. He had cut himself off from them, wholly and completely, with finality. There was no going back from this.

"Return him to where you found him," Horatio ordered flatly. "Let him live to mourn his losses. Let him tell the rest of his people at the Northwoods Inn that their fate will be the same as their friends in Devil's Corner if they do not surrender."

The bodyguards moved to Jackson's side, escorting him to the exit.

"By the way, Jackson," Garrett said cheerfully. "The next time we see you, you're a dead man."

30

ELI POPE

DAY ONE HUNDRED AND THIRTY-SEVEN

"I spot movement," Nash said through Eli's comms. "Looks like a line of vehicles, half a click ahead of my position and headed straight for us."

"The cartel is here," Eli said.

He strained his ears, listening to the whirr of insects. Shades of tangerine and lavender painted the early dawn sky above the silhouettes of the trees. Dew clung to the grass beneath his belly, soaking his pants and shirt, though he barely felt the wetness through his body armor. A piece of damp leaf litter clung to his cheek.

His trusty HK417 rifle with the twelve-inch barrel and nightscope rested beside him. Eli and a dozen others were hidden in sniper hides along the hill overlooking the curve in the road where they'd planted the IEDs. They had been lying in wait for three hours, unsure whether their enemy would show, and if they did, whether the trap would work.

Eli had placed a scout on the hilltop to provide overwatch and ensure the cartel's Hueys didn't sneak up on them. A mile to the north, a QRF, or quick reaction force, of forty of Munising's finest volunteer fighters waited in the old church next to the cemetery. Moreno and Devon were with them.

Eli had instructed everyone on the QRF team to remain prepared with their gear and weapons next to them. They were an untested force. As long as the ambush went down as planned, they'd sit pretty at the church, never lifting so much as a magazine.

At the last minute, Eli had ordered Antoine to relocate to the QRF team. He didn't like losing Antoine, and with Jackson gone on his mission to confront his father, Eli was out two of his best men.

Baker and Flores, two veteran cops who'd proven their skills under pressure, remained back at the Northwoods Inn with a fighting contingent to protect the town. They couldn't leave their most vulnerable people undefended.

"Stay frosty—" Hart's voice cut out suddenly on the radio.

Around the bend, the first vehicle appeared several hundred yards to the east.

Eli waited with bated breath. The vehicle approached, the engine rumbling. His vision narrowed to a tapered point through his field glasses.

The lead vehicle rolled past the cairn marking the first buried IED. It was a Buffalo armored vehicle mounted with a .50 caliber machine gun.

Eli tensed for the explosion.

Nothing happened.

The second vehicle rolled past.

Then the third.

Nothing.

No explosion.

Something was wrong.

The first IED should have blown. It didn't. Neither did the second IED. Or the third.

Horror scythed through him. His palms went clammy, his heart bucking against his ribs. What the hell was happening? He didn't understand it.

He seized his radio. "Echo Three, come in!"

The radio was silent.

"Echo Two, do you read me? Echo, Tango, Alpha? Any call sign, come in!"

Still nothing.

The vehicles drove by at thirty miles an hour, evenly spaced. One by one, the convoy of fifteen trucks and SUVs drove past the ambush point without a single explosion or shot fired.

Most of his people didn't have access to radio comms headgear since they only had a dozen to share between them. Eli had made it abundantly clear that no one should fire until the explosions— the explosions that never happened.

His people had done what they were told. Unfortunately, it was the wrong decision.

In real combat, things went FUBAR and mistakes cost real lives. His heart sank into his stomach. This mistake would have sticker shock.

The final vehicle in the convoy—another machine gun-mounted Buffalo—passed beneath him. Clouds of dust billowed in the air, obscuring the Buffalo as it wound along the curve and disappeared.

Eli cursed into his headset. He'd built the IEDs himself and monitored their setup and placement. Even if one malfunctioned, it made zero sense that multiple devices would glitch simultaneously.

Unless...

The horrific realization punched him in the solar plexus. He reached for the UHF radio that would detonate the last IED. He pressed the button. The blast came immediately.

A hundred yards back, the center of the road exploded. Dark smoke shot skyward. Rocks, stones, and sand sprayed into the air.

Eli cursed again. Anger and self-recrimination warred inside him. "How could I have been so stupid! Damn it!"

"I'm coming in at your nine o'clock," came a breathless voice in his comms set. "Don't shoot me."

A moment later, Nyx slithered into the hide next to him. Black greasepaint streaked her face to hide the bruises left by Sawyer's goons. The unshaved half of her hair was twisted into an elaborate French braid that tumbled down her right shoulder. She smelled of sweat and gunpowder, overlaid with something faintly floral.

The whites of her eyes glowed in the early morning light. "What the hell happened?"

"They must have something like a Maddox Jammer. We used them in Afghanistan to keep IEDs from being set off."

Nyx's eyes widened. "Holy hell!"

"I know."

Eli and Nyx looked at each other. She was close enough that he could smell her fear. Her chapped lips pressed into a worried line. She said what they were both thinking: "The QRF team."

"Bear Claw, this is Alpha One." He spoke rapid-fire into the radio. Bear Claw was the call sign for the QRF team. "Emergency Exfil. I repeat, exfil, exfil!"

A static whine over the radio was the only answer. The jammers were keeping them from communicating. They couldn't warn the team.

Eli leaped to his feet, Nyx right behind him. They raced down the hillside, dodging lashing branches and bulging tree roots that threatened to trip them.

"Bear Claw One or anyone on the Bear Claw net, come in!"

There was no answer but the whine of active jamming.

Panic clawed at his throat. He and Nyx sprinted down the hillside and ran to the truck they'd hidden off the road. It was camouflaged with a cloak of pine boughs. What he wouldn't give for an armored Bradley right now.

He reached the truck. "Get the drone in the air now! I want eyes on the ghost town."

Alexis Chilton sat in the back seat, where she was operating the small field drone. "I'm already on it. Prepping the UAV for flight now."

The Perimeter 12 drone could stay in the air for up to three hours. It was a hybrid that utilized both gas and batteries. Eli would have preferred to use it for the ambush, but the constraints on fuel and charging had forced him to wait to launch it until the ambush started.

The ambush that didn't happen.

Alexis' black-framed glasses slid down her nose as she frowned at the active feed transmitting through the black-and-white handheld screen. The drone was already up in the air and out of sight.

Nyx yanked open the passenger side door. Eli climbed into the driver's seat and twisted around to face Alexis. Dread etched Nyx's taut features. She didn't need to say the words aloud. Antoine had joined the QRF team. She was beside herself with worry.

"What the hell is happening?" Nyx's voice was tinged with fear. "Someone talk to me or I'm going in guns blazing."

"It's not good." Alexis shifted her position so that Eli and Nyx could see the screen in her hand. With her other hand, she shoved her glasses up the bridge of her nose. "I've got them in sight."

The blood drained from Eli's face. On the screen, a handful of their people stood outside the entrance to the steepled church, seeming to study a map spread out on a large boulder.

The rest of the team stayed inside the church. They had been instructed to remain out of sight until and unless they were needed in the battle—which was supposed to occur on the road, not within the crumbling walls of Devil's Corner.

They had posted two sentries ahead on the road leading into the ghost town, who would alert the QRF team with warning shots if they somehow lost radio contact.

Those shots never sounded. Somehow, one of the cartel fire teams must've silenced the sentries first. Now, with their radios down, there was no way to warn them or to reach them in time. They would hear the rumble of the convoy—but far too late to do much about it.

Their friends were about to be slaughtered and they didn't even know it.

31

ELI POPE

DAY ONE HUNDRED AND THIRTY-SEVEN

Nyx slammed the steering wheel with her fist in frustration. "We have to do something!"

"Hostiles spotted!" Alexis cried. "The convoy entered the ghost town from the south.

A bunch of men exited the trucks. They're coming in hot, firing their weapons!"

Eli watched the tiny screen in growing horror. Without sound, everything seemed fake, scripted, a film unraveling reel by reel. Antoine had just arrived at the hotel when the cartel roared past the ambush site.

On the screen, the figures outside the church bolted for cover. They broke into groups of two or three, initially attempting to lay down cover fire as they scattered for the nearest buildings. A couple of men tossed smoke grenades to shield their retreat. It wasn't enough.

The attack was too intense, too overwhelming.

Several dozen hostiles streamed like throngs of ants from a kicked nest. A barrage of firepower blasted the old buildings. Two of the Munising fighters went down fast, their bodies thrown forward in the dirt as rounds pierced their backs.

Eli couldn't see the details of the carnage on the screen, but he could imagine the gaping holes in their chests, the gushing blood and shredded flesh.

Five fighters made a mad dash for the vehicles they'd stashed in the cemetery by the river. A woman with a long ponytail reached the first truck. She ripped open the door. Before she could climb inside, her body collapsed, nearly cut in half by the onslaught of automatic weapon fire.

A second later, the truck exploded. Glass, aluminum, and twisted metal hurled fifty feet in every direction. Shrapnel slashed into unprotected limbs and torsos. Three of their people fell to the ground. Enemy fire pounded the second and third escape vehicles, which burst into flames.

"It's bad," Alexis said. "I count seven of our people down. Three of the escape vehicles are burning. I don't think the cartel has suffered a single casualty. It's a bloodbath."

The remaining QRF force attempted to return fire from the surrounding buildings. Aghast, Eli mouthed orders they couldn't hear, urging them to break into smaller groups and maneuver themselves to safety or better positions using coordinated suppressive fire.

Instead, many panicked, firing wildly and indiscriminately, mostly hitting dirt or other buildings, not the enemy. Despite the training he'd attempted to beat into them, their forces were mainly civilians and law enforcement officers who'd never seen combat.

Many had never been shot at before or experienced the debilitating terror of a firefight.

Even so, many men and women bravely stood their ground and returned fire. However, their lack of coordinated movement was fast becoming the defining moment of the battle in the worst way.

Meanwhile, the cartel fire teams moved with precision, using cover point to cover point from building to building. Each time the first team advanced, a flurry of bullets slammed into the church windows and doors. Another barrage of fire assaulted the church from sister teams embedded behind the cover of one of the stone huts.

As the assault team moved, the hostiles shifted fire from one team to another so as not to hit the advancing team. They maintained a constant flow of fire on the old church, which kept the QRF team from escaping or advancing.

The QRF team was effectively trapped inside the church with limited ability to return fire. The only viable avenue of retreat was out the back door through the cemetery—which would still expose them to enemy fire.

"We have to do something!" Nyx's voice caught, naked fear contorting her features. "Our people are dying. Antoine is—we've got to help him."

"We have to wait for the ambush team to arrive. Otherwise, it's you, me, and Alexis against a hundred enemy fighters."

"We can do it!" Nyx insisted. They both knew they couldn't.

Desperate, Eli tried the comms again. "Bear Claw, come in! Do you read me?"

Finally, the whine of the jammer vanished. He had no idea why, whether they were out of range or it was something else, but he didn't waste another second thinking about it.

The buried IEDs would likely detonate, but the battle had moved beyond the road—they were essentially useless, for now.

"Bear Claw, we've got eyes on you through the drone. The attack is coordinated between several cartel fire teams, with another contingent rapidly moving toward the church, southwest of your position, sixty yards out. Looks like six guys."

"Roger that," came Antoine's distant, fuzzy voice.

Eli had no time to feel relief. "You've got an assault team moving to the north of the building, main entrance. Be prepared to repel an assault. Respond, over!"

"I hear you. I'm watching the doors and windows but hell, we're taking too much fire to return it. My guys are keeping their heads down to avoid getting their tickets punched."

"Get ready NOW! You've got sixty seconds before they breach the church and they're inside!"

"Copy that!" Antoine had to shout to be heard over the gunfire. "Hart, we've got company!"

Nyx sat up straight in her seat, every muscle taut and quivering, but her expression steely. "You've got this, soldier."

There was silence as they waited on tenterhooks, imagining the worst, the terrible ways their friends might be dying that very moment.

A few seconds later, Antoine's voice came again: "The rifle fire ceased."

Eli tensed. He watched the cartel's direct-action team maneuver to the front of the building and stack up against the wall next to the front doors. He relayed the intel to Antoine. "Six guys are moving up. They're going to try to breach the doors."

"Let them try!"

A single blast echoed through the comms set, followed by two more.

"TKO rounds!" Antoine yelled.

TKO breaching rounds were shotgun shells designed to blow the hinges off doors without ricocheting, so a fire team could go through a locked door like it was air and flood a room with men and guns within seconds.

"Live grenade!" Antoine shouted. "Duck for cover!"

With the drone, Eli couldn't see inside the church. He visualized Antoine's frantic attempt to save his team, pulling a grenade and hurling it at the entrance just as the hostiles burst through the front doors.

The grenade detonated with a tremendous *bang*. Shrapnel tore through flesh and bone. Hostiles fell to the floor, screaming in agony.

Through the headset, Eli could hear weapons firing. He imagined Antoine and his surviving teammates shooting double taps at the enemy soldiers. As they dropped, the team would make headshots to keep them down. Screams of the dying echoed within the church's bullet-scarred walls.

"Bear Claw!" Nyx said into her comms set.

No answer.

Nyx leaned over the steering wheel and tapped her headset as if that could make it work. "Bear Claw, come in!"

Still nothing.

Beside Eli, Alexis swallowed hard. She shook her head slowly, heavily. "Please God," she whispered. "Please."

"Tell me you're okay, damn it!" Nyx shouted.

Static hissed through the radio.

No one breathed.

Then, finally, Antoine's wonderful voice crackled in their ears. "Six hostiles down. We're still alive in here."

Nyx sagged in relief. "You're a stupid son of a gun, you know that?"

"And lucky as hell, too. Pope saved my bacon again, damn it! We could use a wildly reckless rescue plan right about now. You got anything in that tactically brilliant head of yours, brother?"

Eli grunted. "Working on it."

Antoine's voice went high and sappy. "If I don't make it out of here, don't forget about me, Nyx."

Nyx rolled her eyes. "Couldn't if I tried. And I've tried."

The few left alive from the QRF team were safe for the moment, tucked in with the dead and dying. It wouldn't last long. Eli had to get them out, and fast.

"More will be coming," Eli warned. "Hang tight."

"Nothing better to do," Antoine quipped. "We'll just sit here, twiddling our thumbs. Moreno told me he's gonna take up knitting. Maybe I'll join him."

Nash appeared through the trees with two of their better shooters. Hart led the rest of the ambush team to the truck and instructed them to pile into the back.

A dozen men and women knelt in the truck bed with weapons up and ready. Their faces were grim, resolute.

They had twelve fighters in total, thirteen including Eli.

Thirteen against the bloody tide of a hundred enemy fighters.

Nash peered through the open rear window. Twigs and leaves stuck to his clothes. He didn't bother to brush them away. "What's the plan?"

"We're going in after our people," Eli said. "It's gonna be rough. Now's the time to bow out. There's no shame in it."

"Screw that," Nyx said.

"We may not make it out," Eli warned. "We're outnumbered, outgunned, and these guys are trained. We have no air or artillery support. They do. I don't know where those choppers are, but they're close. The odds are against us."

No one moved or said a word of dissent.

"To hell with the odds." Nyx started the engine and gave a heart-shredding war-whoop. "I'm gonna shove those odds straight up the cartel's collective ass!"

32

ELI POPE
DAY ONE HUNDRED AND THIRTY-SEVEN

E li took a knee inside the tree line to the south of the ghost town, concealed behind a low hill that created a natural berm. He peered through his binoculars.

Nyx knelt beside him with a map of Devil's Corner spread on the leaf-strewn ground in front of her. Alexis and Nash knelt on the other side, searching for potential threats.

The rest of their team waited behind them within a cluster of jack pines along the riverbank. They'd collected five members of the QRF team who'd managed to escape the onslaught. Everyone was armed and geared up for the battle ahead.

Through his binos, Eli watched the cartel amassing on the grounds before the church. About eighty men nearly surrounded the dilapidated building on three sides. They had dragged their dead and wounded back from the grounds they could reach, likely tending to the injured as they prepared to make a blitz attack.

Eli breathed deeply in the tense stillness. The birds and insects had fallen silent. The sun peeked above the trees, the sky brightening from shades of indigo to rich cobalt blue. Soft scudding clouds tinged sherbet-orange, lavender, and peach-pink rippled across the horizon.

It was the quiet before the storm. Steadying his breathing and pulse, he assessed the situation. They were outnumbered over three to one against a contingent of real soldiers, not untrained and reckless thugs.

Though every fiber of his being longed to jump into the fight and rescue his friends, they couldn't afford to rush in unprepared. He'd already made one mistake. One more could cost everyone their lives.

With one hand, he briefly touched his chest rig over his dog tags and the Saint Michael's medal he wore beneath his gear. For an instant, he thought of David Kepford, the spec ops soldier turned school principal who'd offered his own life to save Eli's.

He didn't want anyone else dying on his watch, not that he had much of a choice.

"Bear Claw, this is Alpha One," Eli said.

"Alpha One, this is Bear Claw. Go," Antoine responded.

"I want you to form two fire teams with the fighters you've got left. My team will hit the north side of the road going into town to pull some of the cartel's attention away from the church. Ninety seconds later, use a bounding overwatch maneuver to escape into the woods on the south side behind the church. We haven't spotted any movement on that side."

"Negative! I would've punched through the south side already, but we've got too many wounded. If I take a team, we'll have to leave at least three people behind, plus I have two walking wounded with CAT tourniquets on their arms and a leg. Over."

Eli cursed. "Copy that. Stand tough. We *will* get to you."

Dread iced his veins. He clenched his jaw, forcing himself to tamp down his emotions. Fear motivated you; panic got you killed.

These people were trapped because of him. His friends, his brothers. He had to get them out, no matter the cost. He wished Jackson was here.

Mentally, he ran through his assets and resources. As far as the cartel knew, the only known threats were the remnants of the QRF team they'd sequestered within the church. They didn't know about Eli's snipers in the woods.

Eli would use that faulty intel against them.

Lowering the field glasses, he gestured to Nyx and laid out the risky plan taking shape in his mind. "Hart's team will take the SAW. Nyx, you'll take the Barrett .50 cal sniper rifle."

They also had two 203 grenade launchers mounted beneath SR-25 rifles they'd stolen from Sykes' dead convicts. Not ideal, but it would have to do.

Eli pointed to Nyx's map. "I want fire teams one and two to attack here, near the town entrance."

"What's our objective?" Hart, the former Marine, asked.

"You have three. First, kill as many of their vehicles as you can so they can't pursue us, or at least cripple them to give us a head start. Two, throw on the firepower to make them believe you're a much larger force than you are. Draw as many hostiles as you can away from our rescue attempt." Eli cleared his throat. "Keep in mind, if you're successful, you could be facing a hundred men, every single one hunting you down."

"That's what you call success?" Hart asked in an appalled voice as if Eli was asking him to jump out of a plane without a chute. It wasn't that far off the mark.

"For five, maybe ten minutes, I need you to punch above your weight class. Fight like a Ranger, not a Marine." Eli winked at Hart.

Hart chuckled. "Yeah right, kid. I was fighting over in the sandbox while you were still in diapers."

Eli continued without missing a beat. "Hold them off for two to three minutes, then send the second fire team down the road and block the road with the SAW in the ambush spot."

Hart spoke up. "Then we take up the fighting holes dug for the original ambush, link the SAWs together, and pour a whole hell of a lot of fire down on them. We pull as many cartel members as possible to give you a chance to rescue the QRF stuck in the town."

"You're getting it, now," Eli said. "Guess Marines aren't as thick-headed as I thought."

Hart rolled his eyes. "After we take on a hundred cartel with only twelve men, what is my next task? Climb a mountain with a thousand-pound boulder on my back? Fight Gault in close-quarters combat with a box of spaghetti and one hand tied behind my back?"

Nash let out a nervous laugh. Alexis adjusted her glasses and managed a skittish half-smile that looked like it might peel off her face like a sticker. She was brave and resilient, though she'd been a desk jockey in her previous life. She disliked killing, but she had shown up, making her stand rather than cowering in fear—Eli respected the hell out of her for that.

He turned back to Hart. "Take a few people and disappear into the woods, then move to the road that skirts the schoolhouse and the cemetery. At the north end of the cemetery, you'll set up a second hasty ambush. After we get the QRF team out of the church, we'll be pursued. When the bad guys follow us, hit them hard before high-tailing it out of there and exfil to the rendezvous point."

His fighters nodded in unison. The whites of their eyes gleamed in the shade beneath the jack pines. The air was dense with the scent of smoke and gunpowder mingled with pine sap.

Hart responded like any former Marine given orders. "Aye aye, sir."

"I need you to pull this off without losing half your men."

"These bones may be getting old and creaky, but my mind and my aim are still sharp as ever, Pope. You can count on me."

"Good." Eli pointed at a cluster of old buildings on the west side of the map. "This building was once used as a general store in the 1800s. It's located one hundred yards from the church. My team will dig in here and here." Eli pointed to the map at two ends of the old graveyard on the opposite side of the church. "This way, any hostiles giving chase will find themselves caught in a very nasty crossfire."

The teams listened without making a sound.

"Nyx, be on the lookout for anyone with an RPG and light them up. Use the Barrett to kill any vehicles in pursuit, or if you see one of those Hueys. When I call for you, bring up the cargo truck."

"Roger that."

"Bear Claw," Eli said into the headset, "if we're taking fire coming or going, don't be afraid to drop smoke to cover us."

"Oui, Monsieur." Antoine's voice was forcibly lighthearted. "Let's get this party started!"

"You heard him," Eli said. "See you all on the other side."

Nyx gave him a sharp salute. "Not if I see you first, suckers."

33

ELI POPE

DAY ONE HUNDRED AND THIRTY-SEVEN

The fire teams headed off in their respective directions, cautious and alert, using the stealthy bounding overwatch method Eli had ingrained into them until it was as natural as breathing.

Alexis remained at Eli's side while she manned the controls, providing constant surveillance intel with the drone. "The cartel is making another approach to the church! They're moving faster this time, not using as much maneuver fire. We better hurry!"

The weapons fire from the cartel's side of town picked up, the *rat-a-tat* of constant gunfire detonating like fireworks.

Alexis used her comms to warn Antoine: "Bear Claw, another assault team is moving to your position."

"From where?" Antoine asked tightly. "How many?"

"Seven guys moving car to car," Alexis said. "South of the church. Each time there's a burst of fire, they move closer, running to the next car. Less than fifty yards from the church."

The teams hurried through the underbrush, zigzagging through the trees, avoiding the branches slapping at their faces or the roots tripping their feet. Thorns snagged at their clothing. The forest was dense and quiet. The tension stretched taut with fear etched in every face.

Eli's team moved as fast as they could while remaining hidden. One fire team took an overwatch position while the second team bounded forward in quick, five-second rushes to the next cover position. Then team two took overwatch while the first team crept to their cover position in a leap-frog movement.

In this way, they could effectively move through hostile territory while minimizing their exposure to enemy fire.

A second barrage of weapons fire echoed in the near distance. Hart's two teams had opened fire on the cartel's flank.

Alexis crouched and studied the handheld. "All elements, the assault team on the church just halted. There seems to be some confusion. They're yelling and waving their arms and the fire teams appear to be falling back."

"Where are they going?" Eli asked, not daring to breathe.

"At least half of the cartel fighters are running to their vehicles and heading down the road. They're going after Hart's teams."

"Good."

Phase one appeared to be working. Eli felt zero relief, only the crushing pressure of keeping his people alive. A delay of even a second could mean the difference between life and death.

Eli's team came out of the trees into the grassy meadow along the banks of the river. The silt-brown water was on their left, mossy tombstones were planted haphazardly in the weeds to their right.

The shadows of the decrepit tombstones stretched across the grass as if the gnarled fingers of the dead were reaching for the living, desperate to drag them into early graves.

As Teams Three and Four took up their positions to provide suppressive fire, Eli's team made their move. Three fighters sprinted from the trees to the one-room schoolhouse across from the church. They turned and scanned for threats while Eli, Nash, and Alexis sprinted across open grass to the church.

Breathing hard, they edged around the corner to the back door. The door was constructed of solid wood. It was locked.

"Lions rule," Eli whispered.

"Packers drool," came the muffled reply.

The door swung open. Moreno beckoned them in with his AR-15. Blood and dirt coated the side of his face, but he appeared otherwise unhurt.

Alexis and Nash slipped inside while Eli provided cover to the rest of his team. Once they'd entered safely, Eli left Nash at the door to watch their six.

The coppery stench of blood and singed smoke filled his nostrils. Dense shadows cloaked the chapel. Wooden pews were shoved against the front doors and piled below the windows. The remains of the QRF team knelt behind the pews and fired out the windows to keep the cartel at bay.

Sunlight poured in narrow beams through the bullet holes that had punched through the walls. Splatters of dark red liquid stained the plank floor. Dead bodies lay among the shrapnel scattered across the floor. The atmosphere crackled with tension, fear, and desperation.

"Where is everyone?" Alexis asked.

Moreno made a pained face. "This is pretty much all that's left."

"Only ten?" Alexis asked in shock.

"Fifteen," Antoine said.

"Out of forty men, only fifteen are still alive?" Eli repeated, incredulous.

He'd feared it was bad. This was catastrophic.

"We have five critically wounded. Nelson's bleeding out from a gut shot that snuck in below his plates. Ray Thompson got hit in the thigh, but we got a tourniquet on him, same with Amanda Martz, but her shoulder got nailed. And Devon got hit pretty bad with some shrapnel."

Eli's heart clenched. He knew how much she meant to Jackson, even if Jackson hadn't figured it out yet. "How bad is Devon?"

"Antoine got her bandaged up. She can walk. The wounded

need a doctor asap. The rest didn't make it inside the church. We don't know what happened to them."

Most of them were dead, judging by the scattered bodies they'd spotted outside.

Antoine shook his head in bitter frustration. "We had no warning. Somehow, they eliminated our sentries before they could get off a shot."

"The cartel used jammers to inactivate the IEDs and our radios. We were up a creek with no way to warn you until their jammers were out of range, and then it was too late."

"I did this," Antoine said. "Good men are dead because of it."

"No, you didn't," Eli said. "I did. I was certain the ambush would kill them long before they made it to town. I should've had you lead the QRF the moment we left the Northwoods Inn. I sent you down at the last moment as an afterthought. You're the reason we have fifteen good men and women still alive. I screwed this up, not you."

Antoine's mouth thinned, but he gave a single, sharp nod. They'd deal with the guilt once they survived this hellhole.

Eli angled his body against the log wall and peered out the window, down the dirt street. He glimpsed movement along the north side of the general store. Several furtive shapes drew closer. Among the clusters of cabins, the wink of muzzles glinted in the sunlight.

The sun rose higher in the sky, bathing Devil's Corner in a warm, cheerful light, incongruous with the death and destruction, the booming guns, and screams of agony.

It was truly a ghost town now.

Alexis perched on a pew near the front, her eyes glued to the handheld screen. "Hart's teams have destroyed four vehicles and a handful of their guys. He's moving to his secondary location."

"Echo Two," he said, raising Nyx on the comms. "If you can get the cargo truck over here, we'll load the wounded and get the hell out of Dodge."

"On it."

Seconds later, the cargo truck roared to life and tore across one hundred yards of open ground. The rumble of the engine attracted enemy fire. Dozens of rounds smacked and pinged the armored vehicle as it raced for the church. It slammed to a halt five feet from the rear door.

Antoine moved to a shattered rear window and hurled a smoke grenade to cover their approach. "Let's go! Move!"

Everyone rushed for the back of the church. Several people paused to gather the wounded. Nelson was unconscious but Antoine hoisted him in a fireman's carry and hauled him to the truck. Moreno helped Amanda Martz to her feet and half dragged her to the truck, Devon right beside him with another wounded man Eli recognized as Ray Thompson.

Nyx hopped out of the driver's side, the heavy Barrett M82 slung over her shoulder. For a second, Nyx and Antoine's eyes met. Despite the chaos, Eli caught the way Antoine's grimy face lit up like a Christmas tree. These two surely had a thing going. He hoped they both survived the day.

"Damn glad to see that cargo truck," Antoine said. "You're not so bad a sight yourself."

Nyx smirked as she slung her arm around Devon's shoulder. "Yeah, well, you smell like cat piss."

Antoine flashed her the middle finger, then turned and hurled another smoke grenade toward the corner of the church. Nash stayed behind to lay down suppressive fire. He fired several rounds out the front window, ejected a spent magazine and seated another, then resumed firing. "They're getting closer!"

"Time to get this party started," Nyx said.

In less than two minutes, they'd loaded the cargo truck with the critically wounded along with two men and a woman who could fight if needed. Thick dark smoke billowed around them, obscuring their vision but blinding their adversaries as well.

Devon offered to drive, but she was in no shape to do so. "I'm fine," she insisted, but her voice wobbled. Blood caked her cheeks and forehead; her face resembled a ghoulish Halloween mask.

"I'll drive," Nyx said.

Eli handed Alexis the keys instead. "Nyx, I need you on the .50 cal to wipe out any hostiles who attempt to follow us. We'll move out first on foot. Once we reach the cemetery, we'll cover you and Nash."

"Copy that," Nash said.

"Get in the truck, Devon," Eli said.

"I can walk," Devon insisted. "Save the cargo truck for the ones who need it."

There was no time to argue. Eli turned to Alexis. "Alexis, drive like a bat outta hell."

"Will do," Alexis said.

Eli gave rapid-fire instructions to the group on foot: "As we move, not only are we using suppressive fire to cover people on foot, we're also looking for anyone with an RPG or any crew-mounted weapon that could take the cargo truck out. This is infantry 101. If you see a threat, engage it and call it out."

Heads nodded soberly. Eli placed Devon in the middle of the group where he and Antoine could cover her. He led his fire team as they raced across the open meadow to the cover of the graveyard.

Pain scythed through his ribs, ankle, and shoulder, but adrenaline dulled the throb and kept him on his feet. Heavy gear clanged and clattered. Time seemed to slow, everything slow and sluggish as if their legs were encased in Jello.

Rounds spat at their feet. Clods of dirt sprayed a yard to Eli's left. He wasn't as fast as usual, slowed down by old injuries. With a yelp, Devon stumbled, but Antoine was there, dragging her up one-handed. "Go, go, go!"

They reached the graveyard. Ducking behind several granite tombstones, they knelt and laid down suppressive fire. Eli fired past the church in controlled, even bursts. He had two magazines left and needed to conserve his ammo.

"Send the cargo truck," Eli instructed through his comms.

"Coming to you now, Alpha One," Alexis said.

"This is Omega One," came a voice through the radio—the scout stationed atop the hill. "I just spotted one of the choppers headed straight for us!"

Then he heard it. His blood ran cold at the sound: the sinister *whomp-whomp-whomp* of an inbound Huey.

34

ELI POPE

DAY ONE HUNDRED AND THIRTY-SEVEN

To the east, a black speck appeared in the sky, silhouetted against the pink-tinged clouds. A raptor of death flew fast over the hills, growing larger with each passing second.

Several fighters aimed machine gun fire at the sky, but the chopper engaged in skilled evasive maneuvers. It just kept coming.

The helo circled the south end of Devil's Corner, zooming low over the log buildings—the houses, the grocery store, the hotel, the school. The rotors throbbed like thunder, the engine roaring in his ears.

"Drive!" Eli screamed through the headset. "Drive, drive, drive!"

"Someone shoot down that chopper!" Alexis cried.

Banking sharply, the Huey headed toward the cargo truck. On the right side of the Huey, a hostile dressed in battle gear leaned out through the opened door, holding a massive rocket launcher aimed at the escaping cargo truck.

The truck jolted across the field, completely exposed and vulnerable, a rabbit fleeing from the diving hawk.

Eli fired round after round at the chopper, but it was no use. A bright whoosh burst from the Huey. The back blast exited out the open door across the helo as the rocket-propelled grenade shot across the sky.

"Incoming!" Antoine shouted.

Alexis jerked the vehicle in a hard right and veered toward the copse of trees to the north of the graveyard. The dense woods provided the only cover within the vicinity. If the truck could get beneath the canopy without ramming into a tree trunk, they had a slim chance.

"Alexis—" Eli shouted. "Go! Go!"

Alexis' panicked voice shrieked over the comms. "Hold on! Brace for impact—!"

The rocket-propelled grenade slammed into the cargo truck. The *boom* echoed like a tremendous blast of thunder. The truck exploded in a massive ball of fiery flames.

The jugs of biofuel they'd loaded in the back only fed the terrible fire. Metal peeled away like an onion. Blood-curdling screams shredded the air. Those trapped inside were burned alive, their skin cooked instantly like steak thrown on a grill.

"No!" Devon screamed. "Noooo!"

Time stopped. The world reduced to tunnel vision. Horror froze Eli in place.

Antoine inhaled sharply and crossed himself, though he was no Catholic. "Holy mother of God."

The surviving fighters stared in shock, too dismayed to move. Their friends, their teammates, the men and women they'd fought beside, had joked with not ten minutes previously—they were gone in an instant, vaporized in a cataclysm of fire and smoke.

Everyone inside that truck was dead. Amanda Martz was dead. Ray and Nelson. And Alexis Chilton. She was too young, too smart, too brave to die. A techie, not a soldier. If they'd had more manpower, she never would have been out there in the first place.

Eli's throat tightened like a vise. Sorrow and regret threatened to choke him. He shook himself out of his stupor. The grief would come later. First, they had to survive.

He seized Antoine's shoulder with his free hand. "Fire at the chopper! Get them before they get us!"

The Huey rose as it banked, attempting to circle back around, and come at the graveyard for a second blitz attack. Eli's men had no cover against the high-powered rounds of a .50 cal rifle or another RPG. They'd be annihilated like the cargo truck.

"You're gonna pay for that!" From the shadowed doorway of the church, Nyx dropped to the ground behind the Barrett, which she'd propped on its tripod. She fired at the helicopter.

The Huey churned upward, veering wildly to avoid the volley of firepower.

She missed, then missed again.

Nyx swore. "It moved behind the church. I can't see it!"

A salvo of rounds smacked the tombstones in front of them. Eli, Antoine, and Devon ducked. Chips of granite punctured Eli's right cheek. Stinging pain made his eyes water.

The Huey swung back around and roared toward them.

It was as if hell had unleashed itself upon their heads. A storm of ammunition rained down on them, impacting the ground on all sides. *Thuds* and *pings* filled the air. Bullets zinged overhead.

The Huey hurled a hail of death at the huddled fighters each time it flew past. The chopper made strafing runs each time they had a break to move to prevent them from escaping to the south.

Nyx was doing her best, but the M2 kept missing the mark. Her position was weak; she couldn't get a good angle. They had to kill it, one way or another.

"We're being torn to shreds!" Antoine shouted.

"Everyone, controlled bursts!" Eli said. "Aim for the engine, the pilot, or the door gunner!"

Eli twisted around to peer to his north, checking for movement through the trees. As he'd feared, furtive shadows darted from trunk to trunk less than a hundred yards from their location.

They were seconds from being overrun.

Antoine spotted the same threat. "We've got hostiles headed this way! We need to push south now!"

Antoine was right. If they stayed, they were dead. "Helo or not, we move in teams. When one team moves, the next lays down fire. We've got to go—"

"Incoming!" Nyx shouted through their comms. "I'm out of ammo!"

As it came back into range, the helo made another attack run. Rounds struck the ground inches to the left and right of their position. The roar of gunfire was deafening. They fired repeatedly at the great metal beast to no avail.

Beside him, Antoine grunted. Eli dared a glance to his right. Blood poured down the man's left arm. Antoine lifted his rifle with a wince. "I'm good."

Maybe this time, but the next shot would likely kill him—or all of them.

The chopper swept too low, aiming its big guns right at the gravestones they hid behind. Eli braced himself. There was no time to think or act. There was no escape.

A great *boom* sounded. It was followed by the familiar whoosh of a stinger. The rocket shot through the air, straight toward the Huey. It struck the back drive shaft that protruded from the rear of the bird.

With a tremendous groan, the helo began to spiral out of control. The rotors spun wildly. The chopper careened left, plummeting rapidly before slamming to the ground fifty yards to the east of the church. The tremendous crash shook the ground. The rotors crumpled and bent, screaming in protest.

The *boom-boom-boom* of firepower quieted. It was as if every fighter was stunned to stillness, absorbing the shock of the downed chopper.

Thick black smoke rose from the wreckage. Flames burst from the cockpit and raced hungrily across the dry overgrown field. One by one, the old log buildings caught fire as the blaze spread into the dense underbrush and woods to the north.

"Who the hell took out that Huey?" Eli shouted over comms. He knelt, peering over the tombstone, searching for threats. He barely had time to feel relief that they were still alive before the next set of hostiles started firing at them.

The chopper was down. At least, there was that.

Static sputtered through the comms radio, then, "You're welcome."

"Jackson," Devon breathed.

Jackson's voice was distant and tinny yet unmistakable. "I found this big ole stinger lying around at one of our hidden caches and figured this was as good a time as any to use it."

"Damn straight," Nyx said. "You saved our butts!"

"I'm gonna save you again," Jackson said. "I'm covering you from the top of the hill. Go now and I'll nail any cockroaches who dare show their ugly mugs."

Eli wouldn't have admitted it under threat of torture, but he was thrilled to hear Jackson's voice. They'd lost good people today. That Jackson lived was no small thing.

Nyx and Nash made a run for the graveyard. Antoine and Eli covered them. Antoine frowned as they prepared to exfil. He'd managed to wrap his upper arm in a makeshift tourniquet to stop the bleeding. "What about that fire?"

The fire was spreading fast. It had reached the schoolhouse. Flames greedily licked the log walls, racing up the east side. The crackling and hissing grew louder as the blaze gained strength. Smoke filled the air in a thick, choking haze.

"Nothing we can do about it now," Eli said.

Antoine nodded. "Then let's blow this joint!"

With Jackson covering their asses, they ran.

35

LENA EASTON
DAY ONE HUNDRED AND THIRTY-SEVEN

L ena rubbed tendrils of hair from her forehead with the back of her arm. Her limbs felt heavy, her mind and body utterly exhausted. Blood stained her scrubs. It wasn't hers; it was Devon's.

Devon slumped on the gurney in a curtained room in the Munising Hospital ER wing. For the last three hours, Lena had painstakingly tugged bits of shrapnel from Devon's face, neck, and shoulders.

Luckily, the shrapnel hadn't torn through arteries or vital tendons and muscles. The superficial wounds bled profusely, but she would be okay. Scarred, but okay.

"I'm so sorry." Lena plucked yet another sliver of shrapnel from Devon's face. An emergency thermal blanket was wrapped around her shoulders. She didn't want Devon to go into shock.

Devon clenched her jaw with stoic determination. Tears mingled with the blood trickling down her cheeks. She'd refused pain meds stronger than Tylenol, insisting they save it for those who truly needed it.

Instead, she kept one hand on Bear's head, her fingers buried in his fur like she was holding on for dear life. Bear sat on his haunches at Devon's feet. His tail swept the floor rhythmically. He leaned into her thighs to offer his particular brand of soft, sloppy comfort. It seemed to be working.

"How bad do I look?" Devon asked with a shudder. "Are we talking gremlin or Scarface?"

"Well." Lena dropped a bloodied, twisted chunk of metal the size of a dime into the tray beside her. The shrapnel had left a quarter-inch tear of flesh directly below Devon's right eye. "You won't be winning any beauty competitions for a while, but this damn piece of shrapnel almost took out your eye. You're lucky."

"Lucky," Devon repeated dully. She appeared shell-shocked, her eyes bloodshot and glassy. Though the room wasn't cold, her whole body was shivering.

Lena examined her face with concern. "Hey, Devon. You with me?"

Devon gave a tremulous nod. Her dark braids were streaked with red like paint. She lifted a hand to touch her cheek, then let it drop limply into her lap. Bear whined and pressed his snout against her ribs. She managed to scratch his ears listlessly.

"I shouldn't care about stupid scars," Devon said. "I'm alive. I'm alive and I shouldn't be. I was supposed to ride in the cargo truck with the other wounded. With Alexis." She swallowed hard. "That should've been me. I should be dead right now."

"You're not dead. You're right here. What happened is not your fault. The cartel killed Alexis. They're the ones to blame, not you. Never you."

Devon nodded again, but she didn't make eye contact with Lena. Her lower lip trembled as if she were fighting an inner battle to hold back a flood of sorrow, guilt, and rage.

Lena didn't blame her, not one bit. She had spent the last ten hours in the operating theater with Dr. Virtanen and a few nurse volunteers, attending to the wounded survivors of the battle. They had irrigated jagged cuts, disinfected lacerations, picked shrapnel from bloody wounds, removed a shallow bullet or two, and bandaged injuries.

Two fighters had perished on the table. It had been a long, tragic, horrifying day.

After she'd stitched the lacerations to minimize scarring, Lena gave Devon a gentle hug, wishing she could squeeze the despair and trauma right out of her friend. "Get some rest, okay?"

Devon attempted to rise, protesting that she was fine. Bear whined, pushing his head against her side more insistently, tail thumping. Lena pushed her back down. "Bear wants you to sit tight."

"I'm okay—"

"Paramedic's orders," she said sternly. "I'll check on you in an hour."

Lena gave Devon another blanket, tucked her in, and set a glass of water on the tray next to her. Bear clambered onto the hospital bed and curled up at Devon's feet. His body heat would warm her up.

Leaving the Newfie to monitor their patient, Lena went to the next room, pulling back the curtain to see if Dr. Virtanen needed help with Antoine's stitches. The ME waved her away. "Get some sleep. There'll be plenty to do in the morning."

Lena moved on. She entered the reception area, where her friends waited for news on Devon.

Eli, Jackson, and Nyx leaped from the row of chairs simultaneously. Their faces were dirty, filmed in sweat and grime. They wore their scuffed, stained battle gear, their weapons leaning against the walls or piled in a nearby seat.

Lena's lungs constricted. She loved these people dearly. How close she'd come to losing one or more of them. How much they'd already lost.

She wavered on her feet. Her shoulders slumped.

Eli crossed the tile floor in three long strides and enveloped her in his arms. She collapsed against him, sinking into that strength, the warmth and steadiness of him. He smelled of blood and gun powder. Sweat soaked his black hair to his scalp.

He'd never been more handsome.

Despite her weariness, her heartbeat quickened. He was on his feet. He was unharmed. Tonight, she would check every inch of him and make sure of it.

"What about Devon?" Jackson asked in a strained voice. "Is she okay?"

Lena forced herself to turn her head and look at him. There was something different about him, something darker, a flinty hardness in his gaze she didn't recognize.

Lena nodded, almost too tired to speak. She felt brittle. Easily broken. Weak. It was a feeling she despised. She'd never felt so useless. At least Devon would live. "She's resting. You can go in and see her. She's in room five."

Without a word, Jackson strode through the ER's double doors and disappeared. His sharp staccato footsteps echoed before fading to silence.

Lena spared a glance at Nyx. The woman shifted anxiously from foot to foot with a conflicted expression, like she was too embarrassed to ask what she badly wanted to know.

"Antoine has a graze on his left forearm. Dr. Virtanen is stitching him up now. He's in room four."

Nyx rolled her eyes to conceal the abject relief etching her features. It didn't work. "He's such a baby. I bet he's crying in there. Just like a man, always needs someone to hold his hand."

Lena's words came slowly and deliberately. Her brain felt fuzzy. She had to focus on every consonant. "You can go see him if you'd like."

"Nah," Nyx said, feigning nonchalance. "Let the man weep in peace. I'll check on him later."

Eli pulled back, studying Lena's face with a frown, his big hands gently gripping her upper arms, as much to hold her upright as to properly examine her. "You're about to collapse on your feet. You need to rest."

"Dr. Virtanen needs my—"

"You can't do everything every second of every day. You're no good to anyone sick. Sit down." There was no give in his steely voice. Absolutely none.

He led her to the nearest chair. She sank into it, the hard metal digging into her spine, but she barely noticed. Her eyes were gritty. Her vision blurred at the edges.

Her pump beeped. It had been beeping off and on for a while; she'd been too busy to check, so consumed with tending to the injured that she'd barely eaten or monitored her blood sugar for hours.

"What's the number?" Eli demanded.

She tugged up her shirt and checked the screen. Her heart sank. "Ah, forty-five."

Eli scowled. "Lena."

Her tongue felt thick in her mouth. It was hard to follow his words, to keep her train of thought. "I know, I know. I ran through the carbs I brought with me last night. I didn't have time to go back to the Inn for more. Theresa Fleetfoot was touch and go all night; I couldn't leave her on the operating table. Then the injured started coming in from Devil's Corner..."

Eli shot her a disapproving look as he unslung his pack, dumped it on a nearby chair, and rifled through it until he pulled out a can of vanilla frosting and a spoon. He always kept it on him, just for her.

"Eat," he growled.

Lena obeyed. She unscrewed the lid and dug the spoon through the thick frosting before popping a spoonful into her mouth. Pure sweetness burst on her tongue. The influx of calories and energy sparked through her cells. She took a few more spoonfuls, then swallowed several sips of water from the bottle Eli handed her.

Holding the can of frosting in her lap, she stared down at her hands. Bits of dried blood limned her fingernails. Her hands didn't seem like her own but a stranger's. Fading bruises still marred her fingertips.

She leaned forward, elbows braced on the top of her thighs

until the dizziness passed and the white spots faded from behind her eyelids. Her hair hung across her face in curtains as she inhaled deep, steady breaths, centering herself.

After a few minutes, she sat back, blinking. She handed Eli the can of frosting, which he tucked back into his rucksack for next time. "Thank you. I feel better."

"How are they?" Eli asked quietly. "The pregnant woman and the baby."

He knew how worried she'd been about the breech birth. She shook her head. "The baby made it. She's with Ana Grady at the Inn. But Theresa started hemorrhaging early this morning around four a.m. We tried so hard to save her. We needed a trauma surgeon. We needed blood transfusions and anesthesia and... everything we didn't have. She...died on the table. It wasn't enough. Nothing is enough."

"You did everything you could."

Lena made an anguished sound and shook her head. All she could see was the stricken face of Theresa's daughter, Miriam, when she had told her the awful news. Her pump beeped again as her numbers rose: seventy, then eighty-five. She drank some more water.

Eli squeezed her shoulder and sank into the chair next to her. She allowed herself to lean against him and rested her head on his broad shoulder. Despite her fatigue, sparks flitted across her skin where he touched her. His mere presence—his touch, his smell, his smile—calmed her.

The double doors into the ER opened. Antoine shuffled out, scowling down at his forearm wrapped in bandages.

"It's fine. I'm fine. It's just a scratch," he muttered when he caught Nyx's concerned glance.

Nyx looked like she wanted to say something sarcastic, one shoulder rising in a disinterested shrug. Instead, she sighed and glanced away. "For a second there, we thought we'd lost you."

"I'm the cockroach of the apocalypse, remember?" Antoine tried for levity, but the joke fell flat. His mouth thinned. There was a faraway look in his eyes as if a part of him remained on the battlefield. Like he was still there, watching his friends die.

"We have to go back," Nyx said. "We need to bury our dead. We can't leave them there for the carrion birds and the scavengers to pick their bones. It's not right."

Eli nodded heavily. "We will. As soon as it's clear and we know the cartel is gone. I'll send out some drones to scout the area in the morning. We need to dig up the IEDs that didn't detonate as well. We can reuse them in the next battle."

The silence hung heavy in the waiting room. Lena glanced from Eli to Nyx to Antoine. Distress etched their faces and radiated from their defeated postures.

"Tell me about the ambush," Lena said.

Eli stiffened, torment in his eyes. "We lost, and we lost badly. Nearly a quarter of our fighting force was obliterated. Alexis Chilton...she didn't make it. She was twenty-five. Nick Drewer, Mike Henderson, Margie Claypool...Thirty-two people. Thirty-two men and women. They were husbands, wives, mothers and fathers, brothers and sisters. All good people. They're gone because of me."

The pain in his eyes was nearly unbearable—it felt like being stabbed in her own chest. Eli's shoulders slumped, crumpling beneath the weight of their deaths.

She reached out, took his hand, and entwined her petite fingers through his large calloused ones. She wanted to make it better for him, to ease that tremendous burden, but she couldn't. All she could do was remain by his side, offering her whole heart as comfort, for whatever it was worth.

She squeezed his hand. After a pause, he squeezed back.

"We're alive because of you," Nyx said. "This isn't on you or Antoine or Nash or anyone. We didn't expect them to have sophisticated equipment like Maddox jammers. A bunch of them were trained ex-soldiers. We had a handful of barely trained civilians. After that fiasco, it's a damn miracle we escaped with anyone alive."

Guilt swam in his eyes. "They weren't ready for combat. Certainly not an organized, multi-pronged attack like the cartel unleashed on us. I didn't train them enough. I should have planned better. There are a thousand things I should've done differently—"

"NO." Nyx's voice was hard, her gaze steely. She pushed herself off the wall and stood in front of Eli's chair. She glowered down at him with her hands fisted on her hips. "Any professional soldier would tell you the same and you know it. If you were in my shoes and the roles were reversed, what would you tell me? You know this as well as I do. Real infantry soldiers practice for an op repeatedly. What to do in an ambush. How to maintain operational security. How to maneuver using fire as a group, as a single organism. You and I endured SERE school—survival, evasion, resistance, escape. They haven't."

She waved a hand angrily, like she could convince him through the sheer force of her will. "The Marine Corps has four-month infantry schools. The Army up to twenty-two weeks, all day, every day, and that's after basic training. They train until soldiers can fight in their sleep. Then they do another year with an infantry company before they're considered competent at practicing basic operational security. Trying to get scared, traumatized civilians battle-ready in a few months was an impossible task."

Eli nodded as if he understood. Lena suspected he was simply acquiescing to Nyx. What the mind might grasp logically meant nothing to what the heart felt, that crushing, soul-deep sense of responsibility. Lena knew Eli felt it more than anyone.

"We didn't even have comms sets for everyone," Antoine said in a gruff voice. He was pensive, absent his usual boisterous, upbeat self. Losing good men would do that to a soldier. "You didn't fail these people—you gave them a fighting chance."

"He's right," Lena said softly. "You gave us a chance. Munising is standing because of you. Without what you just did, the cartel would've already razed us to the ground."

Nyx folded her arms across her chest and glared at Eli.

"Enough with your little pity party. Stop feeling sorry for yourself already and man up."

Eli blanched. He sputtered, attempting to defend himself. "Look, you don't—"

"No, you look." Nyx kept going, raising her voice to speak over him. "Suck it up, Ranger. You've got a job to do. We have to figure out how to stop the cartel. It's up to us. There's no one else to stand in the gap to protect the people at the Inn or the people in town eking out a living. Everyone is doing their best. We need the best from you. Right now."

"I know," Eli said, subdued. "You have it."

Nyx nodded, confident he'd been properly chastised. She returned to her spot against the wall and pretended to examine the dirt beneath her nails, but her sharp gaze kept darting toward Antoine, her brow furrowed, as if she were studying an alien species she didn't quite comprehend.

Antoine, for his part, kept his attention on Eli. "What's the next play? They aren't going to stop, brother. You know that, and I know that."

"He's right," Jackson said from the doorway. He'd returned to the reception area and leaned against the wall beside Nyx. He seemed to have aged a decade overnight.

Wearily, he told them about his clandestine meeting at the cartel's staging area, the so-called deal his traitor father and high-ranking cartel-affiliated brother had offered them, and finally, about Luis Gault's wife.

Lena's heart sank as she listened. Her hand instinctively fell to the pump attached to her hip. "His wife is diabetic."

"The Côté family are vengeful on any given Sunday," Jackson said. "Add the insulin we stole, and Gault will never stop, not until he has the meds and we're all dead. My father and brother won't stop, either. With their intimate knowledge of the area, they're practically unstoppable."

"Practically, but not completely," Lena said. "There must be a way. Tell me there's a way."

Eli leaned forward, his elbows resting on his thighs, his head in his hands. He didn't give her an answer, which scared her more than anything she'd seen or heard today.

"We need to call a townhall meeting," Jackson said. "We can't make decisions in a vacuum. The people deserve to know what's coming, what we're up against. We decide our next move together."

36

LENA EASTON

DAY ONE HUNDRED AND THIRTY-EIGHT

"We have to run," Bradley Underwood said. "Before the cartel slaughters us in our sleep."

Lena settled into the leather armchair next to the stone fireplace and gazed at the tense faces surrounding her. The fire crackled and popped in the massive hearth, casting flickering shadows across the slate floor.

In the aftermath of the failed ambush yesterday, Jackson had called an emergency town hall meeting. Forty of the town's leaders had gathered at the Northwoods Inn to decide their next move.

Some sat in overstuffed armchairs, while others stood in a loose circle, their arms crossed, their postures stiff with worry, every face lined with loss and fear.

Bear stretched out at her feet. His snout rested on his paws, his brown eyes alert as he watched the proceedings. Lately, he'd been sleeping with Shiloh, but tonight, the Newfie seemed to sense Lena's distress and refused to leave her side.

Jackson stood alone in the center of the circle. As sheriff, everyone looked to him for the answer. The twitch in his jaw revealed his frustration and stress. Though he was under tremendous strain, he managed to keep his voice even. "We're here to discuss the options, consider the pros and cons, and come to a decision together."

"Like I said, we have to evacuate." Underwood leaned back, crossed his arms over his chest, and set his mouth in an obstinate line. The ex-sheriff was a stern, imposing black man in his early fifties with a ramrod posture, a shiny bald head, and a clean-shaven jaw. To call Underwood difficult was quite the understatement. "After the FUBAR situation the current sheriff brought down upon our heads, we have no choice but to flee."

"The current sheriff saved my life and many others," Lena broke in firmly, loudly enough for everyone to hear. "Let's not forget that. Jackson, Eli, and our brave fighters defeated Sykes and his convicts. If they hadn't, several of you in this room would be dead."

A low rumble of affirmation moved through the room. The committee knew it was true. Underwood could snark and complain all he wanted, but he couldn't demand his way, not anymore.

She glared at Underwood until he blinked first, his gaze sliding off somewhere to her right, perhaps in embarrassment. He hadn't fought against Sykes. He'd slunk off somewhere to lick his wounds.

When he spoke again, a bit of the aggression leaked from his voice. He waved a hand vaguely. "Just making a point."

"Even if we could run, where do you suggest we run to?" Ana Grady asked. "Is there some stronghold I don't know about? As far as I'm aware, we're the only sanctuary within hundreds of miles."

"She's right," Jackson said. "Where could we go that's safer than here? Where we don't know the strengths and weaknesses of the terrain, where we haven't built defenses? Where are we going to go that can house and feed over two thousand people?"

Underwood sneered like a recalcitrant schoolboy. "That's not my problem to figure out. It's yours, Sheriff."

Jackson spun on his heels to face him. "It's everyone's problem, everyone who wants to survive. How do you propose we transport all these people? With what vehicles? By my last count, we have five working diesel trucks that have been converted to biofuel, a dozen ATVs, and two dozen electric golf carts with a fifty-mile range. We've got about fifty electric bikes and a couple hundred standard bikes with two dozen horses at our disposal. That's it."

Fred Combs had a crew making biofuel around the clock. A scavenging team went out daily within Munising to search for hidden stashes of vegetable oil in every restaurant, school cafeteria, hotel kitchen, and local pantry.

With the cartel an ever-present threat, it was too dangerous to venture beyond the town's boundaries for any reason. The whole town was feeling the pressure, the oppressive sense of claustrophobia.

Jackson continued, "That's before we discuss logistics and supplies. If we can't find a source of safe water, then we're lugging hundreds—thousands—of gallons with us. A gallon per person per day. Sanitized water, food and medical supplies, suitcases of clothing, weapons, and ammunition. We have no way to transport all of it."

Eli paced restlessly behind the circle of chairs. "We lost a quarter of our fighters at Devil's Corner. Even if we had the vehicles, the fuel, and the supplies to transport that many people, how would we guard them out in the open and spread out on the road? We've got a couple hundred men and women who can shoot a gun and have some rudimentary training. Certainly not enough to guard a caravan of this size. If the cartel attacked us on the road, we'd be sitting ducks. They would swoop in, take out the rear and lead truck to trap the middle vehicles, and then methodically wipe out every single man, woman, and child."

Eli paused to let his words sink in. Faces paled. People glanced at each other with trepidation. Fred Combs wrung his hands in his lap. Dana Lutz picked nervously at her fingernails. Michelle Carpenter slumped next to Ana Grady, whose shoulders drooped as the dire reality of their predicament sank in.

Sensing the apprehension in the room, Bear rose on his

haunches and glanced up at his mistress. His head tilted, and his floppy ears pricked in concern. He let out a low, uneasy whine.

She rubbed his favorite spot beneath his chin. He leaned his bulk against her leg, his furry warmth as much a comfort to her as she was to him.

"What are we supposed to do then?" Underwood asked sharply. "You're the genius but you haven't offered any solutions, just shot down other people's ideas."

Jackson's jaw clenched. A tic started at the corner of Eli's right eye. Antoine and Nyx leaned casually against the bar counter toward the rear of the grand foyer, but their eyes were hard as they listened to the arguments ping-pong across the room.

"How do we know the cartel aren't on their way to slaughter us right now?" Tim asked.

"After the battle, the cartel's fighting force returned to their staging area to regroup," Moreno said. "We have eyes on their camp, a few scouts strategically placed to alert us if they start gearing up to move out."

"If you know where they are, why can't you attack them first?" Fred Combs asked. "Drive a truck full of dynamite into the middle of their encampment and set it off?"

"They're too heavily guarded," Jackson answered. "They're dug in inside a castle on top of a hill. An actual castle. They'd repel any assault attempt before we made it to the bottom of the hill. They have roving security patrols and active drones. Machine-gun firing positions are set up in each of the four towers, covering all directions. I've seen their stockpiles of RPGs, rifles, and pistols. They have a ton of ammunition of various calibers. The only thing that castle doesn't have is a moat filled with toothy piranhas."

"What if we surrender to them?" Underwood whined. "Maybe they'll spare us."

Jackson stalked in a tight circle, meeting the gazes of each committee member as he moved from person to person. "The cartel is brutal and merciless. You've heard the rumors, you've seen the refugees with your own eyes. They pick the towns clean as they go, looting, stealing, and rounding people up and shooting or torturing them. They're savages. Make no mistake, they will murder every officer of the law and former military personnel with great prejudice. They will burn and pillage and steal everything they touch. They will do worse things to your daughters."

Underwood flung his arms wide in derision. "Then what's your big play? Your big plan, huh? Did you call us all here just to tell us that we're about to be slaughtered and you can't do a damn thing about it?"

"Absolutely not." A vein popped in the center of Eli's forehead. He looked like he'd enjoy nothing more than to wring Underwood's lazy neck with his bare hands but was fighting to restrain himself. Lena knew the feeling.

A hum of alarmed, fearful voices buzzed through the room. The committee threatened to devolve into panicked chaos. *We're trapped. We're going to die. This is the end.*

The residents of the Upper Peninsula tended to be more reasonable than most. Even still, terror unsettled the most stoic among them. With their homes and loved ones on the line, everyone was scared and on edge. Fear tended to bring out the worst in humanity.

"Calm down, people!" Jackson raised his voice. "I know you're afraid. We're all afraid. But we have to focus and think through our fear. We can't let it cripple us, or we'll lose everything that matters to us, guaranteed."

Nyx cleared her throat. "A wise man once said, 'Fear is a reaction. Courage is a decision.'"

"Winston Churchill," Eli said.

Nyx nodded in appreciation. "You know your history."

"I know war."

"That's what this is," Antoine said. "This is a war. A war we have to win."

"And we will," Jackson said, "but only if we come together. Only if we're smart and brave."

Gradually, people settled themselves. Once the buzz of frantic voices quieted, Jackson spoke again. "Running is not a viable option. Neither is doing nothing and waiting for our enemy to destroy us. We have a plan, but we'll need help."

His tone was even and commanding. Lena had never seen him so confident, so determined. He was finally growing into the mantle of a true leader.

Something had happened during his confrontation with his father—he'd come away different somehow. She hadn't put her finger on exactly what, but it was significant.

"Help from where?" Underwood demanded. "The other towns that haven't been burned or ransacked by the cartel are worse off than we are. The National Guard and State Police abandoned us months ago." He snorted in derision. "Are you mental? No one's coming to help us. We're on our own."

"There's one option," Eli said.

You could hear a pin drop. Lena leaned forward intently, gripping the arms of the leather chair. "You mean James Sawyer."

There was a collective intake of breath. Eyes widened, and heads shook adamantly. The air crackled with tension.

"No," Underwood snapped. "Absolutely not. I will not allow it."

"Need I remind you, you are here as a guest," Jackson said. "I'm the sheriff. We're here to discuss options and decide on a plan together, but ultimately, I am in charge."

Underwood sneered. He opened his mouth as if to unleash a litany of insults, but something in Jackson's stony expression gave him pause. Chagrin, embarrassment, and anger passed across his face in rapid succession. His mouth snapped shut, finally cowed.

Lori spoke up then. "Can you explain your reasoning to us? Please tell us why we would want Sawyer for anything."

"Sawyer has fighters," Eli said. "He has weapons we don't have. He has a vested interest in joining forces with us. Once the cartel burns through us, they'll come for him."

"That man is a criminal. He's a drug dealer and a murderer." The voice was quiet but firm. Fiona hadn't said much since the altercation at the east gate. Fading bruises circled her neck. Her auburn curls were yanked back in a messy ponytail.

"I agree with my daughter," Scott Smith said. "Sawyer and his drugs ruined my boy's life, among many others. He's a scourge, a blight. What's to say he won't see what we've got and take everything we have? What's keeping him from taking over and killing everyone who resists? In my mind, he's as much a problem as the cartel."

"The cartel is worse," Devon said. "Trust me."

As one, the committee turned to look at Devon. She sat perched on the edge of the hearth, the fire blazing behind her. Bandages crisscrossed her swollen features. The bandage taped to her neck oozed red, a grim reminder of the threat they faced.

"It feels as bad as it looks," she said ruefully.

"Sawyer is a devil, but he's the devil we know," Jackson said. "He can be managed."

"To an extent," Antoine said.

Nyx's face turned purple with fury. "I vehemently disagree. So does my murdered grandmother."

Lena understood her misgivings. She felt the instinctive recoil, the revulsion churning in her gut. Sawyer had kidnapped and tortured Eli on his yacht, nearly killing him.

Perhaps he wasn't the worst monster, but he was still a monster, a sociopath interested in nothing that didn't further his own vested interests. His one saving grace had been his affection for Lily. And Lily was gone.

"Who is going to keep Sawyer and his goons in check?" Fred asked. "While you're off fighting the cartel psychos?"

"We will," Nash said.

Eli nodded. "At this moment, we have one goal. To make it too costly or impossible to take the town by force. Right now, we're outnumbered ten to one with a fraction of the cartel's firepower. With Sawyer on our side, we can at least make the battle costly for the cartel. We can slow them down, delay them, and start picking them off guerrilla-warfare style. We need time, additional fighters, and more supplies, which is where Sawyer's men and weapons are critical."

Jackson said, "Without Sawyer's weapons and men, the cartel could overrun us tonight. If they attacked now, we wouldn't last the day."

Eli met Nyx's blazing gaze across the room and held it. "Sawyer must be dealt with, and he will be. We have to barter a deal with the lesser devil to destroy the bigger devil. It's the only way."

Nyx gave him a sullen scowl, but she didn't argue.

"What if Sawyer refuses?" Nash asked.

"That's my problem," Jackson said, "Let me worry about that. Your job is to follow Eli's orders."

All eyes turned as one toward Eli, their expressions frightened and desperate. They longed for a thread of hope to cling to, anything to keep them from drowning in despair.

Eli stepped forward, his jaw clenched. He met Lena's gaze. She gave him a tight nod. She was behind him, one hundred percent.

"Starting first thing tomorrow morning, we build our defenses," he said. "Everyone chips in, every man, woman, and child old enough to swing a hammer. Even our old men can stick an M4 over a fighting hole and shoot. Non-combatants can take care of the wounded and run aid stations, and our teenagers can prepare food and run water and supplies to the fighters. We'll bolster our defensive perimeter around the town and strengthen our fortifications, digging foxholes, sandbagging fighting positions, and reinforcing fallback positions, among other tactics."

A heavy silence descended. People exchanged wary glances. Would it work? Could it work? Was there a way out of this, a chance at salvation? One by one, Lena watched a sputtering spark of hope alight in their eyes.

Jackson paused in the center of the group, his shoulders back, his head high, and his gaze intent. "What do you do when you have a mighty enemy, stronger than you could ever hope to defeat, and then suddenly another enemy appears, equally strong? You are trapped between them. What do you do?"

"It would be impossible to fight both," Antoine said.

"Yes," Jackson said.

"Let them fight each other," Nyx said. "One will kill the other, and the surviving enemy will be wounded, weakened. That is when you—the smaller opponent—may strike."

Jackson's eyes flashed. "Exactly."

"Can we win?" Ana asked soberly. "Tell us the truth. Is it possible?"

"Anything is possible with faith," Lori said.

"With faith and a hell of a lot of guns," Moreno said dryly.

"Let me be absolutely clear," Jackson said. "This is our only chance. There is no other way."

"What say you?" Moreno asked the committee. "Enough equivocating. It's time to crap or get off the pot, metaphorically speaking, of course."

Around the circle, heads began to nod. A chorus of affirmations began as a hum and grew gradually louder. Lori and Tim rose to their feet first.

Tim took his wife's hand. They exchanged a heavy glance, communicating wordlessly in the way of those married a long time. Their expressions were resolute.

Lena watched them, forgetting to breathe. Everyone looked up to the Brooks. They were leaders in the community. The rest would fall in line behind them, whatever they decided.

"We're with you," Tim said.

"So am I," Lena said.

Bear let out an enthusiastic whoof of agreement.

"Well, if the dog's in..." Moreno said with a sly grin. "Guess I'm in, too. Can't let Bear outdo me."

"Whatever you need, we'll do it," Scott Smith said. Fiona nodded, her chin lifting bravely.

"It's decided," Jackson said. "We will stay and fight. Here is where we will make our final stand."

37

JACKSON CROSS
DAY ONE HUNDRED AND FORTY

Jackson stood on the deck of the sleek Honolulu-blue and black Yamaha speedboat they'd borrowed from the marina. Most of the boats had been siphoned of their fuel, but they'd kept a half-tank full in this beauty. The name *Blue Moon* was scrawled along the stern transom in honor of the Midwest's favorite flavor of ice cream.

On his right, Devon stood rigid, her arms stiff at her sides. Her fingers twitched like she was ready to reach for her sidearm at any moment. Nash sat in the captain's chair in the cockpit beneath the black Bimini top.

Several hundred yards behind them, Moreno and Hart idled in a white speedboat, keeping an eye on things. Their only weapons were their sidearms, though they wore their law enforcement uniforms, a reminder that some form of law and order still existed in Munising.

If Sawyer wanted to kill them during this little meet and greet, he would. If things turned sideways, at least they'd take a few of Sawyer's cronies with them. They'd make it hurt.

Grand Island loomed above them, rich with the dense topography of white cedar, eastern hemlock, and black walnut trees, their leaves ablaze with the fiery-oranges and wine-reds of fall. The island boasted fourteen thousand acres of pristine wilderness scattered with cabins, rustic campsites, a visitor's station, and a lighthouse perched atop the bluff.

After the solar flares, Sawyer had transformed the island into his personal fortress. He'd built homes for his army of thugs out of shipping containers and commandeered solar and wind turbines for power. He maintained operational security with roving sentries manned with military-trained watch dogs that constantly patrolled the perimeter of the island.

Somewhere on the island, he'd stashed the cache of weapons they'd stolen from the cartel in Sault Ste. Marie, weapons Munising now desperately needed.

At the top of the sheer limestone cliffs, nestled invisibly within the woods, Sawyer's men provided overwatch. The muzzles of M4s and AR-15s were likely aimed at Jackson and Devon's chests. It was a disconcerting thought.

As they approached the island, a glittering speedboat departed the dock and headed toward them. Sawyer was at the helm, with Pierce, his righthand man, in the cockpit beside him. Three hardened goons stood along the deck at the stern, weapons drawn.

Sawyer drew his cigarette boat alongside theirs and cut the engine. The lustrous, pearl-white speedboat was the Lamborghini of power boats; it could hit one hundred forty miles an hour.

The wind whipped his unruly blond hair into his steely gray eyes. His face was weathered, his skin tanned, a network of fine wrinkles spanning his eyes and mouth. He looked the part of a salty sea captain sailing the Mediterranean or some other tropical locale.

He was tall, lean but muscular, and handsome. His eyes were the most disconcerting thing about him, crafty and cunning, set wide like a shark's and shining with a wily watchfulness. A predator's gaze.

Devon angled her chin at the speedboat. "Nice ride."

The *Risky Business* had burned in their last altercation with Sawyer, sinking to the bottom of the lake to join Lake Superior's graveyard of ships.

"I upgraded, thanks to you. Luckily, there's no dearth of supply. You can have your pick of any toy you want." He winked at Jackson. "As long as you know where to look."

"What the hell do I owe this little visit to?" Sawyer drawled. He lounged in the teak-lined cockpit and shielded his face with one hand, though the day wasn't sunny. His other hand rested casually on the pistol holstered at his hip. "You didn't come out here for crumpets and tea. Spit it out. I'm a busy man."

"We're here to discuss terms," Jackson said, keeping his voice even.

"I'm starting to think you like me or something."

"Or something," Jackson muttered.

Sawyer's flat gaze settled on Devon. "Long time, no see. I hope you haven't forgotten me."

"You're a bit hard to forget," Devon said, intentionally playing to his ego.

Sawyer knew exactly what she was doing and ate it up anyway. He winked at her, like a snake winking at its prey before it swallowed the mouse whole. "Same to you, sweetheart. I mean, before whatever happened to your face. Whatever did you do to yourself?"

"Leave her out of it," Jackson snapped.

Pierce leaned forward, peering across the boat at Devon. "You get attacked by an orangutan high on meth?"

To her credit, Devon didn't react to the insult. Jackson bristled, infuriated on her behalf, but Devon placed a restraining hand on his arm and managed to keep her expression neutral.

Jackson rested his palm on his service pistol. He'd told himself he wouldn't let Sawyer get under his skin. So much for that. "I'm warning you."

"Manners, Pierce. We're civilized, remember?" Sawyer said.

Pierce's expression was smug. His swagger and bearing combined with the way he handled his AK-47 screamed former military.

He was a large guy, much bigger than Sawyer at six-four and nearly three hundred pounds, with enormous, meat-hook hands. His eyes were flinty, his nose a hatchet blade set in his broad, flat features.

He glared at Devon, attempting to intimidate, to humiliate. She glared right back, uncowed. Jackson felt a burst of pride at her strength and courage. Gone was the timid deputy who'd shadowed him during her first week on the job.

Devon gestured at her face. "This is the handiwork of the cartel, which you already know."

"How awful." Sawyer attempted a sympathetic look, trying to approximate genuine emotion but failing, and badly. "We heard things didn't go well for you."

"We drove them back, at least temporarily. That's what matters."

Sawyer frowned as he looked past them, examining the occupants of the speedboat idling behind them. "Where's your bestie, Jackson? I didn't know you went anywhere without him. Hell, you probably visit the ladies' room together."

Pierce snickered. It sounded like nails on a chalkboard.

Eli had wanted to come to the meeting, but the animosity between the two of them would do nothing but cloud everyone's judgment. Jackson needed Sawyer to think clearly and logically, to make the smart decision that would benefit Munising as well as himself.

For the same reason, he'd kept Antoine and Nyx as far away from Sawyer as possible. It was up to Jackson and Devon to broker this transaction.

"We need to talk," Jackson said. "Civilly, man to man. I know you have your code of honor, Sawyer, no matter how twisted or illogical. I have faith you'll do the right thing."

Sawyer's smile widened. He was enjoying this. "You're coming to me for help."

Jackson swallowed the acid crawling up the back of his throat. Sawyer grinned with that cunning, cat-ate-the-canary gleam in his eyes that made Jackson want to throat-punch him. "We have a proposal that benefits both sides."

"We're here to warn you," Devon said. "Consider it common courtesy."

"Warn us of what?" Pierce's sneer appeared etched on his face permanently. "Sounds like more lies to me."

"I may be many things, but I'm no liar. Sawyer knows that."

Sawyer gave a noncommittal shrug. "Maybe. Maybe not. Spill the beans and I'll decide whether to slaughter you now or let you scurry back to the rat hole you call home."

A shiver of dread rattled down Jackson's spine. He was fairly certain Sawyer would hear him out without shooting him in the back. Still, the half-dozen weapons pointed at him were unnerving.

He slowed his breathing, steeling himself to remain calm, cool, and collected. Sawyer had zero respect for weakness or uncertainty.

Sawyer waved a hand at the hazy sky. "Some wildfire, huh?" he asked, changing the subject. "Is that the big bad thing you've come to warn us about?"

Over the last few days, the haze had grown thicker, and darker, as if the air itself was smudged. They couldn't see or smell the smoke yet, but the fire was out there, beyond their line of sight, raging as it burned through hundred-year-old forests like matchsticks.

Devon said, "By our calculations, it's twenty or so miles west of us, currently heading south, but if it changes direction, it could destroy everything within its path. It's hard to tell how big it is, but it's growing."

Sawyer shrugged. "I'm not concerned about a stupid fire. It'll burn itself out or the next rainstorm will snuff it out. We haven't had a wildfire get close in what, eighty years? Longer?"

Pierce nodded, as if he knew a thing about wildfires. Wildfires were uncanny, slippery things. Fire could be unpredictable. With few resources available to adequately fight it, the fire was growing more dangerous by the minute.

Sawyer winked at Devon. "You know what they say, where there's smoke, there's fire."

"We're not here to discuss the fire," Devon said.

Sawyer shifted his attention to Jackson and changed the subject yet again. "I've heard some crazy rumors these last few weeks. Sounds like you've lost control of your family, Jackson."

Jackson refused to rise to the bait. The deck shifted beneath his feet. The waves lapped the bow of the boat. Above their heads, seagulls soared, squawking at each other, occasionally diving for a fish before gliding skyward again with wriggling minnows caught in their beaks.

"I heard your father switched sides on you."

Jackson gritted his teeth. "You heard correctly. That's in part why we're here."

Sawyer cocked his head, studying Jackson intently. "What does your father have to hide, I wonder?"

"I don't care," Jackson said.

"Lily," Sawyer said the word flatly, with no emotion, but there was tension around his eyes, a tautness at his mouth.

Sawyer pretended to be a sociopath, and in many ways, he was, but he'd cared about his son Cody. And Lily, too. Jackson had seen genuine anguish in his face when he'd believed Cyrus Lee had killed her.

Sawyer had taken his vengeance on the serial killer; Jackson had been forced to let him do it. Sawyer was unaware that Lee hadn't killed Lily and Jackson had no intention of disabusing him of that notion. As far as he was concerned, the past would remain in the past.

It was the future they had to save now.

"My father joined the cartel, and he's providing Luis Gault with valuable intel. Our enemy knows our weaknesses, and we do not know theirs. Now, they're coming for us with everything they have."

"Why the hell is that our problem?" Pierce cut in. "Far as we're concerned, Cross, you're an annoying little gnat buzzing around our faces. Good riddance if the cartel smashes you like a bug."

Sawyer's expression darkened. "Let me get this straight. You want my help, but you keep killing my men."

Anger flared through Jackson's veins. "You keep sending your men to the slaughter. We have the right to defend ourselves. You sent assassins into Munising. They killed a seventy-five-year-old grandmother, not to mention the torture of a woman under my protection."

"That so-called woman betrayed her oath—"

"I don't give a damn what she did to you," Jackson interrupted. "I don't care if she skinned your favorite puppy and wears its coat as a hat. She's one of mine, and you have no claim on her. I could arrest you right now."

Sawyer didn't miss a beat. "But you won't."

"This is what's going to happen," Jackson said, his voice stern and unyielding. "You will bury your little grudge and move on like an adult. You'll forget about Eli, Antoine, and Nyx, and in turn, I will overlook the fact that your thugs murdered an innocent citizen in my town. Trust me, it leaves a bad taste in my mouth, too. Do you think I want to be here? We have larger matters that concern us both."

Sawyer's eyes formed into slits. "My best men didn't come back. I lost—"

"Consider it the penalty for their stupidity. I'm going to grant you a pass and assume those men acted on their own, consumed by a personal vendetta. If that's the case, then you and I have nothing further to discuss. They paid the penalty for their crime with their deaths. We can wash our hands of the matter and move on."

Pierce made a move, his weapon rising.

Devon had her gun on him in an instant, the muzzle trained between the man's eyes, her finger on the trigger. "I wouldn't if I were you."

38

JACKSON CROSS
DAY ONE HUNDRED AND FORTY

Devon kept her gun on Pierce.

"Pierce, stand down," Sawyer ordered.

"But—"

"Do it!"

Grudgingly, Pierce obeyed.

"Everyone, take a breath and calm the hell down." Sawyer turned back to Jackson. "Say I agree with you and let bygones be bygones. What then? You've pissed off a very potent enemy."

Jackson cocked his brows, incredulous. "*We've* pissed off— you're the one who stole half their weapons. Don't allow your ego to get in the way. They are formidable, and they will not be deterred. When they attack again, it'll be with overwhelming force and numbers. They intend to obliterate us. All of us, including you. They mentioned you by name. They're coming for all of Munising, and they're going to burn it to the ground."

"What do we care?" Pierce spat. "Let it burn."

Sawyer, though, remained silent, his expression inscrutable. Jackson knew that he cared; somewhere deep down, behind the cruelty and the violence and the thirst for power and control, there lurked the little boy who'd lived his life as an outsider, a pariah, always on the outside looking in, longing to belong.

That was the part of Sawyer that Jackson spoke with now. "The town needs you, Sawyer. So do we. The thing is, you need us, too. Neither of us can defeat this enemy alone. As much as we both might hate it, we must put our animosity aside and work together, side by side. Otherwise, we die and the cartel wins."

They remained quiet as Sawyer considered his words. The wind tugged at their clothing and flung tendrils of hair into their faces. The deck swayed gently beneath their feet. Below them, the water was crystal clear; the shadowy outlines of boulders and downed trees shimmered sixty feet down.

He and Devon waited impatiently. Sawyer would draw this out, he'd take his time. They needed to allow it to happen his way, or it wouldn't happen at all.

"Sawyer—" Pierce said.

Sawyer raised a hand to silence him. "Shut up. I'm thinking." Another full minute passed before Sawyer finally spoke. "I am many things, but I am not stupid. I may be a parasite, but a parasite needs a host. The destruction of my hometown and the murder of hundreds of innocents—many of them my clients— does not behoove me or my business empire."

Pierce shot him a skeptical look. "You can't possibly agree to this—"

"Did I ask you to speak?" Sawyer didn't bother to look at Pierce or raise his voice. He didn't need to.

Pierce's mouth thinned into a bloodless line, but he shook his head. "No, sir."

"Then shut the hell up."

"Yes, sir."

Sawyer's eyes remained hard. "Do you know who leads the Côté Cartel? A Canadian hitman by the name of Luis Gault. He's a myth, a legend, like the windigo that hunts men in the night, seeking to devour their flesh."

"He's human," Jackson said. "I've seen him."

"Humans can be beaten," Devon said. "They can be killed. He's just a man."

Sawyer grunted. He acted nonchalant, but Jackson knew better. Sawyer feared the cartel's brutal retaliation. He was a bully, but he was smart enough to recognize a bigger, meaner version of himself when he saw one.

Pierce sneered. "We can stand on our own just fine. Look behind you. That island is a fortress. No one can infiltrate it."

"Remember their Hueys," Jackson said quietly. "They can, and they will."

"Let them try," Pierce groused. "They'll mow through you and then we'll wipe the floor with the rest of them."

"They have five hundred trained fighters, at least. Probably more if they conscript the low-level thugs and criminals they've brought into the fold. Can you withstand an attack of that magnitude? With air support?"

Sawyer had gone quiet and thoughtful. He let Pierce do the ranting and raving. Pierce was a brawler, a man who used his physical power to obliterate opponents with brute force and violence of action. However, he didn't have Sawyer's cunning or tactical mind.

Sawyer, though, was smart. Jackson could see it in his eyes, that greedy gleam as he considered the pros and cons. He would conclude that an alliance meant fewer casualties on his side and greater strength on the other side of this battle. He was already scheming for the future.

Jackson was counting on it. Sawyer believed he was the smartest guy in the room. His arrogance would be the weakness they would exploit—but only after they'd won.

Jackson breathed deeply, willing his heart rate to remain steady. The air no longer smelled fresh but like something singed. The wildfire was out there somewhere, unseen but dangerous.

"Are you in or are you out, Sawyer?" Devon asked. "We're done equivocating. Man up or stop wasting our time."

"The battle takes place in Munising," Sawyer said. "They never set foot on Grand Island."

"Agreed. As long as Grand Island is a retreat option for our elderly, wounded, and children as a last resort."

Sawyer considered it, then nodded. He winked at Devon, so abruptly convivial it was jarring. He gave her a slow, lingering look. "Maybe those scars won't be half-bad, after all. Makes you look a little dangerous. I like that."

Devon rolled her eyes. "I'm out of your league."

He laughed again. "Why don't you come over here and we'll see, honey."

Devon gave him a strained smile. Her lips were distorted by the cut arcing from her mouth to her nose. She was getting better at playing the game, too. She knew what was at stake. "You wish."

"Watch yourself, Sawyer," Jackson warned.

Sawyer raised both hands in acquiescence. "Don't be jealous, old friend. I can't help it if the ladies love me."

"We're not friends."

This time, the wink was for Jackson. "Not yet."

Jackson glanced up at the ominous sky. Unease flared through him. He tamped it down to no avail. "Do we have ourselves a deal?"

Sawyer's expression hardened. His eyes were flat and emotionless. "We do."

What followed was a tense negotiation between enemies. Neither side trusted the other, but neither side had a choice, either. They discussed how many fighters Sawyer could offer, when they'd arrive, where they'd stay, how they'd handle disagreements, where to store the guns, the logistics of moving troops and weapons. They agreed to meet again at dawn to iron out the details.

Sawyer shifted his position in the captain's chair and turned his attention to the cockpit. The engine growled to life with a low rumble as he spun the cigarette boat in a tight circle and roared toward Grand Island. The water rose in a lacy plume behind the wake.

Two of Sawyer's goons remained at the stern, their weapons pointed at Jackson and Devon until they faded to specks on the horizon. Nash drove the smaller boat in a wide sweeping arc and headed back to the Munising marina.

"How does it feel?" Devon asked after a moment.

"How does what feel?"

"You just made a deal with the devil."

Jackson side-eyed her. "There are worse devils out there."

"That there are."

The unknown filled him with apprehension, a scrabbling dread like spiders crawling on his skin. He had no idea whether they'd just made a deal that would save them or consign them to hell.

39

JACKSON CROSS
DAY ONE HUNDRED AND FORTY

The wildfire that had started during the ambush was growing steadily. The drone footage that Fiona had taken that morning revealed a spreading blaze south of the Au Train River.

It was slowly moving eastward with the direction of the wind —directly toward Munising.

While Eli and his team dug foxholes and constructed firing positions along Munising's perimeter, Jackson had gathered a team of volunteer firefighters.

They stood in a loose circle between towering oaks, maples, and birch trees. Thick fields of ferns carpeted the forest floor, pocked by the occasional decaying, mossy log. Sickly reddish sunlight trickled through the canopy above their heads. The air smelled like charcoal.

"We have to contain this fire or everything we're working for will be for naught," Jackson said. "There's little room for error."

The circle of men and women surrounding him nodded grimly. They wore helmets and orange vests and carried shovels and wheelbarrows, pruning poles, and chainsaws.

Before society's collapse, the USDA Forest Service, Michigan State Police, Great Lakes Forest Fire Compact members, and DNR would band together to fight wildfires that posed a threat to local communities.

No longer. This was up to them.

Jackson had managed to track down two firefighters still in the area as well as Dana Lutz, who'd worked for the Forest Service in her twenties and thirties. She'd volunteered to head a ragtag group of volunteer citizen firefighters.

They'd gathered at a spot a few miles west of Munising. The firefighters had chosen to create a fire line along County Road 577, or Perch Lake Road, which ran north to south parallel to Munising.

The motorsports park was cleared of trees and consisted of wide dirt trails. It should provide a natural break to the wildfire, as would Perch Lake to the south, a shallow thousand-acre lake with a maximum depth of fourteen feet.

To the left of the road was a soft, boggy stretch of land that hugged the road for approximately four miles, not quite marsh-land but wetter than the surrounding woodland.

Their goal was to widen the natural break of the road between the motor park and the lake to prevent the fire from crossing and heading for Munising.

For the last two days, from sunrise to long past sundown, they had dug trenches, cut tree limbs, and raked the ground clear of underbrush. They'd used precious biofuel stores to run tractors and bobcats to cut back trees and move massive loads of dirt along the break line of County Road 557.

No matter what they did, the wildfire might jump the ditches and firebreaks anyway.

Dana stepped into the center of the circle next to Jackson and raised her voice. "We're evacuating everyone from the village of Christmas and the surrounding areas and moving them into downtown Munising. There's no way we can cover everywhere, so we've predicted the area most likely to be able to stop the fire in its tracks."

"Wildfires require three key components to ignite and spread:

fuel, heat, and oxygen. We call them the 'fire triangle.' Fuel is anything flammable, including grasses, shrubs, trees, and even houses. And when burning fuel is exposed to oxygen, the chemical reaction releases heat and generates combustion. For a fire to be extinguished, at least one of the components of our 'fire triangle' must be removed. Also, the intensity and movement of the fire depend on fuel, weather, and topography, collectively known as the 'fire behavior triangle.'

"Now, we don't have the resources to extinguish a fire of this size. Our goal, then, is to construct the fire line like we've been doing—a break in vegetation and potential fuel for the fire. By cutting back the trees and removing the brush down to the dirt, we're attempting to prevent the fire's forward movement into Munising."

"What about a controlled burn?" Jackson asked. By carefully pre-burning a certain area, they could eliminate the fuel before the real wildfire could reach it.

Dana frowned. "I'm afraid we'd lose control of the burn and cause a bigger problem. Last resort, we can attempt a backfire, where we deliberately start a fire in front of the active forest fire to consume fuel, to try to block the path or change the direction it's moving. Best case scenario, it prevents the wildfire from spreading. Worse case, the backfire spreads and joins the original fire, creating an out-of-control blaze that's twice as strong—in which case, we're screwed."

"Just tell us what to do next," Underwood grumbled. Sweat poured down his temples and spread in damp circles beneath his armpits. Scratches marched his dirty face. His reddened eyes watered from the drifting smoke. He was used to demanding authority; he radiated resentment and bitterness at being stripped of his command.

Dana shot him a contemptuous look. Jackson wasn't convinced of their need for Underwood, either. Since Tim and Lori had graciously granted him admission into Northwoods, he'd done little but complain.

"We've got a critical situation here," Dana said. "The landscape is bone-dry. Coupled with the lack of moisture in the dead fuel, plus the strong winds, you have burning conditions that produce fast spread rates and high-intensity fires."

The weather was cool and dry. In late September, the crisp sunny days reached the fifties, while nights were chilly, dipping into the low forties, sometimes the thirties.

It hadn't rained in two weeks. The kaleidoscope of reds, oranges, and purples fringing the trees was spectacular, but the leaf canopy was parched and arid. The grasses, bushes, and pine needles were crisp as kindling.

"How long until the fire reaches us?" Nash asked. "Is there any way to tell?"

The firefighters had explained the math to Jackson. Given a wind speed of sixteen miles per hour, the estimated wildfire spread rate would be about one point six miles per hour during the most severe burning conditions, or roughly ten percent of the prevailing wind.

"The wind is headed northeast at about ten to fifteen miles per hour. Using the ten percent rule of thumb, I'd estimate that if the fire keeps traveling with the wind at this rate, it'll reach this spot tomorrow evening, Munising itself a day after that."

"Will this be enough to stop it?" Devon asked.

"We better damn well try. We have no other choice. Start praying to whatever God or spirit you believe in, because if this wind doesn't change direction and we don't get some rain, it's all over."

Uneasiness crawled beneath his skin. He could see it in everyone's faces—their fear and dread. Better to focus on what they could control versus what they couldn't.

Jackson clapped his gloved hands. "Get to work, people. You've been assigned your tasks. Let's get it done."

With a scowl, Underwood scurried off between the trees, out of sight of the other firefighters. Though he carried a rake in his hand, Jackson figured he had zero intentions of working at a task he considered beneath him.

Jackson put Underwood out of his mind. He didn't have the time or energy to corral the man. Let him sulk.

Jackson and Devon moved to an uncleared area and got to work. They hacked at branches and yanked up underbrush, cut and dragged trees, and dug trenches to scrape the ground to bare earth. It was grueling, back-breaking work.

Jackson chopped back the branches protruding over the road. Weeds snagged his pants, tree roots threatened to trip his feet, and fallen leaves crackled beneath his boots. His muscles ached from the strenuous effort, but he didn't pause to take a break. There was no time.

As they labored, they listened to the twittering birds and buzzing insects, the clink of the shovels on unforgiving soil, and the rhythmic thud of the axe blades.

After a couple of hours, Devon threw her shovel to the ground with a hissed curse. She ripped off her gloves, stretched out her hands, and examined her newest blisters, one of which had burst in the tender webbing between her thumb and pointer finger. "Damn it, but that hurts."

Her scraggly braids were piled into a topknot atop her head. She wore oversized work pants and a long-sleeved shirt, a hoodie tied around her waist. The lacerations on her face were red and angry, though scabs had begun to form.

She ducked her head shyly. "What, Boss? Do I have spinach in my teeth from the omelet at breakfast or what?"

"Nah. You're good."

"Then what? Can't get enough of my new clown face?"

"You look fine, Devon. You're fine."

She gave a resigned shrug. Her hand fluttered near her face as if she wished to hide her scars. "I know it's the last thing I should care about. People are starving. Every day we live under the very real terror of dying. Everything else pales in comparison. It's vain and stupid to care about my looks."

"It's not vain or stupid. You're beautiful, Devon."

She made a face, wincing at the pull of her scabs. "Not anymore."

"A few scars don't change who you are. You're the woman who ran into the lighthouse by yourself and single-handedly saved Lena and Shiloh. Every step of the way, you've been right by my side. You haven't flinched once. That's who you are."

"Maybe," Devon allowed.

"Besides, Nyx said your scars make you look badass. And she's right, by the way."

Devon didn't say anything for a minute. Smoke drifted heavy and thick over the trees. The acrid smell was stronger than a campfire and more sinister.

Their weapons rested on a nearby log. Hart was positioned along the road, providing overwatch, while scouts patrolled a radius of twenty miles around Munising.

They were as safe at this moment as they could be, which meant they weren't safe at all.

Devon paused to tug her neck gaiter from her mouth and nose and took a swig of water from her filtered water bottle. She set it down on a tree stump. She turned to face Jackson. "Can we talk?"

"Sure." He hacked at a branch. "What is it?"

She hesitated. "They say near-death experiences change us. It distills what matters to a few very important things."

He lowered the axe, ran his free hand through his unruly hair, and studied her. "Do you feel changed?"

"I don't know. Maybe. Yes. I mean, I don't want to live the rest of my life worried about *what ifs* and the things I didn't do, the chances I didn't take." Another pause. She chewed her lower lip anxiously. "I need to say this now before it's too late and that chance is taken from me."

Jackson felt something loosen inside his chest. "I'm listening."

"A part of me feels like I shouldn't be here. Alexis should be alive, not me. But here I am. I don't want to waste whatever time I have left on survivor's guilt. Life is too short, too precious. If I've learned anything, it's this. I want to live and I want to be brave." She inhaled a steadying breath and lifted her chin. "So, here's me, being brave."

He waited, a bit confused, unsure where this conversation was headed, but he would wait as long as she needed. He could be present for her the same way she'd always been there for him.

Devon cleared her throat, gripping the shovel handle like it was the only thing keeping her on her feet. She squared her shoulders, steeling herself. "I know you've been grieving Lily, and that's okay. I understand. But now that you've solved her case, I thought... perhaps, you might have room in your heart for someone else."

Jackson gaped at her. It was like she was speaking a foreign language, a language he'd never heard before. For so long, the hollow space in his heart had been filled by Lily, as if her death had stunted his soul in some peculiar, twisted way. His dogged pursuit of justice hadn't allowed room for anything or anyone else.

Looking at Devon now, standing there dirty and raw and vulnerable, he saw her as if for the first time, in a way he hadn't allowed himself to see her before now. Guilt wormed inside him. She was so much more than he could offer her in return. He was unworthy of her.

Chagrined, he tried to explain it, but words seemed to fail him. "It's been so long, I don't remember how to be with someone, how to treat you the way you deserve."

It was the wrong thing to say. He knew it immediately, but it was impossible to take it back.

As if she'd been slapped, Devon took an unsteady step backward. A dozen emotions he couldn't read passed across her face in quick succession: a flash of hurt, of heartbreak, followed swiftly by humiliation. Her expression crumpled. Just as suddenly, it was gone. Her face closed.

"Devon—"

"Forget it." Her hand lifted, hovering near her face, shielding herself from him, protecting herself. "I'm dehydrated and stressed.

I haven't been sleeping. Just ignore me. Pretend this conversation never happened. I'm stupid. I'm just being stupid."

Baffled, he said, "Devon, wait—"

She took several hasty steps back, putting distance between them. "I'm supposed to take the third shift at the West Street checkpoint in less than an hour. I'll send someone to replace me. Catch you later, boss."

Before he could attempt a pathetic apology, she turned her back to him and left the clearing. She walked stiffly along the bank toward the drinking station, where a fifty-gallon container of water sat in the back of a pickup truck.

Jackson watched her go with a feeling like he'd just lost something precious. He felt an ache in his chest he hadn't known existed until that very second. The realization dawned like a sucker punch to the gut: how little he understood the topography of his own heart.

For years, he'd obsessed over a dead girl, blaming himself for losing her, haunted by the killer who stalked his nightmares. Embroiled in his fervent, single-minded pursuit for so long, he'd become conflicted, burdened, and zealous to a fault.

Exposing Lily's killer had freed him. However, it didn't feel like freedom at that moment. He could move on, couldn't he? Open his heart again to something new. It was possible. The thought was both exhilarating and terrifying.

He found himself startled at the forcefulness of the feelings bubbling up inside him. The thought of life without Devon with her mischievous smile and bright eyes was untenable. That was all he knew.

He should go after her. Chase her down, confess his feelings, and lay his heart on the line, as Devon had so bravely done.

An intense coughing fit seized him. The air was becoming dense with hazy smoke. It was getting harder to breathe. Everyone had covered their mouths and noses with handkerchiefs, scarves, or N95 masks if they had them. He had given his mask to Fiona.

Jackson adjusted the damp handkerchief over his nose and

mouth, then carried the axe a hundred yards downriver to where Fiona Smith and her father were busy hacking through branches with handsaws, chainsaws, and pruning poles.

He handed the axe to Fiona. "Take over for me. I'll be right back."

Jackson headed toward the water truck. His steps were light. Despite the dire circumstances, something like happiness surged in his chest.

He hadn't made it a hundred feet, however, when his radio hissed to life. He paused, tugged the handkerchief from his mouth, and coughed into his fist. "This is Falcon. You're a go."

"This is Wolverine," Moreno said, using his call sign. "The scouts on the M-28 E and 448 junctions just reported in. We've got incoming. It's them. The cartel."

Jackson stopped breathing. "How many?"

"Hard to count, but the scouts reported several dozen trucks and transport caravans in the convoy. A bunch of armored, weaponized vehicles and those damn choppers, too. The cartel army is headed our way!"

40

ELI POPE
DAY ONE HUNDRED AND FORTY

E li's heart rate accelerated. Tiny dark objects slowly solidified in the viewfinder of his binoculars. "There they are."

Several hours ago, their forward scouts had notified them of movement along the main corridor of M-94 from the east, turning onto M-28 south of Munising. The main highway was mostly cleared of abandoned vehicles and was the quickest and most direct path from the cartel's staging location.

The cartel appeared like a swarm of locusts, filling both the east and westbound lanes, spilling onto the shoulders on either side of the road, a blight descending upon the town. The rumble of aggressive engines filled the air, vibrating in Eli's teeth.

After determining that the most likely angle of attack would come from the east or possibly the south, Eli had ordered fortifications on Highway 58 along the northeast coast past the North-woods Inn, the hospital, and the visitor's center to the south of Munising, in the direction of the junction with the I-94 and toward Wagner Falls Scenic Site.

Nestled into the curve of South Bay, Munising wrapped around the coast of Lake Superior and spread thin fingers east and west along the shoreline. They had security teams monitoring the shoreline in case of a waterborne attack, though Eli doubted the cartel had the watercraft to mount such a difficult invasion. While the harbor lay relatively flat, great limestone bluffs jutted along the coastline to the northeast and northwest.

He'd also placed scouts at the M-94 intersection, where they could see anything coming from the west or east along 94. To the west, they'd built lesser fortifications to defend M-28 as it wound north, hugging the shoreline past the high school, the marina, and a collection of long-shuttered businesses: glass-bottom boat rides, shipwreck tours, and fishing charters. Only the fishing charters remained in business.

In all, the volunteers had built miles of sandbagged timber barricades and concertina wire entanglements, as well as dozens of anti-tank ditches. Sniper overwatch positions from various rooftops had been selected and fortified. Where possible, they had felled massive trees across the highways leading into the county to slow the cartel's convoy.

In the last few days, Sawyer's men had joined the Northwoods Inn, his fighters significantly bolstering their numbers. His weapons had been moved from Grand Island and distributed throughout the town and the Inn in strategic locations.

"We've got more hostiles coming in on highway 58 from the east," another scout said through their comms. "They just passed the Pictured Rocks Golf Club."

Eli nodded grimly. There were several smaller roads the cartel could take north from M-94 to meet H-58 and turn west toward Munising. He'd feared a multipronged attack, and now, here it was.

A few minutes later, their scout to the west confirmed the worst. "A third contingent is moving closer. They must've made a wide circle to come around behind us. There are dozens of armored vehicles. A couple of trucks are mounted with Ma Deuces."

"Hold your fire unless they attack first," Eli instructed.

This was what the main contingent had been waiting for, then, for their fighting forces to converge on Munising simultaneously, cutting off all avenues of escape except by boat. Luis Gault was banking on the fact that they didn't have the fuel or the number of boats to evacuate their citizens. He would be correct.

As Eli watched, an armored truck that looked more like a tank ground its way closer, nudging past an abandoned minivan encased in vines. Several military-style Humvees were manned by gunners with .50 caliber machine guns. Dozens—hundreds—of weapons swiveled toward their defensive perimeter.

The Munising fighters waited and watched with bated breath, their guns pointed at the enemy. Eli took in the reports from his scouts via their comms. Fiona had taken over the drones, which gave them a high-level, bird's eye surveillance of the army gathering before them on three sides.

"I estimate one thousand to fifteen hundred hostiles. Looks like at least half are fighters, and half are logistical support—fuel resupply, maintenance for transportation and equipment, medical, food and water, etc. Gault has about eight hundred men assigned to companies. Each company has a hundred to a hundred thirty troops. This company is equipped with mortars and drones. They've got two Hueys on flatbed trucks. They've probably got some infantry scouts who can fast-rope the helos."

Gault was in it for the win. He'd brought everything he had.

Eli cursed under his breath. Well, so had they.

"They're cutting off our supply routes," Jackson said. "No one is getting out or in."

"It's a tactical move. They want to finish this thing here and now."

A hundred yards to the south, he spotted movement between the vehicles. He focused his binos on the figure in the center between several bodyguards. "That him?"

Jackson nodded in affirmation.

Eli was surprised that Gault had shown up. He'd suspected Gault was the type to lead from the rear, to let others get their hands dirty. Perhaps he'd underestimated him.

"His wife is dying," Jackson reminded him. "This is personal for him. We took her chance at survival away from them. Whatever happens to her, he blames us."

"It's personal for us, too."

"Bring it, jerkface," Antoine muttered.

The figure remained behind the barricade of armored vehicles. Several bodyguards swarmed around him. He kept himself well-protected.

"Surrender now!" he shouted through a megaphone. Though he was slight in stature, his voice was deep, forceful, and commanding. He spoke with authority as a man used to being obeyed without question. "The offer shall not be extended again. The next time we speak, it'll be as I stand over your dying body before I drive the stake into your beating heart."

"He has a flair for drama, doesn't he?" Jackson asked.

"That's an understatement," Eli said.

No one answered Gault. There was no answer worth giving. The Munising fighters stood firm and silent, brandishing their weapons but otherwise remaining still, as Eli had ordered.

"Why isn't he attacking already?" Nyx asked.

The cartel fighters fanned out behind their line, arrayed in all their might. They didn't attack, nor did they appear jittery or whipped into a frenzy, anxious for the opening salvo; they simply waited.

Gault studied his adversaries: their men, their weapons, their armored SUVs. Their numbers and their firepower were likely more than he'd expected. With Sawyer's men and supplies, they'd more than doubled their fighters and weaponry.

Gault had taken notice.

Eli knew he would; the cartel leader was many things, but he wasn't stupid.

Antoine narrowed his eyes. "They're not attacking."

"Maybe they're planning to starve us out," Jackson said.

"Looks like it might go that way," Eli said.

Nyx cursed under her breath.

"We should move the town's food stores," Jackson said. "Horatio knows their locations."

Eli nodded. "Already on it."

"Remember this moment!" Gault shouted through the megaphone. "Remember how you could have surrendered and saved yourselves from the carnage that's coming. For it will come!"

"He's going to kill us either way," Jackson said in a low voice.

Eli said, "He can damn well try."

Beside him, Jackson tensed.

"What is it?" Eli asked.

"My father is with him. I can see the top of his silver head, next to Gault, to the right. That shorter, thicker man next to him is my brother."

Eli sensed Jackson's anger, the disgust in his voice tinged with sorrow and humiliation. Duty and hatred warred in his expression. This was tearing him up inside, and no wonder.

Eli shot him a sympathetic glance. "You're fighting against your family. Are you sure your head is on straight? No one would blame you for bowing out."

"I owe them nothing. The lines have been drawn in the sand. I'm on this side, they're on that side."

"And if it comes down to it?"

Jackson's gaze was rock steady. "I'll do what I have to do. You know I'll do it. I already have."

Eli didn't doubt Jackson. His old friend was capable of terrible things. He was also capable of tremendous grace, loyalty, and courage under fire.

Sometimes the best people were forced to do the worst things to keep others safe. Eli had done the same and would do it again in a heartbeat. He saw that same gritty determination reflected in Jackson's eyes.

Whatever had happened between them—an entire lifetime of memories, of love and joy and bitterness and betrayal—they were together now.

"I trust you to have my back," Eli said.

Jackson blinked, startled. Then he smiled. "And I have yours."

Eli knew that Jackson would lay down his life for Eli. Eli would do the same for him. Without hesitation or equivocation. Their trust in each other was absolute.

It had taken a war at the end of the world to bring them back to each other. But here they were. At long last, brothers again.

41

SHILOH EASTON POPE
DAY ONE HUNDRED AND FORTY-TWO

"Tell me the truth," Shiloh said to Jackson. "We're screwed, aren't we?"

"I told you I wouldn't lie to you, and I won't," Jackson said.

Shiloh folded her arms and stared up at him, trying to hide her fear, to be tough and strong. It had been two days since the cartel army descended upon Munising's borders, two days since the first volley of artillery fire lit up the sky and sparked fear in every citizen's heart.

As Eli had predicted, the cartel had not outright attacked—not yet. Shiloh almost wished they would, just to get it over with. Waiting for the other shoe to drop was pure torture.

"Just tell me already, damn it."

"I like the bear-fur cape," he said as if attempting to distract her. "It suits you."

Beaming, she straightened her shoulders. The fur cape dwarfed her small frame, but she didn't care. She felt like a great Native warrior from the plains, like she'd been born to this. Besides, the cape kept her warm. The early morning air was downright frigid. This morning, frost had coated the grass.

"Eli helped me make it."

Jackson gave a wry smile. "That doesn't surprise me."

They sat side by side at one of the picnic tables beneath a sprawling oak tree behind the Inn. Shiloh's crossbow leaned against the bench at her feet.

"I have something for you." Jackson reached into his uniform pocket and pulled out a half-melted Mars bar. The wrapper was filmed in a layer of dust, but it was sealed. "I'm sorry it's not a Snickers bar, but hopefully it's second best. I found it at the last house we scavenged, under a little girl's bed."

"She had good taste." Shiloh forced herself not to rip the candy bar from Jackson's grasp. Her mouth watered, her stomach grumbled. She was always hungry these days, her stomach growling within minutes of finishing the meager portions they doled out here.

She took her time unwrapping the treat, inhaling the delicious scents of caramel and nougat before biting into the creamy filling. The sweet chocolate melted on her tongue. "Mmmm."

As she ate, she watched the big white turbines churn along the bluff. Clotheslines hung between the trees near the cabins. Each cabin had a raised garden and a woodshed to store the family's firewood. Some had solar panels on the rooftops, while others used woodstoves for heating and cooking.

People moved about, engaged in various tasks, from plucking the raspberry bushes or collecting fallen acorns, walnuts, and hazelnuts from the orchard in wicker baskets, to weeding the gardens or feeding the goats and chickens. Inside the Inn's industrial kitchen, workers preserved apples, zucchinis, red peppers, cucumbers, and tomatoes in cans and jars.

Everything seemed almost normal except for the criminals marching around, scowling at people, all armed to the teeth, heavily tattooed, with hard faces and empty eyes.

They didn't belong. Their presence was every kind of wrong. These soldier wannabes were thieves, criminals, and thugs. They acted like they'd prefer to slit the townspeople's throats rather than fight alongside them.

They'd invited a nest of vipers to take a nap on their bed. Their mere presence was disconcerting. It was a disaster waiting to happen. And yet, both Jackson and Eli put up with it.

The enemy lying in wait outside their gates was far worse.

It was a tense, untenable situation. Every interaction was strained. Everyone looked at each other with suspicion, mistrust, and resentment. Shiloh could see it in people's strained expressions and their stiff shoulders, their eyes fearful and wary.

People were losing their minds over the littlest things. Daily fist fights and shouting matches broke out over ration portions, cutting in line, and arguments over who fell asleep on watch or who failed to do latrine duty.

Sawyer's crew made everything a thousand times worse.

Shiloh hated it.

Shiloh held out the Mars bar and offered Jackson a bite. "Want some?"

"This one's for you." Jackson waved his hand. "How are you doing? What's going on inside that pretty head of yours?"

Leave it to Jackson to check up on her in the middle of a war. She glanced up at him, studying his strong profile. Jackson was Jackson. Steady, reliable, loyal. He'd always been present for her and Cody. When she'd gone missing, he'd never stopped looking for her.

Back then, she'd resented his help, but she'd been a stubborn, hardheaded, stupid kid. She was fourteen years old now, practically a grown-ass woman.

"I'm fine," she said around a big bite, nougat stuck in her teeth. "Better than ever. Life is freaking fantastic."

It was partly true. She felt strong, smart, and capable. After the initial shock of killing a person faded, so did the anxiety and guilt. The nightmares still visited her sometimes, but they were gradually becoming few and far between.

In her favorite dreams, she and Cody dashed through the woods, just the two of them. In her dreams, they could be together forever with no one chasing them, no one hunting them down.

She always woke up sad, automatically reaching for the lock-pick set he'd given her on the nightstand beside her bed. As the remnants of the dream slipped through her fingers, Cody sank further and further away from her, leaving only an incredible ache in her chest, like a permanent bruise.

Grief wasn't a thing you ever finished. It wasn't a task to complete. It was always there, a hole nestled beside your heart, an absence that could never be filled. It became a part of you, scar tissue that disfigured your soul.

Shiloh consumed the last of the candy bar, licked her fingers, and folded the wrapper into a tiny square. She pushed aside the fur cape and shoved it in her overalls pocket for later when she could lick the wrapper clean in private.

Shiloh ran her fingers over the coarse black fur and frowned. Eli had been cagey with her for the last two days. He'd been so busy she'd barely seen him. Lena, too. "I need you to give it to me straight. No one else will."

"What do you want to know?"

"I've heard the rumors. It's all the patrols can talk about. And last night, on my watch shift, we saw the artillery strikes. What happened?" She and Fiona Smith had watched the impressive streaks of light arcing across the sky, like a spectacular-fireworks show, only lethal.

With a reluctant sigh, Jackson leaned forward and rested his elbows on his thighs. "The artillery strikes hit three of the town's four storage depots. We spent the night moving the supplies, but the cartel must've had drones surveilling the town, or else Horatio anticipated my move. I wouldn't put it past him."

"They destroyed our food because they want us to give up."

"They've surrounded Munising, yes."

"There's like thousands of them."

"Not thousands, but a lot."

"More than we have."

"Yes," Jackson admitted.

They were trapped. Cartel armies crouched just out of sight, waiting them out like a lion skulking behind savannah grass, muscles coiled, ready to pounce.

Occasionally, a rifle shot sounded in the distance. Everyone froze or ducked or screamed. Any moment could be the moment it started, the blitz attack they dreaded.

Shiloh shuddered. "Are we doomed?"

Jackson made a face like he regretted his promise to tell the truth. "I hope not. We're going to do everything we can to keep that from happening."

"Yeah, whatever. That's grown-up speak for 'we're screwed twenty ways from Sunday.'"

Jackson rubbed his jaw. "Shiloh—"

"When are these jerkwads gonna get lost?" She pointed at a couple of Sawyer's goons marching toward the latrines. "I hate them."

"They're a necessary evil."

"That's hard to believe."

"Without Sawyer's men and resources to add to our fortifications, the cartel would've already run right through us. It doesn't benefit Gault if he defeats us but loses half his men in the process, men he needs to subdue the other towns and keep them subdued. The cartel is starving us out instead."

"How are we going to stop them?"

"Eli and I are working that out."

"Work faster."

Jackson snorted. "Trust me, we're trying."

Across the meadow, Lena and Eli slipped through the rear double doors of the Inn together. Eli limped only slightly. They were holding hands.

Shiloh's stomach did a weird little flip. She didn't know how she felt about them as a couple. It made her belly strangely fizzy and also a bit grossed out.

Jackson clambered off the picnic table, stretching as his knees popped in protest. "I need to talk to them."

Shiloh seized her crossbow and slung it over her shoulder. "I'll come with you."

Jackson studied her for a second, brows lowered. She stared him down. Gray streaked his beard. Faint lines spiderwebbed the skin around his eyes. His sandy-blond hair curled at his forehead and around his ears. He looked tired. Tired, and incredibly sad.

"Whatever it is, I can handle it," she said, defiant.

"Of that, I have no doubt. I have a feeling you'd tag along even if I said no, so why bother trying to fight you?"

Shiloh shot him a triumphant grin. "You're finally getting it, old man."

42

SHILOH EASTON POPE
DAY ONE HUNDRED AND FORTY-TWO

S hiloh fell into step at Jackson's side. The thick black bear pelt draped across her shoulders, hanging to her ankles, swishing as she walked.

She snapped her fingers at Bear, who was happily rolling in the dirt near the pigpens. He scrabbled to his feet and shook his mud-crusted coat with great enthusiasm. Globs of saliva sprayed from his jowls.

Tail wagging, he bounded to her side and pressed his snout into the palm of her hand as if to say, *hello again*. She petted his silky ears while they made their way across the field.

Eli and Lena stood in the shade with the Brooks near the chicken coops. Chickens ran here and there, pecking at the ground for worms. The roosters strutted and puffed out their chests like they were the kings of the universe. The animal pens stank of chicken poop and dusty straw.

The goat named Faith lay atop the roof of the nearest coop as she perused her domain. Her ears flicking, she bleated a warning at Bear.

Bear, for his part, gave her a wide berth. The Newfie trotted up to the chickens, sniffing at a couple of russet-colored ones with interest. He wanted to make friends, but the jittery chickens thought he was sizing them up for dinner. They scattered in an explosion of fearful squawks and flapping feathers.

Barking in delight, Bear dashed after them. Incensed, Faith leaped from the roof of the chicken coop. She chased after him, bleating in indignation. With a yelp, the dog turned tail and fled.

The adults watched the shenanigans in amusement before returning to their tasks. Lori was bent over the fire pit, an assortment of materials set on the picnic table beside her. She'd spent the morning burning down a fire to gather the fine white ash to make lye. In a separate fire nearby, she cooked animal fat over low heat in a cast iron frying pan to separate the fat from the grease, which would later be added to the lye to create soap.

These days, making homemade soap was an arduous process. People were running out of store-bought shampoo and toothpaste. They'd resorted to baking powder and other natural ingredients for their personal hygiene needs.

Lori straightened and set the poker in the fire pit as Nash and Moreno approached from the cabins. Antoine and Nyx strode toward them from the opposite end of the property.

Nyx walked with her shoulders back and her head high, her eyes flashing a challenge at anyone who dared meet her gaze. Her expression was surly, like she was ready to bite someone's head off at the merest provocation. Shiloh adored her.

"Let's hurry this up," Eli said tersely. "Hart is manning our defenses. We have to return to the front lines as soon as possible."

Tim glanced at Jackson. "Any movement by the cartel?"

Jackson shook his head. "Not since last night. They're digging in for the long haul."

"It's a siege," Shiloh said. "Like in medieval times when armies would surround castles. Or the Siege of Leningrad in World War II. They're going to starve us to death until we surrender or we're too weak to fight, then they'll come charging in and wipe us out."

Eli's jaw twitched. He met Shiloh's gaze. To his credit, he didn't look away or attempt to sugarcoat the truth. "In a nutshell, yes."

Shiloh crossed her arms over her chest. "Meanwhile, we're

trapped in here with a bunch of criminals who might slaughter us in our sleep until we run out of food and start eating our horses and dogs."

Lori made an appalled sound. "I surely hope not."

Tim stepped closer and took her hand in comfort or solidarity, or maybe both. "It won't come to that. Will it?"

Moreno shuffled his feet. Nash chewed on a fingernail and studied the ground like he'd discovered something fascinating in the grass. Antoine and Nyx stood side by side, their flat expressions unreadable.

A terrible thought flashed through Shiloh's mind. "We're not eating Bear. Not ever, no matter what. He's mostly fur anyway. Empty calories."

Lena gave her a strained smile. "We're not eating our pets."

"Not Faith either. She's so ornery, I bet her meat would taste bitter, like chewing on rawhide or something."

"It's truly that bad, isn't it?" Lori asked.

"It will be," Lena said. "And sooner than we think."

"We have a decision to make," Jackson said. "Here at the Inn, we've been storing up food for winter. Due to Lori's excellent preparations and organization skills, we have enough to feed the two hundred fifty or so residents of Northwoods through most of the winter, since we can also ice-fish and bag the occasional moose. Am I correct on that, Lori?"

Lori's features were rigid. "I just completed a thorough inventory of our supplies. Michelle Carpenter and I went through every sack, pallet, and case of MREs, freeze-dried, dehydrated, and canned items organized by type of food. It seems like a lot, but at fifteen hundred calories a day per person, which is a significant deficit, we're barely feeding our own through April."

Shiloh had seen the shelves of food: boxed pasta; buckets of sealed black and pinto beans, lentils, rice, and flour; the jars of peaches, pears, applesauce, and tomato sauce; the pancake mixes, containers of oats, and stacks of homemade granola bars; and dehydrated bear and venison jerky, not to mention the stacks of dried fish.

"What is the town's status?" Tim asked.

"After the artillery attack last night, not good," Eli said. "Horatio knows this town like the back of his hand. He knew our depot locations and even when we moved our supplies in anticipation of such an attack, he managed to use drones to spot our people transferring the supplies. As you know, those depots were attacked with targeted artillery strikes. He didn't target the Inn because he believes correctly that we're keeping some of the meds here, the meds he needs for his wife. Thankfully, we think those were the only artillery Gault had access to, but he's done incredible damage already."

Jackson nodded. "We have two thousand souls in the town. Some have meager provisions stored away in their homes, but certainly not enough to withstand both a siege and the coming winter. With three of the four storage depots destroyed, they have a week of food left, if that."

There was a beat of heavy silence as the gravity of the situation sank in. Shiloh's stomach knotted in dread. She swallowed the lump in her throat.

Jackson turned to Lori. "Hypothetically, how long would our stores last if we spread our resources further?"

"I'd have to examine the numbers again. The total number of calories available divided by the number of people divided by daily caloric needs. It's basic math. The numbers don't lie. The numbers never lie."

"Can you make an educated guess?" Lena asked.

"Off the top of my head, I'd guess a matter of weeks."

"How many weeks?"

"Two. Maybe three, if we're lucky." Lori's voice was raspy, like the rustle of leaves on pavement, dry and brittle. She stood stiffly next to her husband. Her hands were folded protectively in front of her stomach.

"You're suggesting we share our supplies with the town," Tim said.

"I'm laying out the options," Jackson said.

"We would starve through winter," Tim said gravely. "All of us."

"Yes, that is a real possibility. Though if we win this fight, we could potentially steal the cartel's supplies for our people, in which case we would survive both the siege and winter."

"That's a big if," Moreno said in a dubious tone.

"It is," Jackson admitted.

Nyx crossed her arms and raised an eyebrow as she glanced around the group. "Essentially, we're screwed."

"What do you think, Lena?" Lori asked. "We founded this sanctuary, but it has flourished with you here. We're all a part of Northwoods. It belongs to all of us."

"It's not as if Sawyer is gonna share his food supplies with us," Moreno said. "Hell will freeze over before that happens."

Lena glanced at Eli. "I would do almost anything to protect this place and my family, but we have friends and family outside of Northwoods. We all do. These are our neighbors, our townspeople, our friends. If we abandon them now, what does that make us? Can we live with ourselves if we do this?"

"I could," Eli said without hesitation. "I wouldn't like it, but I could."

"Me too," Moreno muttered, his cheeks reddening with shame. Nash said nothing. Nyx and Antoine exchanged strained glances.

Tim squeezed Lori's hand. "What do you want to do?"

"My selfish side says to keep the people I love alive first and foremost. But my heart tells me that the town of Munising is filled with good people who feel the same way. They're doing their best to protect their wives and husbands and sisters and parents and children. They did not ask for this fight."

"We didn't either," Shiloh said.

"The cartel is here because of the things we did, not the townspeople," Lena said. "If we hoard our food for winter and watch innocent people starve, what good are we?"

"What's the good if everyone starves?" Eli said darkly. "Sometimes you have to put the oxygen mask on your face first, otherwise you're in no position to help anyone else."

Shiloh didn't want anyone to starve, but she also wasn't too worried about a bunch of faceless, nameless people she didn't know. Well, Ana Grady the librarian lived in town. Mrs. Grady had taken in Theresa Fleetfoot's baby along with the deaf boy, Adam. Shiloh adored Mrs. Grady.

Still, they were only responsible for themselves, not for everyone else. They couldn't possibly try to keep everyone alive. It was an unimaginable task.

"It's the right thing to do," Lori said in a firm tone. "It's the just thing."

"If we lose the very thing that makes us human, the best of our humanity, then what's the point?" Lena asked.

"Staying alive," Moreno shot back. "Right and wrong is great for philosophy class, but we're trying to survive. We do this, we could all die."

Jackson stepped forward. "Justice is innate, instinctive. It is a moral code written into our DNA. We're not animals eking out a meaningless existence. We're meant for more than this. We *are* more than this."

Moreno frowned. "I'm afraid I know where you're going with this line of thought."

Jackson met his gaze. "The cost will be high. We don't know how high. However, I couldn't live with myself if I abandoned our people to save my own skin. Some things are more important than survival."

Antoine stared at him in surprise. "You really believe that, don't you?"

"I do. And I think you believe it, too. That's why you and Nyx are standing here."

Nyx gave a wry smile. "Lies. We're selfish mercenaries, only out for ourselves."

Antoine's lips curled in mock horror. "If you tell anyone, we'll have to kill you."

"We've been praying," Tim said. "Our favorite Bible verse is in the book of James: 'And what does the Lord require of you? To act justly and to love mercy and to walk humbly with your God.'"

Lori said, "I've spent my life trying to act justly and to be merciful to others, to show love when it is difficult—especially when it's difficult. We've discussed the pros and cons, the moral and ethical arguments, but in the end, I choose to live my faith. If my actions don't back up my words, then as Lena said so eloquently, what good is it? What good am I? To my God, to myself, to the human beings I profess to love. Love must lead us. Love, and mercy."

"Surely not mercy for our enemies," Nash said, incredulous.

Lori gave him a placid smile. "I'm a Christian, not a saint. May God smite our enemies with blood and fire."

"Amen." Tim wrapped his arm around Lori's shoulder and squeezed her close. She leaned into him, the tension in her face easing. It was obvious how much they loved each other, even after a million years together.

Jackson cleared his throat. "Enough with the sentimental speeches. We set this up as a democracy of sorts, so let's do this thing. We have a quorum. It's time to vote."

One by one, hands raised around the loose circle. Every hand went up, even Eli and finally, Moreno. Despite her misgivings, Shiloh raised her hand. Lena gave her an approving smile.

When Lori spoke, her voice was firmer, more assured. "We'll release our food stores, but under strict rations to share our supplies with the townspeople for as long as the siege lasts or until our stores run out."

"We have a few hundred volunteers from the town on our roster," Eli said. "But we will need every citizen on board for this. Everyone can do something to help fight our enemies."

Tim nodded. "The folks that call the UP home are hardy. They'll fight alongside us to defend their homes, I have no doubt."

Soberly, every head nodded around the circle, Shiloh included.

Jackson said, "Then it's decided."

43

SHILOH EASTON POPE
DAY ONE HUNDRED AND FORTY-NINE

One week into the siege, Shiloh was already going stir crazy. She had spent the morning helping Ruby weed one of the greenhouses, not because she loved weeding but because it was increasingly the only way to spend time with her best friend.

Ruby was one of Lori's top helpers. Her green thumb had proven quite useful. She could make anything grow. Plus, she was an excellent cook, whereas Shiloh was clumsy as an ox in the kitchen and avoided it at all costs—except at mealtimes, of course.

Everywhere she looked, veggies peeked from the greenery: zucchini and cucumbers, plump tomatoes, lacy-leafed carrots, and firm onions. Outside the greenhouse, near the pear and apple orchards, rows of tall corn stalks rustled in the breeze coming off the lake.

She resisted the temptation to pop a handful of cherry tomatoes into her mouth to let the juicy tartness explode on her tongue. She longed to fill her empty stomach with something more than her absurdly small ration of oatmeal and runny eggs.

It was infuriating to be surrounded by food you weren't allowed to eat, not to mention profoundly unfair. She found it disconcerting how quickly hunger became an insatiable thing lurking inside you, your stomach transformed into a ravenous monster willing to eat itself, to consume your own flesh to sate that urgent need.

Ruby tossed a pile of weeds into a nearby wheelbarrow. She paused to cough into her fist. A terrible rattling sound came from deep within her chest.

Concern prickled beneath her skin. She took a step closer. "Hey. You okay?"

"Yeah, I'm fine. This smoke, it just gets in my lungs, you know? I guess I'm sensitive to it."

"You and me both."

Shiloh held out her hand. A fine sifting of ash settled on her open palm. A few days ago, Jackson told her the wind had changed direction. It was blowing from the northeast, pushing the wildfire south instead of east, toward them.

Even with the blaze heading further away, the air was a sickly yellowish-red color, a soupy fog that lowered visibility. It was like some dystopian, nuclear-ravaged world five hundred years in the future.

She could taste the acrid scent on her tongue. The ashy air coated the back of her throat and crawled up her nostrils. The incessant coughing and hacking sounds became a staticky background noise like the *boom* of distant gunfire.

If the wildfire changed direction again and jumped the fire-break they'd constructed, evacuation options were limited. The cartel blocked their exit routes. Eli had insisted everyone have bug-out bags packed and ready to go at a moment's notice.

Jackson had ordered the boats in the marina to be readied for a last-ditch emergency evacuation to Grand Island. They would use fishing boats with small outboard motors, rowboats, kayaks, and paddleboards to transport fleeing refugees across the water from the raging fire.

"Would you rather burn or starve to death?" Ruby asked abruptly.

"And you call me dark." Shiloh rubbed her concave belly. Her hipbones were sticking out like weird knobs. "Burned alive, I guess. It'd be faster, at any rate. Honestly, I'm dreaming of goat burgers. I'm a terrible person."

With a laugh, Ruby rubbed her flat stomach beneath her hoodie. "Then we're terrible together. I could eat an entire horse right now, the tail and everything."

Everywhere they turned, danger lay in wait. Death seemed inevitable: a toss-up between starvation, being burned alive, and serving as target practice for the cartel armies.

The game was rigged against them. It was incredibly unfair.

The agonizing waiting game was the worst. It would have to end eventually. Then what would happen?

The big bell near the Inn clanged loudly, announcing lunchtime.

Shiloh's mouth watered like one of Pavlov's dogs. "About freaking time."

They dropped their trowels and gloves into the wheelbarrow, exited the greenhouse, and sprinted for the outdoor food line the Brooks had set up to serve the masses.

Lori and Tim worked with a local nutritionist to determine everyone's approximate caloric needs. The big muscled soldiers and pregnant ladies got larger rations, including more dairy and protein, as did the kids and teenagers who were still growing. Lena and Keagan also received special meals tailored to a diabetic diet.

Every day, the food rations were a variation on the same themes: cucumber and mustard sandwiches on sourdough bread; cornbread slathered with raw honey; baked beans with a sliver of cooked meat like raccoon, squirrel, or fox; thin slabs of large-mouth bass or whitefish coupled with dandelion salads; or chowders made with chunks of trout and potatoes, thickened with powdered milk or acorn powder and sprinkled with canned peas.

Each morning after her midnight security shift, Shiloh checked her deadfall traps for squirrels, gophers, weasels, or foxes. Whatever they could find, they were willing to eat.

Anything she caught was shared with Bear as well as Ruby, Eli, and especially Lena, who desperately needed the protein.

Nothing went to waste. Even the water used to cook meals was recycled into broth for future stews and soups. Animal bones were saved for bone broth soup. Vegetable peels and eggshells were utilized to fertilize the gardens.

As they took their place at the end of the long line, Mrs. Grady waved to them, one hand on the rump of the newborn swaddled to her chest. Though she lived in town, Mrs. Grady came to the Inn daily to help Lori care for the orphaned children.

Miriam Fleetfoot had named her baby sister Hope. Though she helped with the infant, it was Mrs. Grady who carried her around everywhere in a baby carrier. Little Adam trailed after her, looking forlorn.

Mrs. Grady had cooked up an emergency formula made from boiled water and evaporated milk. It was not an ideal long-term solution, but in an emergency, it was keeping baby Hope alive. That's what mattered these days: staying alive.

Ruby looked around, searching the mass of people in line, and frowned. "I don't see my mom in line."

"I'm sure she's around somewhere—" Shiloh halted mid-sentence. She squeezed Ruby's shoulder. "Look who it is."

Traci Tilton and her son Keagan reached the front of the line. Fiona Smith looked down at a clipboard in her hand, then she served them each a bowl of chili from a big pot along with an apple.

Traci hunched her shoulders, her head down like she was warding off a blow. She gripped her son's hand as she led him away from the line toward a picnic table with a family already present.

There was room at the table. But when the mother caught sight of Traci, she scooted across the bench, filling the space. She glared at Traci. She didn't say a word, but her body language telegraphed the message loud and clear—*you're not welcome here.*

Mortified, Traci bowed her head. She tugged her son's hand. They shuffled past the family's picnic table in search of an empty one.

"Serves her right," Shiloh said. Instead of feeling vindicated, something dark and ugly wriggled inside her. She didn't want to examine it too closely.

Traci and her son hurried to the farthest picnic table, which was unoccupied. She set their bowls on the table, then gestured to Keagan to check his blood sugar numbers. Her face was red with humiliation.

While Keagan lifted his shirt to examine his pump, Traci surreptitiously spooned several scoops of her soup into Keagan's bowl. By the time he looked up, she was seated and eating her own meager serving.

"You think you'll ever forgive her?" Ruby asked.

That familiar spiky anger flared through her veins. "She doesn't deserve it. She deserves to die a horrible death. She should be tied up, slathered with honey, and eaten alive by fire ants."

"You don't mean that."

Shiloh thought of Lena being kidnapped and dragged into the bowels of the abandoned mine. How close she'd come to losing her. Her chest tightened like it was being squeezed by a giant unseen hand. "I very much do."

"Seems like a lot of hatred to carry around."

"I don't care."

"I mean, she's starving herself to keep her son fed. Look at her. Even through her clothes, you can see the divots in her collarbones, the lines of her ribs, even her hipbones, for Pete's sake."

"I can see all those things on you too, Ruby," Shiloh snapped, suddenly irritated. She couldn't articulate why. "Just because she's a good mom doesn't make her a good person."

"Maybe it makes her not all that evil, either."

"Whatever."

"I'm just saying, maybe it wouldn't be all bad to try and understand her side of things."

"Trying to understand some people is like trying to pick up a turd by the clean end."

Ruby snorted. "You don't have to be so sarcastic all the time."

"What's wrong with sarcasm? I love sarcasm. It's like punching someone in the face but with words."

Ruby barked out a laugh.

"It's incredibly satisfying. You should try it sometime."

They moved forward a few spots in line. Shiloh shuffled her feet, bored and anxious. "Whose side are you on, anyway?"

"Yours. Always yours."

Shiloh sniffed. "Damn straight."

A commotion started at the front of the line, drawing their attention. Fiona Smith was shouting and flailing her arms, pointing angrily. "You took two helpings!" Fiona accused the huge man standing on the opposite side of the serving table. "That's stealing!"

Shiloh recognized Pierce. He was big and imposing and relished intimidating everyone into cowering compliance. He loomed over Fiona, all aggression and restrained violence. A bowl of chili was clutched in each ham-sized fist.

Fiona stood tall and refused to back down. "Put it back."

"I'm the one keeping you little princesses safe and sound in your beds. I need energy to do that."

"So do we," Fiona insisted. Her eyes flashed with indignance. "There are rules to follow."

Pierce leered at her. "Those rules don't apply to us, little girl."

Shiloh reached for the crossbow slung across her back, about to march over and give that arrogant asshat a piece of her mind. He might be the size of a rhinoceros, but she was too livid to care.

A hand on her wrist restrained her. "There's a time and place," Ruby cautioned her. "This isn't it."

"You sound just like the rest of the adults."

"Think it through. If you get in Pierce's face, you're forcing a showdown. He can't back down out of pride and you won't back down out of stubbornness. He'll hurt you."

"He can damn well try," Shiloh muttered. "I'll deball him with a rusty spoon."

"Or maybe he breaks a few of your bones with his pinkie finger, big shot."

"Eli would string him up by his bowels for everybody to see."

Ruby made a face. "Exactly. And then Sawyer retaliates, and everything Jackson is trying to do goes up in flames. We implode from the inside. The cartel mops the floor with us. Ergo, everyone dies."

Shiloh grunted in annoyance. Much as she abhorred the idea, Ruby had a valid point. "You suck."

Ruby lowered her voice. "You know Jackson and Eli will take care of this their way. Less...publicly. Trust them."

"You disgust me sometimes with your asinine logic."

Ruby pretended to curtsy. "Glad to be of service."

They returned their attention to the altercation at the front of the line. Pierce was looming over Fiona. He raked her with a contemptuous glare. "I'm not asking again. Get the hell out of my way."

Fiona hesitated, as if debating whether to argue further. Her gaze dropped to the pistols at his hip, the combat blade strapped to one muscular thigh. Fiona stepped back and allowed him to pass.

Pierce kept his double helping of chili and stormed off. No one attempted to stop him. Everyone watched him depart with equal parts fear and loathing.

Shiloh cursed under her breath. "Jackson thinks we can all sing kumbaya and get along like we're at summer camp. It's a fantasy. People are already turning on each other. This is gonna blow up in his face."

"There's nothing we can do about it," Ruby said.

That was the part Shiloh despised the most. "Not yet."

44

JACKSON CROSS
DAY ONE HUNDRED AND FIFTY-SIX

J ackson studied the playing cards in his hand and laid down a Jack of Clubs on the pile of cards in the center of the picnic table. "Beat that!"

He and Lena had played several rounds of two-handed Euchre, a popular card game in the UP where jacks were high, and the favorable suit could change with every hand. They used to play as kids all the time.

Lena had won the last five tricks. Not surprising.

Since phones, iPads, and the internet were out of commission, people had returned to old-fashioned games like Euchre, Rummy, and Cribbage to pass the time in the evenings after their chores were finished.

The act of playing a familiar game eased a bit of the tension. It was a temporary distraction from the war outside their doorstep and the hunger gnawing their bellies.

Bear snored at their feet, stretched out on his side. He'd lost weight, too; the outline of his ribs showed through his thick fur. Jackson had caught Shiloh and Lena sneaking the dog scraps from their rations, which neither could afford to do.

Yesterday, Bear had gone after one of the precious chickens. Dana Lutz had threatened to eat Bear for dinner, which had nearly devolved into a knock-down, drag-out fight with Shiloh. Luckily, the crisis had been averted. They hadn't let the dog out of their sight since.

With a triumphant grin, Lena laid down the "high bower," the Jack of Spades, which was the most valuable card. She'd just won the bid—and the game. "I believe that's ten points, sucker."

Jackson groaned. "I give up."

The sun sank over the bluff, setting water and sky ablaze. Ribbons of burnt orange, coppery red, and grapefruit pink streaked the horizon. The colors were brilliant even through the constant haze of smoke from the wildfire.

Jackson shuffled the cards. The distant boom of automatic weapons fire sounded. The cartel regularly unleashed a barrage of lead at sundown to flex their power, a reminder meant to terrorize and demoralize the citizens of Munising.

Over the last two weeks, several skirmishes had broken out along the defensive lines, a few shots fired here, a grenade lobbed there. A few of Munising's volunteer fighters had been injured. A man in his seventies had been hit in the thigh by a ricochet and bled out.

Each time, Eli managed to reign in the fighters itching for vengeance. The tense standoff continued for another day, then another and another.

Two weeks. Two weeks of hell and hunger.

Jackson had tried to garner aid. He'd sent SOS messages to the Michigan governor in Lansing through their Ham radio. He'd managed to sneak two scouts out of Munising via the water, sending them west along the coastline to Au Train before cutting to shore. They had gone south on ATVs on Highway 41 through Rapid River to the southern shoreline of the UP to avoid the cartel until they'd reached Mackinac Bridge.

It took them almost a week to make it to the Governor's Office, only to be turned away. No aid would be forthcoming from the remnants of the Army Air National Guard, who were otherwise engaged in battling gangs for control of Detroit, Lansing, and Grand Rapids.

The governor had refused artillery or air support or even air drops of food and ammunition. Other than the Soo Locks, which they'd already lost, whatever tattered government remained in Michigan had deemed the Upper Peninsula as nonessential territory. The governor had officially abandoned everyone who called this rugged wilderness home.

Lena let out a hoarse cough as she adjusted the handkerchief wrapped over her face and nose. They'd run out of N95 masks last week.

According to their drone surveillance, the wildfire had spread east into Chatham, then further southeast, burning deep into the Hiawatha National Forest. It could potentially reach as far south as Manistique. Fortunately, the wind had changed from a southwesterly to a northwesterly direction. If it stayed on this heading, it would miss Munising.

"How much food do we have left?" Jackson asked.

"Two days, at most," Lena said.

His heart sank. Even with rationing, they were down to a thousand calories a day. A dull headache throbbed at the back of his head. Waves of dizziness rolled through him when he stood, his thoughts slow and fuzzy. And he was hungry, always hungry.

They were starving. It wouldn't be long before no one would have the energy to fight. He feared someone would open the gates and let the enemy inside just to end their misery.

"When are we going to tell people?" Lena asked.

"We aren't. It would cause a mass panic. People would be fighting in the food line, they'd slaughter what animals we have left."

Lena put on a brave front for everyone else, but he saw the naked fear in her eyes. She couldn't hide her true feelings from him. They'd been friends for too long.

"How are you doing?" he asked gently.

"I can't sleep. I have nightmares. With every patient I lose, it gets worse. My mind keeps spinning with all the things I should have done, all the ways we could have saved them if only we'd had anesthesia, electricity, actual surgeons, a hundred different things."

"You'll get through this. You're strong, Lena. You're a survivor."

She stared at him like she wasn't seeing him, not really. "I don't feel strong. I'm scared every minute of every day. I can't lose you or Eli. I can't lose Shiloh. I don't know what I would do. The thought terrifies me."

"What makes you strong isn't fearlessness, but that you keep going despite the fear."

She nodded numbly, but he could tell she was far from placated. Pretty words sounded good, but reality was something else altogether. They were surrounded, trapped, about to be annihilated. He knew it as well as she did.

"Are you sure you're eating enough?"

"I'm fine." Lena rubbed her eyes. Her pants were baggy, sliding down her hips even with a belt. He eyed the sharpness of her cheekbones with concern. Her face was thin, too thin.

She didn't like people worrying about her, but he made a mental note to talk with Eli. Surely, the kitchen could spare a few more calories for a diabetic. Lena would never ask for special treatment for herself, but she needed it.

She cocked her head, listening to the cartel's nightly barrage, and shuddered. Beneath the picnic table, Bear whined uneasily in his sleep. She reached down and patted his head. He whoofed, his paws quivering like he was fleeing something terrible in his dreams.

"When are you going to tell Devon?" she asked abruptly.

Jackson blinked. "Tell Devon what?"

"That you love her."

Jackson gaped at her. "How—what?"

Lena's lips twitched in the hazy moonlight. "I know you better than anyone on the planet. Trust me, I know."

When he thought of Devon, his heart flipflopped between

desire and guilt. They'd barely spoken since Devon had laid her heart on the line. He'd royally screwed things up. They'd discussed the cartel, security, food rations, and defenses, but they hadn't cleared the air between them. Jackson wasn't sure how.

"You like her," Lena said.

"I—I do. But with everything that's happening..."

Lena leaned across the table and grasped his hand. "Don't let something this good pass you by. Anything worth having in this dumpster fire is worth going after with your whole heart. You deserve happiness, however fleeting, however long it lasts."

"You should've been a therapist."

"Close enough." Lena gave a rueful smile as she lit the oil lamp they'd brought with them. Jackson put the cards back in the box and tucked the box into his pocket.

Night had fallen. The thick haze obscured the stars. Cold darkness pressed in on them. The lamplight cast wavering shadows across their faces.

Lena shivered and drew her jacket tighter around herself. "You're carrying a heavy burden, Jackson. After Astrid, I thought it would go away, but it's still there. You're still haunted."

"It's my family. My father, my brother. What they've done. What they're doing now."

"You aren't responsible for your family."

"I am."

"Your family has had a terrible hold on you your entire life, but not anymore. I can see it in you, Jackson. You're changing. You've changed."

He felt it, somewhere deep inside him, that steely resolve taking hold, an iron hardness in his soul. He was not the man he had been even a month ago. "Maybe you're right."

"There's only one way this ends." He glanced at her out of the corner of his eye. The kind, gentle Lena he'd known his whole life had another side to her. This Lena was sharper, harder. "You're going to have to kill your father. And your brother."

Dread scythed through him. He felt torn down to his soul. The thought was a dark, unformed shadow lurking at the back of his mind, skulking in the corners. It was on him to put things right.

In a world of anarchy, there was one path to justice.

"I know," he said soberly.

Lena held Jackson's hand, her eyes bright and luminous in the moonlight. "You'll be the one to end it. And then, finally, you'll truly be free."

45

SHILOH EASTON POPE
DAY ONE HUNDRED AND SIXTY-NINE

Thick mud squelched between Shiloh's toes and squished beneath her bare feet. The brackish water was icy-cold but nothing like the frigid depths of Lake Superior.

Shiloh and Ruby had spent the morning harvesting the cattails in the marsh along with Dana Lutz, Fred Combs, and Mrs. Grady. Miriam Fleetfoot, baby Hope, and her grandfather Ira were with them as well.

Weeks ago, when Lori had pointed out the edible wild vegetation, Shiloh had considered it an interesting but ultimately useless endeavor. Why eat grass when you can hunt and fish?

But most living creatures had been hunted and fished from the Northwoods property and beyond, even the squirrels. She was thankful she'd hidden some black bear jerky to feed Bear, though he still chased the chickens, damn him.

Now here she was, three weeks into starvation mode, greedily digging up cattails for dinner. They'd been reduced to eating acorns and hazelnuts and consuming dandelions and weeds.

Of course, raw acorns were bitter and contained tannins which were toxic to humans and animals alike, but Lori was teaching them how to leach the tannins once the acorns were ripe and brown. They were edible—barely. Same with the cattails.

The fuzzy cattail reminded her of a caterpillar. Supposedly, you could make flour out of the starchy center part of the stalk. Lori wanted the cattail flour for making pancakes, baking casseroles, thickening stews and soups, and to create tortillas. The cattail flour could also be used to make Eli's favorite fry bread.

Shiloh scrunched her nose. "This is utterly disgusting."

Her stomach growled constantly. Thoughts of food consumed nearly every thought. All day long, she fantasized about Moe's Homewrecker burritos slathered in sour cream and guacamole, or a juicy burger and hot crispy fries from Five Guys. Her traitorous mouth watered.

Shiloh clenched her jaw to keep her teeth from chattering as she worked. As September gave way to October, the days grew chillier, and the nights were downright cold. The haze from the distant wildfires tinged the air a sickly yellow.

Shiloh tossed another cattail into the burlap sack before pausing to study her friend. Ruby had been uncharacteristically quiet all day. Mud smudged her right cheek. She bent over, fumbled in the water, and dug around for the roots.

"You okay?" she asked.

Ruby shrugged her narrow shoulders. "I'm fine."

"No, you're not. Talk to me."

Ruby blinked rapidly. She wiped her filthy hands on her overalls and straightened. "It's my mom. She won't leave our cabin. She's missed her kitchen and trash duty shifts for the last three days. I don't know what to do."

"Is she sick?"

"Kind of."

Shiloh fished beneath the water, grasped the cattail by the roots and wrestled it out of the marsh. She lobbed it into the sack. "What does that mean?"

"It's happened before. More than once. After my dad died... she kind of, like, went away? She'd be there physically but not her mind. She'd forget to buy groceries, pay the electric bill, or make dinner. She'd lay in bed all day and couldn't get up. It's one of the reasons I ran away from home, before... before everything."

Ruby bit her lower lip, regret in her face. "She's okay when she's on her meds. But without them..."

"Can Lena get her the medication she needs? I can talk to her."

"I already did. She doesn't have any lithium."

"Oh," Shiloh said, chagrined. She hadn't realized Michelle Carpenter was bipolar. Her heart ached for her friend. "I'm sorry."

Ruby shrugged, not meeting her gaze. "Not your fault."

A series of loud barks drew their attention. Short, vicious barks —a warning.

Shiloh went rigid. "That's Bear! He doesn't bark like that without a good reason. Something's wrong. Come on!"

She stuffed the last cattail into the burlap sack and lugged it out of the murky water. Silt squished between her toes as she dragged it up the bank and set it next to the five sacks that they'd collected that morning.

Leaving everything but the crossbow, Shiloh and Ruby sprinted up the hill from the marsh. Shiloh's legs felt heavy and slow. She was lightheaded, her stomach a gnarled knot. She blinked away white spots as they followed the dirt path through the trees. They burst into the clearing near the goat pens.

Five of Sawyer's goons stood in a loose circle in front of the goat pen. They wore camo and military gear with chest rigs and long rifles slung across their broad chests.

Bear stood growling in front of the latched gate. He snarled, his hackles raised. Usually a gentle giant, she hadn't seen him this fierce since the black bear incident two months ago.

"Get away from my dog!" Without thinking, Shiloh sprinted ahead of Ruby and forced herself between the mercenaries and the Newfoundland. The dog was clearly guarding the goats from these asshats. Bear might be terrified of Faith, but he was protecting her with every ounce of ferocity he could muster.

The mercenaries kept their distance and stared warily at Bear. He was a big dog. His black jowls pulled back to reveal fangs sharp enough to bite a man's face clean off. It was easy to forget how intimidating he could be.

"Get rid of your damn dog," Pierce ordered. "Or we'll do it for you."

"Were you born this stupid or did you take lessons?" Shiloh snapped. "Get lost!"

The mercenary next to Pierce was in his late twenties with a buzzed head and a sparse beard. He spat on the ground. "We're hungry. We need to eat. We can do whatever we want whether you like it or not."

"You're not killing the goats. I don't have the time nor the crayons to explain this to you. They give us precious milk and cheese. The meat would be gone in a day—"

"I don't give a damn," Pierce interrupted. "We're taking the goats. They're ours now. I'm not gonna tell you again, little girl. Get out of the way or suffer the consequences."

Shiloh stood her ground beside Bear, defiant and thrumming with fury. She seized the crossbow grip, her knuckles white. She hadn't pointed her crossbow at Pierce yet but so help her, she would.

Shiloh glanced around wildly for backup, to no avail. No one else was near the goat pens. The closest security patrol had passed by ten minutes ago and wouldn't return for another twenty minutes. Those not on guard duty were too busy scavenging, hunting, or preparing what little food remained.

Eli and Jackson were gone defending the town, while Lena was at the hospital, and Tim and Lori were busy in the Northwoods kitchen.

Shiloh and Ruby were on their own.

Pierce took a menacing step toward her, his hand on his rifle grip, finger twitching against the trigger guard. "Call off your mutt before I squash you both like bugs."

"This is Eli Pope's daughter," Ruby said bravely. "You better not touch her or you'll answer to him."

Pure hatred flashed in Pierce's flat gaze. "I don't care whose kid you are. One snap of my fingers and I could make you both disappear. They'd never even find your bones."

And yet, a hint of hesitation flickered in his face. Pierce was a brute, but he wasn't an imbecile. He knew Eli Pope would destroy anyone who dared harm a hair on his daughter's head.

Pierce took another step toward her anyway, as if he were so angry—or so hungry—that he no longer cared about potential consequences. There was less than ten feet between them.

Bear lowered his head and snarled.

Shiloh tightened her grip and raised her crossbow.

"I wouldn't do that," a male voice said.

Shiloh turned as Jason Anders and Fiona Smith strode down the path toward them. They'd come from the direction of the Inn. Jason carried an axe. Fiona's pistol sat snug on her hip, and she held a coiled rope low at her side.

"Stand down, Shiloh," Jason said.

Shiloh glared at him. "Traitor."

"He's right." Fiona moved to Shiloh's side. She lowered her voice. "Lori told us to come. She said it was time."

Shiloh recoiled. It felt like being smacked in the solar plexus with a baseball bat. It was suddenly difficult to breathe. "No!"

"We have to keep up our strength. The fighters need calories. And protein." Fiona's face was bone-white beneath her freckles. She didn't like this, either. "I'm sorry."

Jason looked like he couldn't care less. He leaned nonchalantly against the fence post, swinging the axe back and forth. "It's just a stupid goat or two. They're dumb animals."

"About as dumb as you are." Contempt seethed through Shiloh's veins. It took every ounce of her self-control not to raise her crossbow and shoot someone through the teeth. Ruby's presence restrained her natural impulses. Plus, Bear might get hurt in a knock-down, drag-out fight.

One of the thugs burst into cackling laughter. Pierce didn't laugh; he studied her like she was a bug beneath a microscope, a bug he intended to smush.

Shiloh swore at him.

Jason shot her a stern look. "Somebody should wash your mouth out with soap."

"Come try it and see what happens. I guarantee you'll lose a few body parts." She lowered her gaze to his crotch area and fluttered her eyelashes, offering him an evil grin. "At least one, anyway."

A muscle ticked in Jason's clenched jaw, but he managed to reign in his temper. "This is happening," he said. "Move out of the way."

Nausea churned in her stomach. She was unsteady on her feet from hunger. Infuriated, her tense gaze shifted from Jason and Fiona to Pierce and his thugs. Their faces were hollowed out, their features sharpened, their sunken eyes dulled from lack of nourishment.

It wasn't merely the chill in the air that raised goosebumps on her flesh. She couldn't ignore their gauntness or her own, how her body was gradually consuming itself.

The food had run out. Sawyer's men had stolen some of it, she was sure, but it was gone now. The adults hadn't admitted to anything, but she recognized the dismay in their faces, the dread and fear.

The truth was, they were all starving.

"Shiloh," Ruby said in a small, defeated voice.

The fight leaked out of her. She wanted to argue with them, to fight and rage, but it was pointless. Her insides deflated like a balloon stuck with a pin. "Not Faith."

Fiona nodded. "We can work with that."

Shiloh glared at Jason. "Never Faith. You understand?"

Jason sneered. "Not yet, anyway."

She wanted to smash the sneer right off his stupid face—preferably with something sharp, like an axe. Instead, she bent and whispered soothing words in Bear's ear, stroking his back to smooth his hackles.

Grasping his collar, she forced herself to step aside. Though

Bear outweighed her by a good fifty pounds, he obeyed her command, albeit still growling his evident displeasure.

Jason and Fiona entered the gate. With an irate snort, Faith rushed at them, lowering her horns and threatening to headbutt Jason. Shiloh's heart swelled with pride. What a damn fine goat.

Jason waved his axe, cursing at her. Faith had the common sense to trot out of his reach.

Bleating in annoyance, the goat clambered to the top of the shed roof. She glowered down at them from her high perch. Her ribs were visible beneath her ratty white coat.

Pierce and his thugs stood around practically drooling at the thought of fresh meat. They weren't interested in doing the dirty work themselves, but they'd be first in line for dinner, that was for sure.

Shiloh forced herself to watch as Fiona and Jason wandered about the pen and chose four of the largest, fattest goats. They tied ropes around their necks and led them to the back of the property behind one of the sheds, so the little kids wouldn't see the goats slaughtered.

The children wouldn't know the stringy cubes of meat in their stew tonight had come from a spotted goat named Sally, or old Gus with the long gray beard, or Merigold with the gimp leg and tendency to eat candy wrappers.

Maybe they'd be too hungry to care.

"Go run to your daddy, little girl," Pierce said.

His cronies laughed. Bear growled.

Shiloh refused to be cowed, not by the likes of Pierce. She jutted her chin. "I'd slap you, but that'd be animal abuse."

Pierce curled his lip scornfully. "Pope won't be around to protect you forever."

"Shiloh." Ruby grasped her free hand and squeezed. "Let's just go."

Shiloh gave Pierce the middle finger before turning away, her eyes stinging. She kept her grip on Bear's collar. She hated this feeling, despised the sob threatening to crawl up her throat and escape from behind her clenched teeth.

Not even Ruby's hand in hers could soothe her or make her feel better. There was no better, only this endless, agonizing wait that never ended.

Waiting to live. Waiting to die.

Shiloh felt Pierce's greedy eyes on her the whole way back to the marsh.

46

SHILOH EASTON POPE
DAY ONE HUNDRED AND SIXTY-NINE

The next day, Ruby begged Shiloh to come with her to check on her mother.

Shiloh followed Ruby into the cabin. The screen door slapped behind them.

They stood in the darkness for a moment, blinking to adjust their eyes. The stink of sour sweat and something dank struck Shiloh in the face. She recoiled from the stench and covered her mouth and nose with one hand.

Ruby took a tentative step into the cabin. "Mom?"

A low moan emanated from deep within the one-room cabin. Michelle Carpenter lay curled on the mattress on the floor in the far corner. The blackout curtain was drawn over the single window. Clothes spilled from a couple of suitcases stashed in the corner.

"I can't," she mumbled. "I can't do it."

"Can't do what, Mom?" Ruby asked.

Mrs. Carpenter raised her head from the sweat-stained pillow like her skull weighed a thousand pounds. Deep circles ringed her bloodshot eyes. Her face was smeared with tears and snot, her hair a wild corona around her head. In the shadows, she almost appeared possessed.

Her eyes glittered, wide and unblinking. "We're going to die terrible, horrible, painful deaths. We're trapped. Death is coming for us and there's no escape."

Ruby gaped at her mother. "You can't mean that, Mom."

"I can't bear it another second. I tried. For you Ruby, I tried, but it's too much. It's too overwhelming. I can't anymore."

"You're okay, Mom," Ruby said. "You'll be okay."

Mrs. Carpenter pressed her fingers into her temples, digging her fingernails against her skin. She moaned and beat at her skull like she could knock the bad thoughts out of her mind.

If only that was the way it worked.

"We're going to die," she mumbled. "Everyone is going to die."

"No, we aren't," Ruby said, though she knew no such thing.

A part of Shiloh was furious with Mrs. Carpenter. She was a grown-up. She was supposed to have her act together, but if Shiloh had learned anything after the solar flares, it was this: the adults were as scared as she was. And she was scared spitless.

At the same time, a surge of pity welled in her chest. Mrs. Carpenter was in tremendous pain. Worse, she had lost hope. Shiloh saw it in the dulled emptiness behind her eyes. She had succumbed to despondency.

The cartel wasn't the most dangerous thing. Nor was the raging wildfire or the hunger gnawing at their bellies, or the lack of electricity or clean water or hospitals—the true enemy was despair.

They had lost other people not to disease or injury but to this terrible, all-consuming depression. Their minds had broken. There was nothing anyone could do to bring them back from the brink.

Shiloh was too obstinate to give up. As long as you held onto hope, you could fight. You got up no matter how many times you'd been knocked down. You could endure anything, survive anything. But not like this.

"I can't do it anymore," Mrs. Carpenter said. Her words were thick and bleary. "It's too hard. I just can't. I'm sorry. I'm so sorry."

Ruby crossed the tiny room and knelt beside the mattress. She stroked her mother's shoulder to comfort her. "Don't be sorry. You can hang on, Mom. Please, for me."

"I've failed you and I am sorry, baby girl...I love you... I've loved you since...the day you were born."

Ruby gazed at her mother in dismay. "Why are you talking like this? Get up! Get up, Mom!"

Mrs. Carpenter's eyes rolled into the back of her head. Her eyelids fluttered closed. Drool dribbled from the corners of her cracked lips. She muttered something but Shiloh couldn't make out the words.

"I think she took something," Shiloh said.

Ruby leaned over the mattress, feeling beneath her mother's ribs and under the sweat-soaked sheets. She shoved her hand beneath the pillow and yanked out a prescription bottle.

Ruby shook it. It was empty. She looked at her mother in horror. "What did you do?"

Ice water ran through Shiloh's veins. The numbness started in the center of her belly and spread through her limbs. "What pills did she take?"

Ruby examined the bottle. "Pain pills or something. Narcotics prescribed to someone else. Where did you get these, Mom? Who gave them to you?"

Anger sparked through her veins. "Sawyer. Sawyer did this. He gave her the pills, I know it. Him or one of his stupid goons."

Ruby's mother had gone very still and pale.

Ruby shook her. She didn't respond.

Ruby begged, "Please, you can't give up! I need you."

"I think she's unconscious," Shiloh said.

"Get Lena!" Ruby cried.

Shiloh bent and touched Ruby's arm. "I don't think—"

"I said, get Lena! Now! We need to pump her stomach or something! Lena will know how to save her!" Ruby's voice rose an octave. She was shaking, frantic, trying desperately to yank herself free of Shiloh's grasp. "Let me go!"

Shiloh held on tight. "She doesn't want to be saved."

"No! Don't you dare say that! You can't say that!"

Shiloh bit her lip. She pressed her free hand against her concave belly, her fingertips spread across her hipbones. This morning, Eli had cut new notches in one of his belts to hold up her sagging pants, which she'd already downsized two weeks ago.

Even starving, she would gladly surrender an entire platter of barbecue chicken or a whole tray of chicken nuggets to rewind the clock and stop this, to save Mrs. Carpenter from herself.

It was too late. She'd spent enough time with Lena treating patients to recognize when someone was dying. There was no bringing a person back from the cliff once they'd fallen. Or jumped. "You have to let her go, Ruby."

"No! Mom!" Ruby collapsed, half on top of the mattress, half on top of her mother. "She's not breathing...she's not...she's..."

Ruby didn't finish her sentence. She didn't need to.

Shiloh knelt on the plank floor and held Ruby close as she wept and screamed. All she could do was hold onto her dearest friend and refuse to let go.

47

LENA EASTON

DAY ONE HUNDRED AND SIXTY-NINE

It was late evening by the time Lena tracked down Shiloh. She found her at the back of the meadow, near the animal pens where Eli had set up a field with haybales and hand-drawn paper targets nailed to tree trunks.

Shiloh stood thirty yards from a set of targets, her feet spread in a shooting stance, spine straight, crossbow snug against the crook of her shoulder. Her cheek pressed against the stock, the fiberglass bolt nocked and ready to fly.

Lena watched as Shiloh fired. The bolt flew straight and true. It lodged quivering in the center circle of the bull's eye. After reloading, she shifted to the right, aimed at a second target fifty yards distant, and nailed the bull's eye yet again.

"You're getting really good."

Shiloh didn't bother looking at her. "I've always been good."

Lena smiled. "Touche."

She rubbed her sore biceps. Dr. Virtanen had insisted she take a shift off. Instead of resting, Lena had volunteered to drill holes in dozens of maple trees with a spile, a hollow metal tube that dripped sap into a bucket hung on a hook.

Now that the nights were below freezing, with most days still in the forties, they'd begun tapping the maple trees for sap, a process called maple-sugaring.

Fall tapping wasn't as good as in the spring, as the sap contained a lower sugar content, but they could still gather enough sap to boil. Once boiled, the sap condensed into maple syrup. Just the thought of the sweet calories made Lena's mouth water.

Calories were calories; right now, they were desperate for anything, and these days, maple syrup made a meal fit for a king.

Lena watched Shiloh hit several more targets, then waited for Shiloh to retrieve the bolts. "You've been out here by yourself for a long time."

"Gotta stay sharp. Never know when I'm gonna have to shoot some jerkwad."

She wasn't wrong. But Lena could see something wounded in her face. Her niece was out here for more than target practice. She was like Eli that way, keeping the dark, bitter, ugly things locked up deep inside.

"You don't have to be so strong all the time," Lena said gently. "I'm right here to help you carry that burden. You don't need to carry it alone."

Shiloh went rigid, either startled or wary, she wasn't sure which. A memory flashed through her mind: that first night she'd met Shiloh after Eli and Jackson had rescued her from Walter Boone's cabin. The terrified girl had hovered at the edge of the woods, gripping that crossbow like it was the only thing that could save her.

"Shiloh, please. Talk to me."

Shiloh's arms sagged. She lowered the crossbow and let it fall listless to her side. She gazed down at the ground. Her eyes were shiny and red-rimmed. "Ruby's mom killed herself."

It had been two days since Lena had found them in Michelle Carpenter's darkened cabin. "I know."

"Ruby is an orphan now. She has nobody."

"She has you."

"It's not fair."

"No, it's not."

"After everything she's already been through, she shouldn't have to lose anyone else."

"But she did. And she will. Just like you will, too. Everyone dies, Shiloh. No one gets out of here alive. Loss is part of the bargain."

Shiloh squeezed her eyes tightly closed. Wetness glistened at her eyelashes. Even in the twilight, Lena could see the pain etching her features.

Lena stepped closer. She reached out, gently took the crossbow from Shiloh's limp fingers, and set it against a nearby fallen log.

Chickens squawked in the distance. Bear must be chasing them again. Lena would have to go rescue him before someone got upset, but not yet. Shiloh needed her here.

"I can't—I can't lose anyone else." Shiloh's chest rose and fell in rapid panting breaths, her throat hitching like she was holding back tears. "I can't."

Lena took another step closer. Shiloh was fairly vibrating with emotions, with grief and fear, anger and dread. Her muscles were rigid with the effort to hold herself together. Her heart squeezed with tender affection for this brave, fierce girl she loved dearly.

"I'm going to hug you now. Please don't stab me."

Shiloh made a choking sound, but Lena was gathering Shiloh into her arms, pulling her tight against her chest. "You are a survivor, and you will survive this, you and Ruby, together. You can survive anything. You will."

Shiloh allowed herself to sink into Lena's embrace. Four months ago, she never would've allowed this moment of vulnerability, of raw fear and sorrow. She was changing, transforming, no longer a scared little kid but not an adult yet, either. She hovered somewhere in-between.

Shiloh blew out her breath, the warm air crystallizing in the cold. Her voice came out in a strangled whisper. "I...I miss my mom."

"So do I, honey. So do I."

"And Cody."

Lena squeezed her tighter. She was too thin, all sharp bony points, wiry muscle, and no softness. Worry congealed in her empty belly. Shiloh was wasting away in front of her eyes. They all were.

Shiloh twisted around in her arms so she could look up into Lena's face. "What if you die? What if Eli dies? Or Ruby or Jackson?"

"I can't promise you that won't happen."

Shiloh managed a pained smirk. "Anyone tell you that you give terrible pep talks?"

Despite it all, despite her dizziness and hunger, the ever-present threats of starvation and death by extreme violence, she found herself smiling. "All the time."

Bear barked again, closer now. Lena could make out his burly shape near the kitchen entrance, where he was likely begging for scraps. A larger, taller shape crouched next to him. She recognized the familiar form of Eli. He was probably feeding Bear more dried fish sticks to save the poor chickens.

Lena's stomach rumbled painfully. She forced herself to ignore the thought of food and focused on her niece. She squeezed the girl's narrow shoulders.

"I love you, Shiloh Easton Pope. I'll tell you that every single day. No matter what happens, my love for you is right here." Lena tapped Shiloh's chest. "And not just my love, but Eli's and Jackson's, Ruby's, the Brooks', Ana Grady's and Moreno's—everyone who cares about you. You carry their love forever. Their love will give you the strength you need to get through anything. Okay?"

Shiloh cleared her throat. "Okay."

Lena gazed intently into Shiloh's eyes. She needed to make sure the girl heard her and comprehended her words. Words seemed utterly useless in the face of imminent death, but words were all she had. "I can't promise I'll live forever, but I can promise

I'll fight for you to my last breath. I promise I'll never give up on us, not for one second, no matter what happens."

"Me too," Shiloh whispered. She swiped fiercely at the tears sparkling in her eyelashes and pretended to cough. "Must be allergies or something."

"Must be." Lena squeezed Shiloh's shoulder again. "Come on. You need some rest. Let's go find our people."

48

ELI POPE

DAY ONE HUNDRED AND SEVENTY-THREE

"The raids are failing," Jackson said.

"I know." Eli stared across the field where several dozen pairs of fighters squared off, practicing hand-to-hand combat as Eli had taught them. Grunts and groans echoed in the cold morning air.

It was just after eight a.m. Heavy cloud cover mingled with the familiar smoky haze obscured the sun. The air was thick; it felt like inhaling dust, or ash.

"We lost two more fighters last night," Jackson said.

Eli suppressed a wince. Guilt pricked him. For more than three weeks, he'd directed regular raids outside of the wire to attack the cartel's depots of food, water, and ammunition. Small teams would sneak through the defensive perimeter in the middle of the night and hit any supply truck they could find. Then they'd run for their lives.

Each time had been more fraught than the last.

"I have more bad news," Jackson said.

"Spit it out, man."

"The wildfire. Dana Lutz says it's shifted direction. Some kind of storm on Lake Michigan pushing the hot air north. It's heading toward us again."

Eli cursed. "How far?"

"I don't know, but close."

"We'll deal with it later. Right now, we've got to—"

"I have a report, sir," said a breathless voice behind them.

"You're back early," Jackson said.

Drew Stewart hurried up to them. Sweat plastered his hair to his forehead as if he'd been running for miles. Though young, Drew had turned out to be an excellent scout. He had a good eye for detail, could remain still and quiet for hours, and had learned to sneak close to the enemy without being detected.

Three days ago, the Northwoods scouts had started picking up massive activity at the cartel's staging areas. For several days, they had watched the cartel amass troops and supplies—even more than those camped along the town's perimeter.

Drew paused to catch his breath. Jackson handed him a bottle of freshly sanitized water. He gulped it down before giving his report. "They've been building something for days. I couldn't get close enough to make out what it was, but then, yesterday afternoon, they drove a cargo truck into a meadow near the castle. Ten seconds after it stopped, it exploded. The explosion was massive, so big it made a mushroom cloud." Drew swallowed. "It made a huge crater in the ground, maybe fifty feet wide."

Jackson went pale.

"Did you see any boxes or crates of materials near where they were building this object?" Eli asked.

"Yeah. There were a bunch of labeled crates. The ones in English had a warning label. An orange triangle that said 'warning: explosives.' Some of the other boxes were labeled 'Semtex.' There were other boxes, too. They had Arabic writing on them. I took pictures."

Eli studied the pictures on Drew's phone. They were distant, a bit fuzzy, but he could zoom in enough to make out the foreign lettering. "That's not Arabic, it's Farsi. This is PETN, a military-grade nitrate ester explosive made in Iran. Terrorist groups like to mix the two to make car bombs, among other things."

Drew's eyes widened in terror. "They're going to use a car bomb against us?"

"Looks like it."

"Excellent work, scout." Jackson patted him on the back. "Get yourself some acorns drizzled with maple syrup and dandelion salad. You deserve a bit of rest."

Once Drew had departed, Eli looked at Jackson. "We can't wait any longer."

Jackson nodded reluctantly.

"We've held our position for three weeks. If the cartel attacks first, we lose any element of surprise. To have any chance before we're too weakened, we have to go on the offensive."

"I know."

The true purpose of the raids on supply depots wasn't about the food; they had no way to transport the supplies back to Munising, and little hope of success, anyway.

The purpose was to whittle down Gault's men little by little, as well as to make a long-term siege untenable to the cartel and force Gault's hand. In that, they had succeeded.

Today was payday for work well done.

The cartel was gearing up for a major assault. Gault had taken the bait.

"When?" Jackson asked.

Eli said, "Tomorrow morning, we attack first."

49

LENA EASTON
DAY ONE HUNDRED AND SIXTY-THREE

L ena peered up at Eli in the darkness.

He was tense, his expression strained. He thrust a hand-made granola bar into her hand. "Eat this."

"I've already had my daily allotment. This is yours."

Eli grunted in frustration. "Do you ever just listen, woman? How about obeying an order without asking a million questions first?"

She stiffened. "No, I do not ever 'just listen.' If that's what you're interested in, there's a couple hundred soldier wannabes for you to order around to your heart's content."

Eli snorted.

She raised her eyebrows. "Exactly."

Insistent, he held out the bar wrapped in aluminum foil. The foil glinted in the moonlight. "You need to eat."

Her stomach growled traitorously. With reluctance, she accepted the granola bar and consumed half of it in a matter of seconds. Her mouth watered at the delicious taste. Her belly was still an empty knot.

Before Eli could protest, she fed the other half to Bear. The dog licked her fingers eagerly, tail wagging, his hot doggy breath warming her hands. She checked her pump, tugged up her sweater and jacket, and bolused for the carbs.

Eli frowned. "Lena."

"He needs to eat, too. I will not let him starve. I refuse."

With a sigh, Eli tugged a strip of venison jerky from his rucksack and handed it to the dog as well. "Fine."

The Northwoods Inn had finally fallen silent. It was well after eleven p.m. Most people were in bed after nightfall except for the patrols and sentries. Shiloh was sleeping. In the morning, she'd go to the hospital with Lena to care for the injured during the battle.

Eli had been absent for what felt like days. He'd been busy preparing, planning, and training. Everything led up to the next few hours. Whether they won or lost, lived or died, their fate would be decided, and soon.

"It happens tonight, then," she said softly.

"At three a.m.," he said.

Everyone had been briefed. Everyone had a role to play. Even the teenagers and the elderly could carry food and water to fighting positions, relay critical messages, or help Lena tend to the wounded at the hospital.

They couldn't wait any longer. Another few days without food and people wouldn't have the energy to fight. Already, folks were growing listless, some too weak or depressed to perform their chores and security duties.

An image of Michelle Carpenter's rigid corpse seared her mind. The opening salvo had yet to be fired and they'd already lost people to the mental battle. Despair was a contagious disease, and it was spreading. It would destroy them if they didn't fight now.

This needed to end, one way or another.

"What are our chances?" she asked.

"Honestly? Not good."

She studied him in the darkness. His movements were sharp and efficient. He no longer limped. Physically, he had mostly recovered from his death match with Sykes, but the most painful battle scars were sometimes invisible.

"Are you ready?" she asked.

"As ready as we'll ever be."

Lena knew he would protect the town or die trying. Those were the only possible outcomes.

"Come with me," he said. "I want to show you something."

Eli took her hand and led her along the path skirting the bluff. Bear trotted along behind them, sniffing at every fallen leaf and patch of overgrown grass. They passed a couple of checkpoints and roving security patrols. Everyone was tense and on high alert.

Ahead of them, the wind turbines along the bluff loomed like pale ghostly giants in the ambient starlight. Their massive blades turned silently in the breeze sweeping in from Lake Superior.

They stood on the edge of the bluff. Bear flopped down beside them and chuffed as he rested his snout on his paws.

The vast lake stretched invisibly into the darkness. Far below them, the gray roiling waves beat against the sandy shoreline. Stars glinted like specks of ice against the rich black velvet of the sky.

Her chest contracted. She sensed everything: the dirt beneath her feet, the grass scratching at her shins, the breeze ruffling her hair, the crash of the waves. The endless sky, the infinite stars, the vastness of the great lake—it was spectacular.

It took her breath away.

Nature in all her regal splendor would outlast them. Earth would continue its ceaseless spinning on its axis. Galaxies of countless planets and stars would continue their orbits, steady and orderly, as if designed, like some great unseen hand had set them into motion.

Even now, at the end of all things, the world was still beautiful.

A sense of wonder filled her. Never had she felt so close to the supernatural, as if she could reach out and touch the heavens, the stars themselves as if something was up there in all that infinite space, looking down and keeping watch over everyone, the good and the wicked.

"Do you ever feel like there has to be more than this?" she asked.

"More than what?"

"That there's something out there, invisible but real. Maybe its God or maybe it's something else, something we can't see or touch, but it's still real."

Eli grunted. "I believe in what I see."

"You can't see the wind, but it's real. You can see the effects of the wind, in the trees, in the waves, you can feel it on your skin. You can't see love. You can't see hope or faith or truth, but those things exist. They're real and they mean everything."

Lena was a woman of science, logic and evidence, medicine and facts. She was learning she was also a woman of faith. She believed in the inexplicable. This moment of grace amidst the storm—it was inexplicable.

"I want to believe in something larger than myself. That there's a reason for all of this, for existence itself, for our suffering. I want my life to mean something."

Eli took a step closer. "I believe in you."

She blushed. "That's not what I meant."

"All the same, it's true. I believe in my love for you and Shiloh." He reached out his hand and gently placed it on her chest, over her heart. "You saved me."

It felt as if her chest was expanding like a balloon, like her heart and soul could encompass everything, each moment in time from now until eternity.

"I don't know if we'll live through tomorrow," Eli said gravely. "All we have promised to us is this. Right here, right now. I have everything I've ever wanted. I have Shiloh. I have you."

Tears sprang into her eyes. She pressed herself against him. He enveloped her in his powerful arms, the woodsy, musky scent of him strong in her nostrils.

Eli bent his head, tilting her chin up with his finger, and kissed her. At first, his kisses were tender and then harder, fiercer. She kissed him back, her heart a sparkler burning bright inside her chest.

They might have been the only two people in the entire broken world.

Lena and Eli stood together, their fingers entwined as they held each other, balanced on the edge of the cliff, the cold bright stars sweeping across the heavens above their heads, the moon-gilded waters of the great lake below.

"If tomorrow is the end of us, it will have been enough," he said huskily into her hair. "You have always been enough. For too long, I was too young and stupid to recognize it. There has never been anything or anyone else. It's you. It's always been you."

She stretched onto her tiptoes and kissed Eli through her tears. She kissed him like it was the first and last time, the beginning and the end, as if they could kiss every trouble and problem and threat away, erase and rebuild universes and galaxies, and start the world anew.

Maybe this time, they could.

He spoke against her lips. "I love you, Lena Easton." He pulled away, gripped her upper arms, and gazed at her with an intensity that set her heart ablaze. Moonlight glinted in his dark eyes. "We will come home. I am coming home."

"Come back to me," she whispered.

Eli held her close. "Always."

50

ELI POPE

DAY ONE HUNDRED AND SEVENTY-FOUR

"Let's go, people!" Jim Hart yelled. "Wake the hell up!"

Clusters of civilians exited their cabins and shuffled out onto the frost-tipped grass. Frigid air greeted them. Their teeth chattered as they gathered gear and weapons. Flashlights and lanterns gleamed, casting wavering shadows across the ground.

"What time is it?" Jason Anders yawned and stretched, his hair standing on end and his eyes heavy-lidded. He looked young, like the teenager he'd been only a few months ago.

"Two a.m., numbnuts," Nyx drawled. "Wake up kid, or do you need to run back to Mommy for a goodbye kiss?"

Jason flinched. He stared wide-eyed at Nyx, who marched past him like the goddess of war, head freshly shaved on one side, weapons bristling from her hips and thighs. Her favored bandolier of ammo was draped like a sash across her chest.

"Um, no ma'am," Jason stammered. He couldn't peel his gaze from Nyx, mouth agape. His puppy dog crush was as obvious as his beet-red face. "I'm good, ma'am."

"That's what I thought." Nyx winked at Antoine, who rolled his eyes.

They jogged over to Eli, who was reading a couple of last-minute reports from the scouts. Groups of ordinary men and women moved into position, their faces hollow, eyes sunken from lack of sleep as they tried to rouse themselves. Many appeared gaunt, an army of scarecrows armed with rifles and pistols, sporting a mishmash of army uniforms, hunting gear, and civilian attire.

"Get with your group and gather your extra equipment," Antoine ordered.

The fighters formed into fire teams. Nash and Moreno passed out more weapons and ammunition and gave the civilians their assigned posts. Most would defend fighting holes along the route of the advancing army.

Sounds of preparation for battle broke the early morning stillness: the clatter of horses being saddled, the clip-clop of hooves, the low rumble of ATVs and the electric hum of golf carts, and the thud of footsteps and muttered greetings. The smells of sour sweat, unwashed bodies, and gun oil tinged the smoky air.

Eli instructed Hart to distribute the MREs they'd set aside for this moment. Whoops and shouts of excitement erupted as deputies passed out MREs from several large crates.

"What's this?" Fiona asked blearily, staring at the brown package of chili mac MRE in her hands as if she'd never seen something so amazing.

"Breakfast," Hart said with a smile. "Eat up."

"You've had these all along and didn't give them to us, you jerk-wad," Antoine muttered around a massive mouthful of chicken mush strangely tinged green. "I'm so hungry I don't even hate you for giving me Chicken a La King, the literal worst MRE meal on the planet."

"We need the energy to fight today," Eli said. "The fat, protein, and calories will give everyone the best chance to survive the battle."

People tore open the meals-ready-to-eat packaging right there, not bothering to sit, consuming every morsel in a frenzy. It was like Christmas morning.

An army four times their size was determined to slaughter

them, but for a few minutes, their focus had narrowed to the delicious calories filling their empty bellies.

Sawyer sauntered up to Eli and Jackson, a cheese tortellini MRE packet in one hand, his pistol held low in his right hand. He tapped the muzzle lightly against his thigh with each step.

His sharp gaze flicked over Antoine and Nyx as if they didn't exist, then snagged on Eli.

Eli stared back, eyes narrowing. Fresh anger slashed through him. The sight of Sawyer made him want to strangle someone, but he reigned in his hatred and kept his eyes on the prize. This war was far more important than his vitriol for one man.

The two mortal enemies faced each other. For a tense moment, no one spoke, all eyes on the men standing five feet apart, hands twitching on their weapons.

Jackson looked from one to the other with a pained expression. "We're not going to have a problem today, are we?"

Eli's face remained inscrutable. "No problem here."

Sawyer was the first to relax. His handsome features stretched into a smile, all ease and charisma. It was disconcerting how he could transform into anything he wanted at the drop of a hat. "Well, well, if it isn't the savior of Munising."

Eli kept his voice even. "That remains to be seen."

"I guess we'll see if you live up to the hype, huh Pope?"

"Guess so."

"Ready to do this?" Jackson asked.

Sawyer laughed as he finished his meal and tossed the packaging onto the ground. "I'd rather be sailing across Lake Superior, but sure, why not? It's a lovely morning to blow things up and kill a bunch of mouth-breathers."

Eli forced a grim smile. "Now you're talking."

51

ELI POPE

DAY ONE HUNDRED AND SEVENTY-FOUR

E li stood next to Sawyer in a fighting hole overlooking M-28 along the southern defensive perimeter. Hart, Nash, Moreno, and Pierce were with them. Several fire teams were huddled in dugouts along the road just outside of town.

Sawyer had gone surly and quiet. He loathed answering to Eli for anything. Eli didn't like it either, but he needed eyes on Sawyer or he was liable to end up with a knife to the back.

"We good, Sawyer?" Eli asked.

"I have a vested interest in staying alive, Pope. I'm not stupid. You and I have a better chance of surviving the night if we work together." His lip curled in amusement. "I'm not gonna turn on you—today, anyway."

For once, Eli believed him. At this moment, they were brothers-in-arms fighting to stay alive. That was it, but it was enough.

"The convoy is coming down the road toward your position, Alpha One," one of the forward scouts said over the radio. "Approximately a mile distant."

"All teams, maintain situational awareness from your fighting hole and engage anyone approaching your position," Eli instructed. "Until then, do not fire until my command."

The night was pitch black, everything eerily green through the night vision binoculars. The cartel's camp was positioned just out of sight, past the Good Shepherd church on the right.

"I hear them coming," Antoine said. "Party's about to get started."

The low rumble of engines echoed in the crisp air. Dozens of vehicles appeared in the distance behind Gault's dug-in army. Eli recognized a few Bradley fighting tanks, Buffalo MRAPs, mine-resistant ambush-protected vehicles, and M113 armored personnel carriers.

Eli had to hand it to Gault: it was an intimidating sight.

"Wait for it," Eli said to his men. "No one fire. They're about to hit the first trap."

Like any trained infantry, the cartel attempted to spread out their vehicles and men, their cargo trucks remaining on the road while the armored vehicles and tanks spread out across the fields, infantry support moving with them.

This made the machines hard to kill from the air as well as from the ground with anti-tank weapons, but Eli had another plan: version 2.0 of the ghost town ambush. This time, he'd made accommodations for the cartel's jammers.

He watched the cartel's forward vehicles breach an invisible line, triggering the first buried mine. A cacophony of explosions split the air. One by one, the mines buried along the road blew up. The air shuddered with the force of the explosions lighting up the night.

Three armored trucks burst into flames. Twisted metal, chunks of dirt, and rocks flew through the air. Men shrieked in agony. Figures stumbled from the damaged vehicles, writhing as they fell, encased in flames.

For an instant, the cartel hordes froze. Then bedlam broke out. Hundreds of enemy soldiers desperately attempted to backtrack in their exact footsteps while spraying fire into the night to cover their retreat.

"Engage!" Eli commanded. "All teams, engage now!"

Teams of sharp shooters to Eli's left and right began firing.

They dropped Gault's shock troops, who were slowed by the mine field, like sitting ducks. Terrified to dive for cover and accidentally set off a mine, the fleeing hostiles made easy targets.

Eli signaled to Nash. Nash shot a flare high in the air with a grenade launcher. The flare was attached to a parachute so that it floated above them and illuminated the carnage and chaos of men frantic to disengage from the traps they'd set.

However, their adversaries got smart quickly. They dropped smoke grenades to cover the withdrawal back to the road. It was too late to matter. Body parts littered the field on both sides of the road. Four cargo trucks were stuck in mud holes Eli had created for that purpose. Most of the cartel infantry spread out in the field across M-28 were dying or dead.

"They're backing off!" Hart shouted.

"What's happening?" Antoine asked through their comms.

Eli frowned. "The surviving vehicles and men are staying just out of range. For now. Hold your fire."

The cartel fighters seemed to idle for a few minutes as if they were adjusting tactics or conferring with their command and control. After about fifteen minutes, the column started to move again, this time straight down the road to avoid the potential mines buried along either side of the highway.

"Here they come again!" Nash yelled.

Eli and Sawyer watched, tense and still, predators lying in wait, keeping low to avoid enemy fire. Enemy fire tore over their heads, impacting the ground, the trees, and the abandoned buildings near the road.

A Bradley fighting vehicle led the convoy, which rolled forward, drawing closer and closer until they were nearly parallel with the hidden fighting positions.

"NOW!" Eli shouted into his headset.

Several bright streaks flared through the darkness. Rockets streamed out of tubes the Munising fighters held over their shoulders. Milliseconds later, violent explosions shook the ground.

The armored vehicles failed. Shrapnel riddled the insides of fuel tanks and crew compartments. Vehicles were ripped apart, men cooked alive within their metal cages.

The flares were no longer needed to see the battlefield. Vehicles burned bright, flames shooting high in the sky as ammunition cooked off. Men and women fled from several wrecked vehicles, their clothes on fire. The stench of diesel fuel, burning flesh, and munitions choked the air.

Eli watched the carnage unfold. The horrific scene was being repeated along each of the roads leading into town. So far, Gault was losing men and equipment at an incredible rate.

A spark of satisfaction flared through him. He felt a twinge of optimism for the first time in weeks. If the cartel thought they'd reached checkmate, they were sorely mistaken.

It wouldn't last. Gault would regroup and retaliate. They needed to be elsewhere by then.

"Incoming!" Sawyer shouted.

Through the smoke and darkness, furtive shapes appeared between two burning cargo trucks, moving low and fast across the open ground. Four hostiles ran straight for their foxhole. Nash and Hart laid down a steady stream of fire. The hostiles kept coming.

Adrenaline spiked Eli's veins. He dropped the binoculars and went for his weapon. The lead hostile sprinted toward them from across the road, a small object clutched in one hand.

"Grenade!" Moreno adjusted his aim and fired his HK 416 at the hostile's chest.

The man stuttered and fell. The grenade exploded twenty yards from their position. The ground trembled beneath Eli's feet. He turned his head and opened his mouth to dispel the pressure.

Undaunted, three more hostiles sprinted toward them. Sawyer fired a short burst and nailed one hostile in the face as his gun went off, the rounds flying harmlessly over their heads.

Eli fired several shots, taking out the second hostile, but the third made it. He dove headfirst into the hole, rifle forward.

The attacker lunged at Eli with a soul-shredding war-whoop.

He slammed into Eli's chest. Eli managed to grasp the barrel of the rifle before the hostile could fire.

Both men toppled backward. As he fell, Eli managed to jerk the weapon from the attacker's hands. He landed on his back with a hard thud. The hostile tumbled on top of him. The air was knocked from his lungs.

The man's face leered inches from his own—a flattened nose, dead black eyes. They grappled, grunting and sweaty, each frantically grasping for a weapon, for anything to end this fight.

The attacker's weight was crushing. He was strong, powerful, and incredibly heavy. Eli couldn't free himself enough to bring his weapon to bear. He still couldn't breathe.

Eli glimpsed a shimmer of steel. The hostile had managed to wrest his knife free. Eli gripped the wrist of the hand with the knife and held on tight.

The attacker struggled to rip his hand free, only inches from driving the knife through Eli's throat. He growled, viciously shoving the blade against his Adam's apple.

The blade nicked Eli's skin. It pressed deeper. Blood leaked down his throat. The attacker was heavy, too heavy. Eli's muscles strained. His lungs burned. Fear torqued through him. Another inch deeper and he was dead—

Abruptly, the hostile screamed. He ceased moving. The knife clattered harmlessly to the ground. His full weight collapsed across Eli's chest. Grunting from the effort, Eli shoved the two hundred fifty-pound corpse to the side. His chest seized. Finally, he could breathe again.

Sawyer leaned over the dead soldier and extracted his knife from the man's kidney. The blade dripped with fresh blood. He grinned like the cat that ate the canary. "Thought you could use a little help, there."

Eli clambered to his feet, dirty and bloodied but unharmed. He didn't want to admit that he owed Sawyer his life. The words cut like shards of glass on his tongue. "Thanks, Sawyer."

For a brief moment, the two men locked eyes, sharing their

mutual terror, the frenzied rush of combat. People didn't fight for obscure ideals or policies. They fought for each other.

When you were in the foxhole of war, the only thing that mattered was staying alive.

A groan came from behind Eli. He whipped around, weapon rising. Moreno leaned against the sandbagged wall, gun on the ground beside him. His hands were pressed to his upper left thigh. Bright red blood spurted between his fingers.

Moreno gazed up at him with a wide, stunned expression. His eyes were glassy with shock. "I don't know what happened. One second, I was taking out that asshat with the grenade, the next second my leg stopped working. I can't feel it. Dunno if that's a good or bad thing."

"Cover us!" Eli snapped at Sawyer as he dropped to Moreno's side. He reached for his IFAK med kit and withdrew a tourniquet. Rounds flew all around them. He kept his head down as he worked to halt the spurting blood. The bullet had struck the femoral artery.

Moreno's breaths came in shallow, panting gasps. "I don't wanna die."

"You aren't going to die. Not on my watch. You hear me? Not on my watch."

Dully, Moreno nodded. "Gonna...hold you...to that."

Within a minute, Eli had gotten the tourniquet tight on his upper thigh. He ordered two of their runners to transport Moreno to the hospital along with another fighter, young Drew Stewart, who had suffered a gut shot to the pelvis below his armored vest. He was unlikely to make it.

"Moreno's a dead man walking, too," Sawyer said once they had evacuated. "You know that, right? Without proper medical care, he'll bleed out on the operating table."

"You don't know him. Or Lena. Lena won't give up on him. He'll make it."

Sawyer shrugged. "Sure, man. Whatever you say."

Eli pushed his concern for Moreno out of his head, along with thoughts of Lena and Shiloh, safe for now at the hospital. They would stay safe. Eli would make sure of it.

"Enemy reinforcements headed your way, Alpha Team!" one of the scouts shouted into their comms. "All Alpha units, you have an inbound Huey headed your way!"

Through the swirling smoke, a horde of vehicles approached behind the first wave, dozens of cargo trucks and F150s mounted with big guns. The cartel infantry had been slowed by the buried mines, shocked by the sudden carnage, but they'd already recovered and renewed the attack.

Eli picked up the handheld radio. "All Alpha units, disengage and fall back to the next location."

"What's the play?" Pierce asked.

"Gault has mortars and drones," Eli said. "He'll move them into position at any moment, so we'd better move now. Staying too long will be fatal. Our secondary ambush spot is two miles down the road—"

A terrible sound rumbled over the cacophony of the battle. The blood drained from Eli's face. The steady *whomp-whomp-whomp* grew increasingly louder as a dark shape appeared above the tree line, drawing nearer with every second.

The cartel's air support had arrived.

The Huey dipped low above the canopy and flew straight and fast overhead. A constant blitz of fire streamed from the open side of the chopper. The crack and blast of rifle fire was overwhelmed by the deafening roar of the M60 as it lit up the night. The thunderous bursts vibrated inside their skulls.

The doors of the choppers were open; they were loaded with shock troops. The gunner opened up on the retreating teams as they scattered into the tree line. Streaks of light shot across the sky. Tracer rounds tore up the ground not fifty yards to the east of their position.

Four of Sawyer's fighters were caught exposed, crouched in a ditch across the road. They jittered and dropped. Screams shattered the air.

"I'm hit!" one of the men cried.

Instead of looping around for another pass at them, the Huey blew by without stopping. The second chopper appeared over the trees in fast pursuit of the first.

The birds soared above them, headed into the heart of Munising. They flew low with their beacon and anti-collision lights off before disappearing into the night. Eli could still make out the distinct whine and heavy whirr of the blades.

Nausea churned in his stomach. He feared the worst. They might be winning the current battle, but they were about to lose the whole war in one fell swoop.

"Alpha leader to all units!" he shouted. "There are two inbound Hueys loaded with troops heading into town! Do your best to take them down."

"Grab your gear and exfil!" Nash said.

Sawyer ordered his men to comply. "We've got to get down the trail before we're flanked or overrun, there's too many of them to fight."

"What about your injured men?" Nash asked. "At least one is still alive. I can hear him moaning."

"Leave them," Pierce said. "They can't fight. They're no good to us."

A Ranger would never leave a brother-in-arms behind like this, but Pierce was human trash they needed temporarily, not a Ranger. Eli vowed to end him as soon as he dared.

Eli signaled to Sawyer and Nash, who hurled several smoke grenades into the road to obscure their retreat. Rounds zinged overhead, impacting tree trunks to their left as they retreated into the cover beneath the tree canopy. They moved hastily down the trail along the Anna River.

A quarter mile from their fighting position, several horses, bikes, and ATVs had been hidden in the woods off M-28, along with a hidden cache of Sawyer's most prized weapons.

Eli seated himself on his ATV and gestured to Nyx, who'd just arrived, breathless and flushed from exertion. A smear of blood streaked her right cheek. "Bring the Stinger. I'm betting we'll need it."

"You got it."

As he slung his pack across his back and shoved the key fob into the ignition, he thought about a phrase an old friend had said once. The former Navy Seal had called it taking souls, when you beat the enemy so quickly and thoroughly that you stole all hope, crushing their will to continue fighting.

Surviving the night would require a lot of taking of souls.

52

ELI POPE
DAY ONE HUNDRED AND SEVENTY-FOUR

E li and his team exited the tree line to the north of the
defensive perimeter and sprinted into downtown Munising.
Nothing looked familiar in the green glow of his NVGs. The town
of his childhood transformed into a hostile alien landscape.

"Alpha One, this is Charlie Three," came a high frantic voice.
Eli recognized Jason Anders, who was stationed at the Northwoods Inn along with Fiona Smith and several of the local police
officers, including Baker and Flores. Underwood had also volunteered to defend the Inn rather than lead a team into battle. Not
surprising.

"Go, Charlie Three," Eli said as he swung a hard right onto
Munising Avenue, racing through the empty streets of downtown.
He streaked past hunched buildings—cafes and gas stations and
tourist shops—and headed northeast toward the Inn.

"Two helicopters hovered two hundred yards north of our
position, just outside the fence. A whole bunch of bad guys just
came zipping down on ropes, and they're headed for the south
gate to breach the Inn. I'm with Fiona, I mean, Charlie Two. What
the hell do we do?"

Eli imagined enemy soldiers fast-roping from the choppers

like spiders dropping from silken strands. "Slow down, breathe, and tell me how many hostiles. What are you seeing?"

"Maybe twenty or so soldiers. They're dressed in black and have plate carriers and chest rigs, and some have night vision. An RPG just went off and hit the gate! Hurry!"

Gunfire sounded through the radio as civilians traded fire with the mercenaries rushing through the breached fence. The first strike had been meant to soften them up. The ground assault would do the real dirty work.

Eli and his team were still eight minutes out. They'd never make it in time.

"Put some flares in the air, Charlie Three," he instructed. "Take away the advantage they have with night vision. Then start picking them off, one by one. Like we trained."

"Okay—I mean, roger that." Jason sounded terrified. Of course, he was. He was a nineteen-year-old kid desperately holding the line against his worst nightmare.

Eli contacted Jackson, who was stationed further out from the Inn, defending H-58. "Echo One, send some fighters to the North-woods' south gate but not so many that you're blind in other areas."

"This is Echo One," Jackson said. "I've already sent five men on ahead. I can't spare more and defend the town's east perimeter. We're battling a contingent of at least a hundred enemy fighters."

Eli cursed. "Stay where you are, then. If the east perimeter falls, Northwoods will fall in a matter of minutes. They're attacking the Inn to get us to pull our forces from the fighting holes along the road. Stay the course."

With Jackson's fire teams otherwise engaged, it was up to Eli and his small team to save the Northwoods people from being slaughtered. Terror tasted like copper pennies on his tongue.

Using their comms, Eli instructed Antoine and Nyx to break off with him and ordered Sawyer and Nash to continue to the next defensive position. Eli hated leaving Sawyer out of his sight for even a moment, but saving civilians was his most pressing concern.

They needed to keep the Northwoods from being overrun.

"Please hurry!" Jason's panicky voice could barely be heard over the automatic weapons fire. "They've set fire to three cabins, and they're killing anyone they find on sight. Fiona sent everyone not fighting to hide in the wine cellar in the basement of the Inn. Others are hiding anywhere they can. Several tried to surrender and were shot with their hands up. They're butchering everyone!"

Eli went rigid. On one hand, he thanked God that Lena and Shiloh were safe at the hospital, though the people at the Northwoods Inn were his family, too. People he'd sworn to protect were dying.

"Hang tough!" he said. "Help is coming."

Finally, through the smoke-dense darkness, he glimpsed the concertina wire fence of the Northwoods Inn. The south gate had been blown open. Several bodies lay scattered around the abandoned highway barriers.

Eli's team stashed their transportation and made for the gate. Two cartel thugs had been left to guard it. Antoine and Nyx made short work of them before they could alert their friends.

Once they'd disposed of the guards, Nyx relieved the corpses of their weapons and extra magazines. She carried the large FIM-92 Stinger missile launcher across her shoulders.

It was the only one they had. They needed to make it count.

They stacked up beside the broken gate. Steady bursts of gunfire blasted a few hundred yards away. Eli did a tactical reload as he scanned the area directly ahead, then moved deeper onto the property.

Using bounding overwatch, they leapfrogged from building to building, from tree to tree, headed toward the muzzle flashes of the firefight on the east end.

Bullet holes pocked the cabins. Pungent smoke stung his nostrils. Bodies lay everywhere: fighters and civilians, women and old men, even children.

Outrage blazed through him like a forest fire. He would slit every cartel member's throat for this. They would pay, and pay dearly.

"Let's start killing these asshats," Antoine said.

"Amen," Nyx said.

Eli spoke into his comms. "Charlie, this is Alpha One, SITREP."

Fiona answered. "We're seventy yards from the east gate, near the goat pens, about to be flanked!"

"We're moving to you from the southern cabins, so check your fire."

"Yeah, okay," Fiona said, panting as if she were running. "Hurry, please!"

The team moved cautiously from cabin 6A to 7A before halting. Eli bladed his body and signaled to Antoine, who was stacked up beside him. Urgency crackled through him, but a rushed mistake would get them all killed.

Nyx signaled silently and gestured to her right. Eli spotted a figure crouched half-inside one of the cabins—one of their own, not a cartel fighter. On closer inspection, the figure lay collapsed in the doorway, the door wide open.

Eli crept closer and glanced down at the body. He recognized Bradley Underwood. He did not appear to be breathing. His face was slack, eyes glazed and fixed on nothing. Nyx crouched and flipped his body over—a half dozen holes riddled his back.

Underwood had been assigned the front gate and had fled his post to hide in one of the cabins when the cartel began its assault on the Inn. Underwood was a coward. Cowards always found a way to save their own skin—except this time.

Eli shook his head in grim vindication. He didn't feel remorse or sadness, not for this man. As far as he was concerned, Underwood had gotten what he had coming to him.

Antoine touched Eli's arm and motioned for him to keep moving. Leaving the corpse behind, Eli eased past the cabin's front wall and bladed his body, peering around the corner.

Thirty yards to their nine o'clock, five hostiles dressed in black with full battle gear clustered behind cabin 8. Four of the men were armed with AKs and one grasped a drone controller. They didn't notice Eli's team sneaking up on them from behind.

Antoine moved up along the wall in absolute silence. An instant later, he let loose with the Heckler and Koch 320 Grenade launcher. The grenade struck the ground less than three feet from the hostiles. Before they could react, it exploded. White-hot shards of twisted metal hurled into flesh and bone.

Screams and shrieks erupted. Eli took a knee and opened fire at the men falling and writhing in agony. Two seconds later, they were dead.

Bullets sprayed at them from several directions. An RPG ripped across the space between cabins. It blasted into the cabin behind them. Eli and his team ducked, throwing themselves around the corner to avoid the blast force.

"Two Hueys inbound!" one of the scouts alerted them over the radio. "We've fired our last remaining RPGs at them and missed."

Eli had expected as much. Still, his lungs constricted. He turned to his team. "Focus on what we need to do right now. We worry about the choppers when they come."

Antoine nodded. "Roger that, brother."

"They've stopped chasing us! They're moving away!" Jason yelled into the radio. "I think we're safe."

"Okay, stay where you are and wait—"

"Oh, no!" Fiona cried. "There's a team coming around the corner—! They're too many of them—!" The transmission ended in a scream of pain or terror or more likely, both.

"Charlie Three!" Eli called. "Come in! Charlie Two! Do you read me?"

No answer.

"Jason! Fiona!"

Silence from the radios.

"We're almost to you, hold tight!" Eli gestured at Antoine to keep moving. They had to get out of here before the Hueys arrived.

Antoine covered them as they sprinted east, driving back their pursuers with bursts of gunfire. Their boots squelched in the mud along the creek bank. They hugged the creek until they came out behind the animal pens.

Skirting the chicken coops, Eli's team reached the watering station, a collection of thousand-gallon reservoirs built on wooden platforms.

Ahead of them, several darkened figures lay sprawled on the ground behind the water storage tanks. They approached with caution. Dread coiled in Eli's stomach.

He crouched down behind the water storage tanks, Nyx and Antoine at his side. Dressed in black with grease blackening their faces, they were nearly invisible in the deep shadows.

Nyx kept watch as Eli and Antoine knelt beside the bodies. Eli felt for a pulse against Jason Ander's neck. Three holes ripped across his chest carrier; one round had pierced his throat.

His skin was still warm, his eyes open and staring at the empty sky. There was nothing—no pulse, no breath, no sign of life.

A few feet away, Antoine checked Fiona. Judging by the trail of black blood staining the grass, she'd been hit in the thigh, then crawled beneath the reservoir while Jason had attempted to shield her with his body. In the end, he'd fought bravely to keep them both alive.

With his free hand, Antoine gently closed Fiona's eyes and shook his head. She hadn't made it, either. He cursed softly.

Eli swallowed the lump in his throat. The guilt was crushing. Fiona and Jason were just kids, brave stupid kids who'd lost their lives defending their home. Less than a minute ago, Eli had spoken with them. Now they were dead. Gone forever.

The unrelenting barrage of weapons fire ceased. An occasional shot rang out in the abrupt silence. Eli's ears rang distant and tinny, his skull like a rung bell.

"I hear the choppers," Nyx whispered.

Crouched beside Fiona's still form, Antoine glanced skyward. They listened to the familiar roar of an approaching monster. Sans running lights, the mechanical predator was visible only through their NVGs.

It was merely a black silhouette against the black sky, obscuring the stars as it drew closer. The second chopper followed the first.

Instead of opening fire, strafing the buildings, or mowing down scattering civilians, the nearest Huey hovered in midair and slowly lowered toward the ground. The grass was blasted sideways by the beating wind.

"What are they doing?" Nyx asked.

Eli gestured across the field, where a dozen furtive shapes clotted the shadows along the left side of the Inn. He couldn't get off a good shot at this angle. There were too many of them to take on straight up. He wanted nothing more than to murder them all.

"They're picking up their men. Their mission was likely to pull fighters away from the defenses along the roads coming into town, which they've done. They're gathering their assassins before they're hunted down and killed by an overwhelming conventional force. That would be us."

Antoine grunted in disappointment. "Damn it! I was looking forward to more target practice."

"We're not done yet." Eli glanced at the bodies at his feet. A dark rage seared through him. He burned with fury. "You still got that Stinger, Nyx?"

"You know I do."

"Let's make good use of it. Wait until the Huey lands. I want every asshat that butchered our friends and family on that chopper before we blow it."

Nyx frowned. "Will that work? Can you use a surface-to-air missile on a ground target?"

"Stingers use infrared sensors to target aircraft. The sensors search for a heat signature produced by the target's engine. As long as it doesn't confuse ground clutter with the running engine, we're good."

While Antoine and Eli scanned their surroundings, Nyx

unslung the long heavy object, unzipped the case, and went to work attaching the launcher to the missile of the MANPAD, or man-portable air defense system, then rested the tube against her shoulder.

Releasing the safety, she acquired the target through the sights and activated the infrared seeker on the missile. The acquisition tone sounded. "Target acquired."

"Wait for it," Eli said, tensing.

The chopper dropped to the ground behind the Inn in the center of the large meadow. Its rotors churned, stirring up grass and dirt.

"Permission to fire," Nyx said.

"Not yet," he said in a low voice. "Hold."

Thirteen men broke from the corner of the Inn and dashed across the open field toward the Huey's open door. These were the men who had killed Jason and Fiona. Eli knew it in his bones. The first hostiles reached the chopper and climbed inside.

Nyx clenched her jaw. The missile was aimed and locked on its target. They waited, not breathing until the last hostile hopped into the Huey.

"Send it!" Eli said.

Nyx fired. With a tremendous shriek, a streak of white light vaulted from the tube. Smoke blasted from the canister. The seven-pound warhead shot across the field. It struck the chopper's engine near its exhaust.

The result was instantaneous. The massive explosion tore through the night. The air itself seemed to throb. The terrible sound of wrenching, tearing metal scraped their eardrums. A great whoosh of flames blasted three stories high.

Men and women were hurled from the chopper like ragdolls tossed about by a giant unseen hand. Several fighters managed to scramble to their feet, their clothes alight, burning like human torches. Others rolled frantically across the ground, howling as their skin melted from their bones.

The horrific odor of burning flesh reached him. It was small consolation for the carnage these monsters had inflicted upon the innocent. Their enemies deserved to die a thousand painful deaths.

Antoine grinned. It was a ghastly smile. "That had to hurt."

"Not nearly long enough," Eli said.

At least Jason and Fiona had been avenged. It was all he could offer them.

One chopper down. One more to go.

And they were out of missiles. At the south perimeter, Jim Hart still had a few grenade launchers. Hopefully, he could do something with them.

"Is that what I think it is?" Antoine pointed.

Far to the west, a faint glimmer shone in the dense darkness of the night, an orangish light glowed on the horizon above the outline of the trees. "Damn it all to hell!" Nyx cursed. "The wind must have changed direction again."

The blaze was drawing inexorably closer, stirred into a frenzy by the wind blowing off the lake. It was creating its own swirling weather system.

Fire did not discriminate between the good and the evil; it would burn them all.

The seed of an idea sprang to life in the back of Eli's mind. It was wild, crazy, and incredibly reckless. If it worked, it just might be enough to save them—

"Alpha One, we have a problem," Jackson's voice crackled in Eli's earpiece. "I just spotted the truck bomb."

53

JACKSON CROSS
DAY ONE HUNDRED AND SEVENTY-FOUR

"How the hell did the truck get through the defensive perimeter!" Antoine shouted through Jackson's headset.

"It broke through the southern barrier up from M-94," Devon said. "Barreled right through the barricade along with two other armored vehicles. We managed to disable the SUVs, but the truck slipped through."

"Where's it going?" Eli asked on the radio. "I need eyes on it!"

"I see it from my position on the roof of the CVS on Munising Avenue," Devon said. "I've got the drone following it."

Urgency shot through him. He leaned against the sandbagged wall and fired several shots across the street at the grocery store where a team of enemy fighters had taken cover.

The wind bit at his exposed cheeks and chilled the back of his neck beneath his windbreaker. Heavy clouds thickened overhead as the sky gradually lightened from black to shades of gray. Dawn was breaking upon a war zone.

Several hundred yards ahead and to his left, two motorcycles burst through the haze of smoke. As the motorcycles drew closer to the defensive perimeter, Jackson shifted his stance, aimed as he exhaled, and fired several bursts. The bikes were forced to swerve out of his line of fire.

They were fifty yards away. Then thirty. He fired a double tap at the torso of the nearest motorcyclist. The figure jerked, his hands flying up as he lost control of the bike. The motorcycle slid sideways and slammed into the second rider. Both bikes tumbled into the ditch a mere twenty yards from his fighting position.

Jackson wiped cold sweat from his brow with the back of his arm, not daring to blink. "Where the hell is it going?"

"The bomb is barreling out of town on Highway 58!" Devon said.

Jackson stopped breathing. "Is it headed toward Northwoods Inn?"

"I'm still following it with the drone," Devon said. "No, it didn't stay on the road for the turn to the Inn. It turned left, now north, headed toward the...visitor's center?"

"Not the visitor's center," Eli said.

A second of loaded silence passed as the terrible realization sank in.

"They're going to bomb the hospital!" Jackson said in alarm.

Panic swept over Jackson like a roaring wind. His mouth tasted like wet paper towels. Sour sweat glazed his skin. There were only a few guards protecting the hospital's fallback position.

The hospital, the high school, and the Northwoods Inn served as the main fallback positions. They'd placed the weakest citizens in the buildings most likely to endure a sustained gunfire attack, though none were built to withstand a mortar attack—or a bomb.

"They're taking moves right out of the Russian playbook!" Nyx's voice was tinny and staticky from this distance. Jackson was nearly out of radio range. "The filthy pigs!"

She wasn't wrong. It was a tactical ploy used by the unscrupulous, the worst of humanity, to intentionally kill civilians, particularly the most vulnerable ones, to demoralize the enemy to the point of surrender.

Luis Gault didn't simply want to defeat them; he wanted to destroy them, to completely obliterate them all.

"We've got at least two hundred wounded at the hospital along with kids and the elderly," Jackson said.

"Lena and Shiloh are there," Eli said in a strangled voice, his fear crystal clear through the static. "Order the evacuation! I'm out of range. I can't reach them."

"Roger that," Devon said. "I'm warning them now."

Antoine cursed. "That truck is less than five minutes out. There's no way they can evacuate the wounded in time—"

"They can and they will," Eli said. "Someone stop that truck!"

"I'm the closest. I'll do it." Jackson was already moving from his sandbagged fighting position. He kept his head down as lead zinged and pinged around him. Chunks of asphalt sprayed his shins.

He barely registered the stab of pain. He raced for the nearest pickup outfitted with a SAW. His lungs burned as he flat-out sprinted with all his might, legs pumping, ice water in his veins.

"Hurry—!" Antoine said in the understatement of the century.

Jackson stopped listening. He waved down the pickup. A skinny, pimply kid in his early twenties slammed the brakes. He was too young to fight, too young to die.

He rolled down the window. "I was just about to head for—"

"Get out!" Jackson wrenched the driver's door open and hauled the kid out of the truck. "Does the SAW have ammo?"

"Yes, a backpack and three belts in the back, but I was ordered to take the SAW to the south perimeter—"

"Plans changed." Jackson shoved himself behind the wheel, not bothering to adjust the rifle pressed awkwardly against his stomach. He drove like the devil himself was on his tail.

Rocketing up Highway 58, he swerved onto two wheels as he bounced around abandoned vehicles. He roared past several hotels perched along the coast—the Beach Inn Motel, Comfort Inn Lakefront, Sunset Motel on the Bay—all dark and silent, abandoned, home to ghosts and wraiths.

He pushed the pedal to the floorboard. Seventy, eighty, ninety miles per hour. The chassis shook and rattled beneath him. He glimpsed flashes of the lake, boarded-up buildings, and trees crowned with fiery fall colors. He slammed the gas pedal harder.

He raced east as the truck bomb surged north in a race against time he couldn't win. The bomb had a lethal head start. His chest felt like it would explode. He couldn't breathe. He could hardly feel his numb hands gripping the steering wheel.

"Nightingale, come in!" he called for Lena in his headset. "If you can hear me, take cover! There's a bomb! Take cover!"

Jumbled voices exploded in his comms. He couldn't make out individual words in the chaos and panic. It was all static in his head. His ears were tinny, his mouth dry.

Peeling right onto a gravel side road, he took a shortcut to Washington Street. He kept to the left until Munising Memorial Hospital came into view. Though they'd pushed cars and trucks into the roads to block their fallback positions, the terrain was flat enough here that the cartel vehicles could simply drive around them, as Jackson did now.

The truck bounced across the uneven ground. Frantic, he scanned the metal carcasses of a hundred vehicles. Nothing moved in the parking lot but scudding leaves.

He'd managed to beat the bomb—barely.

He had seconds to act. Smashing the brakes, Jackson careened to a halt. The front wheels hopped the curb as he parked half on the sidewalk. He threw open the driver's door and leaped out onto the grassy shoulder.

He slid onto his stomach below the berm and seated his rifle, safety flicked to "off," finger massaging the trigger. Heart hammering against his ribs, adrenaline surging, he waited.

He didn't have to wait long.

Seconds later, the growl of an engine bit the air. The truck with the bomb barreled down the road, straight toward him.

54

SHILOH EASTON POPE
DAY ONE HUNDRED AND SEVENTY-FOUR

Shiloh leaned across the operating table, pressing her full weight across Moreno's blood-drenched legs. She grasped his feet to hold him still as he screamed and writhed, recoiling from the source of his pain.

Lena cursed. "Hold his leg so we can get the bandages on and stop the bleeding."

"I'm trying!" Shiloh cried.

Blood was everywhere. It spattered her face, drenched her hands, speckled her lips. Bright red liquid dripped off the operating table and splashed onto the tile floor. She'd never seen so much blood in her life.

Moreno had been shot in the upper left thigh. His femoral artery was punctured. The artery pumped gouts of blood. Eli had gotten a tourniquet on him on the battlefield, but the tourniquet had to be removed to keep his tissue from dying. They needed to stop the bleeding before he passed out, or worse.

Bear lay near the inert anesthesia machine in the corner. Head on his paws, his ears pricked, his brown eyes followed their every move. His tail thumped the floor. Occasionally, he gave an anxious whine, as though he understood the gravity of the situation.

Lena's radio crackled. Jackson's voice kept breaking up, static filling the room. "—danger—everyone out—bomb—headed for—hospital—"

Dr. Virtanen's face drained of color. "Did she just say there's a bomb?"

Lena spun into instant action. One hand holding a sanitized towel against Moreno's wound, she turned to Shiloh. "Can you warn everyone? We have to evacuate right now. Anyone who can walk, head out the back exit to the shoreline where the boats are hidden, just like we practiced."

Dr. Virtanen stepped back, stripped off her bloody gloves, and wiped her hands on her lab coat. "I'll warn the nurses in B wing."

"What about Moreno?" Shiloh asked as the doctor strode from the room.

"I've got him," Lena said. "You go. Help everyone evacuate!"

Moreno's screams of agony echoed in Shiloh's ears. She raced from the operating theater into the hallway. Her bearskin cape fluttered behind her as she ran, her crossbow strapped to her back beneath it. She had her knife and a Springfield XD-S pistol holstered at her hip.

Eli had relented and allowed her to carry a damn gun. She could shoot better than anyone here, anyway. It was up to her to protect everyone.

Shiloh sprinted from room to room, from the pediatric unit to obstetrics, yelling at people to move their asses. The injured were triaged in the Emergency Room while other units housed the folks too old or sick to fight. The little kids stayed in the cafeteria with their moms or dads, aunts or uncles, or grandparents.

"Evacuate! Right now, people! Calm and orderly. Let's go!"

A cacophony of panicked questions blasted her: *Are we in danger? What's happening? Is the cartel coming right now? Is it the fire? Is it the helicopters?*

Shiloh might be small, but with her bearskin cape draped around her shoulders and the crossbow, she was plenty intimidating. "Ask stupid questions, get stupid answers! Just go! Run!"

Everyone burst into a flurry of movement. Volunteers hefted

the wounded onto stretchers and gurneys and pushed them down the corridors toward the exit out the back.

Shiloh raced for the cafeteria. She reached the double doors and glanced inside. It was pandemonium. At least a hundred kids were crammed into the large room.

The tables were pushed aside. Sleeping bags and blankets had been spread across the tile floor. Some kids slept, played card games, or worked on puzzles. A few ran around in frantic circles. Several were crying. The air smelled of stale crackers, lemony disinfectant, and stinky diapers.

A little boy sat on a chair and howled. Tears smeared his cheeks and snot leaked down his chin. He screamed for his mommy, who was busy fighting on the eastern perimeter, risking her life to save her son and everyone else.

Traci Tilton blocked Shiloh's entrance into the cafeteria. Her eyes widened at the sight of Shiloh. She recovered quickly and managed a tight smile. "How can I help you?"

"You can get out of my damn way."

Traci blanched. She took a hesitant step back, raising her hands in surrender. "I don't want any trouble. I'm just trying to help. Your aunt saved Keagan's life, even after what I did to her. I want to make up for—"

"I don't care!" Anger sizzled through her veins, momentarily overriding her fear. She couldn't handle this ridiculous woman. "I don't have time for your self-indulgent pity party. In case you haven't noticed, we're at war. I have to get the kids out of here before—"

A loud crash sounded in the near distance.

Shiloh whirled around. "What the hell—?"

55

JACKSON CROSS
DAY ONE HUNDRED AND SEVENTY-FOUR

"Take cover!" Jackson repeated, hoping they could hear him inside the hospital. "There's a bomb!"

He never heard a response. His vision narrowed. His absolute focus was on the deadly vehicle barreling toward him. It was a white work van sans windows, the kind handymen preferred. The cargo area could house a bomb large enough to do incredible damage.

The vehicle rocketed toward the parking lot at eighty miles an hour. It headed for the double doors of the urgent care wing.

Jackson would have only a small window to shoot when the truck raced past him.

Scooting to the top of the berm, he targeted the truck through his sights. His position was far from ideal, but he fired anyway, aiming for the windshield and the passenger's side window.

His only chance was to hit the driver. He squeezed the trigger again and again. The rifle bucked in his hands. The stock jolted against his shoulder.

The truck plunged past him.

Jackson's heart sank. He'd missed. It was too late. There was nothing he could do but watch the inevitable explosion, the suffering and death —

The white truck veered wildly. It careened to the left, narrowly avoiding a parked minivan, then skidded sharply to the right, rising up on two tires. It rammed into the side of a sedan not twenty feet from the hospital entrance.

The truck came to a violent, shuddering stop. The entire front end crumpled like a soda can. Steam billowed from the wrecked hood.

There was a millisecond of absolute silence.

Then the bomb exploded.

56

SHILOH EASTON POPE
DAY ONE HUNDRED AND SEVENTY-FOUR

The force of the explosion knocked Shiloh off her feet. Everything was shaking. The walls trembled, the ceiling quaked. The tables tipped over, chairs rattling across the tile. Screams and shrieks split the air.

The floor tremored beneath her as if it were about to open up like a great gaping mouth and swallow them all whole. The entire building groaned. The world seemed to tilt sideways. With a great shuddering crash, the wall next to Shiloh collapsed.

Before she could react, something struck her hard in the back.

The ceiling caved in on top of her.

57

JACKSON CROSS
DAY ONE HUNDRED AND SEVENTY-FOUR

J ackson watched in horror as the brick façade of the hospital convulsed. The doors caved inward, glass panes shattering. Glass shards rained against the asphalt. Roiling smoke burst through the smashed doors. The front entryway toppled in on itself in slow motion.

The explosion hurled bricks across the parking lot. Chunks of warped plastic and metal shrapnel propelled hundreds of feet, impacting nearby cars, trees, the ground, the street.

The shockwave hurtled out from the epicenter of the blast. Dozens of abandoned vehicles in the parking lot jittered and rocked on their chassis.

Jackson's brain rattled inside his skull. He bit his tongue. Hot blood gushed in his mouth. Everything went blurry and distant. His vision wavered, his guts turned to water.

Voices screamed through his comms in desperation, terror, and panic.

Somehow, he managed to push himself to his feet and stand atop the berm, his rifle clenched in his hands, his knuckles white.

In the parking lot, the blackened husk of the truck that housed the bomb was barely recognizable as anything but a harbinger of death and destruction.

Thick black smoke expelled from the wrecked hospital entrance. The front half of the hospital had collapsed. Sections of the exterior wall had crumbled. The windows were shattered like broken teeth.

Fortunately, the rear half of the building remained standing.

Jackson had managed to hit the driver, after all. The enemy's last act must have been to activate the weapon. If the bomb had exploded inside the hospital as intended, the damage would've been multitudes worse, with few if any survivors. The blast wave alone would've ruptured the victims' lungs, instantly liquifying flesh and bone.

If everyone had responded to the warning and moved deeper into the building or evacuated, there would be survivors.

There had to be survivors. He just needed to reach them.

Coughing violently, Jackson covered his mouth with his shirt and headed for the entrance. "I'm coming in!" he said. "Nightingale—Lena!—can you hear me? Shiloh! Moreno! Can anyone hear me?"

"The town's west perimeter has been breached!" Nash shouted into his headset. "I repeat, we've got an entire company of enemy soldiers and at least eight armored vehicles overrunning the barriers near the high school! Team Bravo was forced to retreat!"

"Head to your fallback positions," Eli ordered through the comms. "Defend the hospital."

"We can't! They've flanked us! And the wildfire is cutting in from the west. It's so close we can see the flames crowning the trees. The wind is bringing the worst of the blaze right to us. We're trapped if we don't run."

"Then run," Jackson said. "I'll figure something out."

"Drone footage shows two teams of seven men headed for the hospital," Devon said, fear in her voice. "We've got no QRF team close enough to stop them. They'll slaughter everyone inside!"

Jackson spun on his heels and staggered back to the borrowed pickup. For a second, he leaned over, hands on his knees, and inhaled several heaving breaths, trying to get oxygen back into his seizing lungs.

If they were dead, if Lena and Shiloh were gone, he'd never be able to live with himself.

"Is anyone there?" he screamed into the radio. "Are there survivors? Answer me!"

"I'm here," came a faint, scratchy voice. "We're here."

Jackson straightened, wiping bits of vomit from the back of his mouth, willing the ringing inside his head to dissipate. "Lena! Are you okay?"

"I think so, but—"

"I need you to listen very closely. The cartel breached the town's western defenses. They'll be coming in a matter of minutes. Do you understand?"

"We've got injured and casualties. The front half of the building caved in. People are trapped. I—I can't find Shiloh!"

He had never felt terror like this. Pure, unadulterated horror slashed his guts. "You have to get out! Get everyone and evacuate to the boats. Exfil to Grand Island. I'll hold them off."

"Jackson—"

"Go! Do it!" Jackson stumbled toward the rear of the pickup where the SAW M29 was mounted. With shaking fingers, he dismantled the big gun from the mount. He lugged the mobile machine gun and the ammo belts to the emergency firing position they'd constructed north of the hospital parking lot.

An H&K 320 grenade launcher was attached to a sling on the back of the pack which carried one hundred fifty pounds of ammo for the SAW. He'd use the grenade launcher once the SAW ran out and the enemy attempted to flank him.

"I'll get everyone to the boats," Lena said. "I'll get them out."

"Find Shiloh."

"I will. I swear it."

Jackson knelt behind the half-wall of felled timber shored up with sandbags and got to work. He moved robotically, efficiently.

His only goal was to keep fighting for as long as he could. "I'll buy you a few minutes, but a few minutes is all I can do."

"Jackson, are you sure—"

"No time for that! Go get our girl."

Her voice was edged with steel. "I'll make it count."

58

LENA EASTON

DAY ONE HUNDRED AND SEVENTY-FOUR

Lena crawled on her hands and knees, coughing and sputtering. The medical cart had tipped onto its side. Bandages and scalpels spilled across the floor. Machines had fallen over. Tangles of cords lay everywhere. The ceiling was half-sunken in, with exposed wires and piping snaking downward. The fluorescent lights were smashed to pieces.

And the smoke. Smoke everywhere, blinding her, choking her. The thick smoke stung her throat, her eyes, and her nose.

Scrambling to her feet, she clutched the operating table to keep herself upright. Instinctively, she checked her body for injuries. A couple of pieces of shrapnel protruded from her left shin. Blood leaked down her leg and pooled in her sock. The adrenaline pumping through her veins masked the pain. For now.

Ash rained down on her head. Chunks of drywall lay everywhere. Blinking against the dust in her eyes, she glanced around the operating theater, searching for the Newfie.

"Bear!" she croaked. The word rasped like sandpaper in her throat. She swallowed hard and tried again. "Bear!"

A soft whine pierced the tinny buzzing in her ears. The Newfoundland crouched in the corner next to the anesthesia machine. He growled in terror, his ears flat against his skull, tail low and hackles bristling.

Lena signaled to Bear. "Come on, boy. Come here."

Gingerly, he crept across the floor, belly low, and licked her hand. His fur was matted with dust and debris, but he moved easily without whimpering. He was okay.

Her relief was short-lived. "Shiloh," she wheezed. Then, louder, "Shiloh!"

There was no answer. All the blood rushed to her head. Where the hell was Shiloh? Did she get out in time? Was she trapped somewhere under the rubble, injured or unconscious, or dying?

A groan filtered through the cacophony of screams and the creaking groans of the ruined building.

Lena inched around the operating table. Her legs felt like Jello. There was a distinctive tinny whine in her ears. Her vision kept blurring, going in and out of focus.

Moreno had fallen off the operating table. He was on the floor, curled into a fetal position, his arms wrapped over his head. Blood soaked the floor in a puddle beneath his thighs. Large chunks of drywall had fallen on top of him.

Her main concern was for Shiloh, but she was a first responder: she couldn't leave Moreno behind. The roof could collapse on them at any moment. "Let's go! Come on, we've got to get up!"

The wheelchair was in the corner. Lena shoved the debris off Moreno. Moaning in pain, Moreno gripped her arms, and together they got him situated in the wheelchair. She checked the tourniquet on his thigh. They couldn't leave it on for long or he'd lose his leg, but that was a secondary problem.

First, they had to survive the next ten minutes.

Moreno cursed. "I'm utterly useless!"

"It'll be okay. It's okay." Lena didn't believe it herself. Dread scrabbled up the notches of her spine. She had to find Shiloh.

As if reading her thoughts, Moreno said, "Leave me behind."

"No way."

"I'm telling you, I'm dead weight—"

"Don't you ever shut up? I'm not leaving you so stop wasting your breath."

Moreno shut up. His bronze skin had turned a sickly bone-white. He'd lost too much blood, but Lena couldn't worry about that now. Pushing him in the wheelchair, with Bear sticking close to her side, Lena stumbled out of the operating room and into hell.

Half of the hospital had been reduced to rubble. The ER unit had been sheared off from the rest of the building. Wires and pipes and the bones of the structure were exposed like a macabre corpse. The reception area near the entrance was utterly impassable.

Lena took a step and nearly pushed the wheelchair over a body sprawled in the center of the corridor. Glancing down, she rubbed at her eyes in horror. Her brain dimly recognized the shape of Ira Fleetfoot, Theresa Fleetfoot's father.

Chunks of shrapnel had punctured his chest and neck. He'd been recovering at the hospital from his chainsaw accident. Now, he wouldn't recover from anything.

"Lena!" a distant voice shouted.

Lena looked up from the dead body. Three figures coated in dust scrambled down the hallway toward her. A taller adult and two children. Ana Grady dragged little Adam and Keagon Tilton by the hands. The baby strapped to her torso wailed in terror.

Tears, blood, and dirt smeared their faces. Their hair and clothes were gray and colorless.

Keagan clutched a tattered paperback in his hands—the book of jokes he'd shared with Ruby. Ana pulled him close to her side to keep him from seeing the corpse splayed at their feet.

"I want my mommy," he wailed.

"Bear and I will find her," Lena promised. "Go with Mrs. Grady for now. She'll keep you safe, okay?"

The little boy sniffled through his tears, but he nodded bravely.

"That's a good boy." Lena thrust the wheelchair at Ana. "Can you take Moreno and evacuate everyone you can find? I have to find Shiloh."

"I'll get them to the boats." Ana took the handles. A coughing fit seized her. "Last I saw her Shiloh was headed for the cafeteria to get the kids out."

Moreno gripped Lena's forearm. His hand was clammy. "Go get your kid. We'll see you on the other side."

Lena gave a sharp nod. Ana Grady turned and headed toward the exit with Moreno in the wheelchair. Keagan and Adam clung to her side.

Lena dropped to her knees in front of Bear. Detritus dug into her kneecaps, but she barely felt the pain. She leaned in and held the soft ruff of his neck. Her nose touched his snout. She stared intently into his intelligent brown eyes.

Nothing was more important than this.

"Find Shiloh," she said hoarsely. "We have to find Shiloh."

59

JACKSON CROSS
DAY ONE HUNDRED AND SEVENTY-FOUR

The sun rose on a world gone red with fire and blood.

Jackson's lungs felt seared, his throat and nostrils raw. His hands were stiff like claws as he manned the SAW. The incessant *boom-boom-boom* nearly deafened him.

The enemy approached, their movements practiced and precise as each man in each fire team covered a different angle, moving as an experienced unit. These weren't random thugs but professional soldiers: Russian, Mexican, ex-Army.

Jackson raised himself on his elbows, breathed out, and steadied himself. He zeroed in on the front of the visitor's center, located kitty-corner to the hospital's emergency entrance across the parking lot.

He glimpsed shadowy movement. A hostile peeked out, revealing half of his head and torso, and a sliver of his weapon. Jackson exhaled slowly and squeezed the trigger. He fired several rounds within a second.

The shots ricocheted off the barrel of the hostile's AK-47, smashed up through his chin, and pierced his brain tissue. The man jerked, his weapon skittering across the pavement. He collapsed and didn't move.

"I could use some help here!" Jackson said on his radio. "I'm slightly outnumbered."

"We're coming for you," Eli said into his ear. "There are two hundred enemy soldiers between us, but we'll get you out."

"Anytime now would be great!" Jackson scanned for the next target. And the next. They were closing in. There were too many of them. He kept searching for an opening where he might punch his way through the sea of bad guys, but nothing presented itself.

"I don't know how long I can hold them off. I've only one belt left for the SAW, then I'm down to three magazines for the AR-15, two for my pistol."

"Hold tight!" Eli said.

He wanted desperately to believe Eli, but he saw no escape route. Lead rained down on his position in a hailstorm of bullets. His nerves were raw. He forced himself to use short, controlled bursts of fire rather than shooting blindly.

Soon, the belt-fed magazine ran dry. Swiftly, he swapped it out for a fresh one. Each box held the belts that fed the SAW. It fired from an open bolt position, with the next round outside the super-heated barrel.

The cartel fighters took advantage of the pause in fire and increased their ferocious assault. Rounds whizzed all around him. Hundreds of spent shell casings littered the asphalt.

He figured there were at least ten enemy combatants crouched behind their armored vehicles, perhaps fifteen or twenty, all shooting at him. The thunderous blitz of firepower was overwhelming. He kept his head down and returned fire with punishing bursts of high-powered ammo.

Rounds impacted the sandbags six inches from his right arm. A second later, a round smashed the thick log to his left. Splinters imbedded in his cheek and neck. Another volley of gunfire pounded his firing hole. Muzzle flashes winked from a dozen positions.

Bullets strafed the pickup five yards to his left, punching a zipper of holes across the broad side of the vehicle. Jackson kept a wary eye on the cars, buildings, and trees. He shot anything that moved.

Still, he focused on conserving ammunition. At this rate, he'd run out soon. He was trapped and he knew it. He should be moving from cover position to cover position so the bad guys couldn't flank him, but there was nowhere to go.

He might have tried fleeing up the side road to the west, but that way was blocked by the fire. To the west of the hospital, great columns of thick black smoke boiled upward, lit from within with glowing, winking sparks. The tops of the trees whipped and swayed. A terrible orange glow seared the sky.

"The fire is almost on me!"

"Ten minutes!" Eli said over the radio. "Just hold on!"

He didn't know if he had ten minutes, but he would do his best. He gave regular updates through the radio: "Hostiles fifty yards to the southeast. I spot another team a hundred yards to the north, behind the visitor's center. Ammo is running low—"

Something punched him hard in the stomach. He was knocked backward on his butt. For a second, he sat there, breathing hard, not sure what had just happened. The pain was like a detonation.

Had a round struck his chest plate? But no, the jolt of pain originated lower. Dread slipped like a knife blade between his ribs. This wasn't good.

He reached for the M320 grenade launcher, flipped up the iron sights, took aim, and fired a round. Men screamed and cursed as the grenade exploded. He took out at least two enemy fighters, injuring a couple more.

Before opening the side breech to throw another round in, he swiped his hand across his stomach. Alarm flared through him. His fingers found the ragged hole in his stomach beneath the ceramic plates, an inch below his belly button.

Wetness leaked steadily from the wound. A cold feeling started in his chest and radiated through his limbs. The small piece of lead inside him must have done incredible damage to his internal organs. He didn't know how bad it was, only that it was bad.

Adrenaline kept him upright, but it wouldn't last long. He had to hold on until Eli and his friends arrived. Hold on. Just a little longer. Just hold on.

Already, he felt the strength draining from his body. With every beat of his heart, blood pulsed from the wound. He gritted his teeth and forced himself to focus, to concentrate, to *stay alive*.

Jackson glimpsed movement to his left. Two enemy fire teams leapfrogged between the minivans and SUVs that cluttered the hospital parking lot.

They were coming for him.

60

LENA EASTON
DAY ONE HUNDRED AND SEVENTY-FOUR

"Find her, Bear!" Lena said. "Please, boy, find our Shiloh."

Bear's tail wagged in enthusiasm. She didn't have the PLS, or point last seen, from which to start, or a fresh item of clothing the victim had recently worn to lead Bear's scent work.

But Bear was incredibly smart; he instinctively comprehended what she wanted from him. The dog understood that something terrible had happened, was still happening, and that their girl wasn't with them. Bear wouldn't stop until he found her.

The Newfie raised his snout, swinging his big head back and forth, tail straight out behind him, sniffing for Shiloh's scent. He trotted down the corridor, past the pediatrics wing toward the cafeteria, with zero concern for his own survival.

Hobbling after him, she gasped at the stab of pain in her shin. She was hesitant to yank out the piece of shrapnel in case she caused further damage or increased the bleeding.

It didn't matter. Nothing mattered at this moment but finding Shiloh. She couldn't vanquish the cartel, but she could do this: find the lost.

Lena and Bear were made for this.

Several people ran toward her, Ruby in the lead. The girl was

341

helping Fred Combs, who had his arm around his wife. Their faces were covered in soot but for the frantic whites of their eyes.

They had a woman with them—Miriam—and two children Lena didn't know. Miriam held a broken wrist against her chest. Superficial cuts scraped her arms. The younger child was weeping hysterically. The older one stared ahead, unblinking, his features frozen in a rictus of fear.

Two more survivors appeared from one of the patient rooms: a middle-aged woman with blood caking the side of her face cradled a toddler in her arms, followed by two older men with similar injuries.

"What do we do?" Ruby asked, terrified.

A loud burst of gunfire stuttered nearby. Everyone froze. The *rat-a-tat* of gunfire was somewhere outside the hospital. It was close, too close.

Goosebumps rose on Lena's arms. "Evacuate to the boats. Now!"

Ruby hesitated, as if torn between her allegiance to her friend and fleeing for her life. "What about Shiloh?"

"I'll find her. Just go! Help them. I need you to save these people. Do you understand?"

Ruby nodded. She grasped Fred Comb's arm, pulling him toward the exit. Everyone burst into motion, running and shouting. Ruby called out instructions, making sure the group stayed together as they fled.

They would be okay; Ruby would get them out.

Lena shoved against the crowd, wading deeper into the wreckage of the hospital. Tortured, creaking groans surrounded her. The destroyed structure was like a living thing in tremendous agony, moaning in its death throes.

Bear moved among the ruins, sniffing here and there, darting over rubble and crumbling drywall. Part of the roof had caved in. Thick poisonous dust sifted through the rays of hazy orange sunlight that spilled through the gaping ceiling. Several bodies were scattered among the wreckage.

It was an apocalyptic scene out of her worst nightmares.

Blinking against the smoke and ash, Lena followed Bear's trail, scrambling cautiously over splintered timber, chunks of broken bricks, and slabs of concrete. She was careful of each foothold, yet intensely aware that Shiloh might have minutes or seconds to live. Time was fast running out.

With a loud bark, Bear darted ahead. He darted through the rubble, squeezing through a crevice where a section of brick wall had crashed in on itself.

He alerted. Tail wagging eagerly, Bear pawed at the gap and barked again in excitement.

Lena's heart caught in her throat. Stomach churning, she tugged her flashlight from her pocket, stuck it between her teeth, and began to dig.

Normally, firefighters would arrive and relieve her at this point. The firefighters would take on the perilous task of freeing the survivor from tons of rubble. There was no one here but Lena. Even if the roof didn't fall in on them, Jackson could hold off the cartel for only so long.

Gradually, she became aware of a low roar, a great bellowing beast like a lion. Only it wasn't a lion. It was something much worse.

They had to get out now.

Kneeling, she pulled aside piles of debris, scraps of metal and plastic, and hunks of drywall. Her fingernails split. Her hands were scraped and bleeding.

She had no idea how much time had passed. Seconds? Minutes?

Finally, she reached deep, flailing with her hand. Her fingers touched something warm and soft. A human body.

Bear wriggled his entire torso, beside himself with joy. He barked loudly, as if to say, *hold on, we're coming!*

The body wasn't moving. It was curled onto its side, clothes caked with dirt and dust. She couldn't tell a single distinguishing feature or whether the person was alive or dead.

"We've got you. I've got you," she mumbled around the flashlight.

She hauled aside a chunk of concrete, then another and another, her muscles throbbing with the effort. Once again, she reached down, grasped the person beneath the armpits, and dragged the body up and out of the hole.

The figure's chest did not rise or fall. There was no movement, no breath. No sign of life. Blood matted the person's hair, so coated in debris she hadn't discerned the color at first. The hair was blonde and curly. The person was larger than her niece.

It wasn't Shiloh.

It was Traci Tilton.

A spear of rebar had punched through the center of her chest, impaling her ribs, her heart. Her skin was gray. She was dead. She'd likely died within moments of impact.

Relief flooded Lena's entire body, followed by a wave of guilt and sadness that Traci was gone. She couldn't help the elation that it wasn't Shiloh.

Bear danced around the rim of the pit, tail wagging. He nosed Lena's shoulder and whoofed in agitation.

Within the pit, something moaned.

Bear barked louder, frantic now, digging at the lip of the hole with his paws, his snout pushing deep into the crevice. Lena bent down and yanked aside a slab of drywall.

Beneath the debris lay a second figure. Small and curled like a comma, arms clamped over her head. The figure lifted her chin and groaned.

"Shiloh!" Lena cried.

Dirt covered the girl from head to foot. Her hair was coated in dust. Her face was smeared with a streak of blood. Her chest heaved with great hitching breaths, and her eyes were dull with shock.

Gently, Lena pulled Shiloh from the crevice. She checked her vital signs: her pulse was 110 beats a minute; her respiratory rate was elevated slightly, just above twenty breaths a minute. Fortunately, her skin was warm to the touch, not clammy.

Lena saw no severe wounds except for a handful of superficial cuts and abrasions, though there could be deeper internal injuries she couldn't see. Her vitals indicated she likely didn't have internal blood loss.

Her mouth was moving. Lena had to lean forward to hear her words. "Berlin, Bayern, Niedersachsen, Baden-Württemberg…"

"You're okay, honey," she said. "Breathe, baby girl. Just breathe."

Gradually, Shiloh's hitching chest slowed. Her gasps softened to steady, shallow breaths.

Lena patted her back. "You're alive. You're okay."

Shiloh's gaze fell on the body beside her. "Traci—is she—?"

Lena said, "She's dead."

Shiloh's eyes widened. "Traci—she fell on top of me when the walls caved in. The ceiling collapsed on us. She wrapped her body around mine and she—she took the brunt of it. She died instead of me. Why? Why did she do that?"

Tears in her eyes, Lena stared in awe at the body of the woman who'd lured her into Sykes' trap. The same woman who had sacrificed her life for Shiloh's. She had done both the worst thing and the best thing. In death, she'd redeemed herself.

"Perhaps to prove she was still human," Lena said, "That she was more than her worst mistake."

Shiloh made a strangled sound of disbelief, shaking her head like she couldn't accept the gift Traci had offered her. Well, she had no choice. Lena accepted it for her.

Lena wanted nothing more than to embrace Shiloh and never let her go. To hug her and kiss every inch of her face while she rolled her eyes in protest.

There was no time for anything but survival. "We have to go."

Bear nosed Shiloh's face and licked her dirty tears, chuffing in enthusiastic greeting. She wrapped her arms around his bulky torso and clung to him. "I thought I was going to die."

"You're not going to die, not today. Come on."

Shiloh looked down at Traci in stunned horror. "We can't just leave her."

"We'll come back later, I promise."

"What about her son—"

"Ana Grady has him. He's safe. We need to worry about us." She grasped Shiloh's filthy hand.

"The explosion—"

"Some kind of bomb. The cartel is coming. Everyone else has evacuated to the boats headed for Grand Island. Can you walk or run? We need to run."

Shiloh rose to her feet gingerly. Though her legs trembled from the shock, they held her weight. Bear pressed against her side, and she leaned into his flanks for support. She swiped a swath of dust from her face. Her eyes gleamed like bits of flinty coal.

Lena tugged on her arm. "Come on!"

Shiloh balked. "What about Jackson?"

61

JACKSON CROSS
DAY ONE HUNDRED AND SEVENTY-FOUR

J ackson was losing track of time. His entire body pulsed with the agony ripping through his insides. It felt like he'd been disemboweled by a beast with razor claws.

After several minutes of intense fighting, there was an abrupt break in the shooting. He swiveled his neck, desperately searching for the assault team that would rush his position as the other fighters poured on fire. None came.

An unnatural stillness had descended upon the hospital grounds. No one moved. No shots were fired. The unsettling din of the fire grew louder, which hissed and bellowed as if alive.

The heat of the blaze licked at the back of his neck. A solid wall of fire moving inexorably nearer. It was relentless, unassailable, inescapable. The snap and crackle of the flames in the wind grew louder and louder, a symphony of destruction.

Jackson blinked, wiped the sweat out of his eyes, and forced himself to focus on his next move. He had to keep the bad guys off him while attempting to stop the bleeding from his wound.

With a trembling hand, he pulled a pressure bandage from the first aid kit Eli insisted everyone carry in their chest rig. His palms were clammy against his bare skin. He tugged his uniform shirt up and pressed the bandage to the gushing hole in his stomach with a wince.

His heart flutter-flapped against his ribs. He felt cold, so cold. His thoughts tumbling inside his skull came slow and thick. His movements were sluggish.

He'd used the last belt of ammo for the SAW. He'd also used up the spare magazines for his pistol and rifle. He'd run completely dry.

"Hold out a little longer!" Eli said over the radio. "Five minutes."

"Did our people get out of the hospital? Did they make it?"

"I heard from Moreno," Eli said. "Most everyone is out. Lena is still searching for Shiloh, but everyone else made it already. You saved them."

A sensation of unbearable lightness expanded inside his chest. He exhaled for the first time in what felt like hours. Lena and Shiloh would make it, too. They were too strong, too brave to fail now.

He had to give them more time.

With one hand, he reached down and touched the spot low on his belly. He sucked in his breath, the pain like a white-hot poker. The bandage was soaked. His hand came back slick and red. He frowned, staring at the blood. There was so much of it.

"How are you on ammo?" Eli asked.

"I'm out," he said.

Barely restrained panic laced Eli's voice. "We're coming to you, brother. We're coming."

Jackson had the awful sensation of sand running out of an hourglass. There were a thousand things he wanted to say, but there was no time to say them. Perhaps there was time for one thing. One last thing.

"Devon," he said into his comms, not bothering with a call sign, hoping against hope that he wasn't out of range. He didn't care who else could hear him over the radio. He was beyond caring about inconsequential things.

"I'm here," she said.

"The answer is yes," he said. "I'd love to see where this might go between us. I'm ready. It took me way too long to see what was right in front of me, but I see it now. I see you."

There was a beat of hesitation. "Are you asking me on a date, Jackson Cross?"

"Only if you say yes."

"Yes!" she said happily. "A thousand times, yes."

"That's all I needed to hear."

It was becoming more difficult to speak. Cold sweat filmed his forehead. His muscles burned with fatigue. He was tired, so tired, and hurting all over. The pain was like a hammer bludgeoning his pelvis, radiating through his torso, smashing his ribs.

Movement shifted out of the corner of his eye. He knew then that he didn't have five minutes. He didn't have five seconds.

Ahead of him, two figures appeared through the thick wall of smoke. Their forms backlit against the wall of roaring flames bearing down upon them all. The figures strode between bullet-riddled minivans, approaching warily, both gripping HK417 rifles, one sweeping left, the other right.

They wore black camo gear, chest rigs, and battle belts. Black grease smeared their faces, but he recognized them. He knew the confident sway of the shoulders, the arrogant stride of every step, the way they moved like they owned the world.

How could he not? They were flesh of his flesh, bone of his bone. His only family. And his mortal enemies.

He managed a bittersweet smile. "I have to go. I've got company."

He did not flinch from the truth staring him in the face. There would be no happy ending. No rescuers blasting the enemy to smithereens at the last instant, no heroes swooping in to save the day. It was just him.

This, then, was the way it ended.

He'd spent his life believing he was a force for good, and yet he had committed horrific acts. He had framed an innocent man and sent him to prison. He had murdered his sister. Justified or not, he had done these terrible things. He had tried to reconcile the darkness within him and he did not know if he had succeeded.

Now, here at the end of the world, he could do this one thing. This last good thing. Maybe the best thing he'd ever done.

He would make his stand while the people he loved escaped.

Lily's family would live. That's what mattered.

"Jackson." Eli's voice was loud and firm in his ear. "You need to get out of there, right now!"

"I can't do that."

"Jackson—"

"It's Horatio. My father, my brother. There's no one else to stop them but me. It has to be me. Tell Lena and Shiloh that I love them."

"Jackson, wait—!"

He couldn't wait. It was time. Time to end this.

Jackson turned off his radio. He pulled a small object from his chest rig and balled it in his fist, holding it low by his side. Eli had tucked it into his hand that morning. He'd saved it for something like this. This was the moment. He waited.

"Jackson!" his father shouted. "I know it's you! Hold your fire!"

Jackson moved back from the empty SAW, sank back on his heels, and dropped his useless pistol to the ground at his knees. Splashes of blood darkened the ground beneath him.

He refused to raise his hands in surrender. He would never surrender, not to them.

Horatio rounded the sandbag wall first, his rifle aimed at Jackson's chest. Garrett followed his father, his stance wide, his expression smug. His eyes burned with hatred. They were angry, bitter, out for vengeance. They'd found it.

"It's a pity it came to this," Horatio said. "You could have been on the winning side. You could have dined on steak and wine with us tonight. Instead, you'll die squealing in your own filth. We'll leave your carcass to be burned to ash by the fire."

"Go to hell," Jackson said.

"Gault said it should be me who finishes you." Garrett stared down at him with an expression of pure loathing. "You're my brother. You've always been my brother. Blood for blood."

"Yes," Jackson said. "You're right. Blood for blood."

Garrett raised his rifle.

Jackson released the pin of the grenade.

His brother's face registered a brief moment of shock. His father's features twisted in a murderous outrage as the terrible realization struck him. He half-lifted his weapon. It was the last move he ever made.

Pulling the pin did not initiate the fuse within the grenade, as it was merely a safety device. But releasing the lever—the concave handle on the side—that got the party started.

He felt himself fading. He wasn't yet too far gone to do what needed doing. Jackson released the lever. He tossed the live grenade at his brother and father.

His last thought was not of Lily but of Devon, smiling at him, beckoning him onward into a new world where he could begin again. In his mind's eye, he stepped into her arms.

There was a blinding flash of bright light. Then everything went dark.

62

LENA EASTON
DAY ONE HUNDRED AND SEVENTY-FOUR

Lena grabbed Shiloh's arm and yanked her out of the cafeteria and down the corridor toward the exit sign. The hospital was groaning, cracking, and splintering. The building might fully collapse at any moment.

"Jackson," Shiloh gasped. "He's fighting them for us—"

Lena pulled her harder. "We've got to go!"

Shiloh dragged her feet. "Wait—We have to go back for him. He's all alone—"

"We're not going back for him. He'll meet us on Grand Island."

"NO! That's not right." Shiloh fought Lena, trying to jerk her arm out of Lena's grasp. She was in shock. She wasn't thinking clearly. "He needs our help—"

"We can't help him!" Lena shouted.

The sorrow she'd been holding back threatened to overwhelm her. If it did, she'd be worthless. She couldn't think about it, couldn't feel it. Instinctively, she knew the truth in some deep primal part of her brain: Jackson was gone.

He had made a final stand to save them. He hadn't needed to say the words aloud—she had known what he was doing, what he was going to do.

And she had let him do it.

Her best friend was dead or as good as dead, and she couldn't do a thing but keep going, one foot in front of the other, to get herself and her dog and her niece out of this hellhole alive.

Shiloh stopped in her tracks. Bear nearly barreled into the back of her legs. He panted, hackles raised, growling at every crash and boom. All around them, things shattered and toppled and caved in.

"We have to help him!" Shiloh twisted around, ripping free of Lena's grasp, about to dart back through the collapsing hospital as if she could single-handedly rescue Jackson Cross from an army of killers with nothing but a crossbow.

Lena gripped the girl's shoulders. "Shiloh! Listen to me. Jackson is dead. He's gone, do you understand? We can't help him now. We can only help ourselves."

Shiloh gaped at her. "You're wrong!"

"We have to leave!"

Aghast, Shiloh shook her head, hard and furious. Her eyes sparked with frantic tears. A wretched despair contorted her features. "You're lying! Tell me you're lying!"

Wetness stung Lena's eyes. It felt like a giant hand tearing her beating heart from her chest. "I'm not lying. I'm so sorry."

"NO!" Shiloh moaned. She fought Lena, trying to free herself, to escape, her tiny ferocious fists striking Lena's chest and shoulders. Lena held on, she held fast. Her heart shattered into a thousand pieces along with Shiloh's. "No! No! No!"

Gunfire blasted again. Closer now. It sounded like it was coming from just outside the hospital entrance. Shouting filtered through the tortured groans of the wreckage.

Somewhere, something massive crashed. The floor trembled. The walls quaked, undulating in precarious waves. Dust swirled around their feet.

The dull roar in the distance was no longer dull. The dreadful sound like a mighty wind. It wasn't the wind. At the end of the corridor, through the window in the exit door, the world outside had gone a terrible, nuclear red.

Shiloh went rigid in Lena's arms. The horrified whites of her eyes glowed in the crimson light. "What is that—?"

But they knew. They both knew.

The fire. It was finally here.

Lena took Shiloh's hand. They ran for their lives.

63

ELI POPE

DAY ONE HUNDRED AND SEVENTY-FOUR

After hours of unrelenting attack, the cartel pulled back momentarily to regroup, lick their wounds, and prepare for the next round of brutal warfare.

The Munising fighters had taken advantage of the break in the battle to reconvene for a desperate plan B.

Sawyer and Pierce stood on one side of the table, Antoine and Nyx on the other side. Hart and Nash were squished between them. Dana Lutz was with them, too. After what happened to Jackson, Eli had brought Devon in from her post. He wanted her close.

Everyone was exhausted, tense, and acutely aware of their missing brethren.

Eli had been forced to call off Jackson's rescue attempt. Much as he was loathe to admit it, it was a futile cause. Devon had recounted the explosion she'd seen through the drone footage. There was zero chance that Jackson had survived it.

He didn't have absolute confirmation that Jackson was dead, but he knew the truth in his gut, in the painful twist of grief as if a hole had opened up inside him he could not fix or heal.

He'd lost many good people in combat, but none hit as hard as this one.

"He's gone," Devon said, her face stricken. Her skin was ashen, her features slack, her arms limp at her sides. "Jackson is gone."

Eli went to her. He met her sorrowful gaze with his own. He didn't lie to his people. He refused to start now. "He is."

A whimper escaped her lips. Agony flared in her scarred face, her features contorting in loss and grief and horror.

He touched her arm in an attempt at comfort. "Everything you're feeling, put it in a box in your mind and put that box on a shelf for later. Jackson wouldn't want you to die now, after all this, after all we've fought for. He'd want you to fight. We will destroy them utterly for what they did to him. I swear it to you."

Devon gave a tremulous nod.

Eli would do the same. He had no choice. The grief would have to wait.

Right now, Lena and Shiloh should be fleeing the bombed hospital, then rowing across the water to the safety of Grand Island.

He hadn't heard from them in hours, but radio communication had been a crapshoot all day. At least Moreno had reported that he'd escaped the hospital and was about to cross the channel to Grand Island. Eli had to believe his family was with Moreno.

He had no choice but to believe, or else he'd fall to pieces here and now.

There were a thousand things he wanted to say, a million things he yearned to do. To cradle Lena in his arms, take Shiloh's small hand in his and bring them out of this hellhole safely into the light. To hold them both and never let go. He could do none of those things.

"You good, soldier?" he asked Devon.

Devon nodded again. She raised her chin, brushed a hand across the scabs marring her cheeks and throat, and rubbed the tears from her reddened eyes. She was tough; Eli trusted her to keep it together until the battle was either over or they were all dead.

He pushed out every thought, every worry. His total focus

narrowed to one point: neutralize whatever enemies threatened his town, his county, his people.

"What's the plan, brother?" Antoine said in a subdued voice.

"I may have an idea," Eli said. "It's not an honorable one."

Nyx scoffed. "No one is gonna give a flying fart that we lost honorably. They'll be dead. Their children will be dead. Their wives and sisters and daughters..." Her voice trailed off. "Honor only matters if we win. We have to win."

"Oorah!" Hart said, repeating the Marines' battle cry.

Eli nodded tightly. "Okay, then. Gather around. Here's what we're going to do."

The plan was simple enough to describe, but quite another matter to implement. It would take incredible skill and a whole hell of a lot of luck. They were down to a handful of elite, trained fighters.

He turned to the weary group gathered around him. Eli pointed to a spot on the map a quarter-mile wide, where a small meadow formed a valley that sloped up between two hills, creating a sharp ravine to the north. "We're going to draw the enemy into this area here."

The valley was located three miles southeast of town. The top of the hill where the ravine ended lay at the northernmost point of the valley, with the open valley stretching to the south.

There was an ORV trail for dirt bikes and ATVs that went through the valley before zigzagging up the middle of the narrow end of the ravine. The trail was too steep for trucks or other vehicles. To summit the ravine, they would have to climb on foot.

That's what Eli was counting on.

Pierce scowled. "Once we have several hundred cartel fighters chasing us, just what are we supposed to do?"

Hart smirked. "Run."

Pierce's scowl only deepened. "Sounds like a great plan."

"It'll work," Antoine said. "We'll make it work."

"You'll draw them into the mouth of the upslope to the north, right here," Eli continued. "Once you make it to the top of the hill, we'll use drip torches to start a fire behind the enemy soldiers, here and here and here. My team will light the fire to the south, while the wildfire blocks their escape from the west. We're going to trap as many of them as we can in the valley. Then we'll cook them alive. The defensive line at the top of the ridge will clean up any hostiles who escape the flames."

Hart offered a wry grin. "You're planning a cartel wiener roast."

Eli's lips twitched. "Damn straight."

Nyx rubbed her hands together with glee. "Hell yeah! I can get behind that."

"For weeks we've been doing hit-and-run raids. Twice we've escaped by ducking into these woods and going up this ravine. This time is different. We're going to slow down at the base and hold our position long enough for the cartel to call for support and backup. I want them to think they've found an important base of operations or some command-and-control point."

Eli looked at Pierce and Sawyer. "Keep your men hidden at the base in the woods, far enough from the offroad trail to remain unseen until it's too late. When you retreat up the hill, they'll pursue you, thinking they're going to wipe us out. That's when you open up and clobber them."

Pierce looked downright contentious. "What keeps the fire from getting us? Seems like the stupidest idea on the planet. I for one don't feel like getting roasted like a rotisserie chicken."

Eli angled his head at Dana. "You want to step in, here?"

Dana Lutz stepped forward from where she'd been hanging back, quietly listening. Eli had brought her in based on her expertise with fire. She'd proven invaluable already.

She cleared her throat. "You and your men will summit the top long before the fire makes it to you. As an extra precaution, we won't start the fires until you reach the top and give us a signal—say, fire a flare from one of the grenade launchers. If there's no flare, we'll assume you're too close and the fire will be a no-go. Same if the wind picks up too much."

"There's a front moving in off Lake Michigan," Hart said. "Heavy winds and precipitation."

Dana nodded. "The hot air from the wildfire will affect the wind currents. The winds can pick up to forty miles per hour in that small canyon. There's plenty of fuel and a steep slope up, which will push the blaze north right up the valley to the ravine. Fire travels faster uphill."

Antoine peered at the map. "At the top, we'll have a clear field of fire shooting downhill. We'll bring the fireworks. We have a couple of SAWs and several M240 lightweight machine guns, though we're running low on ammunition. And we can put our remaining vehicles here at the bottom of the other side of the hill, to evacuate men if we can't hold the line. Best case scenario, finish them from the top."

Pierce shook his head, his stance wide and combative. His eyes flashed with suspicion. "No way! You're using us as bait. This is an insane plan. It's crazy! Sawyer, tell them."

Sawyer remained silent. His face was cool and composed, implacable. He seemed to be
weighing the options in his head. "It could work."

"Sawyer—"

Sawyer shot Pierce an aggravated look. "Do you have a better idea? I want Luis Gault's head on a platter. He'll make a delicious meal for the fish."

Pierce showed his teeth like a cornered animal. "You're trusting Pope to light a fire at our backs. I'd sooner trust a wolf."

Sawyer wheeled on him. "Enough! We're going to do this. Do I make myself clear?"

Pierce grimaced. His eyes glittered with pure, savage hatred. He made no attempt to hide his contempt for Eli or the rest of the Munising fighters.

"Clear as crystal, boss," he muttered darkly.

Eli maintained his neutral expression. He kept his thoughts to himself. Pierce was going to be a problem, though he was predictable if nothing else. No matter. Very soon, Pierce would no longer be a concern.

"We in or what?" Nyx asked.

Everyone was silent for a sobering moment as they contemplated the long odds, the significant risks. Devon stepped forward first. "We're in. For Jackson."

64

SHILOH EASTON POPE
DAY ONE HUNDRED AND SEVENTY-FOUR

The wildfire crackled, popping and hissing, roaring as loud as a freight train.

With Bear right behind them, Shiloh and Lena exited the rear of the hospital and sprinted for the thin band of forest that separated the hospital grounds from the shoreline.

They'd just reached the beach when flocks of birds arced across the sky, dark and fleeting as loosed arrows. Loons and herons, hawks and swallows, woodpeckers and blue jays.

Shiloh blinked rapidly, trying to clear her foggy vision. Her brain felt thick and cottony. Her body was reeling from the trauma of the explosion. Her head throbbed. Every muscle in her body was bruised and sore, but the adrenaline masked most of the pain. That would come later.

She couldn't think about what had just happened. Traci Tilton's sacrifice. The sour-sick panic of being buried alive. She couldn't think about Jackson. Whether he was alive or dead.

She did what Eli had taught her. She pushed it all out and focused on staying alive. There was no time to recover, only to act.

Dozens of people were already on the beach. About fifteen small watercraft were already in the lake rowing for Grand Island.

Several people were still frantically pushing kayaks and canoes into the water.

Hundreds—thousands—of birds clotted the horizon in a dreadful migration. The strange, sinister sight struck sheer terror into Shiloh's heart.

"They're fleeing," she said, horrified. "Fleeing ahead of the fire."

"As should we!" Lena said. "Hurry!"

Before they could react, something large shook the under-brush behind them. Adrenaline kicked her heart. Shiloh whirled, reaching behind her for her crossbow. Bear plunged in front of them, barking fiercely in the direction of the woods.

"What is that—"

A dozen feet to their left, a pair of moose broke from the scrim of spruce trees, a big bull moose and a smaller female. Shiloh and Lena watched in shock as the huge animals lumbered across the sliver of beach and plunged into the lake.

Their harsh chuffs echoed in Shiloh's ears. The moose looked neither left nor right, nor did they seem to notice the humans huddled on the beach beside them. They appeared oblivious to Bear, who continued barking, hackles raised.

The moose waded deeper into the water. Within moments, two angular brown heads bobbed above the surface of the lake. The moose angled themselves toward the shore of Grand Island and swam hard. The water parted in twin arcing lines behind them.

Fifty yards down the shoreline, a black bear appeared. It hurtled into the water without hesitation. The moose and the bear didn't seem to be aware of the other, natural predator and prey oblivious to anything but the monstrous threat bearing down upon them.

More creatures emerged from the forest and burst onto the narrow shelf of the beach. A family of foxes appeared, then hares and chipmunks and squirrels. Five coyotes sprang into the water, yipping and howling while a wolverine scurried out onto a bleached piece of driftwood.

Shiloh stared, utterly mesmerized. Bear raised his snout and sniffed the air. He whirled, growling and barking at the wild animals. She kept her hand on the scruff of the dog's neck, holding him back.

"Stay!" Lena shouted at Bear. The dog trembled, muscles quivering, but he obeyed her command. The tremendous roar at their backs grew louder. Lena pointed to a two-person canoe no one had claimed yet. "Get in! Go, go!"

Shiloh's mouth had gone dry, her palms clammy. Her fingers fumbled in terror as she freed the canoe from the rope tied around a nearby beech tree. The oars were balanced precariously on the seat bench.

One hand still on Bear's ruff, she and Lena dragged the canoe across the sand and pebbles and pushed it into the shallow water.

"Get in!" she screamed at the next family waiting in line. People were wailing, screaming, weeping. Ana Brady sat in one of the boats with a bunch of kids. Moreno was with them, the wheelchair abandoned on the shoreline. Ruby had gotten Fred Combs and his wife into a rowboat and was pushing them out into the water.

Booming sounds like gunshots sounded over the roar overwhelming every other sound. The trees were exploding with great cracks like thunder.

A tremendous wave of heat blasted her back. The heat was incredible. It felt like she was being roasted alive. The hairs on her arms were singed. The heat struck her in swirling flurries like the forest fire had created its own blistering wind, its own terrible weather.

Shiloh risked a peek behind her. Far above the trees, an enormous dark cloud rose, expanding across the entire sky, swirling and cresting, a seething storm of smoke about to descend upon them. The warning flare of what was coming.

The wildfire grew closer, like an advancing front: ferocious and unrelenting, unstoppable. All along the shoreline, flames flickered and danced among the tops of the trees.

"Shiloh!" Lena shouted.

Shiloh spun around. Everyone else had clambered into the boats except for Bear. He crouched low on his belly, ears laid back against his skull. He was growling and snapping in a panicked frenzy. He was terrified of the fire but even more afraid of the stupid canoe.

Shiloh hopped into the canoe with Lena, who was desperately trying to coax the balking Newfoundland to leap into the middle section. Bear whined louder.

"Come now!" Shiloh seized his collar and yanked at him with all her strength. The dog protested every indignity. She didn't care if he hated it; she wasn't leaving him behind. "This is no time to be a scaredy cat, you big oaf!"

Though he outweighed her, Shiloh managed to drag him reluctantly over the bow and into the watercraft. He growled in disdain at the unsteady rocking, his paws slip-sliding on the slick, water-logged belly of the canoe. He whipped his head from side to side, snapping at the overheated air.

"Get down!" Lena ordered him. "Stay down!"

They rowed as hard as they could, the heat a solid wall against their backs. The smoke thickened, swelling and eddying and billowing all around them. A dense, molten fog closed in on all sides.

The surface of the water disappeared, then the shoreline vanished. Behind them, only the fiery tops of the trees were visible.

"Row! Row! Row!" Moreno's voice echoed dimly but Shiloh could no longer see him. Ruby was yelling something she couldn't make out. It sounded like a prayer, or maybe a distraught cry for help.

She couldn't focus on the others. Her palms blistered as she rowed harder and faster. Her muscles screamed in protest. Her arm hairs felt singed.

Sparks churned and roiled with the smoke. Hot embers

swirled over the caravan of boats rowing madly across the channel. The lacy tatters of glowing leaves and strips of bark fluttered past, on fire.

The fire was a great dragon, a malevolent creature that lived and breathed. The frenetic flames crackled through the crowns of the trees. The whole forest flared a radiant, pulsing crimson.

Horrific sounds echoed all around them: popping and hissing, cracks and bangs. The air was on fire. Everything burned. The blaze turning everything into molten lava.

People were weeping and crying, praying and begging for their lives. Every breath hurt. Her lungs felt coated with char and soot. Steam sizzled off the water with every splash of the paddle.

She couldn't see Grand Island through the smoke. They had to be near the middle of the channel, but they were not safe. No one was safe. Not the fleeing wild creatures nor the humans flailing across the water. They were caught in the mouth of the dragon.

She didn't know how far a fire could jump across water, only that it could. The wildfire was big enough, powerful enough. It could cross the channel in a flashover. If that happened, they would all be boiled alive.

Behind them came the ominous cracks and shrieks of burning tree limbs breaking off and falling to the ground. Flying sparks landed on Shiloh's shirt. She managed to bat them away before her clothes burst into flames.

Flaming debris flew over their heads and landed hissing in the water or on the kayaks and row boats. People screamed in terror. A fluttering spark landed on Bear's haunches. Startled, he whimpered in pain.

"Don't move!" Shiloh said, her throat raw.

There was a bucket lying near a pile of rope next to the dog. Pausing for even a second would slow them down. She refused to allow Bear to burn to death.

Swiftly, she tossed the paddle inside the canoe, reached for the bucket, dunked it into the lake, and poured water across Bear's back. The dog yelped. The water had the desired effect; it drenched his fur and put out the tiny flames.

"Keep rowing!" Lena shouted.

The boats pulled further from shore. Finally, the fierce wind seemed to lessen. The raging roar of the dragon stalking the shoreline weakened to a growl. The blizzard of sparks lessened to the occasional flaming pine needle or molten leaf.

The fire crouched, balking at the wide expanse of the water, stymied at last.

Then the looming shape of Grand Island materialized through the smoke. Glossy white yachts floated along the dock.

The first rowboats and kayaks reached the shoreline. People tumbled out of the watercraft, spilled into the water, and sloshed for the pebbled beach.

Using her paddle to steer, Lena angled them to the left of the dock, away from the bigger boats and toward a shallow sandbar. She hopped out and reached for Shiloh. Together, they hauled the bow of the canoe onto the gravel-strewn beach.

Bear scrambled out of the canoe, nearly tipping it in his eagerness to escape. He stood in the lake up to his haunches, his snout pointed toward the mainland, barking fiercely at the fire.

Ashes twirled from the sky like powdered snow. It silted in Shiloh's hair and clung to her eyelashes. She waded into the lake next to Bear and sank onto her bottom, letting the water cool her scorched skin.

She gazed across the beach in search of Ruby. She was standing in the sand a few dozen yards away, soaking wet but alive, so very alive. Their gazes met: Shiloh's questioning, Ruby raising her chin in answer. She was okay. They were okay.

Everyone who'd fled the hospital had made it.

Lena came and stood next to Shiloh. Neither spoke a word. Lena took Shiloh's hand. They stood and watched the mainland burn in astonishment.

They had escaped through the flames but everything they

loved had remained behind to be devoured by the dragon. Their home, their town, everything burning.

What would be left standing? Who was still alive? Shiloh didn't know. She was alive but in shock, too numb for the grief and rage to sink in.

"Jackson," she whispered, heartbroken. "Eli."

"I know." Lena squeezed her hand. "I know."

65

ELI POPE
DAY ONE HUNDRED AND SEVENTY-FOUR

E li crouched in a hidden fighting hole to the south of the valley. He'd chosen a spot that gave him a clear sightline of the entire valley and the steep ravine ahead of him.

He barely felt the chill of the wind stinging his cheeks. Though he was positioned to the east of the wildfire, a dense red haze had settled over everything. The stink of smoke was strong in his nostrils.

Hours earlier, he had ordered volunteers to collect the trash from empty ammunition containers and weapons crates, as well as the used MRE packets, and toss them around the valley.

The cartel pursuers would believe they'd stumbled upon a base of operations command-and-control center and would immediately call for backup. Hopefully, Gault would send a significant portion of his army to mop up the fleeing Munising fighters.

Sawyer shifted beside him, staring through a pair of field glasses as he studied his men's dug-in positions. A hundred of Sawyer's best fighters hid among the trees surrounding the valley, waiting for their moment to strike. Jim Hart and his team waited atop the ravine armed with grenade launchers in case the last chopper showed itself.

Eli had planned for Sawyer to lead his own men, but Sawyer

had put Pierce in charge and remained at Eli's side. Perhaps he suspected a double-cross, or he was smart enough to cover his bases.

"Ready to do this?" Eli asked.

"Frankly, I'd rather be sailing." Sawyer shot him a shrewd smile. "You should come with me sometime."

Eli's lips twitched, barely. "Been there, done that. Think I'll pass. I can't say much for the catering or dining service, though you do have good taste in beer."

Sawyer laughed out loud. "We could have been friends, you and I."

Eli thought of the torture he'd experienced at Sawyer's hand. He thought of David Kepford, shot in the spine by Pierce. "Perhaps in another life."

"Perhaps."

Eli's radio crackled to life. "I've got their camp in sight," Antoine said. "Several hundred people, logistical support as well as soldiers set up in tents. They've consolidated forces. The sentries are half-asleep, drinking their coffee from metal cups and bundled up in winter jackets. Piece of cake."

Eli spoke into his headset. "You're a go."

The sound of multiple gunshots shattered the silence. Eli listened to the comms as Antoine and Nyx opened fire on the camp from the armored SUVs they'd borrowed from Sawyer, racing past with strafing fire before fleeing.

The hornet's nest exploded. Automatic fire broke out from multiple directions. Shouted orders spat through the radio. The sounds of gunfire and screams echoed in tinny blasts.

Nyx whooped. "I think we got their attention!"

"Alpha Team!" Antoine said. "We're two miles out and being pursued by a blue pickup and several vehicles behind it. Be ready to light it up!"

"Good copy," Eli said.

"Now what?" Sawyer asked.

"Now we wait."

KYLA STONE

They didn't have to wait long. Three armored SUVs came flying into the valley from the ORV trail, jolted across the meadow, and careened toward the narrow dirt road leading up the northern point of the ravine. The trucks slammed their brakes at the base of the hill. Several Munising fighters leaped out and began the ascent on foot. Quickly, they reached the top and disappeared from view.

Dozens of vehicles poured into the valley in hot pursuit. At the base of the ravine, they were forced to halt. Armed men spilled out and began moving toward the hillside like an army of ants. They broke into fire teams, one team moving quickly for a few seconds while the other provided cover. They alternated roles until they reached the tree line and disappeared into the dense foliage, headed up the ravine in pursuit of Eli's men.

"Now?" Sawyer asked.

"Now." Eli fired a starburst flare into the sky.

Seconds later, Sawyer's men opened up on the cartel from their hidden fighting positions. They unleashed hell on the pursuing vehicles. Two trucks went careening across the meadow and slammed into a cluster of jack pines. One burst into flames.

Screams and curses echoed between volleys of gunfire. After the shock of first contact, a murderous volume of fire headed the other way. Branches snapped as a barrage ripped through the canopy, shredding bushes and dense underbrush. Twigs and bits of bark hit the ground all around them.

"There's an element moving toward us on the right through the woods," Pierce said into their headsets.

At the same time, Eli spotted another contingent in the woods on the other side of the creek. "Twenty to thirty men are moving through the woods to the west of you. They'll be slowed by the ravine and the dense underbrush, but you need to move now."

Sawyer looked at Eli for confirmation. Eli nodded.

"Tango One to all Tango groups," Sawyer said. "Start moving up the ravine. Leap frog up and cover each other. Don't panic. Good luck."

Eli signaled to Sawyer. They inched backward out of the hide

Eli had constructed. Ducking, they made their way a few hundred yards southeast to where Dana Lutz and her team of volunteer firefighters were positioned deeper in the woods, concealed until the cartel troops passed through.

"Scouts just spotted that last chopper!" Hart shouted through their comms. "No surprise, it's headed our way, coming over the valley from the east."

Eli tensed. "You have to take it out or the Huey will pulverize our men, making it pointless for the cartel to chase them up the ravine. The entire trap will fail. Take it out, Hart!"

"I've got this!" Hart said. "I've only got the one grenade left. No problem."

A minute later, the helicopter appeared to their right. The percussive blows of an M60 machine gun were deafening, drowning out the crack of rifle fire. The gunner shot bursts indiscriminately across the narrow valley, as if the shooter didn't care who he killed as long as his enemies ended up good and dead, too.

Sawyer crouched, cursing. "That thing could take us all out."

"It won't," Eli said. Then, into his radio: "No pressure, Hart. It's all on you."

"Easy as stealing candy from a baby!" Hart said. "Watch the magic and weep."

A bright light flashed. The rocket streaked across the sky. It arced perfectly, striking the chopper's front right side before the pilot had time to attempt evasive maneuvers.

The Huey careened, spinning out of control. It struck the tops of the trees a couple hundred yards to the south, slicing through the canopy and shearing off branches. The chopper shuddered as it smashed into trees and underbrush. It cascaded down the slope of the hill on its side, rotors snapping off and flying dozens of feet before plummeting to the earth.

Eventually, the helicopter came to a crumpled heap against the base of a large outcropping of rock. Steam billowed from the wreckage.

Weapon up, Eli shifted to the left, moving out from behind a large jack pine. He kept the mangled chopper in his sights. Nothing moved inside. The gunner and the pilot were dead.

Through their headsets, Antoine let out a fierce whoop of delight. "Hell yes!"

"Who knew Marines could hit a target," Eli said.

"I heard that!" Hart groused.

"The cartel is gaining on my men," Sawyer hissed. "What the hell are you going to do about it?"

They listened to the panicked radio chatter coming from Sawyer's goons. Hordes of
cartel fighters scrambled up the hillside after them.

"They're about to flank us!"

"I'm hit!"

"I've got a wounded man. He's been shot in the leg. We're about to be trapped!"

"Leave him," Pierce growled. "Get your ass up that ridgeline."

"They're right behind us!"

"There's too many of them!"

"Where the hell is our cover fire!" Pierce shouted. "They're gaining on us!"

Sawyer shot Eli a suspicious look, his eyes narrowing. "Thought your guys were gonna protect mine, Pope."

Eli shrugged. "They are. The underbrush might be too dense for our fighters on the ridgeline to fire accurately. Your guys need to climb higher."

In truth, Antoine and Nyx had already evacuated from the top of the ridgeline and swiftly descended the opposite side to the escape vehicles waiting on the other side of the hill. Eli had given them private instructions out of earshot of Sawyer and his men. Now that the chopper had been eliminated, Hart would do the same.

Sawyer scowled up at the wind whipping the tops of the trees. Some trees had lost their canopies, but many leaves still clung stubbornly to gnarled branches. There was plenty of fuel for the wildfire to burn for a long time.

"It's windy. Too windy to light the fire. My men aren't far enough ahead."

Eli went still. "Sure, they are. They'll be fine. This is the chance we've been waiting for."

Sawyer stared him down, his gray eyes flinty and cold, his expression stony, revealing nothing of his thoughts. Eli braced himself for a confrontation.

This was it. The moment it all came together, or everything fell apart.

66

ELI POPE
DAY ONE HUNDRED AND SEVENTY-FOUR

E li waited with bated breath, giving nothing away. Pulse even, gaze steady. *Wait for it.*

After a tense moment, Sawyer relaxed. He thrust out his hand. "Fine. Give me one of the torches and the jerrycan of fuel. I'll light the fire on the east end."

Eli waited until Sawyer had stalked off and disappeared behind a row of birch trees, then he turned to Dana. A solid wind rushed up the ravine, just like he'd hoped. "Start lighting the other two fires."

Dana's eyes widened in surprise. "It will kill everyone in that ravine."

"I know."

She lowered her voice. "What about Sawyer's men?"

Eli made sure Sawyer was out of earshot before he spoke. "If we manage to win this battle, next week we'll be fighting for our lives against Sawyer's goons. Sawyer is a blight on this community. Without him, good people would be alive: Cody Easton, Nyx's grandmother, and David Kepford, not to mention the countless others who've died from drug overdoses. Trust me, I'll sleep like a baby after this."

Dana tilted her chin in the direction Sawyer had wandered. "Are you going to kill Sawyer, too?"

He wanted to. With every fiber of his being, he wanted that man dead. But Sawyer had saved his life on the battlefield. Did that mean something? He wasn't sure yet. "First things first. Light the fires."

Eli watched Dana and her crew light their drip torches and set the dry grasses at the base of the ravine ablaze, which they'd soaked with what little remained of their biofuel. Their limited supplies were precious, but this was worth the sacrifice.

Tiny flames ignited. Little flickers danced along the dry grasses and brittle underbrush. Fed by the wind, the fire grew quickly. It spread rapidly along the base of the valley. The three separate blazes snaked toward each other, growing in strength.

The first trees caught fire. Tiny saplings crackled and burst into flames. The flames licked up the trunks and leaped from branch to branch. A strong gust of wind churned between the hills and drove up the small canyon.

Meanwhile, the battle progressed between the cartel and Sawyer's men. Volleys of gunfire traded back and forth, echoing loud as thunder. The men engaged in the fight seemed not to notice as the fire crowned in the trees at the base of the hill.

The wind took the flames and whipped them into a ferocious blaze. Smoke poured into the valley and rose in dark menacing columns. Scarlet-stained clouds blotted out the sun.

"The fire is too close!" Pierce shouted, panic in his voice. "We aren't even halfway up the hill!"

Eli ignored him. He tugged out his radio and in a low voice relayed a specific set of instructions to Antoine, who was headed back to Eli's location on his ATV via a circuitous route around the valley. "Take care of Sawyer. Like we discussed."

"You've got it, brother."

The fire in the trees on the sides of the ravine burned hot and bright. A sound like rushing wind grew steadily louder, drowning out the gunshots from the AK-47s and AR-15s, mingling with the cracks of exploding tree limbs and bursting pinecones like fire-crackers.

It fascinated him how the fire moved faster uphill; at a thirty-degree incline, the fire doubled its speed. It seemed an evil trick, but one that would work for them.

Even with Dana's warning ringing in his ears, he hadn't predicted how swiftly the blaze would consume everything within its path. The deadfall, the parched grass, the dry trees shorn of leaves—it was all fuel, the perfect combustion.

The fire pushed hard and fast up the slope, impossibly fast. Flames licked at the heels of the cartel now. It raced up the hillside not fifty yards behind them. Screams rent the air as they realized the lethal danger chasing them. Once the predators, they had suddenly become the prey.

In desperation, the cartel men dropped their weapons and packs and ran with everything they had. They scrabbled up the steep hillside, boots slipping on slick leaf litter, tripping on roots, thorns snagging their skin.

The inferno was close enough that they could feel the heat scorching the clothes on their backs. Their boots melted, and their hair started to burn.

Shrieks pierced the air, terrible inhuman sounds that prickled the hairs on the back of Eli's neck. One by one, the cartel fighters fell as the fire consumed them.

Flesh cooked on bone. Airways swelled, internal organs smoldered. Through the trees, their bodies glowed like lit matches.

The blaze seemed to gain fuel from the human corpses. It surged up the ravine, faster than Eli could have anticipated. Rather than a simple chemical reaction, it seemed alive, a monster bent on destruction.

The ravenous beast was still hungry. It was eyeing its next food source—Sawyer's men.

"Sawyer!" Pierce cried, not bothering with call signs. "Come in, Sawyer! We're trapped! We need help!"

"Sawyer is...incapacitated at the moment," Eli said.

A moment of tinny silence. Eli could almost hear the mental energy crackling as Pierce worked it out, the thing Eli had done to him. Pierce let out a howl of fury and fear. "YOU!"

Eli only smiled. His silence said everything Pierce needed to know. Eli had orchestrated every moment of this massacre, and he didn't regret a second of it.

"You did this!" Pierce screamed. "You trapped us!"

With one hand, Eli reached beneath his plate carrier and tugged out the Saint Michael's medal he wore around his neck next to his dog tags. "Remember the school principal you murdered on your island by shooting him in the back? You tossed his vest and his medal on the table in front of me while you laughed."

"I don't know what the hell you're talking about—"

"Do you remember, Pierce? Because I remember. I remember it all."

Pierce sputtered, speechless in his rage. "You—you—I'll kill you for this!"

"I don't think so."

"You're done, Pope!" Pierce shrieked. "You hear me? I'm going to cut open your girlfriend, then your daughter, while they beg for mercy, and then I'm going to gut you like the pig you are—"

"Goodbye, Pierce." Eli clicked off his radio.

Pierce was trapped, as good as dead. Eli only wished he could be present to see the man roasted alive in person. It would be immensely satisfying. He touched the spot on his chest over the Saint Michael's medal and mouthed the prayer he'd memorized: *Saint Michael the Archangel, defend us in battle...*

Screams and shouts of fear echoed through the comms. Sawyer's crew had almost reached the top of the ridge where there was a break in the trees along a ledge of stone outcroppings. They sprinted for it as if that small clearing could save them, the cries of their dying pursuers searing their eardrums.

Eli watched the massacre unfold through his binoculars, his breathing slow and even, imagining Pierce as he fled the inferno, the smoke choking his throat and lungs, the ten-pound rifle he carried growing heavier as he fought against the steep incline of the slope, scree kicked loose beneath his scorched boots, panic a hot coal in his chest.

No matter how fast Pierce ran, it would not be enough.

One by one, the fighters tossed aside their rifles in a last-ditch effort to outrun the flames snarling at their heels. It was no use. The fire overtook them and they fell writhing to the ground as they burned.

Less than a minute later, the screams stopped. Everything stopped but the fire.

Eli gazed up at the impressive curtain of flames rising thirty feet high. The orange glow pulsed and throbbed. Sparks flew through the air. He found himself dazzled at the astonishing beauty of it.

He doubted Sawyer's men had found it beautiful as they died. Certainly not Pierce.

"What have we done?" Dana breathed, in awe at the fierce display of nature's power.

"What we had to do," Eli said.

To save themselves, they'd burned the world to the ground.

67

LENA EASTON
DAY ONE HUNDRED AND SEVENTY-FOUR

The fires raged for the rest of the day. The front sweeping up from Lake Michigan finally arrived. The dismal rainfall drenched the town and the nearby forests, stifling the fire though not putting it out completely.

As swiftly as it had arrived, the inferno passed by, leaving a swath of smoldering destruction in its wake.

Hours passed. The hospital survivors waited on the beach, watching the fires burn, praying for rescue, desperate for a reprieve. People were injured, crying and scared, devastated but alive.

Lena huddled shivering with Shiloh and Ruby beside some driftwood. Bear paced restlessly beside them. It felt like an eternity passed in that terrible unknowing.

Eventually, a tiny rowboat appeared from the mainland, rowing across the channel to Grand Island. Eli had returned from battle. He had come for them as he'd promised.

Shiloh sprinted across the pebbled sand and waded into the water without waiting for the boat to dock. Nyx reached over the hull and yanked her dripping wet up onto the deck. Shiloh tackled Eli, wrapped her arms around his waist, and refused to let go.

Eli had held her close and met Lena's gaze across the stretch of water; a whole lifetime of things unspoken passed between them in an instant. Relief and sorrow, grief and love.

Lena couldn't wait a second longer, either. The thought of another minute separated from Eli Pope was unbearable. She splashed into the water after Shiloh, love and relief pulsing with every beat of her heart, the fear knotted in her gut untangling at the sight of Eli's beloved face.

Still holding Shiloh, he reached for her, and she melted into him. Eli drew them both close in his strong embrace. He kissed the top of her head.

Tears streamed down her cheeks. She wept with mingled joy and sadness. They had lost so much, but she still had her family.

"You came back to me," she whispered against his chest.

She felt rather than saw his weary smile. "Always."

Shiloh didn't even complain when they kissed.

From the shoreline, Bear barked in enthusiastic greeting. The survivors on the beach looked on, too traumatized to whoop or cheer. Still, the abject relief was evident on their soot-smeared faces. Against all odds, they were alive. They'd been saved.

"We did it," Eli said into her hair. "We won."

68

LENA EASTON
DAY ONE HUNDRED AND SEVENTY-EIGHT

F our days after the battle, Lena and Eli returned to Munising, along with Nyx and Antoine. Tim and Lori Brooks came with them. Tim's right arm was cradled in a sling from a stray bullet. Lori helped Moreno on his crutches. Moreno had survived with a blood transfusion, although he might never walk on his own again.

Shiloh had demanded to come with them. Though she sported some ugly bruises, she had survived relatively unscathed. She insisted she had to see for herself. She needed to see. So did Devon.

In awed silence, they stepped cautiously through the wreckage. The moment felt reverent, almost holy as they witnessed the devastation, solemnly counting the cost. How much they had lost. How much more they could have lost but had salvaged instead.

The aftermath of the battle was a dreadful thing to behold: a ruined landscape out of a nuclear holocaust. The scorched earth pulsed with the remnants of the wildfires, little patches of flames still alight, red embers glowing from blackened stumps and burnt branches.

Charred tree trunks speared the sky, saplings like spindles with their tops sheared off, the trees burnt skeletons. Here and there a spruce or jack pine or cluster of beech trees remained unburned, singed but still standing. The forest along the coastline of Lake Superior for twenty miles was naught but fiery embers.

In town, the scars of the battle were everywhere: buildings reduced to rubble, streets lined with the husks of burned cars, razed apartment buildings, houses cut in half. Bullet holes scarred boarded-up cafes and shops.

Half of Munising had been burned to the ground. The hospital was charred rubble. The fire had scorched the high school but spared the middle school. The paper mill had burned, but the marina had not. Remarkably, the Northwoods Inn had been spared.

Eli's desperate Hail Mary plan had worked. Luis Gault and his cartel had been destroyed. Gault's corpse was recovered with burns covering eighty percent of his body.

Sawyer's goons had perished with them. Except for Sawyer himself. He was held under guard until they decided what to do with him.

Two hundred citizens had lost their lives in the fighting or died in the fire; eighteen hundred more had lived. Alexis Chilton and Amanda Martz had died in the failed ambush weeks ago. Last night, Drew Stewart had passed away from his gunshot wound. Jason Anders and Fiona Smith had lost their lives bravely defending the Northwoods Inn from the cartel's blitz attack. And Jackson Cross, who had sacrificed everything to save others.

In a few days, they would prepare a mass funeral. People needed to mourn, to gather together, to find ways to say goodbye in an ancient ritual as old as time. In addition to those lost to the war, they were also grieving Ira Fleetfoot, Michelle Carpenter, and Traci Tilton.

Violence was bloody, senseless, and sometimes necessary, but never without a cost.

This time, they had paid an incredibly high price.

They had won the war. Their town was razed, but they were still standing. And the job of rebuilding had already begun.

Three days ago, scouts had discovered the cartel's supply caches hidden in a few key locations, including at the castle, which they'd reclaimed after a quick skirmish, eliminating the last few cartel members within a hundred miles of Alger County.

Afterward, they'd hauled everything back to the Northwoods Inn. The food would be enough to get them through this winter. Next winter would be another challenge, but they would prepare; they'd be ready for it.

A few days ago, Moreno had spoken to the Michigan governor, who had made the trip north on horseback to personally thank them for removing the thorn of the cartel from her side. It seemed they were worth the trip once the cartel no longer posed a threat.

While a remnant of the cartel still controlled the Soo Locks, their numbers had been summarily decimated; they'd be easy pickings for the National Guard now.

Moreno looked at Lena as he spoke. "The governor told me that the National Guard has begun creating outposts in strategic locations throughout the country, mostly coastal for now since their carriers have power and on-board medical bays, food storage, et cetera. What remains of the national government is operating in Mount Cheyenne. Congress has been making deals with South America for critical medications. There's a good chance that in two years, there will be enough restored infrastructure to store and distribute the most critical medications to citizens, even if we have to travel to get them."

Lena nodded, her hand instinctively straying to the pump at her hip. She glanced at Eli, unable to hide the relief from her face. Perhaps it was too good to be true, or maybe they would finally catch a break. They deserved a few miracles.

Moreno explained that the governor had promised that the first transformers would be arriving in Michigan within the month. It would take years to restore even the local power grid system, but the process of recovery had begun. Humanity had started the long journey back.

Back to what, exactly? What would a new world look like once law and order and civilization had been restored? What parts of society did they want to keep and which parts should they abandon to build something newer, brighter, and better from the ashes?

It was a conundrum for another day.

Heat radiated from the scorched earth. It felt like walking through an oven. Ash coated the asphalt and the bullet-riddled cars. Though the smoke had mostly dissipated, the air smelled faintly singed.

At the hospital, they found the remains of the fighting position where Jackson had made his last stand. The sandbags were ripped, the sand melted, the logs burned down to charcoal. Lena recognized the horrible shapes of bones scattered among the ashes. It was impossible to tell which bones were Jackson's.

They stood in a loose circle, mourning their friend, their hearts shattered by loss and grief.

"I took him for granted," Shiloh said. "He was the only grown-up watching out for me and Cody. He always made sure we were okay. I never even said thank you."

"He knows," Devon said. "He knew."

Shiloh gazed at a section of rubble still glowing with embers. "He worried about not being a good person, but he was. He was good. He was the best."

Tears sluiced down Devon's cheeks. Her eyes were red and swollen from weeping. "He was."

Shiloh hugged her. Devon hugged her back. "He loved you very much," Devon said, looking around the circle. "All of you."

"And he loved you," Lena said in a choked voice.

Devon made a strangled sound of grief, but she squeezed Shiloh closer and managed to keep herself together. Even amid her grief, she was strong and brave. No wonder Jackson had fallen in love with her.

The bitter unfairness of it bit deep and painful. Outrage flared in her chest, beating in tandem with her anguish. It was all gone.

That hope, that future—a lifetime of love and friendship ahead of him, snatched away in an instant.

Jackson had been her best friend. Even before Eli, Jackson was the constant, loyal, reliable presence in her life. They'd held onto each other when they had nothing else.

"That love you shared isn't gone," Lori said quietly. "It's still here, still alive in your hearts. As long as you remember and share that love, a part of the person lives on inside you."

"Thank you for reminding us," Devon said. "I just hope he's at peace."

Lena prayed his soul was at peace, too. Jackson deserved that peace. In death, she hoped he had found it in a way he never had in life. He had died heroically saving innocent lives, single-handedly eliminating the threat of his father and brother.

In the end, he'd found the redemption he'd sought his entire life.

Her heart surged with sadness mingled with a bittersweet joy. This life had been hard-won, with many sacrifices, but she would do it again—all of it, every awful thing, for these people, for their courage and resilience. And for the beauty that could still be found, even here, even now, standing among the ashes.

On their return to the Northwoods Inn, they passed by the lighthouse. Seagulls swooped and dove along the jagged bluffs. The wind rasped their hair into their faces, but they barely noticed.

Miraculously, the lighthouse remained untouched. The gleaming white tower with the bright red cupola roof rose eight stories above them. Built into the base of the tower was the single-story brick cottage. Lena and Shiloh had sought refuge in the lightkeeper's home not so long ago.

Lena's rickety Honda Pilot sat in the driveway gathering dust. Dust filmed the windows, spidery cracks marred the windshield, and duct tape wrapped the bumper, holding it in place.

The Tan Turd may have been old, ugly, and falling apart, but it had brought Lena and Bear from Tampa safely home to the Upper Peninsula.

For that, she would always hold a soft spot in her heart for the Tan Turd.

Beyond the lighthouse, the great lake stretched as far as the eye could see, the horizon broken only by the humped shape of Grand Island. The emerald water glittered like jewels. Lacy plumes topped the waves tumbling against the shoreline strewn with sun-bleached driftwood.

Lena and Eli stepped into the shadow of the lighthouse tower. A seed of hope sprang to life inside her chest. They could rebuild the beacon, find a generator somehow, and get the lighthouse functional.

Finally, they could go home again.

Tears glistened in the corners of Lena's eyes. She blinked rapidly but made no move to wipe them away. "It's a mercy."

Eli put his arm around her shoulder. "A mercy from whom?"

She gazed up at the looming tower, standing tall and stalwart, a beacon of light in a sea of darkness, a lodestar to guide the lost home. "Maybe from God, maybe from fate. I don't know, I don't need to know. It just is."

69

LENA EASTON
DAY ONE HUNDRED AND EIGHTY

James Sawyer stood at the outskirts of town with his hands zip-tied behind his back. Lena and Eli had brought him to this spot along M-94 East past the Econo Lodge. The motel had also escaped the wildfires.

"I should kill you," Eli said. There was no malice in his voice but a cold flatness that chilled Lena to her core. "You deserve to die."

"Do what you have to do," Sawyer said.

Sawyer stared down the empty road at the barren trees, the iron-gray sky, the clouds heavy with rain or possibly snow. He didn't blubber, cry, or beg for his life. Neither did he bother to defend himself.

Sawyer's men were all dead. Gault was dead, as were Horatio and Garrett Cross. Sawyer had lost his army, his fortress. Everything he'd built had been burned to ash. Grand Island still stood, but Eli's people had taken command.

Even his body bore the scars of his defeat. Ugly red burns marred the right side of his face. Half-melted skin sagged in a hideous approximation of a smile. His windblown blond hair had been seared off in patches, his scalp raw like charred meat. He shuffled with an evident limp with every step.

Lena had spent the last few days tending to his injuries, ensuring his burns didn't turn septic. It seemed counterintuitive to spare the life of a man like Sawyer, but Eli had asked her to do it. For him, she would do anything.

Eli hadn't told Lena the details of what happened when Antoine took Sawyer into custody after the fire had destroyed his men. Lena didn't need to know, but she could guess plenty. Antoine had obtained some semblance of vengeance for Nyx, after all.

Sawyer was beaten. He knew it, too. It was evident in his slumped shoulders, his bowed head, the resigned expression on his disfigured face.

He kicked at a stray rock, blackened with soot, then winced from the exertion. "I'd like my final resting place to be Lake Superior, if that's not too much to ask."

Eli smiled. It was an empty smile, hard and dangerous. "Sure thing. We'll wrap you in chains and drop you over the side of your yacht."

Sawyer offered a lethargic shrug. He didn't seem angry that Eli had double-crossed him. He was subdued, diminished, as if he'd expected the betrayal all along. He couldn't prove it, and perhaps some deep-down part of him didn't want to. He was finished. Maybe he was ready to be finished.

Everything about him seemed smaller than she remembered.

"You fought with us. You kept your word. You also saved my life." Eli frowned as if the admission pained him. He ran a hand through his hair. "That means something to me, much as I wish it didn't. I wish I could serve your head to Nyx on a silver platter like she wants."

Sawyer snorted. "That doesn't surprise me."

"You could've been a better man," Lena said. "This didn't have to be your path."

"Yes, it did." He turned and met Lena's gaze. Something flickered for a moment in his sea-gray eyes, a spark of something like remorse. As quickly as it appeared, it was gone. "I regret nothing. Nothing except Lily. And Cody."

He didn't have to say the words aloud. He'd abandoned them both, rejecting his chance to be a father and husband. A chance to be something different, something more. Something better than the sum of his poor choices.

"I can't absolve you of anything," Lena said. "I am not my sister."

He offered a bitter smile. "I'm not asking for your forgiveness. There's nothing that could make a difference, not for me."

Long-buried memories fizzed to the surface. She saw Sawyer as a boy, his neediness, his boasting, his desperate loneliness. How he'd tried so hard to gain entry into their exclusive clique, the insular world Eli, Jackson, Lena, and Lily had created for themselves.

Despite his best efforts, he'd remained forever on the outside, destined to be a loner, excluded, always standing in the shadows, out in the cold.

Sawyer deserved to pay for the things he'd done with his life. And yet, he'd also fought side by side with Eli. He'd saved Eli's life. He'd lived up to his end of the deal with honor. Much as Lena hated it, she felt a thin thread of kinship with Sawyer, a blood debt for Eli's life.

She didn't pity him, but perhaps she understood him a little.

Sawyer nodded wordlessly at her, as if in mutual understanding. Gone was his arrogance, his cruel confidence, his swagger. He had lost everything. That tremendous loss had humbled him. His eyes, once cunning and predatory, were now haunted.

He was a broken man.

"What do you say, Lena?" Eli asked. "Should he live or die? His life is in your hands."

Lena tried to muster contempt for Sawyer but felt nothing. She was sad, tired, and numb. She had hated him once, but no longer. She had no more energy for hatred.

The time for fighting was over.

"No more death," Lena said wearily. "Life is more than survival. There is a place for killing, but there is also a place for healing. It's time to heal."

Eli hesitated for a moment, then nodded, his expression unreadable. He stepped forward, drew his knife, and slit Sawyer's zip-ties. "Lena speaks for you, you lucky bastard. A life for a life."

Sawyer rubbed his bruised wrists and said nothing. He pressed his lips into a thin bloodless line, his gaze on the ground.

Eli pointed down the road. "Start walking. You will not turn around nor look back, not for a hundred miles. If I ever see you again or hear a word of your existence, I will hunt you down, pry open your chest cavity with a crowbar, and peel out your beating heart with my bare hands."

Convoluted emotions swept across his face. His mishappen features hardened in resolve, his eyes bright as coins against the garish burns searing his skin. To his credit, he did not look afraid.

Turning his back on them, he shuffled down the center of the road rutted with potholes and clotted with weeds. Without his army of thugs behind him, he was only human, shrunken, small, and weak. One man, alone, with no one and nothing to call his own.

A king without a kingdom.

Eli took Lena's hand. They stood amid the destruction and watched Sawyer grow gradually smaller until he was a mere speck in the distance. There one second and in the next, he vanished.

70

ELI POPE
DAY ONE HUNDRED AND NINETY

The air smelled cold and clean. Eli inhaled fresh air into his lungs.

Eli, Shiloh, and Lena had hiked three miles from the trailhead to reach their destination. Bear pranced around their legs. They'd trekked past gurgling creeks and splashing waterfalls and through dense hardwoods shorn of leaves.

Ahead, the jade-colored waters of Lake Superior winked through the barren trees. They paused at the lip of a sandstone bluff streaked with colorful minerals, the red of iron, the orange of copper, the green of manganese. Fortunately, the Pictured Rocks National Lakeshore area had been spared from the wildfires.

The cold wind stung his exposed face and made his eyes water, but he didn't care. The temperature had dropped into the thirties during the day, even colder at night. Frost clung to the grass in the mornings.

Eli wore a hoodie beneath his windbreaker; Lena was dressed in a thick cable-knit sweater and jacket. In her bearskin cape, Shiloh looked like an ancient native warrior goddess, and she knew it, too.

"This is what I wanted to show you." Shiloh paused and pointed. "Chapel Rock."

Chapel Rock jutted from the lake—a tall rock formation separated from the bluff. Once, a natural rock archway had stretched between the bluff and the unusual rock formation, but it had collapsed back in the 1940s, leaving Chapel Rock disconnected from the rest of the coastline.

A single white pine grew from the center of the rock like a spire. It was connected to the mainland by a long thick root system that crossed the wide expanse like a tightrope. It should not exist. Yet it thrived, clinging to unforgiving stone, spreading its ropy roots far across the expanse to seek vital sustenance, to survive.

"I've come here before, but it never meant what it does now. This tree shouldn't be able to grow here, but it does. It defies the laws of physics, gravity, and nature. Despite the impossible odds, it's still here." Her lips twitched into the tiniest smile. "Like us."

"Like us," Lena echoed.

They stood for a moment in awed silence, contemplating the resilient pine tree standing proud as a sentinel.

Beyond Chapel Rock, Lake Superior was flat as glass, a burnished silver that reflected the gunmetal gray of the sky. The horizon blurred, water and sky bleeding into each other, creating the sensation that they were gazing into a distance that went on forever, to the edge of the known universe and beyond.

Lena shivered from the cold. Eli wrapped his arm around her shoulder. She sank against him, snuggling against his ribs. Holding Lena never got old.

Bear darted back and forth along the edge of the bluff, barking at the seagulls who dared to swoop low, squawking at him for drawing too close to their nests. He trotted up to Lena, sticking his snout against her palm and licking her hand, his tail wagging joyously.

Shiloh stared at the white pine jutting from the rock, absently fingering the arrow jammed into her ponytail. She removed the hair tie attached to the arrow from her hair, stepped to the edge of the bluff, and threw it across the void to the rock ledge. It fell with a plunk at the base of the white pine. It nestled among the tangle of gnarled roots.

"For Jackson," she said. "So he'll never forget us."

Lena said, "He won't forget us, and we certainly won't forget him."

Shiloh said, "This should be where we bury him."

There wasn't much left after the grenade, but Eli knew what she meant. They needed a marker, a monument to his courage and sacrifice, a place to pay their respects and recall their fondest memories of him.

"I think it's perfect," Lena said.

Shiloh tickled Bear behind his floppy ears. She raised her face to the horizon. The first snowflakes of winter tumbled from the slate gray sky. Laughing, Shiloh held out both hands and caught the flakes on her palms. Bear tried to chase them, sticking out his pink tongue, whoofing in startled delight.

They had brought flashlights. They remained at the bluff until the sun sank into the lake. The night was dense and starless. Everything coated in a felted blackness soft against their skin. They listened to the slap of the waves against the sheer cliff below, the sigh of the wind, the splash as a fish leaped from the water.

They were alive. They had each other. There was little else he could ask for but this: his heart beating against his ribs, reminding him of everything he had endured, everything he loved.

"Look at that," Shiloh said.

Eli and Lena turned and looked where Shiloh pointed. For six months the world had gone dark, and it would remain dark for years longer. In honor of the loved ones they had lost, for this single night, the Northwoods Inn was aglow with candles.

They could just make out the Inn nestled on the bluff across the inlet. In every room, in every window, a necklace of fairy lights had been strung along the ridgeline. Tiny flickering flames like a thousand stars lit up the night.

It reminded him of the times he'd looked down at the world from an airplane, everything dark but the twinkling, welcoming lights of a town or a city beckoning him to a place he could never call home.

At the Northwoods Inn, Lori and Tim would be cooking dinner as Faith frolicked beside them, gobbling everything within sight. Despite the incredible odds, Faith had survived, apparently too obstinate to die.

Later tonight, they would gather with everyone they cared about: Devon and Ruby, Antoine and Nyx, Moreno, Nash, Hart, and the Brooks, as well as Ana Brady with her adopted children— Keagan, baby Hope, and Adam—and everyone else that mattered in this world.

There would be songs and conversations around campfires, stories and tears and bittersweet laughter. Tales told of fond memories of Jackson, Alexis, Jason, and Fiona, and the others who had courageously sacrificed their lives so others might live. The Northwoods Inn was home.

Eli's heart swelled in his chest. At long last, he'd found where he belonged.

"Do you think things will ever go back to the way they were?" Shiloh asked.

He thought of cages, of prisons, both the manmade kind and the kind people made for themselves. He inhaled deeply. A strange sensation was growing inside him—expansive, bright and airy, and incredibly satisfying. It was hope.

"Maybe we don't want them to," Eli said.

"We can start anew," Lena said. "It'll take an entire lifetime."

"We have time," Eli said.

"Then let's get to work." Shiloh grinned in the dark, her teeth flashing. Her first smile in days, genuine and raw, brimming with joyful abandon. She took his hand in hers and looked up at him, beaming. "Dad."

AUTHOR'S NOTE

I hope you enjoyed *The World We Burn* as much as I enjoyed writing it! It is always a bittersweet experience when I finish a series. I've come to love these characters we've spent so much time with, cheering for them to survive, to find love, to make a life for themselves despite their difficult circumstances. The end of the world can be the beginning of something beautiful.

It's always hard to kill a character I love as much as Jackson. As I was brainstorming story ideas for this last book, the hospital scene came to me as vibrant, raw, and real as if I were watching the scenes play out in the movie theater of my mind. I knew that Jackson wouldn't hesitate to lay down his life to protect Lily's family. I know it's bitterly unfair that he lost his life just when he had truly found himself, but that's what makes his sacrifice so meaningful.

I pour my soul into every book I write, but this one in particular meant a lot to me. Eli, Shiloh, Lena, Bear, and Jackson are beloved characters I won't soon forget. I hope you won't, either! I like to imagine them making a life for themselves long after the last page has been read.

Thank you so much for joining me on this epic journey through the apocalypse. Until next time!

-Kyla

ACKNOWLEDGMENTS

As always, a deep heartfelt thanks to the behind-the-scenes readers who give early feedback on the raw manuscript as I shape the final story that you hold in your hands. They catch those pesky typos and watch for plot holes and make sure I have my facts right. Any errors are my own.

To my loyal Patreon members for their enthusiastic support:

Gregory Hoyt

AJ Flowers

Reece Chilton

Jon Carriker

Annette Cairl

Michelle (Misha) Kinsel

Steve Tradd

To my fabulous BETA readers: Ana Shaeffer, Fred Oelrich, Melva Metivier, Jim Strawn, Sally Shupe, Annette King, Cheryl WHM, Kathy Schmitt, Cheree Castellanos, Mike Neubecker, Bavette Battern, David A. Grossman, and Courtnee McGrew. Your thoughtful critiques and enthusiasm are invaluable.

To Donna Lewis for her excellent line editing skills. Thank you! Thank you to Joanna Niederer and Jenny Avery for detailed feedback and proofreading. Jenny catches the tiniest details and makes sure every aspect of the book is accurate. I owe her big time!

And yet another heart-felt thank you to David Kepford for his tactical expertise and experience in everything from undercover work to paramedic gear and psychological insights into the twisted mind of a killer. This book is so much better with his input.

To my husband, who takes care of the house, the kids, and the cooking when I'm under the gun with a writing deadline, even when the septic system backs into the finished basement! To my kids, who show me the true meaning of love every day and continually inspire me.

Thanks to God for His many blessings. He is with us even in the darkest times.

Thank you.

ALSO BY KYLA STONE

The *Lost Light* Post-Apocalyptic Series (CME):

The Light We Lost

The Dark We Seek

The Hope We Keep

The World We Burn

The *Edge of Collapse* Post-Apocalyptic Series (EMP):

Chaos Rising: The Prequel

Edge of Collapse

Edge of Madness

Edge of Darkness

Edge of Anarchy

Edge of Defiance

Edge of Survival

Edge of Valor

The *Nuclear Dawn* Post-Apocalyptic Series (Nuclear Terrorism):

Point of Impact

Fear the Fallout

From the Ashes

Into the Fire

Darkest Night

Nuclear Dawn: The Complete Series Box Set

The *Last Sanctuary* Post-Apocalyptic Series (Pandemic):

Rising Storm

Falling Stars

Burning Skies

Breaking World

Raging Light

Last Sanctuary: The Complete Series Box Set

No Safe Haven (A post-apocalyptic stand-alone novel):

No Safe Haven

Historical Fantasy:

Labyrinth of Shadows

Contemporary YA:

Beneath the Skin

Before You Break

ABOUT THE AUTHOR

I love writing stories that explore how ordinary people cope with extraordinary circumstances, especially situations where the normal comforts, conveniences, and rules are stripped away.

My favorite stories to read and write deal with characters struggling with inner demons who learn to face and overcome their fears, launching their transformation into the strong, brave warrior they were meant to become.

Some of my favorite books include *The Road*, *The Passage*, *Hunger Games*, and *Ready Player One*. My favorite movies are *The Lord of the Rings* and *Gladiator*.

Give me a good story in any form, and I'm happy.

Add a cool fall evening in front of a crackling fire, nestled on the couch with a fuzzy blanket, a book in one hand and a hot mocha latte in the other. That's my heaven. I also enjoy traveling to new places, hiking, scuba diving, and the occasional rappel down a waterfall or abandoned mine shaft.

I love to hear from my readers! Find my books and chat with me via any of the channels below:

www.KylaStone.com
www.Facebook.com/KylaStoneAuthor
www.Amazon.com/author/KylaStone
Email me at KylaStone@yahoo.com

Made in the USA
Las Vegas, NV
18 January 2024

84511425R00239